About 1

Mark Yarwood has worked in animation, edited a small press magazine, written for television and the Plymouth Evening Herald. He was born in Enfield, North London and now lives in Plymouth, England with his wife and daughter.

His website is: www.markyarwood.co.uk

Also by this author

SPIDER MOUTH
MURDERSON
LAST ALIVE
THE AMOUNT OF EVIL
WHEN THE DEVIL CALLS
THE FIRSTCOMER
HOLMWOOD
JAIRUS' SLAUGHTER
WELCOME TO KILLVILLE, USA
UGLY THINGS
FIRELAND

JAIRUS' SACRIFICE

MARK YARWOOD

BiscuitBooks

This novel is entirely a work of fiction. The names, characters and incidents portrayed in it are the work of the author's imagination. Any resemblance to actual persons, living or dead, events or localities is entirely coincidental.

BiscuitBooksPublishers

A Paperback Original 2018

Copyright © Mark Yarwood 2018

The Author asserts the moral right to be identified as the author of this work

Printed and bound by Createspace.com

ISBN-13: 978-1722790530

All rights reserved. No part of this publication may be reproduced, stored, or transmitted in any form or by means, electronic, mechanical, photocopying, recording or otherwise, without the prior permission of the publishers.

Cover by Andy Hall of Frank Design Associates Limited

ACKNOWLEDGEMENTS

It seems to have taken forever to get this book to this point, but it wouldn't have been possible without the help of a number of people who I'm very grateful to.

I'm hugely grateful to John Hudspith, my editor, who once again has taken my rough, fluff filled first draft and turned it into a book I'm very happy with.

I don't think I've mentioned the following person before, but I'm grateful to my friend, Rich Vivash, who has in the past advised me on technical issues and inspired the character of Rich Vincent. Thanks old friend.

Big thanks to Ross Mackenzie, my good friend, who took time out of his busy and hectic schedule to pose for this book's cover image. Just like Jairus, he's six foot five and he'll "kick your ass". Talking of the cover, this book would not have one if it wasn't for the expert skills of Andy Hall of Frank Design Ltd, my Brother-in-Law, who I am extremely grateful to.

Also I would like to thank my former school friend, Helen Kirilov, for taking the time to proofread this book and for giving me technical advice.

Thanks to my mum, Dad and brother for all their love and support. But most of all, I'm forever thankful to my wife and daughter, especially my wife for putting up with me. And thanks to Maggie, for all she does, and for never forgetting to feed Gary, the fish.

Lastly, this book deals with the issue of child abuse carried out by people in positions of power, and I'd like to acknowledge the suffering of their victims and all the survivors of child abuse who are all too often not believed.

For Terry and Trystan,
you'll never be forgotten

PROLOGUE

The gunshot had come from her neighbour's house on the right. There was no street lighting along the overgrown lane that curled and snaked for five hundred yards beneath Lynne's house from the main road and down towards Looe. Everything was woodland, a canopy of branches enclosing most of the road. There were only five houses dotted along the lane, all of them raised up and away from the road. There was no sound after the shot, not even the distant rumble of traffic, only the constant clicking of the crickets.

Lynne stepped out onto the front decking, then blinked when the security light blazed on above her. She could see the uneven stone steps that led from her garden down to the lane, soaked in the golden light, but only darkness beyond. She walked through the wooden gate which squeaked loudly into the night, and listened, watching the blackness beneath her.

Another shot boomed out. She froze. Then another ripped through the night. Each shot remained in her ears, echoing as she stared towards the next house. She could see very little, just the murky outline of the porch that jutted out, held up by concrete stilts. She'd never liked the house, all concrete, steel and glass, a mishmash that didn't fit with the old-world cottages on the lane.

She hesitated, one foot on the first step, staring

into the gloom that seemed to stare right back at her. They were her neighbours, fellow human beings, and even though she hardly ever spoke to them, and they seemed a little offish, she decided she needed to make sure everything was all right and went carefully down the steps to the lane.

There was movement, somewhere down the lane, the brush of something against the hedges that surrounded the next house. She pulled out her phone and shone its light towards it, watching as the soft blue glow highlighted little but jagged shadows.

It could've just been gunshots in a film, she thought, or a car backfiring somewhere, or some other reasonable explanation. But something had chilled her blood when she heard the first shot.

She jumped as yet another shot pounded through the blackness as if it tore through her own flesh and bone. She hit 999 on her phone but nothing happened. No signal. There usually was a weak signal outside her house, but there was nothing down here on the lane.

Her heart thudded again. Something moved near the undergrowth surrounding the concrete struts of the house and Lynne had the sensation that something was observing her from the darkness. Whatever or whoever was watching her seemed to be moving towards her, the sound of it brushing against branches and stepping on twigs was growing louder, closer.

Her heart was booming in her skull. She stepped backwards, reaching out her free hand, trying to find the gate and the steps back up to her house. She swung round and found the first step with the light from her phone, then spun back round to face the black lane, and the outline of the trees. Her foot found the step and she began to climb, never taking her eyes off the darkness.

It was only when she reached the gate that she hurried to her front door, rushed inside and slammed it behind her. She turned on every light before hurrying to the landline phone and ringing the police. Then she sat in her kitchen, the biggest of her kitchen knives in her hand, staring at the front door.

Her eyes had started to droop by the time the police arrived in their droves, cutting off the lane with their police cars and vans. She stepped out and watched them swarm over everything like ravenous rats. Eventually a dark-suited man with a craggy face and slightly greying hair came up her steps, stopping occasionally to look down at the scene.

She watched from the porch, seeing him taking his time, and making a phone call before smiling to her briefly as he put out his hand.

'Detective Inspector Robert Johnson,' he said in a flat voice that seemed to have little detectable accent. 'Lynne Pearce? You called us to report the sound of what you presumed was gunfire?'

'Yes. It sounded like gunfire to me. Was it?'

The detective looked over her shoulder, towards the open front door and perhaps her kitchen beyond it. 'Can we go inside?'

She nodded, then allowed him to go first. He stepped in, his eyes jumping all over the room before he gave her another short smile and stood by the Aga, arms folded.

'Something awful has happened in your neighbours' house, Mrs Pearce...do you live alone?'

'Yes, I do. What's happened? Are they hurt?'

'They're...' The detective looked past her for a moment, a calculation or decision wavering in his mind. 'I'm afraid it was a fatal shooting.'

She put her hand to her mouth, saw the chair pulled out of the kitchen table and sat down. 'The kids? Are they all right?'

The detective shook his head.

'Oh...oh my God...what happened...I mean, I heard the shots...'

'Did you know Mr Pinder and his family?'

She couldn't honestly say she did, and suddenly felt a little ashamed to admit it. Nonetheless, the truth seemed the only important thing at that moment so she said, 'No, not really. I keep myself to myself and it seemed they did too. I saw him and his wife and their two kids...oh God the kids. Who could...'

The detective seemed completely unaffected by events as he said, 'It's a terrible thing to have happened.'

'Was it a burglary gone wrong, do you think?'

'No, we're not looking for anyone else in connection with this.' He turned his head, then took out his phone and stared at it.

'I don't understand...'

He looked at her. 'Oh, right, I'm sorry. It looks likely at this moment in time that Mr Pinder murdered his family then took his own life. Please don't repeat that. Seeing as you knew them, I'm happy telling you at this juncture.'

'He...he killed his family and himself?'

'I'm afraid so. Please keep that to yourself. You know what the media can be like. We have to think about the family's living relatives...'

She nodded, but something began to gnaw at her- the feeling she had in the darkened lane came creeping back, the sensation that someone else had been waiting in the shadows. 'This...this might sound strange...but...I went down to the lane after I heard the first shot...I wanted to see what was going on...'

'That could've been very dangerous.'

'I know, but...I thought someone might have been under the house. I thought I saw movement...I heard something.'

'Probably an animal...a cat or something.' He turned and stared right in her eyes.

'I don't think so. I got the sense that it was a person. I'm sure it was...'

'Mrs Pearce,' he said, his voice harsher. 'Don't repeat that. Ever, I mean. Some things are best unsaid. Some things can put you in danger. Very serious danger. So, please, never speak of that again. Do you understand?'

'Yes, of course.' Lynne said the words, but felt a terrible coldness wash over her as the policeman kept staring at her.

CHAPTER 1

A grotesque sound layered over the cacophony of violence beneath him, rising, beating, vibrating through the structure of the concrete estate until it found Jairus lying on his bed half drunk, staring at the cracked ceiling. It was meant to be music, but it had no real structure or melody, unlike Johnny Cash's tunes which were…

His hangover blew any clear argument from Jairus' brain. He took his hearing away from the ugly noise. A baby was crying somewhere, while a woman and man's screams battled for supremacy. One day they'll kill each other, but he couldn't do anything about it, he was no longer qualified to clear away the mess, to try and bring any kind of closure.

He was lying on the sofa bed he'd bought from IKEA, still wearing the shirt and trousers from last night. The sofa was the only large, solid piece of furniture in his new flat. His stereo sat on the worn carpet in one corner; the TV sat on a storage box at the end of the bed.

Jairus turned his head towards the doorway that led to the short flight of stairs and his flimsy front door. Another door slammed somewhere along the balcony, followed by the hurried slapping of trainers which came in his direction. He pulled himself up and looked about the small room, at his stuff, the remnants of his life strewn about, and the two empty vodka bottles by the bed. Half a bottle sat near his pillow.

They'd suspended him. Indefinitely.

It must have been a pleasure for them to see him burn, to see his police record go up in flames and his character and name blackened.

He grabbed the half bottle of vodka and took a couple of long swigs.

His doorbell rang but he knew the person forcefully pressing the button couldn't be after him because nobody knew where he was. He'd moved to the very epicentre of North London crime and depravity because he knew it would be the last place his colleagues would expect to find him, the last place they would search. Also, he moved there because he felt somehow it suited him to spend some time in hell, or purgatory. He'd surrounded himself with the most perfect camouflage, now that they had marked him out as a criminal. He was like the chameleon, masked by that which surrounded him.

Someone thumped the door, hammered their fist against it.

'Oi! Yous there, man? Come on, man, answer the fuckin' door. Don't be a cunt. I need help, man.'

Jairus pulled himself off the sofa bed and took his own bitter time going down the stairs to the front door, but didn't open it. 'Go away!'

'You're a copper, innit?' the person shouted through the door.

'No, I'm not. Go and bang on someone else's door.' Jairus went to turn away, thirsty for another swig of firewater, anything to keep the bridge of numbness between him and real life.

'Yous a copper. Everyone says yous the filth. Come on, man. Me fuckin' nan's going to get knifed if yous don't open this fuckin' door.'

'Yeah, that right? I don't fucking care.'

'It's me fucking nan, man.'

Jairus huffed out a harsh breath. This was all he needed, reality banging on his front door. He had to make it go away once and for all.

He pulled open the door, tore his hand towards the scrawny white kid in the bright red baseball cap, baggy jeans and hoodie, and gripped him by the throat. He pressed his thumb into his windpipe, making him cough and fight for breath. 'Don't knock on my door. I don't care who's going to get knifed. I'm not at home to you. You got that?'

The kid gagged and nodded his head, so Jairus released him and watched him cough and rub his neck. 'Fuck me, man. I just wants yous fuckin' help. You telling me you ain't no copper?'

'Yeah, that's what I'm telling you. Now get lost and take off that stupid looking hat and stop making that Godawful sound with your mouth.'

'They says they's going to rape her, man.' The scrawny kid put his hands together as if he was about to kneel and pray. 'Please, man, I'm telling yous, these fuckers will do it.'

Jairus stared at him for a moment, hating him, wanting to punch him just for bringing real life back into his world. A bunch of thugs threatening an old lady wasn't exactly fair. How could he face himself if he shut the door and crawled back inside his vodka bottle?

Jairus reached round the back of the door and grabbed hold of the baseball bat he kept there in case of emergencies. 'My car's downstairs. You can show me where your nan lives.'

'Yous going to sort them out?'

'Yeah, I'm going to sort them out.'

The kid's nan lived only a few streets away in an old redbrick council house that sat on a grid of identical roads on the outskirts of Hornsey. It was rough, dirty like all the other estates that surrounded it. Jairus parked at the end of the street, his eyes fixed on the gangs of youths sitting at either end, one lot positioned by a graffiti-daubed playground, the others by a small square of dying grass about five hundred yards away.

'This is where they do their deals, right?' Jairus asked.

'What do yous mean, man?' the kid said, avoiding Jairus' eyes.

'If you start feeding me lies, then I'm out of here. Your nan can fend for herself.'

The kid started fidgeting, messing with his baseball cap. 'What yous expect me to say, man?'

Jairus started the engine, put the car into reverse.

'Fuck me...yeah, yous got me. They's fuckin' drug dealers. But they's was on me. They got to be gone, man.'

'Yeah, I bet you want them gone, so I get rid of the competition for you. Where does your nan live?'

The kid held up his long bony hand. 'Sees the red door. She lives there, man. I swear. Cross me heart and all that shit.'

'Fine. They don't get here soon, I'm gone.'

'Yous a copper, yeah?'

'Yeah...no, I was a copper.'

'Shit. Yous don't look like filth.'

'Yeah, that right?'

'Yous look like a caveman, bro. No offence, man, but you smell like a wino.'

'Yeah, well, you dress like a twelve-year-old.'

'Fuck me, here's they come!'

Jairus fixed his eyes on the end of the street where a gang had emerged, spread out, all in hoodies, a snarl set in each and every face. Five of them. One of them looked Chinese, another was black. The rest looked white. The one out in front, carrying a nine iron, spinning it in his hand, was a thick-set mean-looking white lad. He was sticking his middle finger up at the other gangs, who were gathered in greater numbers, but now seemed to shy away.

'See what I means? They's going to me nan's house.'

Jairus let out a deep sigh, lowered his forehead to the steering wheel, realising it was too late now, even if his usual stool in his local was calling to him. He pushed open the door, grabbed the baseball bat and pulled himself out on to the pavement. The scrawny kid hurried to get behind him as Jairus took his place at the end of his nan's front garden.

Like a school of hooded fish, the gang turned all at once and approached the garden gate and stopped dead when they saw Jairus stood there.

The leader swung the golf club around in his hand, his dead eyes crawling up and down Jairus with disdain before they jumped to the scrawny kid. 'Didn't I warn yous, Darryl? I recollect telling yous that the money or the gear better be in my hand this PM. You got my money, Darryl?'

Jairus snatched the golf club from the leader's hand. 'Don't talk to him, talk to me.'

The leader sneered, kissed his teeth and squared up to Jairus even though he was at least six inches shorter. 'And who's the fuck is yous when yous at home? Who's this old cunt, Darryl?'

'The old man who's about to give you two choices.'

Jairus threw the club to the pavement.

The leader looked round at his gang and they joined in when he started laughing. 'That right, you old fucker?'

'Yeah, that's right. You either walk away now and leave my friend's nan alone for good, or I have to stop you.'

The leader laughed again, looked round at his crew, probably counting, Jairus decided, then said, 'There's five of us, chief. You don't wants that kinda beef. Yous don't want this to get on top, does ya?'

'I'd answer you if I knew what the fuck you were saying. Stay or go. Up to you.'

The leader nodded, then stepped back, paced around a bit, whispering something to his gang. One of the crew stood back, arms folded, probably keeping an eye out for the police, while the leader reached into his jacket and brought out a knife.

Jairus gripped the baseball bat tighter, watching the knife glint as the young thug clenched and unclenched his hand round the blade.

'Going to cut you up, chief,' the leader said, holding up the knife, grinning ear to ear, jabbing the air a few inches from Jairus.

'Yeah, well, do your worst.' Jairus was ready, his heart pounding, the same old tension headache beginning to beat at the top of his skull. He watched the knife in the kid's hand, and kept looking up at the other gang members, staring them in the eyes, trying to ascertain who would stay and who would run.

The knife slit the air, thrusting towards Jairus' stomach. He lurched back, swinging the bat and delivering a blow to the leader's knife hand. He caught him on the wrist, making him yelp. The knife clattered to the pavement, so Jairus swung back round, smacking him nicely on the chin, sending him sprawling to the floor.

The black thug behind him had a cosh and charged towards Jairus, swearing, making growling noises, lifting the weapon far above his head. Jairus jabbed the bat at his gut, knocking the wind straight out of him, doubling him over.

The last three, including the lookout, froze, staring at Jairus, then looking down at their fallen comrades, confused about what to do next.

Then their minds were made up for them when an incident response car came roaring towards the scene. As the remainder of the crew ran, along with Darryl, Jairus spun his head round to see the police car braking hard, climbing the pavement.

Great, that was all he needed.

The uniforms, both men, both just as thuggish looking as the gang members who'd just left the scene, came swaggering up to Jairus. The first one said, 'We've had reports of a disturbance. You wouldn't know anything about it, would you?'

Jairus looked at the baseball bat in his hand and dropped it. 'No, constable, I wouldn't.'

The other uniform, his hand clamped on his radio, said, 'That's funny, because we've got a description of a man who's assaulting people, and it seems to match you.'

Jairus smiled. 'I don't see anyone around to press charges.'

The first uniform looked round, then nodded. 'No, you're right about that. You used to be on the job, didn't you?'

'Yeah, once upon a time,' Jairus said, expecting that he was about to receive a get out of jail card.

'I thought so. You're former DCI Jairus, yeah?'

'Yeah, that's right.'

The first uniform nodded. 'That was a shame what happened. Really not fair. Get in the car.' The uniform jerked a thumb towards the incident response car.

'Why?' Jairus stayed where he was.

'Believe me, it's in your best interests.' The first uniform walked towards the car and opened the back door. 'We've been told to keep an eye out for you. Someone wants a word.'

Jairus moved towards the car, more curious than he was thirsty, for a change. 'Who?'

The constable shrugged. 'I don't ask questions. Someone high up. That's all I know.'

Jairus looked into the car, his mind whirring, trying to think who high up might have a grudge against him. No one came to mind, only the lowlife scum he'd put away.

Jairus climbed in the car.

CHAPTER 2

Dusk was setting in by the time the police car came to crawl along the bush-lined country lane that ran through Hatfield in Hertfordshire. Jairus looked beyond the tall gates that sat to his right, and the sun that was submerging behind the grand old country house about a half mile behind it, bathing everything in long brown shadows.

Hatfield House. A Jacobean house built in 1611 by the first Earl of Salisbury. Jairus had visited it before, and read the leaflet to death, a long time ago with Karine, in another life that had yet to be tainted by death.

'Yes, he's here,' the first constable said, talking on his mobile. 'OK. We'll send him up.'

The uniform turned and faced Jairus and nodded towards the house. 'Head through the gates. Keep walking. They're sending someone to meet you.'

'Who are THEY?' Jairus asked.

The uniform shrugged. 'I don't know. My job was to get you here. Shame you didn't have time for a shower, because you stink of booze.'

'Yeah, I know. Come on, you must have some idea.'

'You'll soon find out, won't you? Now, hurry up so we can get back to work.'

Jairus pulled himself out of the car and faced the tall gates as the police car roared away behind him. He stepped through the small archway to the right of the gate and then joined the long tarmac driveway that snaked all the way to the magnificent redbrick house with the protruding chimneys in the distance.

All the time he walked, Jairus was trying to piece things together, to get some idea of what or rather who he might be facing at the end of the long drive, but his mind remained clouded in a fog created by the alcohol he'd consumed the night before.

Everything was hazy, and as the sun drifted low behind the great house, leaving the sky soaked in a blood red, a shape emerged from the shadows. It was a slender woman in a long flowing black dress, he could make out that much. He focused on her face as she came closer and saw bright red and full lips against a pink oval face under a flourish of glistening brunette hair.

Then the hauntingly beautiful face came into focus and he stopped walking and stood staring as the woman, now so familiar, yet so strange, smiled at him.

'Hello, Jay, it's been a while,' Cathy Durbridge said, bathed in the shadow of the house.

She'd lost weight, her curves had gone and now a smooth, sleek and glamorous woman stood before him, looking as if she'd been carved out of ivory. She had come far from being the unashamedly sexual forensic expert he'd known several months ago, the woman he'd considered spending the rest of his life with. Perhaps, he'd decided over the months of limbo, waiting for the axe to fall, he'd only wanted to be with her because she represented the dark side of life and that's where he felt he fitted in and deserved to be. Still, as he watched her step closer to him, and the scent of her body, her hair, filled his nostrils, he felt his desire for her awaken.

'Yeah, it has,' he said. 'I've been busy.'

'You refused to see me when I visited,' she said and turned and headed back towards the house.

Jairus fell in-step with her. 'Yeah, I know. I wasn't in a good place. You look like a 40's femme fatale.'

She smiled. 'I'll take that as a compliment.'

'It was meant as one.'

'Just so you know, I don't blame you for cutting yourself off.'

He stopped and watched her elegantly striding towards the grand house. 'You don't?'

She stopped and faced him. 'No, of course not. You were drowning and you didn't want to take anyone down with you. In a way, you probably wanted to save me.'

'Yeah, something like that.'

She looked him up and down, then shook her head. 'You look terrible, Jay, and you smell like a tramp.'

'That's what people keep telling me.' Jairus walked on, overtaking her, heading through the giant hedgerow that had been carefully crafted into a massive archway and entered the enormous garden that led to the back of the house. 'Who exactly am I meeting?'

The closer they got to the house, Jairus could make out several elegantly dressed bodies on the stretch of perfectly manicured lawn, everyone moving among the stone statues and sculpted hedgerows with champagne glasses in their hands, while a powerful and dramatic classical tune was playing loudly from somewhere. He could not make out any faces, as if each man and woman's face was dipped in darkness. Masks. Every one of the figures was wearing a mask.

'Have you heard the name Douglas Burdock before?'

Jairus stopped moving and grabbed her elbow. 'Douglas Burdock? As in the son of Robert Burdock, the media mogul who owns most of the TV companies and newspapers in this country?'

'The very same,' she said and began walking towards the house again. 'Douglas is very different from his father though.'

'Yeah, right. Are you very intimate with him, Cathy?'

She looked at him and he saw the flames begin to rise beyond her eyes. 'To a point. That shouldn't matter to you. And by the way, I don't like to be called Cathy anymore. I prefer Cat. Cathy sounds too...'

'Nice?'

'Exactly.'

As they passed through the masked partygoers, Jairus said, 'What sort of party is this?'

'The kind you don't want to know about.' She reached the French doors that were wide open and passed between two white curtains that billowed gently into the massive hallway beyond them.

'Yeah, I thought as much.' He followed her into an endless hallway, the floor patterned with black and white tiles, the giant windows beaming moonlight onto the wood panel walls and the enormous fireplaces, oil paintings, and suits of armour that decorated their journey.

Cathy stopped at a large armoured decorative door halfway along the hallway and faced him blankly. 'Douglas is waiting for you in there. Listen to what he says. Listen very carefully.'

'How did you end up mixed up with the likes of the Burdocks?'

Cathy knocked on the door. 'Ask me afterwards. He's waiting.'

He looked into her eyes for a moment and saw little that convinced him she was the same woman he'd spent many passionate evenings with a few months back. Something had happened to her since then, something so traumatic it could even affect someone as battle-hardened as her. He tucked away his wonderings and opened the door.

He found himself in a small library, which was made up of a ground level and a mezzanine. The walls of both levels were crowded with ancient volumes. At the very back of the room was a grand oak desk, which a suited man sat at. Jairus recognised the square face, and the neat and slicked hair of Douglas Burdock as he stood up and smiled. His eyes seemed deeply black. He recalled it had been commented on in the papers that Douglas Burdock was a damn sight better looking than his craggy-faced father, which Jairus knew had to be something to do with his mother, who had once been a much sought-after model.

'Ex-DCI Jairus,' Burdock said, walking round the desk and holding out his hand. 'Cat has told so many colourful stories about you.'

Jairus kept his hands by his side. 'Yeah, that right? Why don't you tell me what you want?'

Burdock lost his smile and stared at Jairus. 'So you can go back to pickling yourself in vodka? You know there are far more enjoyable ways to truly destroy yourself.'

'Is that what you think I'm doing?'

Burdock sat at the desk and leaned back in the chair. 'Why else does an alcoholic drink or a junkie take drugs? That's one of the main design faults of the average human being. The self destruct button was put too clearly on display. Tell me, Jairus, why do you think you drink?'

'Are we having a bloody counselling session now?'

Burdock smiled. 'Indulge me, please.'

'If you must know, it's because it helps dilute the feeling of self-hatred and misery I feel thinking about the people I could've helped in the future. Satisfied?'

Burdock nodded. 'Beautifully put. You know, you don't have to be a policeman to help people, Jairus. Have you considered private investigation?'

'Yeah, for about a millisecond. It's not the same. I'm either a police officer or not. Now, are you going to hurry up and tell me what you want or do I walk out of here?'

'Very well, Jairus. I want to hire you to look into a case...'

'I'm not for hire. Weren't you listening?'

'I was listening. I chose not to hear.'

'Yeah, I guess that's how you newspaper people do things. Pick and choose what you hear.'

Burdock's face became almost solemn for the first time. 'You've mistaken me for my father, Jairus. He's the newspaper man. At least he was until the Alzheimer's started eating his mind. Now I'm in charge of his empire.'

'Bully for you.'

'Did you know that my family pretty much own Australia? I'm not even making a joke. It's quite an audacious feat of Machiavellian cunning by my father, don't you think?'

'Yeah, quite a feat, but not beyond him. People think he's the devil.'

Burdock grinned and sat up. 'That they do. And they're very nearly on the money. I should know. But let's talk about you. If I'm going to have someone working for me, I like to know all about them.'

'You're not listening...' He thought about walking

out, making a stand against the establishment figure sitting in front of him, grinning like a crazy person. The party that was happening outside the library was organised by Burdock, and Jairus shivered at the thought of what might be going on behind closed doors. Jairus pressed pause on his thoughts as he saw Burdock take out a thick file from out of nowhere and open it.

'This is the file I had put together about you,' Burdock said, nodded to himself, then started shaking his head. 'A very interesting read indeed. You've lived quite an exciting life so far. You had a very good clearance rate. You put quite a few notorious criminals away. In my opinion the Met are making a big mistake getting rid of you.'

'Yeah, I think so too.'

'Then I took a look at your early years. Comprehensive school. Art and English seemed to be your area of expertise. But it was your father who really piqued my interest. A big man, brutal some people have said about him. A professional criminal most of his life. Then he double crossed the wrong people and had to go on the run, as they say. On the run with his young boy. Your old man had to change his name. So, Jairus isn't your real name?'

'No, it isn't. Can we cut all this out...'

Burdock sat back, smiling. 'No, we cannot. How would you feel if I said I could get you reinstated, arrange for you to be a police officer again?'

Jairus stepped closer and stared in the black empty eyes that looked back at him. He was good at reading people, and could usually tell if they were having him on or not, but he saw little in Burdock's face to give anything away. 'Is this what it's about? You drag me here just to pull my leg for a while? Yeah, this is how you get your kicks, right? I've met your kind before. You have more money than you know what to do with, and you've done everything, been everywhere, so you have to resort to fucking with people's lives. Well, not my life. You got it?'

'I'm not fucking with you, Jairus. Surely, you've heard the rumours... about how my father had several high-ranking police officers in his pockets. It wouldn't take much for me to flex a little fourth estate muscle and bring you back from the dead. How would you like that? How would you like to be Lazarus for a change? I mean, because of your father you spent your time on this earth with one biblical name, why not exchange it for another? By the way, was he a religious man, your father?'

'No, not that I know of. Look, let's get back to...'

'If I'm going to bring you back from the dead, and expend that kind of energy, I want a return on my investment.'

The irritation became spiders crawling over Jairus' skin. The room seemed to be getting smaller, which meant he was getting closer to Burdock, breathing in the same poisonous air. 'You said you wanted me to look into a case for you.'

'True. And I do, very much so. But you see, I have a gap here in my information. I don't like gaps. Call it my OCD, if you will.'

'What do you want to know?'

'I want to know how your father came to pick Jairus as your surname. If he wasn't a religious man...'

'They were going to kill him, the people he'd double crossed... so he went to the police. They wanted to give him a new identity so he could disappear after testifying. They told him to pick a new name. He told me that he went and jumped on a train, just to get away for a bit. Ended up in Bath of all places. It was raining so he walked into an art gallery or museum or something... the way he told me it happened was he was walking up the stairs and he looked up and there was a painting right in front of him. It was a scene taken from the bible. Jairus' Daughter, the painting was called.'

Burdock nodded and smiled, seeming satisfied as if he'd just eaten a delicious and filling meal. 'I know it. It's a beautiful painting. And here you are. A big man with an even bigger name to live up to.'

Jairus felt his hands involuntarily clench into fists. He could hardly bare to spend another second in the smug, self-congratulatory man's presence. He didn't know his father, but he'd heard the rumours of his depravity and sadistic nature. The apple never falls far from the tree. 'Let's talk about the case.'

Burdock nodded and reached down and put another thick file on the desk. 'And so to business. It's a shame, I was so enjoying the conversation. Have you heard the name David Coulson before?'

'Yeah, if I'm remembering right, he was a journalist that was found hacked to death in a car park in the East End of London.'

Burdock clapped his hands together. 'Well done. David Coulson was an investigative Journalist who was always trying to bring to light the terrible injustices caused by police failure or general corruption of the legal system. He was found after apparently being savagely attacked by someone wielding a machete. One of his arms was separated from his body, as was one of his hands. His head had almost been severed. It seemed to be the attack of a madman.'

'Yeah, I read about it. You said seemed. The inquiry found nothing that would substantiate the allegations that the Met were somehow involved in his death. They arrested Mickey O'Neil.'

Burdock laughed. 'He was killed by another inmate. Conveniently. The inquiry you spoke of was a police-led inquiry. Come now, Jairus, you don't really believe they looked very deeply into the issue, do you? No, of course not. Because they were scared of what they would find, the same way a terrified child doesn't get up in the middle of the night to look in their wardrobe.'

'You think it was covered up? And you want to me to try and find out who killed him?'

'Exactly. I want to know what David Coulson was looking into.'

'Not interested.' Jairus went to turn away, heading for the door.

'Think of all the people you could help. All the dead you could help avenge.'

He stood there for a moment, his hand on the door, feeling the burn of anger and frustration pumping through him. 'Yeah, I do every second of every day, but I don't trust you.'

'Of course you don't. There's no reason for you to. But you trust Cat, don't you? Talk to her. She'll tell you what you need to know. Then you can think about it. One simple investigation and you get to play policeman again.'

'If you've got high-ranking police officers in your pocket, why don't you get them to tell you the truth?'

'For many complicated reasons, I cannot be seen to be involved in this. No one knows you're here. There'll be nothing tying us together. I just want you to find out the truth behind his murder.'

'You can get me reinstated?'

Burdock nodded. 'Yes, I can. May God strike me

down if I'm lying.'

'Then get me back to work and I'll look into this on the side.'

Burdock laughed. 'You're more slippery than an eel. You know, Cat said you'd be tricky. She wasn't convinced that you would agree with this, because you would feel like you'd be selling your soul to the devil. How much is being a police officer worth to you, Jairus? Is it worth your soul?'

'Fuck you...' Jairus faced the door again, ready to walk out, telling himself there'd be another way back from the dead.

'I'm joking, Jairus. Please. Don't walk out just yet. If I get you reinstated first, they'd never let you look into Coulson's murder officially or otherwise. They'd keep you on a short leash. You know you want this more than anything.'

Jairus turned to see him now without the smirk on his face, looking almost as if he was being genuine. He knew he couldn't trust Burdock or his kind. He wasn't stupid or naive, but he also couldn't ignore a lifeline either, a way back into the light. He was drowning slowly and he knew it, could feel the sting as his lungs filled up with self-loathing. He had lied before. It wasn't just the future cases, the lives he could possibly save if he caught another psycho killer, it was the past deaths, the endless parade of ghost faces that appeared in his head at night. Their blood was on his hands, and without the job to keep his mind busy, his brain was an old empty house for them to haunt.

'If I take this on,' he said, unable to stop his words and ignoring the awful feeling filling up his bones. 'You reinstate me. No other strings. Have I got your word?'

Burdock nodded. 'You have my word, Jairus. You

won't regret your decision.'

'Yeah, well I better not.'

'Cat will be your liaison. She'll give you whatever you need. You'll need this too.'

Jairus nodded, took the file he was holding out, said nothing more and left the room.

He found himself standing in the monstrous hallway, the moonlight soaking the floor, while dust swirled in the air.

The sound of clicking heels came towards him. It was Cathy. Her eyes were fixed on the file in his hand. She almost looked a little disappointed, he thought.

'So, you're taking the case?' she said, then lifted her eyes to his.

'Do I even have a choice?'

'Of course you do, Jay. You can walk away from this, tell Douglas thanks but no thanks.'

'Yeah, I know, but I need to get back to work or I'll die. You know that more than most.'

'Or maybe you forget this and go and help the people that need help. Who says you need to be a police officer?'

Jairus felt the burn of anger again. 'I say. I can't... I can't give up. I'm nothing if I'm not... listen, can he really get me reinstated?'

She stared at him for a while, her words seeming to flutter on her lips for a moment.

'Cathy? Can he?' Jairus touched her shoulder, and she looked at his hand as she said, 'Yes. He can get you back on the force. He can pretty much do anything.'

'That's all I need to know.' Jairus tucked the file under his arm and stormed back the way they had come.

'Jay?'

He stopped, then slowly faced her. 'Yeah?'

'What if the path you're taking ends up leading you to an even worse place than you are now? Have you thought about that?'

'Why, do you want to tell me something?'

He couldn't see her face as it was blanketed by shadow, but he saw the movement her head made, the slight shake. 'No, I don't. I've arranged for a car to take you back home. It'll be waiting where you were dropped off.'

'Good. I'll be in touch. I may need your help.'

'Be careful,' she said, but Jairus was hardly listening, he was thinking about what his first step would be. But something in her voice was bugging him, the delicate sigh of doubt and fear that tainted her words. He'd never known Cathy speak like that before. He wondered what had changed her so much.

He pushed the dark thoughts from his overcrowded skull and allowed himself a smile, knowing that he was closer to getting his life back.

CHAPTER 3

Early the next morning, dressed in his trademark dark suit, Jairus took a fleeting look at Wandsworth Prison as he drove by. It was enough to fill his veins with ice. A few minutes later, as he sat cradling his black coffee in the greasy spoon about a half mile from the prison, which looked more like a medieval castle, he shuddered at the realisation of how close he had come to being another of its inmates. He shook his head and felt his stomach churn, knowing he couldn't have survived it. It wasn't only the confinement that would have got to him, it was the fact he was an ex-copper that would have turned him into fodder for the lowlife scum who had taken up permanent residence among its forbidding walls.

Jairus pulled the shutter down over his dark wonderings, and looked at his notebook in which he had started sketching out a plan of action. It was weird being out on his own with no one to back him up, but the same old buzz of excitement rose through him at the prospect of solving the case.

He picked up his coffee and watched his hand tremble, the black liquid sloshing about in the white mug. He'd not started the day by having half a bottle of vodka, which was an enormous shock to his system and his body was in the midst of a tantrum, demanding the fiery liquid it was used to consuming.

Job number one was to find out about Mickey O'Neil, or Mickey the Machete, as he came to be known. His MO was usually a random attack on anyone unfortunate enough to be close by after he had consumed a cocktail of drink and drugs. And of course, a machete was his weapon of choice as it allegedly was in the case of the journalist David Coulson. It seemed on the surface to be an open and shut case, but the more Jairus read the file put together by Burdock's people, the more his skin began to itch. Mickey had confessed a few hours after he was caught, and told the interviewing officers he'd been drinking in the pub that Coulson had been murdered outside of. There were no solid eye witnesses to say he was definitely drinking in the pub before the murder. But no one had come forward to say he was elsewhere either.

Jairus needed to get into the prison and talk to Frank Saunders, the man who stabbed Mickey the Machete in the throat five times two years ago. Before the stabbing, the inmates had shared a cell together for sixteen months. If anyone knew about Mickey, it was the man who'd killed him. And if anyone knew how to get into Saunders' head, it was Jairus as he'd helped hunt him down five years ago and put the cuffs on him. It would be a pleasure to see him in the place he belonged.

But he wasn't a detective and couldn't waltz in and demand to see Frank. Also, he didn't want anyone to know about the visit or that he'd even been anywhere near the place. He wanted to stay off the radar.

The cafe door opened and a tall and thickly built man in a prison guard uniform came stomping in. He looked twice as mean as any of the prisoners that he guarded, which was the whole point, Jairus supposed.

Tony Fenton. He was ex-police too, but found he couldn't handle the roll and all the rules they kept slapping on an already difficult job. Keeping a watch over the people they'd already put away always seemed a strange choice to Jairus, but he never really thought about it too much.

Tony sat down with a heavy sigh and then smiled sadly at Jairus. 'Sorry, mate. Heard about what happened to you. A real fucking shame.'

'Yeah, a real shame.' Jairus sipped his coffee, not really wanting to make small talk.

'How did you get off a murder charge?' Tony leaned in, his eyes burning with curiosity. 'Didn't they find him dead in your flat?'

'Yeah, but a couple of witnesses came forward to say I couldn't have been there when he was killed. Plus some CCTV footage turned up.'

Tony nodded, smiled, but Jairus saw the doubt in his eyes, the plethora of rumours that would never stop haunting him.

'You're a lucky fucker,' Tony said. 'You always were.'

'Doesn't feel like it. Listen, I need a favour. A big one.'

'I thought as much. Go on, what is it?'

'I need a word with Frank Saunders.'

'Apply for a prison visit.' Tony eyed him suspiciously.

'I can't. You know I would if I could. I can't be seen to be entering the prison. I need a chat with him, but I also need never to have been there either.'

Tony blew out a heavy breath. 'Jesus, mate. You don't ask a lot, do you? Fuck me. That's not going to be cheap. I'll have to pay...'

Tony stopped talking when Jairus took the thick

manila envelope from his overcoat and slapped it on the table.

'Jesus!' Tony looked round at the other customers as he snatched the envelope and dropped it into his lap. 'Careful. How much is in there?'

'Five ton.'

Tony smiled. 'That'll do it. I'll get a uniform and bring it here. You can change in the toilets. Then I'll drive you inside. There's some cameras dotted about, but they're easy to get around. Problem is, where you going to have this chat?'

'Is there an office or somewhere?'

Tony rubbed his face, then snapped his fingers. 'I got it. There's a spare cell. It's on another wing, but I can get Saunders there no problem.'

'Good. Thanks for this, Tony.'

'No problem. Knowing you as I do, I can die happy in the knowledge that all this is for the greater good.'

'Yeah, you can.'

Tony nodded, then stood up. 'Right, let's do this.'

Jairus waited in the darkness of the cell, shaking a little, mostly from the lack of alcohol in his system, but partly from imagining he was an inmate. He felt the panic he suffered as a kid in his dark room at night, imagining there was a monster under his bed. Slowly imagination would turn into almost certainty. He was free, this was not his home, he kept telling himself, as he listened to the prison soundtrack playing on a loop.

The metal staircase creaked as boots hammered along it.

The cell door was unlocked and the square of light beamed in at Jairus until a short, but broad figure stood in the doorway.

The cell door closed and was locked again. Jairus

turned on the lamp light that Tony had leant him. Frank Saunders blinked and held a hand over his eyes for a moment before he took Jairus in.

'You're no prison fucking guard,' Saunders said, almost spitting out the words.

'I'm not? How do you know?'

'That uniform's too fucking small for you for starters. You have to wake up fucking early in the morning to pull the fucking wool over my fucking eyes.'

Jairus looked over the stubby man with the greying, receding hair. He somehow reminded Jairus of Bela Lugosi's Dracula. 'Sit down, Frank. Let's talk.'

The Dracula spell was broken when Saunders broke into a rattling laugh and showed off his blackened, crooked teeth. 'Hang fucking on. Yeah, I knew it! You're the fucking pig who put me in here!'

'Yeah, the ex-pig,' Jairus said. 'Which means I don't have to follow the rules, not that I did anyway. You see I always took the rule book to be more of a guideline.'

Saunders sat on the bed, his sharp eyes burrowing into Jairus. 'Got a fag?'

Tony had made sure Jairus was equipped. He took out a pack of Camels and slipped one to Saunders, even gave him a box of matches. The inmate took a few seconds to enjoy the smoke, then half closed his eyes. 'You know it was just luck... the way you got hold of me back then.'

'Yeah, maybe.'

'If it was today, right now and I was outside these walls, I'd run rings round you. You wouldn't know right from wrong. Good from evil.'

'I know people like you, Frank. I know how you get your jollies. You can never fool me.'

'Maybe, maybe not. What the fuck is this all about?

The way you've sneaked yourself in tells me this ain't fucking exactly above board.'

'Yeah, you're right. I want to know about Mickey the Machete. The man you knifed in the throat.'

'I know who the fuck you mean. You never seen so much blood in all your life. I swear I could see a fucking line in his face as the blood drained out of him. Beautiful it was. Modern art. Not like the shit they call modern art these days.'

Jairus felt his whole body tighten with loathing, the old headache returning to the top of his skull, beating hard. 'Yeah, I know what you mean. So, tell me about Mickey. Why did you knife him?'

Saunders' eyes narrowed, his free hand began to fidget. 'Because I felt like it.'

'You just felt like knifing him after months of sharing a cell with him?'

'Yeah, it's what us psychopaths do.'

'You're not a psychopath, Frank. I've seen your file. You're just evil. You like to see the innocent suffer, like them to beg for mercy, like to see the relief in their eyes when they think you might show it. But what you love more is the look in their eyes when they know it's over. Isn't that right, Frank?'

Saunders grinned, but Jairus saw that his eyes were full of menace. 'You don't want to get inside my head, boy. You think you're hard, you don't know the meaning. No one knows you're here. Fuck me, that could give me a field day with you. I'd cut you open and piss on your heart, see the steam rising off it.'

Jairus gave his best blank look, staring straight into his empty eyes. 'Try it. See what happens.'

'Maybe I will. If I tell you about Mickey, what do I get? Reduced sentence?'

'You get a very cushy life. I can arrange that.'

Saunders took a long drag of his fag and sneered. 'You think I'm fucking stupid? Stone me. I ought to rip out your...'

Jairus launched himself forward, clamping an arm round Saunders' neck. He pulled him off his feet, squeezing, making him choke, the cigarette still hanging from his lips. 'Now, Frank, tell me about Mickey.'

The inmate's hands tore at Jairus' arms but he just squeezed tighter. 'You...fuck...you can't do this...you can't kill...me...'

'Can't I, Frank? Look up, Frank.'

Saunders' eyes lifted up to the ceiling and the beam that cut through the cell, where Jairus had created a noose from some clothes and an old sheet. 'The way I'm holding you won't leave any marks. I know what I'm doing, Frank. When you're unconscious, I put the noose round your neck. No one's none the wiser. Do you think they'll carry out much of an investigation over a scumbag like you?'

'I'll... fuck...'

'You'll tell me about Mickey, that's what you'll fucking do.' Jairus eased off the pressure a little, enough to allow Saunders to talk.

'Alright, what the fuck do you want to know?'

'Why did you kill him?'

'I can't fucking say, can I?'

Jairus squeezed, and put extra pressure on his windpipe. 'Yeah, you can.'

'Fuck you! You're not going to kill me! You think I'm fucking stupid!?'

Jairus laughed as he choked him harder and saw his face changing colour, slowly going purple. 'You don't even know who I am, do you? You think I'm just some pig who happened to nick you.'

'I know who you are! A... wAnnebe hard man, ex-fucking pig. Suck my cock... just like you did to your boss every fucking day.'

'You remember my name, don't you? It's Jairus.' He whispered the words in his ear. 'You've heard the rumours about me, the things I've done since putting you away. I'm the pig who got away with murder. Not just once, but twice. All I got was a slap on the wrist. Think I can't get away with it again? Just remember I'm not even here!'

As Jairus squeezed even tighter, Saunders tore at his arm, fighting for breath, trying to say something.

'What's that, Frank?' Jairus said, laughing, his heart now pounding, his whole body feeling alive again. 'What're you trying to tell me?'

With the pressure released, Saunders coughed and rubbed his throat, his eyes still bulging. 'You... you're a... fucking psycho!'

'Yeah, tell me something I don't know. Like, tell me why you killed Mickey.'

Saunders broke away and stood panting, leaning his back against the cell door, rubbing his throat, his eyes rising towards the makeshift noose. 'They'll kill me and my mum,' he said, staring at Jairus. 'That's what the fucker said to me. My mum's riddled with cancer now, so I don't suppose it matters. They can come for me if they want, I won't go without a fight though.'

'Who threatened you, Frank?'

'I don't know. The word came through a screw. Took me aside one day and laid it on the line. Showed me fucking photos they'd taken of Mum when she was out and about.'

Jairus watched him go from the tough prison-hardened killer to little boy lost, who only wanted his mum. They were all the same underneath, he'd seen it so many times before. All they want at the end of the day is Mummy's love. 'Who was the screw? You got a name for me?'

'You're a greedy bastard, ain't you? Alright, I'll tell you. Ain't no skin off my nose no more. Get yourself killed for all I care. His name's Darren Parker. He doesn't work here anymore. Find that fucker and give him a whack from me, would you?'

Jairus nodded and stepped closer to Saunders. 'Yeah, I'll do better than that if you tell me what you and Mickey discussed late into the winter evenings.'

'You're fucking trying to get me in the shit, aren't you?'

'You got yourself in the shit when you stuck that chiv in Mickey's neck. Now, just get it off your chest, Frank.'

The inmate sat heavily on the bed, then looked up at Jairus. 'You do something for me then. Go see my mum, tell her I love her and that I'm sorry. You got that?'

Jairus nodded, so Saunders buried his face in his hands, then took them away and stared at the opposite wall. 'He told me he did it. He hacked up the journalist, but what he also told me was that he didn't do it in the car park.'

'Bollocks.'

Saunders stared at him, fury bubbling behind his eyes. 'I'm telling you that's what he said. He cut him up in some house somewhere...'

'The police were sure he was cut up in the car park.'

'Then they're either incompetent or they're fucking lying, ain't they?'

'Or Mickey was lying.'

'Why would he?'

Jairus' headache was back, punching into his skull, sending a strange sensation down his spine. He didn't like what he was hearing. 'Where was this house?'

Saunders shrugged. 'London somewhere...'

'Where?' Jairus lurched towards him, making Saunders flinch.

'Hackney. It was a basement flat, I remember that. Nice place. Done up nice, he said. That's all I fucking know.'

Jairus stared at him for a while, trying to read the Dracula face staring back at him, then jumped up and pulled down the noose. 'If I find out you've been bullshitting me, you know what I'll do, don't you?'

As Jairus banged on the cell door, Saunders said, sounding tired, 'You'll have to use fucking CPR on me first, because chances are, pig, I'll be fucking dead.'

CHAPTER 4

He had a pretty good view of the suit who was sat in the battered Peugeot on the other side of the playground. He probably thought he was being inconspicuous but he really wasn't. The sweat and desire was practically dripping off the old pervert as he lifted his tiny pair of binoculars and pointed them towards the kids on the swings. He knew the one who had caught the old perv's eye, and that was the pretty little blonde thing on the far swing.

He sat up a little from his position as his back was beginning to twinge. Too many days spent watching people like the old filthy bastard in the Peugeot. Even though he knew the old man, they were practically strangers. It did nobody any good building a relationship. It was more a business deal anyway. Yes, they were on first name terms, but the name he'd given the old perv wasn't even his real name. He'd told him his name was Tom.

Almost a year had past, but Tom didn't have to think too hard to work out where he could find him. He lacked imagination, and was made weak by his deviant desires. It was probably the main reason no one had entrusted the old deviant with any notable responsibility.

Tom began to laugh and sunk back into the undergrowth, hiding himself behind the large tree at the edge of the park. He was laughing, but he was concerned too. He'd arranged everything for tonight's activities, and now there was a chance things could get totally fucked up. Even so, he couldn't help laugh, as a lump with a shaved head came swaggering up to the battered Peugeot and thumped the roof, making the old dirty bastard flinch and cower.

'Wot the fuck do yer fink you're doing?' the lump pushed out his chest, his big workman's hands balled into giant fists, his face prickled with scarlet fury. 'You fucking lookin at those fucking kids?'

Tom moved back as he saw another lump, this time black, but just as livid as the first lump, come pounding towards his friend. 'What's going on?'

The first lump started jabbing a thick finger towards the old pervert. 'Fink we got ourselves a paedo, mate. This fucking shit's been spying on the kids over there.'

If they dragged the old bastard from the car and beat him to death it would be no less than he deserved. So many times, the enraged public had stepped up to call out someone for being a paedophile, usually because of mistaken identity or misreading a situation, but for once the mob had hit the dirty nail right on its twisted head.

Tom watched as the old Peugeot rumbled to life and the suit struggled to get it into reverse while the two lumps began shouting and jumping up and down like a couple of irate rhinos. Then the car roared backwards, making a screeching sound and narrowly missing a red-headed young woman pushing a pram. Soon everybody and their mothers seemed to be shouting and waving their fists at him as he raced off.

After waiting for the small angry crowd to stop furiously discussing the whole incident and dawdle off, Tom picked himself up and rubbed his aching back. Too many years hiding, crawling into spaces far too small for him had taken their toll. He was barely thirty-two years old, he reminded himself as he took out a fag from the battered packet in his jacket pocket and lit it. His hand was trembling, his heart beating heavily. He put a finger to his pulse and looked at his watch. He tutted and sucked in a lungful of smoke. Too fast. He was definitely heading towards a major heart attack in the near future.

Fuck it, he said and stubbed out the fag, then walked hurriedly to his battered old Mini. He jumped in and drove off and headed back towards Enfield, Brimsdown industrial estate to be precise. He drove past the Alma pub that sits proudly but awkwardly on the corner, then pulled up outside the set of old rundown warehouses, factories and garages that sat back rusting a few hundred yards from Durants Park. Nobody walked this way during the night except the drug dealers, and he couldn't care less about them.

He lit another fag and stared at the rusting old factory to his left. It looked pretty secure, but Tom knew there was a gap in the fence that surrounded the place. It was easy for him to slip through and enter the dank interior where there was still factory tables lining the dusty shop floor.

Tom took another long drag of his cigarette, wound down his window and flicked the butt into the road. Then he looked at his hands, feeling his pulse and his heart ring throughout his body, bringing with it a wave of nausea, and self-loathing. His past started to flicker in front of his eyes, playing like an old black and white movie.

His hands were trembling as he lit another fag and kept it in his mouth, sucking, as he pulled up his jacket sleeve, revealing his bare left arm. He stared down at the scars that lined his forearm, deeply made cuts that symbolised all the bad things he'd done.

What would one more bad thing matter?

He sucked on the cigarette, then snatched it from his mouth and stubbed it into his wrist. He gritted his teeth, balled his free hand and slammed it onto the steering wheel, a growl escaping his throat.

He flicked the cigarette, breathing hard, shaking, a tear beginning to travel down his face. He wiped it away, and stared at the old factory, where another night of terrible things would happen.

Jairus dug his hands deep into his jacket pockets and stormed down Seven Sisters Road, glancing over the steady stream of heavy traffic heading south, the flicker of brake lights going on and off. A red double decker bus hissed loudly as it pulled into the bus stop next to him. There was a young black man and an old white man screaming about God to his right, most of the pedestrians ignoring them both. His eyes jumped to the word SIN written in bold red letters on a board leaning against the wall. He wasn't going upwards when he died, that's for sure, he thought, and decided he couldn't care less. Do all you can to avenge the dead and get out, sink into the nothingness, the great void, he told himself.

He took out his mobile and checked the address. There was a glass-fronted record shop on the next corner, positioned next to a kebab shop. Apparently, there was a steady rise in the desire for vinyl again, a piece of useless information that somehow pleased him, gave him a sense of continuity with his old distant, younger life.

This was where Darren Parker had set up shop, weirdly leaving the Prison Service to open a record shop. He could understand it in a way, how years of abuse, having prisoners spit at him, scream in his ear, threaten all kinds of terrible things, might weaken his resolve and send him running for the vinyl hills, but Jairus' stomach tightened as he stepped into the nearly empty shop.

It was all laid out perfectly, neat racks of vinyl, labelled in genres. Rare records lined the walls. A till sat in the far corner, a door marked private behind the till and the skinny young black kid at the counter. He was reading a dance music magazine.

Jairus found the few Johnny Cash records they had and pretended to examine them while he kept watching the boy on the till. 'Darren around?' Jairus said.

The young lad flickered out of his dream and looked blankly at Jairus. 'What yer say?'

'Darren around? Darren Parker? Fella who owns this place?'

The young lad narrowed his eyes, his body tensed. 'You a friend of his?'

'Yeah. Darren through that door?'

'I dunno.'

'You dunno? Well, you pop in there and tell him John's out here. I used to work at Wandsworth with him.'

The lad had a scowl creasing his face, but was standing still.

'Go on, run along. I'll keep an eye on the place.'

The lad walked backwards a couple of steps, his suspicious eyes on Jairus, then hurried through the door and shut it behind him.

Jairus stepped up to the till and waited, thinking he could hear distant voices. When the lad came back, he looked even more suspicious and nervous, but said,

'He's coming.'

'Good. I'll wait here.' Jairus went on flipping through the records, his eyes rising to the young lad whose eyes were permanently fixed on him.

A couple of minutes passed, so Jairus walked up to the lad and dug his hands in his pockets. 'Darren's not coming out, is he?'

The lad shrugged. 'I dunno.'

'Is there a back way out of there?' Jairus nodded to the door. 'Yeah, he's slipped out, hasn't he? Where is he?'

Jairus saw the lad's eyes flicker to his left, so Jairus swept round and saw a stocky man with blond short hair, dressed in shirt and trousers, walking past the shop window. His shifty eyes fell on Jairus, then he quickened his pace and looked set to run at any moment.

Jairus rushed through the door, breaking into a jog as he turned right and spotted the blonde man hurrying into a narrow back street of grotty terraced houses, most of which had front gardens cluttered with bin bags.

'Oi, you, Darren Parker,' Jairus shouted.

The blonde man looked back at him and shouted, 'Fuck off!'

Jairus caught up with him as Parker took out his keys and unlocked a black sporty VW Polo. 'I'm not a police officer, if that's what's worrying you?'

Parker stopped as he was about to open the door, looked down at the pavement and said, 'You're not? Then who are you? Cause I don't know any prison guard called John.'

Jairus smiled. 'My name's Jairus.'

'Jairus? Jairus what?' Parker stared at him, his concern fading and being replaced by suspicion.

'Just Jairus, like Madonna, Prince. Get it? I want to talk to you about Mickey O'Neil.'

The ex-prison guard's expression changed, the colour racing from his face as he tore open the car door. 'Fuck off.'

'Yeah, I will eventually.' Jairus kicked the car door shut. 'You paid for him to be killed. Why?'

'Did you just kick my fucking car?'

'Yeah. Get over it. Why did you want Mickey dead?'

The guard stepped up to Jairus, rage now sparkling in his eyes, his frame rigid, his hands balling. 'Don't fucking kick my car. Now fuck off! I've got nothing to say to you!'

'I'm guessing someone got you to pay Frank Saunders to knife Mickey. Maybe they paid you. Is that where you got the money to buy the record shop?'

He saw the twitch of Parker's right shoulder, the turn of his arm, the telegram that told Jairus that a punch was coming. As the fist twisted towards his face, Parker's gritted teeth behind it, Jairus grasped his wrist and twisted, spinning him around and pulling his arm behind his back. He cracked him in the knee with the heel of his shoe, sending Parker to his knees as he yelped and swore.

'Fuck... you fucking,' Parker screamed, but Jairus twisted his arm, sending his hand in the opposite direction.

'So, Darren,' Jairus said. 'Who persuaded you to get Saunders to kill Mickey?'

'Fucking... your mum did.'

'Yeah, did she?' Jairus applied more pressure, making the ex-guard let out a cry between his gritted teeth. 'Have a medium handy, did you? Come on, mate. Do you really want me to snap your arm?'

'That... all you're going to do?' Parker forced a

painful laugh out of his mouth. 'Go on then. You can't arrest me, can you? No, so fuck off.'

The wave of anger morphed into fury, making Jairus' heart ripple, his hands begin to shake. Without knowing it, he applied more pressure, blocking out the screams of pain coming from the man kneeling on the pavement. 'You going to tell me? Or do I have to come back?'

'Fuck you!' Parker looked around, then started shouting, 'Help me! I'm being attacked! Someone help me!'

Jairus spun his head round to see who might be looking at the scene he'd created, but the few passers-by there was were avoiding looking at them, not wanting to get involved. Thank God for the usual neighbourly love, Jairus thought, even though he also knew Parker wasn't going to talk. He didn't have any leverage, apart the physical kind he was inflicting.

Jairus pushed him forward onto his face. 'I'll be back to talk to you another time. You better get ready to talk to me.'

Parker rubbed his arm and shoulder, his twisted eyes scowling up at Jairus. 'You better not come back. If you know what's good for you, you'll stay away.'

'Yeah, but you see, I've never known what's good for me... or even cared, for that matter.'

Jairus turned and walked away, heading back in the direction of his car, thinking about his next move, deciding that keeping a close eye on Darren Parker would be his best bet now that he'd kicked the shit out of the hornets' nest.

The street light gave a cosy violet glow to the proud Victoria building which wrestled shoulders with all the other grand palaces along the wide London street.

This was where the toffs lived, all the Barons, Lords and a scattering of greedy MPs.

Tom was watching the grand windows, seeing the lights go out, smoking his fifteenth fag since he'd been stood opposite the old perv's London abode.

The lights had been out now for nearly an hour, and as Tom knew that the aged suit and his wife no longer shared their marital bed, he was sure he would find him fast asleep in the back bedroom.

He crushed his fag under his shoe, pulled up the hood of his jacket and walked quickly across the street, avoiding the glow of the street light. He was soon under the shelter of the grand doorway, hidden by the two pillars on either side. He took out the front door key and slipped it quietly into the lock. He quietly let himself in, and looked into the dark and empty hallway which was awash in the same dismal light from the street lights. He went up the wide and thickly carpeted stairs that wound up the centre of the house and stopped on the top landing, listening to the heavy snoring coming from the wife who was lying comatose in a giant four poster. He went to the last bedroom and achingly slowly opened the door and stood frozen for a moment, his eyes jumping to a regular sized double bed and the skinny old man lying sprawled across it.

He sat heavily at the end of the bed, hoping that the old pervert would feel it in his sleep and wake, but he only muttered and coughed a little before falling silent again.

Tom put his face in his hands and sighed, then looked at the gangly white foot hanging off the bed. He grabbed the icy foot and yanked, but the old perv moaned and tried to pull his foot away.

Tom grabbed hold, tightly and kept yanking until

the old perv coughed and spluttered and jumped up in bed. He couldn't help but laugh when the old man stared at him, spittle on his chin and his bleary eyes trying to take in what was happening.

'Oh, Lord,' the old perv reached over and grabbed a pair of spectacles from the bedside table and put them on. 'What the devil do you think you are doing here, Tom?'

'Don't worry, the old dear's out of it and snoring the house down.' Tom patted his pale, withered leg and felt puke rise to his throat.

The old man swung his legs over the bed and stood up, his head swinging about as if he expected somebody else to jump out. 'How the bloody hell did you get in?'

'You getting Alzheimer's? You gave me a key, remember? Just in case of emergencies.'

'I took the bloody thing back!' the old perv ripped a dark blue robe from the back of the bedroom door and threw it on. 'I don't do those things anymore, Tom. I'm a changed man.'

Tom couldn't help but break out into almost hysterical laughter while the old perv stood staring at him, his face filled with horror and confusion.

'What?' The old perv slung his arms up in anger. 'Stop laughing. She'll hear you!'

Tom looked up, and let the old man, who looked rather feminine in his dressing gown, see his sneer. What the old man didn't see, couldn't know about, were the black worms that burrowed into his skull and slowly consumed his soul. 'I saw you today. At the playground.'

The old perv's face changed, seeming to dissolve from haughty condemnation, to fear and embarrassment within seconds. 'I stopped to eat my lunch... there is no...'

'You're not standing in front of a judge,' Tom said. 'You don't have to persuade me. But I did happen to spy a pretty blonde thing. Your favourite kind, if I remember rightly.'

The old perv looked down at his hand, his face becoming paler, a glisten of sweat on his wrinkled top lip. 'I'm not... I do not do those...'

Tom held up a hand. 'All right. You don't have to repeat yourself. Then I'll be off. I had a little treat for you, but it's all right. I know others who might want a taste.'

Tom went to leave the bed, but found the old man's claw griping his arm, his old watery eyes wide, his mouth slowly opening. 'Do you mean what I believe you mean? Please, do not play games with me, Tom. Have you brought... pictures?'

There was laughter and great sickness rising through Tom as the black worms dug further into him, but he kept it all down, just like he had for years. So many years of darkness. One more night of darkness would make little difference in the grand scheme of things, would it?

'I'm not playing games,' Tom said, and put on the mask of sincerity that he'd become expert at donning when the situation demanded it. 'It's not photographs this time.'

The old perv leant forward, hungry. 'Video?'

'No. This time it's the real thing.'

He flinched back a little, his watery eyes widening. 'The real... you've never... how did you?'

'Do you really want to know all that? What if you get pulled in by the police again?'

The old perv shook his head, remembered horror filling his eyes.

'She's waiting for you right now,' Tom said. 'That's all you need to know.'

After a couple steps backwards, the old perv found his voice and said, 'Is she... is she a golden child?'

Tom's stomach churned. 'She is. Or rather platinum, you'd say.'

'How old?'

'Barely eight.' The worms burrowed so fiercely that Tom almost cried out.

A pasty, oily tongue protruded from the old pervert's mouth and caressed his lips. 'Where is she?'

'An old disused factory. But we have to go now. We've wasted too much time already.'

The old man was hesitating, practically dancing with indecision.

'One last time for old times' sake,' Tom said and watched the old man nod and crumble easily into his inner well of dark desires.

CHAPTER 5

He got himself comfortable in his car, his overcoat wrapped tightly round him, a takeaway coffee clasped between his chilled hands. The early October sun had retreated, leaving an iciness in the air that Jairus did not appreciate one bit. He thought his days of carrying out surveillance and other menial police tasks were behind him, but there he was, sitting in his cold car and staring out at the newly-built flats.

But he wasn't a policeman anymore, something he was having to repeat to himself like a mantra, although a whisper of an echo suggested that he would be again. He grasped hold of that thought and wrapped it around himself, knowing there was a way back through the fog his life had become surrounded by.

His hands were shaking more violently than ever, and twice he almost lost grip of the coffee and swore aloud as if he'd actually dropped the scolding liquid onto his lap.

There was no movement from the flat, which went against his notion that Parker was scared and would try and contact whoever had set up the hit on Mickey O'Neil. The other problem that kept racing around his brain, chasing its own tail, was how exactly he was going to find the house where David Coulson was allegedly murdered. All he had was an area and the rough description of the type of building it was. None of what Frank Saunders had told him seemed useful and was becoming less so as the night drew on and Darren Parker stayed at home.

Jairus looked at his watch and saw it was nearly 11 p.m. He was very close to giving up and heading home, although he knew that his mouth would begin to salivate the moment he saw the half-drunk bottle of vodka still sat by the sofa bed. Then his eyes rose to the rearview mirror when he saw a pair of headlights enter the street and a car begin to parallel park a couple spaces behind him. He blinked and held his hand over his eyes when the car's headlights caught the mirror.

Then the lights went off, leaving the street in a blanket of hazy indigo darkness. He sat up when he heard the sound, the clicking, scraping sound that comes from heels moving along the pavement. He adjusted himself and the rearview mirror, trying to see who was coming. He wondered if they were heading for one of the flats, perhaps they were even a friend of Darren Parker.

He flinched when there was a loud tap at the passenger window. A woman, probably about thirty-five, dark complexion, luscious long dark hair, full red lips, was looking in at him. She was smiling, her beautifully shaped eyebrows raised above her dark glistening eyes.

He lowered the window. 'Yeah, can I help you?'

'On a stakeout?' she said, in a nicely spoken voice, a hint of an Enfield accent beneath it. 'That's what you policemen call it, don't you?'

'I'm not a policeman,' he said and turned his eyes back towards the flat. 'What's it got to do with you anyway?'

'If you're stalking who I think you're stalking, then

it's got everything to do with me.'

Jairus looked at her, saw her dark eyes glistening, seemingly full of mischief. 'Who do you think I'm stalking?'

'Darren Parker?' She raised one eyebrow. 'Look, it's actually quite cold out here. Can I get in?'

'It's not much better in here, but all right.' He opened the door for her and she gracefully slipped in, a movement that very few people seemed to be able to pull off.

Now he could see she was wearing a cream blouse, a pinstripe skirt, black tights and heels. She was full figured, beautiful, and there was definitely some Mediterranean blood pumping through her veins.

She turned to him. 'So, you're ex-DCI Jairus.'

'How did you come by that information?'

'I spotted you earlier. I took the registration number of your car. Pretty straightforward. Have you turned private investigator?'

'No. Who are you? Why do I smell journalist?'

The woman raised her arm and sniffed underneath it. 'Do we really smell that bad? I'm Helen Chara. Yes, I do belong to that dirtiest of dirty professions. I'll admit it, I'm a journalist. Guilty as charged.'

'Don't worry. You're in good company. Everyone thinks all coppers are dirty too. Who do you work for? And why're you interested in Darren Parker?'

She smiled. 'Well, I work for myself, since I got fired from my last job. I guess I wasn't sleazy enough... and the reason I'm interested in Darren Parker is a piece I was putting together about the regime of violence in some British prisons.'

'Do people really want to read or even care about that?'

She moved herself closer, her dark eyes piercing his

skull. 'You don't think prisoners should have rights?'

'No. They give up their rights when they commit crimes. Simple as that.'

'Really? And I thought you had kind eyes.'

Jairus looked down and saw that her hand, and her perfectly manicured dark red nails, was almost touching his leg. Then his eyes jumped to her nylon-covered legs. Her skirt had ridden up a little, revealing her legs to be very shapely. 'Are you trying to bewitch me, Helen?'

'The thought had crossed my mind. But I can see you're too sharp for me.' There was that smile again, the full lips, the playful dark eyes. Jairus realised that early in her life she must have learned that her smile got her almost all she wanted. He felt himself being drawn in, a burning star being pulled towards a black hole. He cleared his already foggy mind and found a thought in among the detritus that drifted through his brain. 'Did you know David Coulson?'

Her smile faded, and a look of polite sobriety came across her. 'The journalist that was hacked to death? No, I never met him, but I think we all felt anger and sadness when we heard the news. The same way you police officers get furious and vengeful when one of your own gets targeted.'

'Ever hear talk that his death wasn't all they made it out to be?'

She rolled her eyes. 'You're heading into conspiracy theory territory.'

'Am I?'

'I've heard talk that Coulson was knocked off because of some story he was looking into. Although no evidence that he was looking into something dangerous or inflammatory has ever come to light. Anyway, your lot seemed happy enough.'

Jairus huffed. 'Sometimes that's not good enough, not even for me.'

'Are you suggesting that sometimes officers like things to a bit neater than they actually are? Can I quote you on that?'

'Don't you dare.'

She put the smile back on. 'So, what's put you on Darren Parker's scent? I take it, seeing as he used to be a prison guard, he has a connection with the man who was put away for murdering Coulson? Mickey O'Neil? Am I right?'

'Yeah, something like that. But you better not go printing any of this.' He looked into her eyes, gave her his best menacing look.

'Why not? What're you going to do if I did?'

'Believe me, Helen, when I say that I can make life very difficult for you.'

A cunning smile lifted the corners of her full lips. 'That may have been true when you were back on the force, but I'm not so convinced now. But I'm thinking of proposing a deal... except, I did some quick research on you and found out that you'd stitched up a couple of journalists in the past.'

'Like you said, that was when I was back on the force. I'm all alone now and I need allies. I don't have many friends left. You help me get to the bottom of this, and you get to write the story. That what you were thinking?'

She sat back, still digging her dark eyes into his, seeming to examine him carefully. 'OK. It's a deal. What's our first job?'

Jairus nodded towards the building. 'I need his mobile number, so...'

'Why didn't you say?' Helen dug out her notebook from her coat and opened it up. 'Here. I managed to charm Parker into giving me his number when I first talked to him. Didn't take much. Most men are easily manipulated.'

Jairus smiled. 'Yeah, don't I know it.' He entered the number into his own phone, then opened the car door.

'Where are you going?'

'I need to call one of the few friends I do have left. If he's still talking to me.'

She frowned, folded her arms across her chest. 'I thought we were building trust.'

'Yeah, we are. I trust you when it comes to me and what I need to do. This is someone else, a friend. I don't want to jeopardise their safety.'

She let out a strange huff.

'What?'

'Well, you say all that but you're going to drag them into your business anyway?'

He didn't answer, just climbed out and got the number up that he wanted and dialled as he walked away from the car. Of course, as he dialled, he knew Helen had a point; once again he was preparing to drag one of his friends into his own personal hell, but he had little choice as there were aspects of the case he needed expert technical assistance with, and Rich Vincent was the most technical person he knew. He was the best IT person Edmonton Police Station had and also lead guitarist in a heavy metal band at the weekends. Jairus had been dragged to a pub on quite a few occasions to see him torturing a guitar, looking the part with his long black hair, Iron Maiden T-shirt, black nails and tight black jeans.

As the call was answered, Jairus pulled his ear away from the phone as a blast of distorted music screamed into his ear. A familiar voice was shouting out through the wave of sound.

'Rich?!' Jairus shouted into his phone. 'Rich? That you?'

The music died away, becoming faint as Jairus said, 'Rich, you there?'

'Jairus?' Rich said, his astonishment coming through the line. 'Jesus... I didn't think I'd ever hear from you again.'

'Yeah, well, I'm back from the dead.'

'Good to hear your ghostly voice, man.'

'You too, Rich. I take it your band's getting ready to play a gig?'

'That's right. Listen, mate, I've taken a long break from work. Doctor reckons it was messing with my head, you know all the child abuse stuff they had me doing. I've seen too many bad things, he reckons.'

'Yeah, I'd agree. I was just going to ask you to look into some stuff for me.' Jairus' stomach tightened, the guilt and awkwardness ripping through him. He'd already dragged Rich into too many dodgy situations in the past and was quite aware that Rich's mental issues were probably partly down to him.

There was a pause on the other end, so Jairus said, 'Don't worry, Rich. I don't want to drag...'

'It's OK. What do you need?'

'I knew you wouldn't let me down. I've got a mobile number. I need to know any calls made from the number from this morning up until I tell you to stop. I need to know where the phone goes and all that type of thing.'

'Yep, I know the routine. Lucky for you I've got a few contacts that owe me, and plenty of hardware at home. Anything else?'

Jairus turned and looked at his car, where Helen Chara was also on her mobile. 'Yeah, could you look into someone for me. Helen Chara. She's a journalist, or so she says.'

Rich laughed. 'I should've known a woman would be involved.'

'Yeah, there always is. She says she wants to help, but I'm always suspicious of people who turn up out of the blue offering help.'

'All right, Jay, I'll dig up what I can.'

'Thanks, Rich, I'll be in touch.'

'Jay...'

'Yeah?'

'Watch your back, won't you?'

Jairus laughed. 'Don't I always?'

The line went dead, so Jairus turned and walked back towards the car, where Helen Chara was climbing out.

'You leaving me to watch him on my own?' Jairus said.

She smiled. 'I'm afraid so. As much as I was enjoying your company, I need to go and see someone.'

'Boyfriend?'

She stared at him, a smile beginning at the edge of her mouth. 'I'm not going to answer that. Think I'll keep you in suspense. Anyway, I'll be in touch. Here's my number. Let me know what I can do to help out.'

Jairus watched her red nails pushing the business card across the roof of the car, then he put it away in his pocket. 'Yeah, I will. Tell me, do you know Robert Burdock?'

He noticed the minutest change in her face, a slight tremor, telling of a possible earthquake to come.

'Everyone's heard of Robert Burdock. Look, I've got to go. Call me.'

He watched her walk away, slip into her car and start the engine, then climbed into his. He drove away, heading for home, satisfied that Rich would tell him all he needed to know about Darren Parker.

He knew he wouldn't be able to sleep though. The ghosts were already moving into his mind, ready to haunt his entire night.

Tom parked the car outside the factory, lit a cigarette, his fingers trembling, and turned to watch the old perv, who was staring disbelievingly at the battered building.

'In there?' he said, his voice shaking with either fear or excitement. Probably a bit of both, Tom thought, knowing how the filthy bastard enjoyed as much pain and discomfort as he did pleasure. Enjoyed inflicting it too. Tom held back a belch filled with the stench of vomit. He sucked on the cigarette and said, forcing a smile to his lips, 'Yep, Goldilocks is in there. Waiting.'

The old perv's eyes were glistening as he opened the door, his head still fixed towards the building. For a moment, Tom thought he might cry, and wondered what percentage of him was suffering guilt, if any at all. It was a special kind of monster that could do the things he'd done and still go about his day, eat breakfast, kiss his wife, and go to work as if his soul had not tasted evil.

'You never did anything like this before, Tom,' the old perv said, his eyes digging deep into him. 'It was only the photographs with you. You always said it was only the dealing, never the making.'

Tom nodded, swallowed down the vomit taste rising to his mouth. 'People change... I need the money... I know... I know you'll reward me for this. Won't you?'

The old man put his withered old hand on Tom's. 'Of course. Of course I will. But this will be the last time. I promised myself.'

Tom took a few deep breaths, a last drag and opened the door. He pressed the butt into the ground with his foot, watching the old man stumble out of the car towards the building, obviously drawn towards the moment, unable to help himself, addicted to the darkness that had opened up inside himself, and began swallowing the goodness it found and turned it to dirt. That's what Tom felt his lungs were filled with, the blackest earth, drowning him in pure emptiness.

Tom caught up with the old perv and redirected him round the back where there was a gap in the fence. He looked at Tom, with myriad questions presenting themselves in his watery eyes, but Tom pushed him onwards.

She was inside, waiting, tied up.

Tom stopped halfway across the uneven concrete ground, and bent over, retching. Nothing came up. He expected blackness to pour out of his mouth, like some smelly, evil filled oil, but just a trail of saliva emerged from his dry lips.

'You all right, Tom?' the old man said, fear stamped into his wrinkled skin.

Tom nodded, then pointed to the large metal doors that were heavily chained and padlocked.

'How do we get in?' the old man looked horrified, his face stamped with impatience like a kid told he had to wait to open his Christmas presents.

Tom walked to the doors, grabbed the chain and yanked it down. It clattered loudly to the ground, making the old man jump out of his skin and spin his head round to see if anyone was watching. He then grabbed one of the doors and pulled it open. It screeched all the way, revealing the dusty and dark interior. Tom's eyes adjusted and he could see the deserted factory floor, chains hanging down, discarded machinery covered in thick dust.

'You hear that?' Tom asked and looked at the old man, who overtook him and walked inside.

'Hear what?'

'Listen.' He knew the sound would soon greet the old perv's ears and fill him full of desire. He knew it assuredly as he knew tomorrow the sun would come up, and the sky would look radiant and beautiful for a while, just before all the badness would bleed into it.

The old perv reacted, his head flinching, his eyes widening. He looked at Tom as if for confirmation, but he didn't need it. He heard the faint sobbing as well as Tom did, and as much as it made Tom want to vomit and cry, it would make the old perv want to laugh and smile.

They were lost in the darkness for a moment until Tom took out a torch and shone it across the blackened shapes. He found the large green bag that was tied up with rope, and held it in the beam so the old pervert could see it and begin to fantasise.

'This will be the last time,' Tom said.

The old pervert nodded enthusiastically. 'Open it. Let her breathe.'

'She's all right.' Tom knelt down and placed his hand on the bag, but felt no movement. The sobbing had stopped.

'What is it?! Is she OK? It's no good if she's dead.'

The words stung him, a giant stinger through his gut, forcing the vomit to rise up his throat. He swallowed it with much effort, then turned and looked at the old pervert, shining the torch in his face. He flapped at the beam as if he believed he could actually knock it away. 'Don't! I can't see.'

Tom removed the torch light, undid the bag and

then stood back. 'She's fine. Goldilocks is fine. Ready for you.'

The old pervert in the grey suit didn't waste any time and sunk to his bony knees, his desperate hands grabbing for the bag's zipper, struggling to undo it.

Tom stepped back into the darkness, his hand reaching behind him where he knew there was a workstation. He gripped the crowbar that he knew was there, because he'd placed it there, just as he had placed the bag on the floor.

The old perv gasped as the blonde hair flourished over the edge of the bag. He started talking to the girl in a soft voice, like a father trying to calm an upset child. He lifted her out with trembling hands.

Tom gripped the small, but heavy crowbar, feeling the chill of it burning his palm. The old perv had stopped dead, his head shaking, questions rising from his confused mouth. Then his knees were moving as he scrabbled to turn round and face Tom.

'Is this a joke?' he said.

'What's wrong?' Tom held the bar behind his back.

'This is a dummy. What's wrong with you?'

Tom stepped towards him. 'What's wrong with you? Do you know there's something very wrong with you?'

The old pervert's face changed, his anger flowing into suspicion as he fought to get to his feet.

Tom rushed forward, raising the crowbar above his head, his whole body trembling, his heart burning, pounding. The old pervert raised his arms, tried to cover his head as he screamed.

The bar landed with a wet sounding thump. The old man was still for a moment, his eyes swimming in his head, trying to focus, while the blood trickled from the gash in his skull.

Tom couldn't move, hypnotised by the wavering movement of the old sex offender as he tried to drag himself back into consciousness.

The bony hand snapped at the air, then grasped hold of Tom's jacket. 'No, no. Why? Why?'

Tom lifted the crowbar high above his head and slammed it down again. He stood back as the old pervert slumped to the floor, his face buried in the dummy's hair, the recording of the sobbing started up again. But his body was still moving, twitching, a faint breath escaping his mouth.

Tom cracked the bar twice over the back of his skull, then stepped back. He was dizzy himself, his head pounding. He couldn't breathe. He was going to suffocate if he didn't get outside. He grabbed the bag and dragged it behind him as he ran towards the doors and out into the blue-black night. He sucked in large breaths but his heart wouldn't be still.

He was bent over, panting, fighting the urge to vomit. With shaking hands, he found his cigarettes and put one between his lips. He lit it, took in the smoke and then searched in his other pockets for the piece of paper he'd been carrying around for months. It was dogeared and stained, but he unfolded it and read again the computer printed list of names, each one of them as guilty as the last.

He found the biro and shakily ran a line through the old pervert's name.

CHAPTER 6

Jairus was feeling worn out by the time he'd arrived home, ready to drop, and thought it might actually be possible for him to sleep without the aid of vodka.

He was wrong.

His mind rattled on like a slow rollercoaster fixed in a loop. His brain beat, beat, beat on, joining together in rhythm with the rain that had begun to hammer at his windows. He turned over and came face to face with the blurred logo on the half-drunk bottle of vodka. He snapped upright, grabbed the bottle and pulled himself out of bed. In the kitchen, he poured the remainder of the clear liquid down the sink. He looked at his trembling hands, then out into the rain-soaked night.

An hour later he found himself dressed and in his car heading for the East End, the glistening dark streets racing past. He seemed to be the only soul left awake, sent out to be on guard, watching over the population. He laughed at his own ridiculous thoughts and put his foot down, racing through a junction before the lights changed.

The Isle of Dogs was as much a wasteland as the rest of London that night, with the wind and rain attacking the streets and pushing litter in every direction.

He parked at the very edge of the car park that sat behind the Ship Inn, one of the original London pubs left on the Island. It was sat alone, with empty overgrown lots on either side ready for a development of flats to be built.

The rain hardened its attack on the streets as Jairus sat for a moment watching it strike at the asphalt and ricocheting back into the air. When the rain calmed, he climbed out and headed for the outlined space where Coulson had been found in pieces. He stood looking down at the ground, picturing the murder scene as he recalled it from the crime scene photos contained in the file he'd been given by Burdock. He turned his head as the rain tapped at his skull, looking towards a CCTV camera to his right, too far away to have caught sight of the body. Same with the camera to his left, which meant the body had been placed in that blind spot on purpose.

Jairus looked up when a heavy clanking sound echoed round the empty car park and saw the pub's emergency exit had been opened. He could make out the tall and broad silhouette of a man holding two bin bags full of rubbish. Their eyes seemed to meet for a moment before the figure dropped the two bags into a wheelie bin and went back inside. Jairus went back to his vigil, feeling the rain soaking into his skin, hoping it would wash away the disease he felt had invaded his body and soul.

Then there were wet footsteps coming towards him and he looked up to see the tall man standing looking at him, now covered by a blue waterproof jacket.

He was in his early fifties, Jairus estimated, had a neatly trimmed grey beard, and piercing grey blue eyes that looked at him through craggy slits in his face. He had a bulbous stomach that hung over his trousers.

'Can I help you, son?' the man asked in a deep

gravelly East End accent.

'Just standing around minding my own business.'

The man stared at the parking space that Jairus had been concentrating on. 'That's where that reporter died. Hacked to death by that bleeding lunatic.'

'Mickey the Machete.' Jairus nodded.

'That's right. You look like old bill.'

'Yeah? Good-looking man is he, this old Bill?'

'You're a bleeding comedian. Why else would a man be stood in the rain staring at that God-awful spot?'

'Yeah, I'm... I mean I was on the job. Not anymore.'

The man turned and gestured towards the pub. 'You should definitely come inside out of the rain then, my pub's full of people who used to be something.'

'Thanks. I'm OK.'

'If you come in, I can get you a towel to dry you off and if there's anything you want to know about the murder, then I can tell you all that I know.'

There was a tinge of pity in the landlord's voice, and Jairus hated the sound of it. But even though the last place he needed to be was a pub, he also wanted as much background material as he could get on Coulson's murder. And landlords sometimes had a lot of information, because people drink, and when people are drunk they tend to talk. 'Yeah, OK. Let's go.'

Jairus followed the tall man, his coat soaked with rain, back towards the pub. The man let him inside the warm interior of the bar, then shut and locked the door behind him.

It was a big oblong room with a matching old style bar at the centre. Scratched and stained wooden tables filled the place. An old upright piano stood in one corner near the toilets, along with a scattering of fruit machines. Jairus felt as if he'd travelled back in time to the kind of pub his dad used to take him to.

'Sit at the bar, take the weight off,' the landlord said as he took off his coat. 'I'm Terry, by the way. Terry Stephens. I own this shithole.'

'I'm Jairus.' Jairus shook his hand.

'Jairus? Jairus what?'

'Nothing. Just Jairus.' Jairus sat on a stool at the bar. 'Anyway, I like this shithole. Has a certain amount of charm.'

'I'm pretty fond of the shithole too, but the developers keep offering me cash to sell it.' Terry headed behind the bar. 'Too early for a drink?'

'Black coffee, two sugars, cheers.'

'Nothing stronger?'

'No, I don't drink anymore.'

Terry nodded sagely. 'Can't say that I blame you. My doctor keeps telling me to lay off the sauce. Keeps on about my blood pressure. He can go fuck himself. I come out clean from three tours of Belfast with the paras, so I'm bleeding well having a drink when I want one.'

Jairus watched him start the coffee machine over the other side of the bar, then pour himself a pint of ale.

'So, tell me about the murder,' Jairus said.

Terry sipped his drink, then wiped his mouth. 'What do you want to know?'

'Anything you think's relevant.'

Terry pointed at him. 'I'll tell you one bleeding thing. That reporter wasn't knocked off outside this pub.'

'Yeah? How do you know?'

'Cause I bleeding well saw him lying there. There was blood, but not enough. The whole thing just wasn't right. You know that feeling you get when something isn't right? You ever get that?'

'Yeah, all the time.' Jairus had had the feeling far too often, and he had it right then. Everything about the case had the same stench, the same tinge of strangeness. All definitely wasn't what it seemed. 'The body was dumped in the blind spot between the two cameras, so nobody would see what happened. Did Mickey drink in here regularly?'

'Never had the whole time I've owned the dump.'
'Police said he was a regular.'
'Bollocks. When I was down that nick they kept on about Mickey, showing me his photo, trying to brainwash me into saying that I had seen him in here. Hours they played that game.'

Jairus' stomach did its usual manoeuvre of tying itself in a heavy knot as Terry fetched his coffee and placed it in front of him.

'I told 'em,' Terry said, his anger starting to burn. 'He never was in this bleeding pub. They didn't like that. Didn't want to talk to me anymore. Then some of the regulars started talking to your lot, telling them they'd seen Mickey in here. Someone slid them some cash.'

Jairus' trembling hands picked up the coffee cup and he took a sip. 'I'm kind of reliably informed that Mickey did kill Coulson, the reporter.'

'He may well have done, but he didn't do it outside here!'

'I believe you. But I need to find where and why.'

'Probably stuck his nose into something he shouldn't have.' Terry sipped his pint and shrugged. Then he looked up, his brow scrunching up. 'Hello, who's this?'

Jairus turned round as someone battered their

hand against the pub doors. He could only make out two figures through the darkened frosted glass.

'We're closed!' Terry shouted as he walked halfway to the doors.

'We'd like a word with Mr Jairus,' said a well-spoken voice.

Jairus put down his coffee, his stomach twisted, the old skull-crushing headache arriving just in time.

'I don't know who the bleeding hell you're talking about,' Terry said, and engaged questioning eyes with Jairus.

'His car is parked outside,' the voice said.

Jairus mouthed, 'Ask them what they want.'

'What do you want?' Terry shouted.

'Just a short chat with Mr Jairus. That's all and then we'll leave you in peace, Mr Stephens.'

Jairus sat up, thinking, trying to workout who exactly would be wanting a chat with him in the middle of the night.

'You got anything to defend yourself with?' Jairus whispered.

Terry zipped round the bar and produced a sawn-off shotgun, then a baseball bat and smiled.

'Let them in,' Jairus said, 'then stand where you are. Don't let them see the shotgun though.'

Terry agreed and went to the double doors and unbolted them.

Two men were stood waiting, both neatly suited. One was smaller, aged about forty, dark hair, sharp, watchful eyes. Jairus watched him taking everything in about the room and the two men inside it. The other man was taller, bulkier, definitely ex-army of some kind, and looked as if he could do some serious damage.

The bigger man took a chair and sat facing the

door, positioned halfway across the room so nothing escaped him, while the shorter man approached Jairus and stood there. He refrained from looking down for a while, and kept his sharp eyes on the room and Terry.

'I promise you will not be needing your shotgun tonight, Mr Stephens,' he said and looked down at Jairus. 'Ex-DCI Jairus. It's almost a pleasure to meet you. I've read so many interesting things about you.'

'Yeah? That's nice for you.' Jairus finished his coffee, then put his hand into his jacket pocket and felt the roll of one pound coins he kept there. Contained inside his fist they made his punch ten times more effective. 'What do I call you?'

'Nothing.' A brief smile flickered across the man's lips. 'You don't get to call me anything.'

'Do I get to know where you're from?'

The man looked down at the chair in front of him, then placed his hand upon it. 'Do you mind? I've been on my feet all day.'

Jairus nodded then watched as the man sat down and folded his arms. 'Let's just say I'm from a government department.'

'Yeah, OK, but what government department?' Jairus' headache became a fist that was kneading his brain.

'That's not important. What is important, is that you have been delving into matters that really are none of your business.'

'Have I?'

'Yes. For example, you gained illegal entry to Wandsworth Prison. I don't know how, and I don't really care, but seeing as you then visited Darren Parker, and you're now sitting inside the public house that David Coulson was murdered outside of, it doesn't take a genius to work out where your little private investigation is headed.'

'Yeah, you're right about the genius bit... so they sent you.'

The man's expression remained blank. 'I'm here to ask you to stop your investigation, Mr Jairus.'

'Ask me?'

'Tell you. Warn you. Pick whichever one suits you best. Mr Jairus, you seem to be under the misapprehension that you are still a police officer. I must remind you that you are not. Being a police detective afforded you some protection, but now you are merely a civilian, that protection you enjoyed has gone.'

'You're wrong.' Jairus sat forward, holding back the anger that was building up in his throat. But he allowed each word to carry a hint of the fury he kept chained up deep within. 'I'm quite aware that I'm not a policeman anymore. It keeps me awake at night, knowing that scumbags are out there getting away with the terrible things they do. I don't sleep now. I can't. There's no rest for the wicked. I know that's true now. All I've got is my little investigation, so if you think you're going to take it away from me, you've got another fucking thing coming.'

The man looked round at his partner for a moment, then sighed. 'As I said before, the protection you had is gone. Anything that happens to you now is your own fault, no one else's.'

'Are you threatening me? I don't like being threatened. It doesn't sit well with me. It gets my back up. You go and tell your boss, whoever the fuck he is, to go fuck himself. You understand?'

'You're not being very subtle, Mr Jairus. My boss, as you put it, would also like to know who put you on this trail you're following.'

Jairus sat back and laughed loudly. 'Yeah, I bet he would. He's a nosey bastard, your boss, isn't he? I repeat, tell him to go fuck himself. Now why don't you and your pet gorilla leave me in peace?'

The man didn't react for a moment, and kept staring at Jairus. Eventually, he stood up and nodded to his partner, who also stood up. 'Very well, Mr Jairus, you have been duly warned. We will be in touch. I hope you change your mind before it's too late.'

'Don't go counting on it.' Jairus got to his feet and watched as both men headed for the door. The bigger man opened the doors, pushing them out towards the heavy rain.

The smaller man stopped and looked at Terry, who was still behind the bar. 'I'd be a bit more fussy about the company I keep, if I were you, Mr Stephens. Good morning, gentlemen.'

When the doors were slammed shut, Terry hurried over to them and bolted and locked them, then turned to Jairus. 'Who the bleeding hell were they?'

Jairus sat back down and found his mouth bone dry, as if he'd swallowed a bag of cement dust. His body trembled and ached for a proper drink. Sweat was beginning to break out over his forehead and down his sides. 'Government department, they said. Could be spooks. Someone sent them to scare me off.'

Terry stepped over to him. 'And are you? Scared, I mean?'

'No, I'm not scared. Just angry. Tired. Bloody thirsty too.'

'You want that drink now?'

Jairus shook his head. 'No thanks. I've got work to do.'

Douglas Burdock stopped halfway along the glass

corridor and faced the London skyline and the wave of angry weather that was blasting at the walls of the hospital. The Thames looked black and almost evil as it slithered through the ancient buildings that surrounded it, all filled with the darkest of histories. He loved the city because it was so steeped in evil and myth.

His father could claim a fair amount of recognition for creating some of the history and myth of London, even of Great Britain itself, and quite often had claimed it in the privacy of one of his homes. He had created so many myths, he boasted, constructed so many political situations, but without anyone actually knowing anything of his part in the whole scheme. That was his gift, his father would say, and he revelled in his own ghostly brilliance. As with Satan, his father would say, having true power comes with a kind of invisibility.

Burdock walked on, wondering what point in the investigation former detective Jairus had arrived at, and knowing with almost certainty that he was the right man for the job. After all, Cat had recommended Jairus and she knew him more than most – in fact, she had got to know him intimately and knew all his darkest secrets, although she would not divulge them. He was happy enough for her to keep his secrets, as it guaranteed that she would indeed keep his own, and of course the nature of their arrangement insisted on the ability to keep secrets.

Burdock reached the end of the glass corridor and headed for the large square desk that sat at the centre of the white tiled, clinical room. The same dark-skinned guard sat at the desk watching something on a portable DVD player. He looked up, then quickly stood to attention.

'Morning, Mr Burdock, I was just...'

Douglas held up a hand. 'It's quite all right. I know you wouldn't let anything happen to my father.'

The guard nodded. 'No, sir, I wouldn't. I appreciate being given this position, I really do.'

'Is Nurse Wright in there?' Douglas gestured towards the reinforced glass doors that served as an entrance to his father's private hospital room. Why they insisted on calling it a 'room', he had no idea, as it would be more fitting to call it a suite or even an apartment. Most of the hospital had been funded by his father, solely for the reason that he always said he wanted to have somewhere comfortable to die in peace. He didn't want to die at home, he insisted, because since leaving New Zealand all those many years ago, he no longer considered himself a citizen of any particular country. He wanted a place, somewhere neutral and plain for his last days. And so he had created it to fit his needs perfectly, as he had done with many things that he'd desired but did not yet exist.

The guard informed him that Nurse Wright had indeed been with his father for most of the day. It was a situation that would infuriate his father and send him into a fit of swearing, or at least it would if he wasn't in a wheelchair, forced to sit silently, staring at the view out of his window.

Douglas smiled to himself and headed through the security doors and into the hospital apartment. Apart from the clinical atmosphere, there was little else to mark the place as being part of a hospital but he supposed that was the point. No one wants to die in the infectious wasteland of such an institution, least of all his father.

Nurse Wright was reading a book, which seemed to have the half-naked figure of a man on the cover.

The nurse, who was somewhere in her mid-thirties, and quite attractive, with dark brown hair, looked up and smiled, glad to see him as always. She had put makeup on, and he wondered if she was aware of how fatuous she looked. He knew she had a child that she had been forced to bring up alone, after the father had sensibly ejected himself shortly after the kid arrived. Something surprised him every time he laid eyes on her. It was a sexual curiosity that invaded his usually uniform mind when he was in her company. It wasn't as if she was beautiful, because she wasn't. Pretty, certainly, and her body was lithe despite the rigours of childbirth.

So, he was curious as to what she would look like naked, and how she would behave if he made a sexual advance.

He couldn't though, at least not yet. She was his father's nurse. But he promised himself some fun at a later date.

'Thank you for being here, Nurse Wright,' he said, smiling. 'I really appreciate it. I know it's hard on your home life.'

'Not at all,' she said and hid the book as if she thought he hadn't seen it yet. 'I'm a nurse. That's what we do. I'm afraid your father hasn't changed much since the last time you were here.'

He nodded and looked towards the white leather sofas that sat opposite the line of tall and wide windows. He could just make out the wheelchair silhouette of Robert Burdock, the media emperor.

'I didn't really expect him to. It's a slippery slope they inform me.'

She smiled and blushed a little. 'Can I get you a cup of tea or...'

'No,' he said and saw by her expression that he'd

been too abrupt. He smiled. 'Another time. Then you can tell me all about the terrible pitfalls of being a nurse.'

'It'll have to be quite a few cups of tea then.'

He did his best to look amused, then said, 'Excuse me, but I have a few things to speak to my father about. You know how he likes to be kept up to date.'

'All right,' she said and grabbed her bag. 'I'll see you next time.'

Within a few seconds of Wright's exit and the security doors closing, Douglas made his way up the long corridor and towards his father's silhouette, listening to his own smart shoes slapping the hard, white floor. His father didn't move, not even a blink of his eye as he stopped by his chair, then sat down and stared deeply at his profile.

'Daddy, dearest,' he said, quietly.

There was the smallest flicker of his eyes, then his dry lips parting, as a harsh breath escaped his mouth.

'Don't call me fucking daddy,' Robert Burdock said and looked at his son, his eyes full of brimstone. 'You know I fucking hate being called that. Always have.'

'I know, father. I'm glad to see you've made such a miraculous recovery.'

'Has that cunt gone?'

'Yes. Nurse Wright has gone home. I think she has the hots for me. In fact, I think she might be in love with me.'

The old man's eyes blazed as he knew they would as he said, 'Don't make me puke! What about the paki? He still here?'

'Father! Could you at least try and reel in your racism for at least ten minutes?'

'See, that's your fucking problem, Douglas, you're a fucking pansy. How's my media empire? You fucked it up yet?'

'As you well know, Father, everything is in order. All your employees, all the editors and the like, know what they're doing.'

'It's a good fucking job, isn't it? I couldn't rely on you or your halfwit brother, could I?' Robert Burdock wheeled himself closer to the window, his withered arms working furiously.

Douglas followed and looked into the rain that hammered the glass and cascaded down it. He looked at his father and saw only the terrible things he'd done. Evil things, the general public would say, and denounce him as an agent of Satan, if they were in anyway religious. Luckily, at least for his father, religion was dying in the people's hearts. 'How long do you have to hide here, Father?'

Burdock senior's eyes ignited again as they burned up at Douglas. 'How many fucking more times I have I got to tell you? I'm not fucking hiding.'

'I know. You're just pretending to have Alzheimer's so when they do drag you to court, you can simply stare at them blankly...'

'Deny everything, Douglas. That's the key. Don't even deny it, just fucking babble and let the very fucking expensive doctors do the lying for you. You've got to have a good defence or you're fucked.'

'I know, Father. Anyway, would you like me to tell you all I've been up to over the last few days...'

The old man pointed a liver-spotted finger at Douglas, 'Are you sure that fucking pig is up to the job?'

'I'm quite sure. Once he bites down on something he doesn't let go. He'll take it right to the bitter end.'

'What's his fucking name?'
'Jairus.'

'Jairus? What sort of fucking name is that? Sounds like a bloody foreigner! Fuck me, you fucking pick them, don't you.'

'Trust me, he'll do his job.'

'He'd better, Douglas. If he doesn't, then we'll have to have him killed, won't we?'

Douglas nodded. 'I don't think there's any doubt that we'll have to have him killed anyway.'

CHAPTER 7

The sun was bleaching up into the indigo sky when Jairus arrived back on the estate he regretfully called home. Living in the midst of all the hell and debauchery that the estate could muster was a kind of punishment, he'd decided. His time spent between heaven and hell, a kind of limbo as he waited for some kind of retribution from whoever was looking down on him and messing with his life.

He stood for a moment on the concrete balcony, smelling the drifting earthy scent of marijuana coming from one of the other flats, and watched the morning develop in slow motion like a polaroid photograph. The beat of dance music, or whatever they called it these days, had already begun to vibrate up through the floors. He unlocked his door and headed up the stairs to his place.

He stopped halfway, sniffing the air, smelling the sweet and pungent aroma of perfume. He walked into the living room and found Cathy lying on his unmade sofa bed, her head supported by one hand as she smiled up at him. Her now more slender body had been slipped into a tight-fitting, low-cut light green dress. She had one of her finely carved legs up. He tore his eyes away as he felt the yearning growing inside himself once again.

'What're you doing here, Cathy?' he said and took

off his coat and hung it up.

She sat up. 'I'm the liaison between you and Douglas Burdock, remember? He wanted to know how it's all going.'

Jairus looked at her, his entire body already itching with irritation at the mention of the Burdock name. 'Tell him it's going swimmingly.'

'I will,' she said, then reached behind her and produced a small bottle of vodka. 'Look what I found hidden in the toilet cistern. Probably doesn't do your plumbing much good.'

'That's for emergencies, and I'd forgotten it was there. Pour it down the sink.'

She sat up, eyebrows raised. 'Are you sure? Don't want a quick gulp?'

'Yeah, I'm sure. I'm done with all that.'

'Really? Done with all the self-pity, the dark soul-searching? You ready to live your life again?'

The irritation grew, burning across his skin, tightening his heart. 'What does it matter to you?'

She stood up, came closer, and so much so that all he could smell was her perfume. It engulfed him and put fire into his veins.

'Of course it matters to me,' she said. 'You matter to me, Jay. Remember you're the one who went away. I tried to get in contact...I wanted to see you...but you wouldn't let me.'

'I didn't want to see anyone. I couldn't. I felt like... like I was damned. I don't know.'

'I know. I'm damned too, remember? We're the same. We're as damaged as each other.' She pushed herself forward, her face tilted up towards him, her full lips open a little.

Even though almost every part of him, at least all the parts that counted, were shouting for him to grab her and kiss her and let himself fall all over again, something in his head switched on, a flicker in his brain, like a warning light. She was part of another world now, and it was part of Douglas Burdock's world. 'I can't, Cathy. I'm sorry.'

'Why not?' She stepped back, and he thought he saw a flicker of fury in her eyes.

'Because of what we're like... The two of us together.'

'And what are we like exactly?'

'Like two supernovas.'

She smiled. 'Exploding stars, lighting up the galaxy for a brief moment... luminous, beautiful and destructive.'

'Yeah, exactly.' He walked to her, touched her arm. 'What about you and Douglas Burdock?'

'You mean you want to know the nature of our relationship?'

'Yeah.'

She turned away, walked towards the window as if she was staring out, then turned and stared into his eyes. 'I belong to him.'

'What? What does that mean? You belong to him?'

'I don't expect you to understand.'

'Good, because I don't. People don't belong to people. It doesn't work like that.' He was suddenly right in front of her, gripping her shoulders.

'Maybe not in your world, or the soft and pretty and pink world that most people live in... but in my world, and especially in Douglas' world, it most definitely works like that.'

He looked into her eyes, ready to debate it further and try and discover what exactly she meant, but he saw that the shutters had already come down. It was a lost cause, and a big part of him didn't want to know what had happened between them in case the rage grew inside him again. 'Fine. I hope you're both very happy.'

'Happiness has nothing to do with it.' She looked solemn for a moment, then her smile was back. 'Tell me, Jay, do you still think about Karine? Do you still blame yourself for what happened?'

'You know I do.'

'See, there it is, the need to take on the blame and the suffering, and feeling that you have to punish yourself for ever more. Do you ever think that perhaps she started that argument on purpose? Maybe she wanted you out of the way that day, so she could die without you knowing?'

He sat down on the bed and stared at his trembling hands. He didn't tell Cathy about the runaway rollercoaster of self-loathing and regret that constantly looped and curled in his mind throughout the wee hours. He didn't have to, she knew because it was written in his eyes, his skin, and was ever-present in his voice, echoing with every word. And, of course, Karine was always there – her face, the way she smelled, and how she looked, laid on the bathroom floor so lifeless. But something else had been coming back to him lately, as if now that his job was gone and he had no real detection to do, his mind had decided to turn savagely on itself.

'I keep,' he said and the words piled up in his mouth.

'You keep what?' She placed a hand on his shoulder.

'Those weeks before Karine had her heart attack... she seemed... distant. I mean, she was never one for blurting out her emotions, but I just keep remembering her seeming like...'

'Like she had something to hide?'

He nodded. 'Maybe it was her heart. She knew she didn't have long and didn't want to tell me.'

'But you don't believe that?' Cathy knelt down in front of him and looked him in the eyes.

'No. I remember coming home one day and I walked into the kitchen and she had her phone in her hand. Then she hid it, put it away too quickly...'

'Perhaps your mind's trying to create a false memory. Helping you through the regret and pain by creating a version of Karine that had secrets, or was having an affair.'

Jairus looked at her and saw that she didn't believe what she was saying, was merely trying to placate him. 'Yeah, maybe.'

'Perhaps it's time to let her go and stop haunting her?'

'Perhaps.' He rubbed his face and stood up, forced a smile to his lips that was almost painful to keep in place. He'd struggled with the notion of telling her about the two suits who'd threatened him, but decided to see what their next move was before he let on to Burdock about it. 'Anyway, Cathy, or Cat, whatever you call yourself these days... you can tell Mr Burdock that it's all going fine.'

Her face had changed, and now she had gone from looking sympathetic to almost blank. 'I'm starting to regret getting you involved in this. I did it so you'd have the chance to be a policeman again, but I'm not sure that's the answer for you.'

'Trust me. It is. If I'm not thinking about murder, then I'm thinking about me, and we both know that's not healthy. I need this.'

'Walk away from this. Find something else to look into.' She touched his arm.

He pulled away. 'I can't. I've started now. Go and

tell him.'

She stared at him for a few seconds, let out a heavy breath and nodded. 'Very well, Jay. I will. Until next time, look after yourself.'

A few hours later after a long shower and breakfast, Jairus headed down the concrete stairs of his building, listening to the echoes of life all around him. There was screaming, dance music, babies crying, all bleeding together into one nauseating soundtrack.

He took out his mobile and called Rich. All the way to the car park his phone kept ringing, and only when he unlocked his car did the call get answered and a gravelly and painfully hungover Rich Vincent answered.

'It's the middle of the bloody night,' he said, then started coughing.

'It's half eight in the morning, Rich,' Jairus said and laughed. 'Out late were we?'

'Of course. God knows how much I drank last night. Can't remember a thing, mate.'

'Nice. Sorry to bother you, but have you been keeping tabs on the mobile number I gave you?' Jairus got in his car and started the engine.

'Yep. Darren Parker. He could be dead. The phone's on, but hasn't moved. No calls, no texts either.'

'You're joking?'

'Nope. Looks like he has that number for that very reason.'

Jairus slammed his hand against the steering wheel. 'Fuck. I got that number off that bloody journalist.'

'You mean, Helen Chara, the incredibly hot reporter? Please tell me you've nailed her?'

'No, mate. I'm a monk these days. Plus, I don't trust her. She said she got fired from her last job, so who did she work for?'

'The News of the Day. Apparently she fell foul of the owner...'

'Robert Burdock by any chance?' Jairus lowered his head to the steering wheel and butted it lightly.

'The very same. She crossed the line, bugged someone or the like... you sound pissed off.'

'I am. Jesus. Something funny's going on. I feel like someone's taking the piss. Look, can you find where David Coulson's widow's living now?'

'Coulson? The journalist that was hacked to death?'

'Yeah, that one.'

'Jesus. You're onto a messy one, aren't you? Do you know how many conspiracy theories come up when you type his name into a search engine?'

Jairus drove out of the car park and onto Wood Green high street. 'No, how many?'

'A fucking lot. All right, I'll find your widow for you. I'll email you her address when I track her down, and I'll send some background info too.'

'Thanks, Rich, I owe you.' Jairus hung up and kept driving, his eyes jumping to the rearview mirror more often than needed. He was feeling slightly paranoid after his run in with the suits who said they were from the government. That statement could have meant a lot of things, but it'd left him with a very bad taste in his mouth.

After a few minutes, Rich emailed through the address. Alice Coulson and her two children were still living in the home they'd shared with David, which was a nice big house in Crouch End, one of the trendier parts of North London. He recalled with a little sadness how Karine had dragged him there to have lunch in one of the trendy restaurants so she could try and spot a few celebrities. All they managed was an

80's comedian and a young lad from Eastenders, but Karine had seemed thrilled.

Along with Alice's address, there was a little background information, which included the fact that Alice Coulson was a primary school teacher. Knowing that teachers were nowhere near paid enough, Jairus assumed it was David Coulson's job, and his two successful true crime books that afforded them the four-bedroom house in much sought-after Crouch End.

The house he parked outside of pretty much matched the image his mind had created as he read the email. Large, red-brick, big double black door at the end of a medium-sized gravel drive, on which a silver compact car was parked. She was probably in, in the midst of getting the kids ready for school, he guessed, and headed to the front door and rang the bell.

After a couple of rings, a flustered slender young woman, adorned in a red flowery dress answered the door. She had shoulder-length hay-coloured hair that framed her hollowed-out face. Stress had stamped its mark under her bright blue eyes.

'Alice Coulson?' he asked, noting that her eyes kept jumping to some kind of tablet device in her hand.

'Yes, I'm sorry, but I'm running a bit late,' she said, reaching to grab a jacket off a hook near the door.

'It's about David.'

Jairus cringed inwardly, as she lowered the device and stared at him with a thousand questions piling up in her eyes. 'David? What about David?'

'I wanted to ask you some questions about him.'

Her eyes switched from curious, to sharp, angry, ready to cut him to pieces. 'You're from the papers, right? You can get lost...'

'I'm not. I swear. I'm looking into his death and I was hoping...'

'Are you a policeman? Where's your ID?'

'Look, I'm going to be completely honest with you. I was a police officer, I'm not now.'

Her hand moved to the door, ready to close it. 'So, you're a private detective or something like that? Quite frankly, you can go... look, I'm sick of people coming round to ask me questions about David and what happened to him. He was killed... murdered in cold blood by a lunatic that shouldn't have been walking the streets!'

'I know, I'm sorry.' Jairus held up his hands. 'Just please hear me out. I believe the man that they say murdered your husband probably did, but the police said he was killed outside that pub, and I don't think he was...'

Alice Coulson sighed heavily, and rubbed her eyes. 'You've got another theory, yeah? Yet another theory about what happened to David and why it happened. Tell me, I've read them all. Every time I go online, on Facebook or something like it, I see yet another tosser with a conspiracy theory. There are even books about it. Why don't you go and write a book about it? Now, please, just...'

Jairus was about to turn away and leave the poor woman in peace, knowing very well what it is to be hounded. Sickness filled his stomach as he recalled the press at his door after Carl Murphy died. He pushed it all aside, knowing full well that he couldn't leave her alone, that she could be key to the investigation. 'Yeah, I know how many people are saying things about David,' Jairus said and made eye contact, held her angry and sad eyes. 'I know what it's like. Believe me. I know you've got a lot of questions yourself about what happened. Why? How? How does a psycho like Mickey O'Neil get to walk the streets? It's not fair. But I'll tell you one thing, I think I'm onto something because yesterday two suited men, who said they were from a government department, warned me off. Now, if you look inside yourself and if you find you're happy with the official explanation of what happened to David, then I'll walk away. But if there's part of you that has any doubt... well, I promise to get to the bottom of it. If you're doubting if I'm who I say I am, then Google my name. You'll find plenty about me. Most of it not very flattering.'

She stared at him for a moment, her face slipping away from anger, perhaps defrosting, he thought. She opened the door a little as she said tiredly, 'OK, I'll talk to you. Ask me what you want. I don't suppose one more crazy theory will make any difference.'

Jairus stepped into the wide hallway, made of real wood flooring that seemed to stretch on for miles, or at least to a massive and bright kitchen at the far end of the house.

'Keep going down to the kitchen,' she said. 'I take it you'd like a tea or coffee?'

'Yeah, thanks.' He headed through a large archway to the kitchen, which glistened with early morning sunlight coming through the big windows. He stood at the island at the centre of the room, while Alice Coulson filled the kettle. 'Your kids not here?'

She turned and faced him, resting her back on the side. 'No, my sister takes them on for a couple of days a week. They'll be at school by now. I should be on my way to work.'

'I'm sorry, but I really need to ask you about David.'

She nodded. 'It's OK. I'm not actually in a classroom until this afternoon. I'm only missing a boring meeting about the curriculum. So, what did you want to know?'

'Do you know what David was looking into before he was killed?'

Alice made a face that told Jairus she'd been asked the same question a million times before.

'Like I told everyone else, the police, the reporters, I didn't know what he was looking into that would get him murdered. I suppose you also want to know what he was doing outside that pub?'

Jairus nodded.

'I don't know the answer to that either. David's job took him to some unusual places and he sometimes mixed with dangerous people. He'd been threatened before. None of the threats seemed to concern him or the police. I don't know... maybe he should have walked away... he wrote two books that were quite controversial. But I don't think there was anything in there that would make anyone want to murder him.'

'OK. Has anything unusual happened since his death? It doesn't matter what it is... something out of place or a strange feeling, or... has anything gone missing?'

'Well, yes... actually, no, that's not true. It's nothing really, but David had a blue folder with some papers in. He carried them around with him before he was killed. The police gave me his personal effects, but the blue folder never turned up.'

Jairus felt the tightening at the back of his skull. 'Did you ask the police about it?'

'Yes, but they just told me that they gave me back all that was found next to his body. So, I have no idea what happened to it.'

'Have you told anyone else about the blue folder?'

She shrugged, then turned to the kettle as it boiled. 'Only the police.'

'Why're you telling me now?'

She faced him, smiling a little, but sadly. 'I don't know. I suppose you're the first person I've talked to like this who I actually believe wants to do the right thing.'

'Yeah, you're right, I do want to do the right thing. But believe it or not, doing the right thing is what usually gets me in trouble.'

Alice laughed, knowingly.

'What?' Jairus asked.

'Nothing really, it's just that you sound like David. It's when he was trying to do the right thing that he found life or people getting in his way. Never stopped him though.'

'The more I hear about him, the more I like him.' Jairus took the mug of coffee Alice handed to him. 'Thanks. So, this blue file, did you see him with it in his office? I take it he had an office at home?'

'Oh yes, a big one right at the back of the house. I've kept it just how he left it. I'll show you if you want?'

'Yeah, that'd be great.'

'Take your coffee. Go up the stairs and it's right at the back of the house. I'll meet you up there, I've got to call the school.'

'Thanks.' Jairus followed her directions and found himself alone in front of a large solid wood door. He turned his eyes to the left and right and looked into the two bedrooms either side of him. Both boy's rooms, with football posters, computer games consoles. He felt like an intruder, not used to being alone in someone's home when there wasn't a dead body to give him reason to be there. It should have been a refreshing change, but he felt on edge and the same old headache was beginning to pulse at the very top of his skull.

Something wasn't right. That's what his headache was telling him as he opened the door to David Coulson's office and found a relatively neat, quite large office decked out with a big antique mahogany desk, expensive looking leather desk chair, and shelves stuffed full of books. There was a PC, a few files and pieces of paper on the desk and an empty mug that said, 'World's Greatest Dad'.

Jairus stared at the mug for a while, feeling a bite of sadness dig into his stomach, then turned to take in the computer as he heard footsteps behind him.

'It's just like he got up and went to the toilet,' she said, a note of grief in her voice. 'But he hasn't. He isn't coming back.'

He turned in time to see her swallow down the tears that threatened to overflow at any second, glad that she had retaken control. 'Did the police examine his computer?'

'They took it away for a while,' she said and put her hand on the flat screen monitor. 'But they never said if they found anything. What do you think's on there?'

'I don't know. But I'd like to get someone over here who might know what to look for.'

CHAPTER 8

'I'm supposed to be on fucking holiday,' Rich said, standing at the front door, rubbing his bleary eyes.

Jairus grabbed him by the arm and dragged him inside, taking a quick sweep of the quiet street before he shut the door. 'Yeah, I know. I wouldn't have got you over here if it wasn't urgent.'

Rich walked up close to him, close enough for Jairus to smell the stench of stale alcohol oozing from his pores as he said, 'Please, promise me there's going to be no dodgy stuff or bodies to tidy away.'

'I wish I could promise that, mate.' Jairus put his finger to his lips when he heard Alice Coulson's footsteps coming down the hall. 'Alice Coulson, this is Rich Vincent. Don't let the look or stench of him put you off. The man's a genius.'

Rich took the delicate hand she held out. 'Thanks, Jay, I think. Nice to meet you, Alice.'

'And you, Rich,' she said, smiling, while her eyes looked over his pony-tailed hair, Iron Maiden T-shirt, leather jacket and black jeans.

'Right, where's this PC?' Rich said.

'Upstairs. Office at the back of the house.' Alice pointed towards the stairs.

'Do you have another computer in the house?' Jairus asked Alice.

'Well, yes, I've got a laptop. Why?'

'Did David ever use it?'

She frowned, then shook her head. 'Not really. Only when I needed help with something. Why?'

Jairus followed Rich up the stairs with Alice coming slowly behind. 'I'm thinking that if David wanted to hide anything, then putting it on your laptop would be his best bet.'

'What do you think he was trying to hide?' Alice asked as they stepped into David's office.

'I don't know. Maybe what was in that blue folder, or maybe it's nothing. Where is your laptop?'

'Hang on.' Alice headed out of the office, her footsteps trailing off to somewhere else in the house. Jairus turned to Rich and saw that he was already sat at the PC, waiting for it to boot up.

'Windows,' Rich said, rubbing his face. 'I hate Windows.'

'I know. We all do. See if he's wiped anything off.'

Rich stared up at him. 'Mrs Coulson, is she really all right with this?'

'Yeah, I think so. She wants to know what happened to her husband. Who wouldn't?'

'But what if it's something she really doesn't want to know, or something that puts her in danger?'

'Then I'll protect her.' Even though Rich nodded and went back to tapping away at the keyboard, he saw the doubt in his eyes, the hesitation in his fingers. It was the price of not being a copper anymore, not having the weight of the law behind him. When he said he'd protect her, he meant it with every atom of his being, he just didn't know how he would go about it. It all needed to be kept under wraps – that was the best way to keep her out of danger.

'I can't find much that's been wiped off the hard drive,' Rich said. 'But I did retrieve a J-peg of an aerial view of an island.'

'What island?'

'Tebel Island, a small island near the Isles of Scilly.'

'Here it is,' Alice said, handing Jairus the battered looking silver laptop. 'But I don't think David would've used it.'

'Let me have a butcher's,' Rich said, put it on the desk, opened it up and turned it on.

'Why would David have been looking up the Isles of Scilly?' Jairus asked her.

She shrugged. 'We had talked about going there one day. I've heard good things about the islands.'

Jairus picked up his tepid coffee and took a sip. 'OK, we'll forget that for the moment and concentrate on your laptop.'

'This is a bit surreal,' Alice said, shaking her head.

'Is it?' Jairus said.

'Yes. I mean, one minute you're knocking on my door, the next you and your friend are searching through my computers. Do people usually trust you after an hour of knowing you?'

He laughed and rubbed his stubble. 'Sometimes. Tell me, did you Google me?'

Her cheeks reddened. 'Yes, I did. You've been in a lot of trouble.'

'But his heart's in the right place,' Rich said. 'He's a good man despite what they've written about him. Right, there's one file on here that someone tried to delete. They used a special package to delete it. They've done a pretty good job too.'

'Can you get it back?' Jairus asked.

'Do politicians take backhanders?'

'From what I've heard. Alice, did you try and delete anything off your laptop?' Jairus turned to her.

She looked confused and shook her head. 'No, no I

didn't. For one thing, I wouldn't know how to.'

Rich bent over and pulled up a printer that was tucked under the desk. 'I'll attach this printer and print it off.'

'Yeah, good.' Jairus stuck his hands in his pockets and watched Alice as she was biting the inside of her mouth and fidgeting. 'Hey, it'll be all right. Whatever's on the that file, there'll be an explanation.'

'Really?' she said, her eyes a little wide. 'But explaining what? Why David was killed? I mean... why would he have anything on my laptop and try and wipe it off?'

'Maybe he knew it would be found one day?' Rich said as the printer rumbled into life.

'Yeah, it's possible.' Jairus leaned over the printer and watched as the sheet of A4 paper appeared. He picked it up and looked at it. 'Is this all there was?'

'That's it.' Rich shrugged.

Jairus turned the piece of paper around and showed Alice. 'It's two columns of names. Three on the left, three on the right. You recognise any of the names?'

Alice scanned the list. 'No, none of them. What does it mean?'

Jairus looked at the sheet of paper again, running through the names in his head. On the left was written: Neil Grant, Matthew Pinder, and Ben Samuels. On the right: Arthur Davidson, James Howard, and Leonard Jameson. 'I don't know. But David put this on your laptop, then tried to erase it. My gut's telling me this means something.'

'Could be nothing,' Rich said.

Jairus looked at him. 'It's the only thing I've got to go on.'

'You want to run those names against the computer's Internet history?' Rich asked.

'Yeah, good idea, and then you better do a better job of erasing that list than David did.'

Rich smiled. 'Already done. All right, the names on the left are not coming up in his search history. They could be anyone basically. Now, the names on the right have been searched for but a long time back, but not in connection with each other. Arthur Davidson and Leonard Jameson were former MPs, while James Howard...'

'Created the first British-made mobile phone,' Jairus interrupted. 'What about the laptop?'

'No, nothing on there.' Rich sat back. 'That it? Should I pack up?'

'Yeah, thanks, Rich,' Jairus said and watched as Alice walked towards the window and seemed to stare out into the street. 'Alice? You all right?'

She looked at him, tried to smile, but it faded quickly. 'Yes, I'm fine. Just... talking about David... I...'

'Yeah, I know. I've been through it and I know it isn't easy. Look, I'm going to get to the bottom of this...'

'There's a police car coming down the road.' Alice indicated to the window, so Jairus looked down into the street and saw the incident response car crawling along towards the house.

'They might not be coming here,' he said, but the biting pain at the top of his skull told him otherwise. 'Better hurry up, Rich.'

'I'm good to go.' Rich picked up his rucksack and heaved it onto his back.

The police car parked close to Rich's beat-up blue Audi. Two male uniforms climbed out, one talking on his radio, while the other seemed to pay special attention to Jairus' car. He was taking his number and checking it. Jairus turned and looked into Alice's eyes.

'I didn't call them,' she said, and he saw no lies in

her face, none of the usual telltale signs.

'Good. Let's go out the back.' Jairus led the way, his hands stuffed into his pockets, with Rich and Alice hot on his heels.

As they all reached the back door, the front doorbell rang. Alice spun her head round towards the front of the house, then looked back at Jairus and Rich. 'You two go, I'll talk keep them talking. Follow the back lane to front of the house.'

'Thanks,' Jairus said, then pushed Rich out of the back door and along the path that cut through a long and bumpy lawn. They went through a tall wooden gate and into a narrow lane that, as Alice said, ran along the back of the houses and then joined the main road at the very end. Rich and Jairus hid at the end of the street, masked by two big chestnut trees, and watched the two uniforms as they talked to Alice on the doorstep.

'What the fuck do we do now?' Rich asked.

'You head to your car and start the engine like you haven't got a care in the world. Chances are they're not looking for you.'

Rich rubbed his eyes, shook his head and pulled his rucksack up his back. 'What do you get me involved in?'

'Just go!' Jairus pushed him on and watched as Rich headed for his battered Audi while one of the uniforms turned to stare at him. Seemingly satisfied that Rich wasn't heading to the car they had targeted, the uniform turned back to Alice.

Jairus looked up as he heard the screech of Rich's car as it reversed towards him as he crouched down by the trees. He saw his moment and crawled towards the driver's side of the Audi and slipped onto the back seat and kept down as Rich drove out of the road.

'So where did those uniforms come from?' Rich asked as Jairus sat up and put his seatbelt on.

'Someone sent them. The more I keep digging into this, the more I keep getting a terrible feeling. I mean, if Alice didn't call them, which I believe she didn't, then who did?'

'Nosey neighbour? Thought we looked dodgy?'

'Yeah, could be,' he said, then sat back, feeling another skull-crushing headache arriving while his hands trembled and his entire body cried out for a drink. 'I don't think so though.'

'Where am I taking you?'

'Did you happen to find an address for Helen Chara?'

'Of course.'

'Then take me there. I want a word with her.'

DI Jake Brenton was sitting in his car, smoking and staring towards the ramshackle building in front of him. He wound down the window and tapped the cigarette on the door. He was wondering what he was doing there on a rundown industrial estate in North London, and scratched his two-day stubble. He'd got the call an hour before from his boss, Detective Chief Superintendent Paul Carron, and was told bluntly to head to the crime scene.

Brenton got out of the car and groaned as he did, threw the butt of his cigarette to the floor and crushed it under his foot. He caught sight of his tired round face, his receding dark hair. He shook his head, took out another cigarette and poked it between his lips. He stood for a moment, watching a couple of SOCOs, all dressed up in white, leaving the building carrying cases. Something was up. He knew there was definitely more to the whole scene than just some random person turning up bludgeoned to death. Why else would he be there instead of the local firm?

He saw someone waving out of the corner of his eye, and opened his eyes wide when he spotted DS Kate Wood coming towards him dressed in her usual grey trouser suit. It'd been a while since they'd worked together, but she looked just the same; oval pretty face, porcelain skin, red bobbed hair. He liked her, always had, but he'd never told her for obvious reasons.

'Hey, Kate,' he said, lighting his cigarette. 'What's the score?'

'I thought you gave up the fags?' she said, looking with disdain at the cigarette in his mouth.

'I did. I think I've given up eight times nearly. It's difficult.'

She made an unamused sound in her throat. 'How's the wife?'

'Gone. Left me, I mean.'

Wood scratched her chin, then put on a pair of latex gloves. 'That's not good. How're the boys? They must be teenagers by now.'

'Yes, they are. I don't think they're too impressed with their old man these days.'

'Are any kids impressed with their parents?' she said, then gestured to the old factory building. 'DB. Approximately sixty to sixty-five years old. No ID. Prints have been taken, the usual business. Local pathologist is in there poking about at the moment. Want to take a walk with me?'

Jake took a last lungful of his cigarette, then stubbed it out. Wood held out a gloved hand. 'Give it to me. Let's not contaminate the scene.'

He did as he was told, then put on some overshoes and followed DS Wood into the building. The place was blazing with artificial light. The SOCOs had set up lamps in just about every grotty corner. The floor was stained by oil or something similar, while old work benches were dotted around, cluttered with old pieces of machinery. There was a deep earthy smell to the place that managed to scratch right at the back of Brenton's nose and throat.

The white bodies of the SOCOs blazed in the light while they moved slowly around picking up the pieces, ready to try and put Humpty back together again.

The victim was crumpled on the floor, his right arm across his face as if to guard it. Blood covered his head and part of the floor.

'Looks like blunt force trauma,' Brenton said, already itching for another cigarette.

'That's pretty much what I said,' a voice commented behind Brenton.

He turned to see a slender and quite tall middle-aged man decked out in a green forensic suit.

'You're the pathologist?' Brenton asked, turning to see Wood crouching by the body.

'Dr Jeremy Garrett,' the pathologist said and looked at his gloved hands. 'Nice to meet you. I'd shake your hand, but...'

'It's all right.' Brenton stood behind and watched Wood take out some tweezers from her pocket. 'How long's he been dead?'

Garrett came forward, also watching DS Wood. 'I'd say between thirty-seven to forty hours. Lividity and blood pooling would suggest he was killed where he was lying. Didn't take long to die. I'll give you more when he's on my table.'

'Thanks. What's that, Kate?'

Wood gently picked something out of the small pool of blood by the victim's head. She held it in the tweezers and turned to show Brenton and the doctor.

Brenton took out his glasses and put them on, and focused in on the long blonde hair she was holding between her tweezers. 'A blonde hair? Well, it's not the victim's.'

'Looks like a blonde was here, or...' Garrett began.

'Or the victim or killer brought it with them on their clothes,' Wood said as she stood up.

'Could I have that?' a voice said behind them.

Brenton turned to see a plump white forensic suit. The round face of the woman who stared out at them from the hood did not look happy. 'When you've finished contaminating the scene.'

Wood dropped it into the evidence bag she held out. 'OK, keep your hood on.'

At that particularly awkward moment, Brenton spotted a bulky male uniform striding towards him and prayed he was there to take him away. He was pleasantly surprised when the uniform said, 'DI Brenton, sir?'

'Yes?' Brenton took out his pack of cigarettes in eagerness.

'You're wanted outside.' The uniform pointed a meaty thumb towards the doorway.

'OK, thanks.' He stuck a cigarette between his lips and turned to face Kate Wood. 'I take it the murder weapon wasn't found?'

She shook her head. 'Nope. But uniforms are still searching.'

'Good.' He walked out into the natural and burning daylight, blinking and preparing to light his cigarette. He stopped, frozen for a moment, and put his lighter back in his jacket. Parked across the yard outside the factory was a shiny black Jaguar. There was a smartly dressed man sitting at the wheel, while a thick-set, greying middle-aged uniformed police officer was sat reading a newspaper in the back. His weary eyes turned towards Brenton; he waved him over.

'Shit,' Brenton muttered, pushing a smile of politeness to his lips and walking to the car. Like any police officer with half a brain knew, when the top brass turns up to a murder scene, Brenton knew a pile of shit was heading his way.

'You're not smoking that thing in my car,' the Commander said as Brenton looked in the window. He recognised the spangle-suited stuck-up bastard as Commander James Swanson. They were all the same, thinking only of the budget and smudging the figures.

Brenton put away the cigarette and climbed in. 'So, Commander, what can I do for you?'

He put down the paper and folded his arms. 'There's a dead man inside that building, yes? In his sixties?'

'Yes, that's right. We haven't ID...'

'Leonard Jameson. Former Conservative MP of this area.'

'Right...'

'You're wondering how I know that.'

Brenton nodded, sensing the ship of shit sailing clearly in his direction.

'I just do.' Swanson looked away. 'No doubt it won't take you long to officially identify him. I take it I don't have to say that you're not to repeat anything you hear in this vehicle?'

Brenton scratched at his beard, making all kinds of faces.

'Do you have a problem with that, DI?'

'I just get a little uncomfortable when I don't know the full story.'

Swanson huffed. 'DCS Carron said you could be

relied upon to keep in line, to follow orders. Are you calling him a liar?'

Brenton groaned inwardly, knowing that it was of course only a matter of time before his own past came back to slap him in the face. 'No, he's not a liar. What exactly do you expect me to do?'

'Do your job. Find out who murdered Leonard Jameson and stop the person who killed him from doing any more damage.'

Brenton was suddenly filled with doom. 'You think that his killer might do it again?'

Swanson opened his jacket and took out an evidence bag. Inside there was a small square of cream-coloured paper. Something had been printed on the paper but it had lines drawn through it. The Commander handed him the evidence bag.

Brenton saw that the name Leonard Jameson had been printed in black ink at the centre of the piece of paper before someone had drawn through it. 'The killer sent a message?'

'Yes, it would seem so.'

'Who did the killer send this to? They could be in danger.'

The Commander sat forward and engaged his eyes. 'That's not important. Do you understand?'

'I see. Maybe the paper will tell us something.'

'Forget the paper. It's just a piece of paper. There's no importance in it. Only the message has relevance. Now, I want you to follow the evidence in that building and find his killer. When you do, let me know before you make an arrest, or travel down any official routes. Have I made myself clear?'

'Perfectly.' He needed a cigarette to get rid of the rotting taste that had filled his mouth.

'You know your career is riding on this, don't you?'

'I do get that feeling, sir.'

'Good. Have a shave, there's a good man. Try and look like a police officer. Now, go and do your job.'

The Commander picked up his paper and started reading again. Brenton climbed out of the car, reaching for a cigarette. The more he thought about what Swanson said and wanted him to do, the more the repulsion and anger raced through him. Shakily he put a cigarette to his lips and lit it as the car rumbled away.

'Who was that in the flash car?' Wood said, appearing next to him and making him start.

'Jesus.' Brenton nearly dropped the cigarette and lighter. He took a deep breath and then looked at her. 'That was Commander Swanson poking his nose in.'

'What did he want?'

'He's keeping a close eye on things.' Brenton sucked hungrily on the cigarette.

'Why's he so interested?'

'Search me. You know what the brass are like. Listen, Kate, the blonde hair you found... let's keep a lid on it, shall we?'

Her eyes narrowed, weighing him up carefully. 'It's in the system now, the SOCOs have them. What do you mean?'

'I mean, any results that come back, are for our eyes only. Got it?'

She gave him the same suspicious look. 'All right, but if anyone tries to pile any crap on me, I'm not going to fucking lie.'

'Of course not.'

'What exactly is going on? The brass don't just show up at any crime scene.'

'This is going to be a sensitive one. Swanson wants to be kept abreast of any developments.'

Wood shook her head and huffed. 'Great. That's fantastic, and all we need.'

Brenton looked back towards the building, then patted his jacket, feeling the evidence bag he'd secured there, wondering what information, if any, the paper the name was printed on might give up, if he dared to have it examined.

CHAPTER 9

His fingers were moving, so was his mouth, and words were tripping out one after another in no discernible order. He was walking. He looked down and saw the grey pavement beneath his dirty trainers. The cracks whizzing past.

Tom stopped moving, causing a man behind him to nearly crash into his back. The man swore under his breath as he stormed off, turning occasionally to stare back at Tom, a threat clear in his mad eyes.

He looked round and saw he was on a high street somewhere. He took in the names of the shops as the dizziness spun round his head and made his stomach rise up to his throat. The flavour of puke was on his tongue.

What had he done?

He backed up against the window of a phone shop and gripped his face and began to weep uncontrollably. He didn't realise it, but somewhere in the darkness of his hands, the crying became crazed laughter.

He looked at his hands, expecting to see blood on them. No, of course there wasn't blood. He'd washed himself, scrubbed himself with bleach. His skin burned with it, stunk of it, just like after he'd been swimming as a kid.

He began walking again, recognising the street he was on, suddenly aware that only two streets away was a large shabby house with people inside that he knew and trusted.

The house was set back from the street a little way, and a weed-strangled garden led to the front door. The place had been painted cream a long time back when it had been loved and cared for. Cracks now ran through the exterior where the constant stream of traffic had done its worst and discoloured the once pleasant paintwork.

He hurried to the peeling blue front door, put the key in the lock and stepped inside the wide and dusty hallway. The pile of junk mail and letters for the old occupants was still on the welcome mat. He headed along the hall, pulling a piece of the already flaking wallpaper with him.

The television was on, so he stood in the living room doorway, staring into the darkened room. The curtains were drawn tightly as always.

Linda was sat on the sofa, her legs drawn up to her skeletal body, her bony arms wrapped around her knees. She was lit up by the glow of the TV, but still she remained delicate and ghostly and not like a real person at all. He could never think of her as real, only as a human-shaped piece of skin that a real person has shed moments earlier.

She toyed with her unkempt blonde hair, then her head jerked as if she'd sensed he was there. She jumped up, clutching herself, her giant sad eyes burning out at him.

'Oh my gawd,' she screeched and rushed towards him. 'Tim! For heaven's sake, luv, where have you been? We thought you'd been taken.'

That's right, he thought to himself, and nodded. They knew him as Tim, not Tom. When they asked him to pick a name, a nice new shiny name to hide behind, he'd chosen Tim. It had been his best friend's name when he was growing up. Timothy. The little Nigerian kid with a giant heart and big toothy smile. The shiny coin amongst the dirt. The name was close to Tom, and he didn't ever want to forget that he was also Tom.

'Tim? Where've you been, luv?' Linda reached out to touch him, but her hands wavered and then fell to her side. 'I was worried. Scared, really.'

'I needed to get out.' He went and sat in front of the TV and saw that some skinny teenager was screaming at his girlfriend, accusing her of sleeping with his best friend. A slimy man in a suit was offering them ridiculous advice.

There was thudding down the stairs and a bulky man appeared in the doorway doing up his trousers, a newspaper tucked under his arm. Tom looked at the bulky man and his bulbous arms that were daubed with army tattoos. He had the face of a boxer, but the blue eyes of a scared child. Ex-soldier, ex- policeman. Derek.

'Tim?' Derek rushed over and put a giant hand on his shoulder. 'Where the fuck have you been, son?'

'Out.' Tom picked up the remote control and began flicking through the channels, trying to find the news. Had he killed the old pervert or had his violent fantasies become so real to him?

'Out? Where?' Derek crouched down and tried to look into his eyes. 'You know it's not safe for you out there, son, don't you?'

'I want the news.'

Derek stared at him for a while, then grabbed the remote control and put on the twenty-four-hour news channel. There was nothing. No breaking news about an old pervert MP having been beaten to death. He didn't know whether to laugh or cry.

He got up and barged past them both and went upstairs to his room, which he unlocked and locked again once inside. He sat on the single bed they'd bought him and stared at the little electronic safe they'd also provided. He pressed the right numbers, held his face, sat in silence, breathing in the nothingness.

The blackness moved, formed into a shape. The shape came towards him, a face now appearing, and it was snarling and ready to bite.

'Daddy,' he said and screamed into his hands.

No, he wasn't there. He'd been gone a long time.

He opened the safe and looked at the sheets of cream paper. He took them out and placed them neatly on the floor. He sat on the bed and looked them over, reading each name printed on the paper.

He closed his eyes and waved his hand in the air, then pointed, and opened his eyes again.

His finger was pointing at a name. The name brought a face to his mind, another craggy old man whose face was stamped with evil.

He took out a pair of latex gloves and pulled them on, then kneeled down and took out his scissors. Carefully he cut the name out, dropped it into a small plastic bag, then placed it under the bed.

'One down, five more to go,' he said.

Jairus stood across the street, watching the constant stream of black cabs and tourists. He looked towards the grand building at the end of the driveway, and the steady stream of visitors headed up the white stone steps of the British Museum. The place breathed history, exuded Britishness, whatever that meant. That's why so many foreign tourists were heading towards it, hypnotised by the imposing building.

Jairus straightened up and put his hands deep into his pockets when he saw her coming out and walking with confidence down the steps.

Helen Chara. He had to admit she was attractive, and he couldn't help feel something awaken in him when he fixed his eyes on her curvy frame. She was wearing a black dress, knee-length boots and a burgundy fitted jacket.

He pushed away his longing and brought back his inner suspicion to the surface as she clocked him and began striding towards him, a knowing smile forming on her dark red lips.

'Well, look who it is,' she said, stopping barely a few inches from him. 'Are you stalking me, former DCI Jairus? There's got to be something else I can call you.'

'Jay,' he said. 'No, I'm not stalking you. But I will buy you a very over-priced coffee.'

She looked behind him and towards the little Italian-style coffee house on the corner. 'So, it's coffee, and then you decide whether you want to take me for dinner?'

He held back a smile. 'Yeah, you'd be lucky. I don't do that stuff anymore.'

'Oh, so now you're a monk?' She smirked.

'Yeah, that's right. Come on, and I'll tell you about the vow of chastity I've taken.'

'OK, I'll have a cappuccino.'

Helen insisted on sitting outside in the sun, the last that October could afford to shine down. She stirred her coffee, all the time taking him in as if she was taking him apart like a piece of machinery.

'OK, there's obviously something on your mind,' she said after putting down the spoon.

'Yeah, there is. Robert Burdock,' he said and sat

back and examined her as she rolled her eyes and sighed.

'What about him?'

'You used to work for him, didn't you?'

She leaned forward and smiled. 'Somebody's been checking up on me. Have you been stalking me online, Jay?'

'Just answer the question.' He was thinking what a nice smile she had, but caught himself, and shut it away.

'Yes, OK, I admit it. I used to work for Robert Burdock. I was a reporter on a paper he owned. He gave me a job to do. Let's just say it wasn't exactly above board. When the shit hit the fan, he denied any knowledge and I ended up fired. I was the sacrificial lamb.'

'I know how that feels.'

'So, we have a lot in common. Both left out in the cold. Talking of lamb. I cook a very good...'

'Have you ever met his son, Douglas Burdock?'

She huffed. 'Oh, yes, I've met Douglas. A lot of women reporters have met Douglas Burdock. He's a very... sexual... animal. Very controlling of the women who fall under his spell. Why do you ask?'

'A friend of mine... she's... well, I think she's somehow involved with him.' Helen made a sound in her throat, and it didn't sound good to Jairus. 'What does that mean?'

'I've heard things about him,' she said, 'How he likes to possess people. He finds things on people and uses it against them. He basically buys the women that he wants by offering to make the thing they fear go away.'

'What does he do with these women after he BUYS them?' The headache began to pulse at the back of his skull.

'I don't think you want to know.'

'Yeah, I need to know.'

Helen shrugged. 'Let's just say he's into the darker side of sex.'

'How dark is dark?'

'Pitch black.'

'Jesus...' Jairus' stomach tightened as an image of Cathy flashed into his mind. He tried to halt the images of her tied up, abused, beaten, but they kept flooding in.

Helen sat forward, touched his hand. 'Is she an ex, this friend?'

He took his hand away. 'No. Just a friend.'

'Can I ask, who's paying you to look into Darren Parker?'

'No one's paying me.' Jairus stood up, getting ready to leave.

'No one's paying you? But you're doing it for someone?'

'Yeah.'

She sat up. 'Oh... right... now the penny drops. It's Douglas Burdock, isn't it? He's got something on you... or he's promised you something...'

Saved by the bell, Jairus thought to himself as his phone started ringing. He took it out and saw that Rich was calling. He held up a hand to Helen as he said, 'Yeah, Rich, what's going on?'

'I Googled those names we found on that list. One of the names, Matthew Pinder brought up a news story from a couple of years back.'

'Go on.'

'Seems this Matthew Pinder got up in the middle of the night and shot his family and then himself.'

'Do you know anything else about him?'

'He was a businessman. Quite successful. It says he was suffering from depression. What do you think?'

'Where did this all take place?'

'Looe. Cornwall. But he was originally from London. Do you think there's a connection?'

'I don't know. But it's the only thing I've got to go on. Can you text me the address?'

'On its way. You going to head down there?'

'Yeah, why not? I'll send you a postcard.' Jairus hung up, put away his phone and faced Helen, who had her eyebrows raised. 'I've got to go.'

'Where are you going exactly?'

He laughed. 'That's for me to know and for you to keep your nose out.'

She finished her coffee and stood up. 'Does that mean you don't trust me?'

'Yeah, that's right. I don't. For one thing, you're a journalist. Secondly, you're a journalist who's out in the cold with only scraps to eat. You're too hungry for my liking.'

Jairus pushed his hands into his pockets as he began to head away from her, but stopped when she said, 'Don't you want to know what I dug up?'

He took a few steps back and faced her. 'Tell me.'

She smiled. 'First, you have to tell me where you're off to?'

'You go first.'

She narrowed her eyes. 'You swear to tell me where you're going after I tell you my info?'

'I swear.' He could smell her perfume, could see her smooth olive skin.

'I started to dig around a bit, mainly looking into what else David Coulson might've been up to before he was killed.'

'Yeah, and?'

'Did you know he had a close female friend? No, you didn't, did you? They met up a few times, had drinks...'

'You think they were having an affair?'

Helen shrugged her shoulders. 'David Coulson was good-looking. Apparently, he was pretty charming too. I've heard that quite a few women were taken with him.'

Jairus thought of Alice. She hadn't mentioned a close female friend, and talked about him as if she was still very fond of him. 'What's her name?'

'Julia Robins. She was a model in her younger days. Blonde, leggy. If you like that sort of thing.'

'I don't.'

She smiled, and played with a strand of her dark hair. 'I didn't think you did.'

'Where does she live?'

'She was living in Victoria Road, Hackney...'

Jairus stepped closer to her, feeling the burn of excitement ripple through him. 'In a flat?'

'Yes, actually. A basement flat. Why?'

'No reason.'

She raised an eyebrow. 'I saw that look in your eye. The little twinkle.'

'Where does she live now?'

'That I haven't found out yet. She was living there with her husband, but they split up a short while after Coulson was killed. He still lives in the flat, but he wouldn't answer any questions. It's like she's vanished. So, where are you going?'

'Cornwall.' Jairus turned and began heading back to the tube station.

'Hang on,' Helen said, sounding annoyed and grabbing his arm. 'That's it? Cornwall? Cornwall's a big place.'

'Yeah, it is. Look, you go and find out where Julia Robins lives. When you find that out, I'll tell you what I've got up to. Deal?'

She narrowed her eyes. 'OK, but you better not be mucking me around.'

Jairus didn't answer, just stuffed his hands into his jacket pockets and walked towards the tube station and kept turning everything over in his mind, trying to put the few pieces he had together. Nothing really fitted, apart from the fact that Coulson's female friend having a flat that fitted the description of the one Mickey O'Neil had boasted he'd killed Coulson inside of.

The feeling he had that things were going to keep getting worse was growing. Being on his own meant spreading himself thin, but he had no choice. First he'd look into deaths of the Pinder family, then find that flat where Coulson might have been murdered in.

Tom was standing at the bus stop but kept forgetting why he was there. He looked at his watch, then up at the sky. It was cloudy. Some of them looked as if someone had scorched them with a naked flame. He kept asking himself why someone would set fire to a cloud, just to keep his mind from the things he'd done, and would do.

When he looked around, he saw a fat old lady with white hair staring suspiciously at him. He'd been talking about the clouds, asking the question aloud.

The car's engine roared as it pulled into the bus lane and stopped, making Tom jump.

That's why he was here.

There was the young, dark-skinned man driving, while the middle-aged woman was sitting in the back like she was the Queen or something.

'Please get in, Tom,' the young man called out.

Tom did as he was ordered and climbed in the back, and sat next to the woman, who had a tablet device on her lap. She was dressed in a sharp tailored grey trouser suit. It's what she always wore. She had dyed blonde hair disguising the grey. The perfume too, the kind old ladies wear, which clawed at the back of his throat.

The car was driven not far away, and parked at the outskirts of a supermarket car park.

Seemingly satisfied with their location, the woman looked up, raised her pointy nose and sniffed. 'Oh dear, Thomas, when was the last time you had a bath?'

He didn't say anything, but looked up at the driver, Joe, probably not his real name. Nobody had their real names, he'd learnt that over the years. Joe looked him over with utter contempt, then faced front again.

'Thomas?' she said, her voice rising with anger. 'Thomas? Look at me. That's it. Listen, you have to take better care of yourself. Smelling as you do does not inspire confidence in people, or sympathy. People do not stop to give smelly tramps money. No, they step over them... or worse. Do you understand?'

He nodded.

He could feel her examining him with the same contempt as the driver. The question was there too, hiding among the dyed blonde hair and deadly perfume, waiting to jump out.

'Where are they?' she said, the anger lessening in her voice, but still there, barely concealed.

'I don't know... yet...' He flashed her a look.

She pinched her nose, let out a harsh breath. 'You don't know? What good are you, Thomas? I've given you one simple job to do. Find out where they are hiding them. I thought you said they trusted you. Was that a lie?'

'No. They do trust me. They believe my story.'

Joe turned around again. 'They believe it, because it's true, Tom. All you have to do is open your mouth and let the ugly things they did to you spill out. They'll see the truth in your eyes. Truth is very important when telling a good lie.'

'Listen to Joe,' she said. 'He knows what he's talking about. How many more interviews are there going to be? I take it they want to interview you again?'

'Yes, they do. They've asked to meet with me again.'

'Where this time?'

He shrugged. 'I don't know. They only tell me at the last minute. They're scared.'

She stared at him for a while, then gently touched his chin and turned his face around. 'You understand that we need to find the house where they're keeping those poor people, don't you, Thomas? They have suffered enough. We can look after them. Protect them, as we are protecting you. You do understand, don't you? We protect you, don't we? Imagine what terrible things could befall you if we took away that protection.'

'I know.' He could taste her lies like poison on his tongue.

'What about Jessica?' Joe said.

The mention of the name bit into his stomach and drove an icy blade into his heart. He looked up and saw the black eyes digging into him.

'She needs to be kept safe too, doesn't she?' Joe smiled. 'She's about the only family you've got left. How old is she?'

'Twelve.'

'That's right. Pretty too. She's going to break a few hearts. I know. I've seen a photograph.' Joe smiled, then licked his lips. 'You don't want what happened to you to happen to her, do you?'

Tom couldn't trust himself to keep his rage from his voice, so kept his response to a simple shake of his head, which he knew would satisfy them and give them the sense that he was beaten and weak.

'That's settled then,' the woman said and patted him lightly on the shoulder. 'You'll feed them the last piece of the information that Joe provided, and convince them that you are the genuine article. When they take you to the house, you will let us know where it is. We will deal with the rest.'

Their collective silence seemed to signify that they wanted a response. He nodded.

'Don't disappoint us, Tom,' Joe said, setting his serious dark eyes on him again. 'Think about Jessica.'

'Don't hurt... don't let her be hurt,' he said and looked down at his hands.

'That's up to you, Tom.' Joe nodded.

'Now, please remove yourself from my car,' the woman said. 'There's a supermarket over there. Buy some soap and deodorant.'

Tom was shaking as he found the handle and let himself out of the car, and then watched it rumble to life and drive away from the car park. He was left standing among the other vehicles and the discarded shopping trolleys.

He opened his jacket and patted his pocket, feeling the plastic bag he had concealed there. Inside there was another envelope, which contained a sheet of the special paper he'd stolen all those years ago.

A single name was printed on the square of paper. Soon, two of them would be gone.

CHAPTER 10

Jairus watched it all whip past, the green flashes of grass and bushes, the grey of metal and concrete as acres of warehouses, giant car parks and wholesalers turned into fields and farmland. The distant white cloud-like shapes of sheep grazing. The acrid, stomach-churning smell of the countryside was almost comforting, reminding him of an innocent time, sitting in the backseat of the family car when they were still a family, before his dad's life of crime tore it all apart.

On the way, he'd stopped off in Plymouth, a city once flattened in World War Two, now a strange hybrid of the new and the old. He booked in to a concrete monstrosity of a hotel on the edge of town, a symptom of the misguided sixties attempt to rejuvenate post war Britain. Then he started driving again, heading in the direction of Looe as the sun began to hide beneath the ragged rural horizon.

It was pretty much blackness by the time his satnav informed him that the road he wanted was on the next left. The turning, which was arched by dense foliage from the trees above, narrowed into a small country lane. On the right there seemed to be the shape of houses, which were raised up, overhanging the road. On the left was more thick woodland that was encroaching on the thoroughfare. The thick trees did an excellent job of keeping out the little light from the moon, and so Jairus parked his car at the first chance he got, stopping on what seemed to be part of the one of the house's drives.

He found himself partly parked under the struts of a more modern house of steel and glass, which stood out among the cottage-style buildings beside it.

He climbed out and took his mobile from his pocket and brought up the email he'd been sent by Rich. He looked around into the gloom, then opened the gate that led to the paved steps that led up to the house. He climbed up, using the glow from his mobile phone to light the way, and eventually stood on the concrete landing in front of large glass doorways. The whole front of the house was mostly glass. How could anyone live in a house where everyone could see in, he wondered?

The house was now empty, having not attracted one person who wanted to live in a house of murder and suicide, although Jairus was sure there would be someone somewhere that would revel in the death that surrounded them as they slept.

It was too dark to see into the house, but he was itching to get inside and was pondering whether to let himself in when a light from next door caught his eye. It had come on for a few seconds then gone off again. A curtain had moved too.

He turned and watched the house, feeling the curious eyes on him, burning out to him, wondering, and probably scared of who he was. He smiled, even though they wouldn't be able to see. But people could tell you were smiling even in silhouette, he remembered being told by some science program.

Either way, he wondered, as he went back down the steps, whether they were calling the police or not.

He reached the bottom of the house, walked through the gate, ready to get in his car and head back to his hotel. But something told him to stop where he was, then look up. He raised his eyes, following the stone steps that led up to the cottage next door. His eyes widened when he saw a figure coming towards the edge of the veranda. A security light blasted golden light down towards him, prohibiting a good view of who ever stood there. For a moment, he thought it was a woman.

'Hello,' he said, covering his eyes from the burning light. 'I didn't mean to disturb you. I just came to take a look at the house next door.'

No voice came back and the silhouetted figure remained looking down at him, motionless. He decided another tactic and headed towards the gate to their steps. He put a hand on the gate and opened it slowly. 'I'm going to come up. Is that all right?'

The figure moved this time, hurrying to block the gate at the top of the stone steps. 'Stay there!'

It was a woman's voice that shouted down to him, and he heard the trembling fear within it. Who ever she was, she was terrified. Of course, it was perfectly understandable that she was scared, having a strange man coming towards her in the dark of night. But the fear she was exhibiting was something that had already been set in place before he ever arrived.

'I'm not going to hurt you,' he said, staying where he was. He held up his hands.

'I'm not stupid!' her voice came back, hardened, trying to hide her fear now. 'I've seen you down there, sitting in your car, watching my house. I'm not scared of you!'

'I'm not who you think I am. I've never been here before. My name is Jairus. I used to be a policeman.

I'm here to find out what happened to Steven Pinder and his family.'

There was silence for a while, then she said, 'He killed them all, then killed himself. That's what they said in the papers.'

'Yeah, but you sound like you don't believe that.' He took another step towards her.

'Why shouldn't I believe it? Why would they lie?'

'Exactly. Why would they lie? Unless you know something they don't.'

Her voice trembled as she said, 'I don't know anything.'

Jairus looked round, then took out his wallet and threw it so it landed close to her. 'There's my ID, so you know I am who I say I am. Nobody's here but us. Nobody knows I'm here. Whatever you tell me, I'll never tell anyone the information came from you.'

The woman slowly crouched down, her hand reaching out for the wallet, her wide eyes never moving from him. Something caught the harsh beam of the security light, glinting out at him. The woman had a knife at her side that he could see was trembling.

'I can see you're scared,' he said, smiling kindly. 'I used to be a policeman, now I work on my own. If you can tell me anything about that night, it'll be really helpful. Then I'll be on my way.'

She opened the wallet, looked at whatever she saw there, and then looked up at him. 'You used to be in the police?'

'Yeah, for my sins. I hope I get to be once again. That's why I'm looking into this.'

'I don't think you should be looking into this.'

'Yeah, and why's that?'

The woman looked towards her neighbour's old house. 'Something awful happened that night...I mean, I know...what they say happened, that he killed them all then killed himself...'

'Did you hear the gunshots?'

She nodded. 'Yes. I didn't know what it was at first. Then I came outside. They sounded like...crackers going off, not like you hear on TV...'

'No, they don't sound like they do on TV. Were they far apart, the shots, or close together?'

The woman rubbed her eyes and looked down at the knife in her hand. 'Not close together. There seemed to be a minute maybe more between each one. I can't be sure though.'

He nodded. 'What makes you think that something wasn't right about what they told you happened? Was it a feeling or...?'

'No, I went down there, down those steps. It was probably a stupid thing to do, seeing as someone was firing a gun, but I needed to find out what was happening...does that make sense?'

'Yeah, perfect sense. It's natural curiosity. Shows you were concerned for your neighbours.'

She nodded and looked down at the road. 'It sounds crazy...and you might not believe me, but...well, I know there was someone there that night. I thought I saw movement...and I sort of sensed someone was watching me from under the house. I think they were hiding behind the trees.'

'What do you think they were doing there?'

She gave a tired laugh, and shook her head. 'I don't know. Maybe I imagined it...but, when I mentioned it to the police officer that came to see me...he looked at me strangely and warned me not to mention it again. It sounded like he was almost threatening me, without really threatening me...if that makes sense?'

'Yeah, it does. What was this police officer's name?'

'Detective Inspector Robert Johnson. I didn't like him to be honest. Came across as cold, unfeeling.'

'Is there anything else you can remember that stands out from that night?'

She raised her shoulders. 'Nothing really. I guess, I was left with a feeling of unease about the whole thing. I've still got this feeling in the pit of my stomach that something's not right. Do you ever get that?'

'Yeah, all the time in fact. Thank you for your time. You've been really helpful. I'd keep all you've told me to yourself. In case anyone does come round asking any more questions, or you start being watched again, you can call me. If you look in my wallet, you'll find one of my cards. Ignore the top number, that's my old work number. My mobile's at the bottom.'

The woman took out a card from his wallet, then held it out to him. He walked up the last few steps and went to take back his wallet, when he was overcome with dizziness. He looked at his hand and saw it was violently shaking. His heart began to thump manically in his chest.

'Are you OK?' the woman said, still holding out his wallet. 'You don't look very well.'

'Yeah, I'm fine.' He snatched the wallet and turned back down the steps. 'Thanks again.'

He stopped at his car and leaned on the door, holding himself up. His whole body seemed to be vibrating uncontrollably as his heart raced. He looked around him at the darkness and wondered what he was doing there. Where was he?

Yes, he remembered, he was in Cornwall, following up a lead. He breathed hard, trying to get his body to listen to him, to get it to calm down long enough for him to get back to Plymouth and then to bed. Maybe he was suffering from flu, he thought or just extreme exhaustion. When was the last time he'd slept through the night? He couldn't be sure.

He got into his car and started driving back the way he had come, heading around dark bends, the bright beam of headlights the only warning that another car was coming towards him from the gloom.

Hold it together, he told himself, don't crash now.

By the time Jairus made it back to Plymouth, his symptoms seemed to have dissipated. He was a little hot and cold, and sweat had broken out all over his body, but his heart had calmed and he'd stopped shaking quite so violently.

He parked in the underground car park beneath the hotel and took the stairs up to the reception area. He stepped out in the large plush area and walked past the glass partitioned bar on his right. He stopped as he heard what sounded like a raucous party going on inside. He turned towards the bar and saw all the upside down bottles of spirits lined up behind it. His mouth was salivating at the sight of the bottle of vodka. He could've killed for a drink, easily murdered anyone who got in his way. He closed his eyes, opened them again and began walking towards the lifts.

'You look terrible,' a female voice said to his left.

He turned and saw Helen Chara looking him over with concern plastered on her beautifully made-up face. She was wearing a dark red dress, her long raven-black hair pouring over her shoulders. 'What're you doing here? You following me?'

'I'm starting to realise you're always where the action is...seriously though, you look ill.'

'Yeah, do I? Well, I'm fine. I just need some sleep.' He went to walk towards the lifts, but Helen grabbed his arm.

'Oh my God, you're shaking.'

He looked down at his hands and saw that he was indeed violently trembling again.

'Come and sit in the bar,' she said and started directing him towards the frosted glass doors.

'No, the last place I need to be is a bar.'

She looked at him, her face flooding with realisation. 'Do you have a drink problem?'

'No, I don't.'

'You do, don't you? When was the last time you had a drink?'

'A few days ago. I haven't got a problem...'

She shook her head and started dragging him through the doors and into the noisy bar. A large TV over the bar was blaring out a football game while a group of men pushing thirty screamed up at the screen. Helen directed him to a booth in a far corner and made him sit down.

'You wait right there,' she said, pointing one of her red nails at him.

'Where are you going?'

'To get you a drink.'

He stood up. 'I can't have a drink. I've come this far...'

She squared up to him, poked him in the chest. 'Do you want to go to hospital? Get a load of drugs pumped into you? No, I didn't think so. You're in the early stages of alcohol withdrawal. I've got a sister who's a nurse, so I know all about this stuff. You either go to A and E or you start drinking. Seeing as you're probably a bit obsessive, you won't want to go and spend a lot of time in hospital and then rehab while the case you're on goes cold. Am I right?'

He nodded, then looked at his hands trembling. The sweat was pouring down his brow. He looked up towards the bar, but the bright TV screen and the bar lights merged and burned into his retinas. He blinked and rubbed his eyes, tried to focus and make sense of the shapes in front of him.

No!

He shook his head as he saw a familiar hooded shape by the bar. Two twisted, evil eyes burned into his. Then the figure was falling to the ground, begging for mercy as he tried in vain to keep the blood from pouring out of the knife wound in his gut.

Jairus looked down and saw the bloody kitchen knife in his own hand.

He looked up at Helen who was staring at him as if he'd gone crazy and stripped his clothes off.

'I'm seeing things,' he said. 'I used to see things... but...'

'I'm getting you a drink.'

Jairus nodded. 'Vodka. Straight.'

He sat down with a thump after Helen headed for the bar, and gripped the table as if he was in danger of spinning off across the room. When Helen came back with a tray of drinks, mostly consisting of glasses of vodka, he grabbed the nearest one and downed it in one.

'Easy there, tiger,' she said, picking up a glass of white wine. 'This is a short-term treatment. It's not a cure.'

'Yeah, I know.'

'You need help.' She reached across the table and gently touched his hand.

'You've already helped me, thanks.' He picked up the next glass and took a sip, and already he felt the symptoms fading away. His hand seemed steadier, and when he looked towards the bar, the hooded figure had gone.

'I've been reading up on you.' Helen sat back in her

seat, her glass almost touching her lips.

'Yeah? I probably don't make very interesting reading.'

'Oh, I disagree. You've beaten two suspicion of murder charges so far. That's pretty impressive.'

'I'm glad I impress you.'

She leaned forward. 'Tell me about Carl Murphy.'

He automatically looked towards the bar where the apparition, or rather the hallucination, had manifested itself. Helen turned to see what he was looking at, then she looked at him again, another smile of realisation spreading through her face. 'That's who you saw over there? I see now. He haunts your dreams.'

'Dreams suggest sleep. I don't really sleep. Not properly.' He took another sip of vodka, but suddenly it didn't taste so good and left an acidic flavour in his mouth.

'That's even worse, if he haunts your waking hours. I read that you killed him in self-defence. Did you?'

He let out a laugh to mask the fact that the memory was crawling through his brain again, like worms burrowing beneath his scalp. He drank some more, even though the drink tasted bitter to him. 'Yeah, that's right.'

'What about the man found strangled in your home?'

'Someone tried to set me up. It nearly worked too. But luckily, a witness came forward and some misplaced CCTV footage surfaced that proved I couldn't have been there when he was killed.'

'Lucky.'

'Yeah, very.'

'But the police cut you loose anyway? That must've hurt.'

He sighed, sat up and finished the second glass of

vodka. 'I don't want to talk about me anymore.'

She smiled. 'OK. What shall we talk about?'

The truth was he was too tired to talk, especially about himself, but he knew he was starting to realise how her mind worked. She was a kind of huntress, always on the prowl, and she had set her sights on him, and would not be sated until she had devoured him. He would be left as an empty carcass, while his skin would be hung out for everyone to stare at.

He needed a distraction.

'I'm sure there's a mini bar in my room,' he said and smiled at her.

She raised her eyebrows. 'Really? Both of us go up to your room and crack open the mini bar?'

'Yeah, why not?' He smiled even though it almost caused him physical pain to do so.

Jairus slid the card into the lock, then opened the door and flicked the light switch. He stepped into the glaringly white bathroom as Helen walked further into his room. She was saying something, but he couldn't hear. The pulse of his headache was too loud, too intrusive to let in anything of normal volume.

He ran the tap and splashed some water onto his face and then looked into his own red eyes. When was the last time he'd actually slept properly without waking up after an hour, without his heart thudding madly, and his mind racing with dark and horrific thoughts and memories?

Close it off. Smile. Have another drink.

Jairus joined Helen in the main room, then opened up the small fridge that was secreted under the desk. There was a half bottle of vodka and a small bottle of wine. He poured them both a drink, the handed Helen hers.

The journalist smiled, then pointed towards the glass doors that separated the room from the concrete balcony. Jairus looked beyond the glass and out towards the scattering of distant lights on the horizon.

'Not a bad view,' she said.

'That'll be the Hoe,' he said, stepping closer to the glass. 'Where Sir Francis Drake played bowls and then along the Barbican there's the Mayflower steps where the founding fathers left from.'

'You know a lot about Plymouth?'

He shrugged. 'I just like to read about stuff.'

'Are your parents still alive?'

He looked at her, trying to decide what her angle was, then gave up. 'My mum died a long time ago. My dad was a career criminal, then a grass...'

'Is he still alive?'

'I don't know.'

'Any brothers or sisters?'

Jairus took a drink, dredging up old memories. 'There was a rumour my old man had another family somewhere, but I never wanted to find out if it was true. What about you? Where are your parents?'

'Crete. Living the life of Riley.' She moved closer to him, looked up into his eyes. 'I find you strangely fascinating. I can't work you out, which is why I'm so obsessed with you.'

He almost laughed. 'You're obsessed with me?'

She nodded. 'A bit. Does that freak you out?'

He shook his head, then found himself bending towards her and kissing her lips. He straightened up and smiled.

'Is that all?' she asked.

He took her wine glass from her hand, set it down on the desk, then pulled her close and kissed her. Her arms slipped round his neck and pulled him tighter to her as she kissed him back, almost desperately.

Then they were lying on the bed; he wasn't sure how they had got to that position, but decided he didn't care. For a long time, he hadn't found a moment when his mind didn't romp onwards and around to bite its own tail like a crazed dog, so when his mind seemed to clear as he kissed her, he decided to enjoy it. For once, he let himself go as they kissed and touched each other. There was nothing to say, and nothing to think for a while, and he sunk into it, his mind left abandoned like a deserted boat on a stormy sea that was now calming.

The tower was glistening with the blue light that ran up its steel body and vanished somewhere in the black sky. Tom was leaning against the wall of the coffee shop across the street, his head tilted back, staring up at one of London's tallest buildings. It wasn't the tallest, not by a longshot. That title had been taken by the Gherkin, or whatever they called it. There were so many skyscrapers being erected across the city, it was difficult to keep up with them. Slowly, but surely, they were turning London into New York, or was it Los Angeles? Someone had told him that years ago. There was a plan that some people – the real power behind the curtain – had come up with to meld Britain to Europe and then to America. A one-world government would emerge sometime in the near future, as well as a world currency, growing from the desire of the Free World to protect itself from the threat of terrorism.

Who had told him that?

He had an image of a slightly overweight, grey-haired man in a suit looking down at him from a leather chair. He was smiling, sickeningly so, trying to seem kind, when Tom knew he was anything but kind.

There was a rumble in the late-night traffic. Tom snapped out of his thoughts and tucked himself around the corner, his eyes fixed on the shiny black limo that was heading towards the tower. It slowed and pulled through the gates of the skyscraper's courtyard and parked by the large glass doors of the foyer.

A few minutes later, Tom watched, as a man, average height and bulky, squeezed into an expensive tailored pinstripe suit, came striding towards the glass doors flanked on either side by two younger and much hungrier, leaner looking suits. He could see how they stuck to him, and fawned over the older man as they escorted him to his car.

When he appeared in the blue beam of the spotlights, Tom found he could get a better look at the man, could see his beady dark pupils peering through his hooded eyelids. His grey and neat beard was in place as it had been all those years ago.

The man slipped inside the limo as the chauffeur opened the door for him. Then the car turned and headed back out of the courtyard and into the stream of traffic.

Tom saw him race past, sat upright, his phone to his ear.

Tom felt the puke rise in him and rushed into the tiny alley next to the coffee shop and vomited by some wheelie bins. He wiped his face, then stood up, feeling his brain swirling and bouncing around his skull. He took out a cigarette and shakily lit it, took a deep puff, then put one hand in his pocket and removed the addressed envelope.

James Howard.

He read the name and the vomit tried to rise again into his mouth. He took another puff and started walking down the street, looking for a post box.

In twenty-four hours' time, the old businessman in the suit would see him for what he had become, what they had turned him into.

And it would be the last thing he'd see.

CHAPTER 11

DI Jake Brenton checked the address again, took another draw on his cigarette, then looked up the high street and saw the broad concrete building wedged between the takeaways and sports shops. The front of the old Southgate police station was stained with rain marks, the metal shutters still pulled down over the windows. He could even see the old pole sticking out of the front where the fake blue light box would have sat.

When he got close to the entrance, he saw a uniform standing guard, ready to point any lost souls in the right direction. He dropped his cigarette, stamped it out, and took the old battered concrete stairs that stank of urine and headed to the next floor. The rest of the place smelt like school. It was the waxy floors that did it. He found himself in one long dusty old room with small modern desks lining the walls. A whiteboard had already been set up at the far end of the room, and a few computers had been placed on the desks huddled nearest to it.

As Brenton was looking about the office, DS Kate Wood came out of an office on his right carrying some sheets of paper.

'You're early,' she said. 'Thought I was going to be the only mug who showed up.'

'Couldn't you find a more rundown place than this

to use as our headquarters?'

Wood stuck up her middle finger. 'Very funny.'

'I was half expecting Dixon of Dock Green to be here.' Brenton walked up to her, and took a quick look inside her sparse, damp-smelling office.

Wood started waving her hand in front of her face. 'Jesus, Jake, how many fags have you smoked this morning? You stink like an ashtray.'

'That's my new aftershave. Eau de ashtray. Do I get an office?'

'Next door. Listen, I need you to come into my office and shut the door behind you.'

He saw her troubled expression. 'All right. I can see you're worried about something.'

Brenton stepped in and leaned against an old battered desk and watched Wood close the door, then face him as she said, 'They managed to speed through the results on those hairs we found.'

'The blonde hairs?'

'Yes, the blonde hairs.' Wood went over to the desk and opened a file. 'They got a DNA match from another murder case.'

'Oh, bloody hell.'

'Yep. Remember the disappearance of Mandy Rose?'

Brenton looked down at the post mortem photograph of the lifeless, blue-ish skin of the blonde young girl. 'How could I forget? You're telling me the hairs belong to her?'

'Two of the hairs. The others were horse hair, more than likely from an old blonde wig.'

Brenton rubbed his face. 'So, what are we saying? How did they get into our crime scene?'

Wood pulled out a chair and sat down. 'Leonard Jameson MP.'

Brenton sat down. 'Go on.'

'It's been alleged in the past that he has an unhealthy interest in young girls. There was a family that came forward about fifteen years ago claiming that Jameson sexually assaulted their daughter. The case was dropped, and a police officer came forward a few years ago to claim that he had arrested Jameson when he tried to abduct a young girl from a playground. Apparently, Jameson gave a false name and address.'

Brenton had a sinking feeling and found himself itching for another cigarette while his conversation with Commander Swanson kept spiralling in his mind. 'What're you getting at? That we've got a vigilante on our hands who believes Jameson murdered Mandy Rose?'

'He has to be more than just a vigilante, doesn't he? I mean, the forensic department confirmed that those hairs were taken from Mandy Rose before she died.'

'A family member? So we interview her father and...'

Wood sat back. 'What about Edward Foreman? He's inside for murdering Mandy Rose and four other girls.'

Brenton buried his face in his hands, trying to keep Foreman's ugly mug from poisoning his mind. 'You want to talk to Foreman?'

'You said you wanted to keep this on the quiet, so we'll have to go and see him.'

Brenton stood up and looked down at the almost serene photograph of the young murdered girl. His stomach bit down on itself. 'All right. We'll go and see him.'

'This afternoon.'

'Have you already arranged it?'

'Of course.' She smiled.

'Fuck me, Kate. I feel sick.'

'You still want to keep this under your hat?'

'Yeah, not a word.' Then Brenton remembered what he had stuffed in his coat pocket and took it out.

Wood stared at the plastic evidence bag he was holding in his hand and the piece of paper contained inside it. 'What's that? Are you carrying around evidence in your pockets?'

'This piece of paper was sent to someone, I don't know who, with Leonard Jameson's name printed on it, and then crossed out. A message from his killer.'

'Oh my God. Has that been examined?'

'No. I was told there was nothing significant about the paper itself. Which means there must be.' He looked up at Wood. 'We need to know all about this piece of paper, without anyone knowing we examined it.'

She picked up the evidence bag and stared at it, then raised her eyes to Brenton. 'Who exactly gave this to you?'

'I don't think you want to know.'

She handed him back the bag. 'Then you keep hold of it. Let's go and pay Foreman a visit. See what he says, and if he shines a light on any of this...shit, maybe then we take a closer look at that piece of paper.'

Jairus found a place to park in the narrow street that ran behind Charles Cross Police Station, and picked up his takeaway coffee. He carefully prized the lid off, then looked around to make sure nobody was watching him as he took out the small bottle of vodka he'd bought and poured a couple of shots into his drink. A Russian coffee, he muttered to himself and put the lid back on. He took a sip and then looked towards the fenced-off compound behind the police station where all marked and unmarked were cars were secured. The police station looked more like a rundown office block. It was sat on the corner of the street, opposite a derelict church, which had been hit by German bombs and left as some kind of monument to the city's brave stand against the Nazi war machine.

Jairus could find no existence of a DI Robert Johnson working out of Devon and Cornwall constabulary, but Rich informed him that the contact number for the case that was printed under all the news articles was for a DS Simon Davies. After another quick financial check by Rich, Jairus had a sketch of his habits, which included a mid-morning breakfast at John's café, which was situated almost directly behind his car. Rich was also helpful in pointing out a few other unusual purchases and stays at out of town hotels that stood out in Davies' recent financial dealings.

Jairus had woken to find Helen gone and a note left on the bedside table. She'd gone back to her room to have a shower and had some other errands to take care of. She also left a reminder at the bottom of the note telling him to make sure he had a drink sometime that day. For the first time in several months, he felt like he had a hangover, and to make matters worse, his old iron fist headache was pounding against the top of his skull. It was his body's way of telling him something wasn't right with current events.

Jairus sat up when he saw two uniforms coming down the narrow alleyway that ran past the police station. Behind the uniforms came a tall and slender suited man with thinning straw-coloured hair. He had his hands in his pockets and had a tired look on his face as he strolled past and headed into the cafe. Jairus looked down at his phone as he brought up the ID photograph of DS Simon Davies, confirming to himself that the policeman he was after had just entered the eatery behind him.

Jairus climbed out and headed into the cafe and watched the suited man as he queued up at the counter and then ordered a coffee and a bacon sandwich. Jairus ordered a black coffee, then walked over to the table in the corner at which DS Davies had sat at. He was reading that day's Sun newspaper which had been left on the table.

'Mind if I sit down?' Jairus asked and pulled out a chair opposite him.

Davies looked round at the other empty tables, then shrugged as he lifted his paper up to his face. 'Help yourself.'

Jairus sat down and sipped his black coffee, then said, 'You're DS Simon Davies, that right?'

The paper came down, revealing Davies' creased brow. 'Who are you?'

'My name's Jairus. Ex-DCI Jairus. I wanted to talk to you about the murders of the Pinder family.'

Davies didn't say anything for a while, just closed the paper and put it to one side. 'You're an ex-police officer?'

'Yeah, you catch on fast.'

'What are you now... a private detective?' Davies folded his arms.

'No. I'm just really curious.'

'Right, well, when my bacon sandwich turns up, I'll be out of here and back to work.' Davies picked up the paper again.

'Were you satisfied that Matthew Pinder had killed his family and himself?'

Davies didn't say anything.

'OK, let me change the subject...you're married, right?'

The police officer looked up. 'What's that got to do with anything?'

'Does she know you're having an affair?'

Davies looked round the room again. 'Who the bloody hell are you?'

'All I want to know is, if you were satisfied with the whole murder suicide bit? Talk to me and your wife remains ignorant of your infidelity, or at least until she finds out by herself. Because they always do.'

Davies huffed. 'Wasn't my call.'

'Was it DI Robert Johnson's call?' Jairus sipped his coffee.

'Yes, it was. He was happy with murder suicide.'

'Where's Johnson now?'

Davies shrugged. 'Moved on. Fast tracked, I don't know. He wasn't down here long.'

'Don't tell me he turned up here shortly before the Pinder deaths and then left shortly after?'

'That's about the size of it.' Davies smiled up at the young lad who placed his bacon sandwich in front of him. 'Is that it?'

'Don't you think it's a bit odd that he turned up just before the murder suicide, then left after?'

'Extremely. What do you expect me to do about it? Murder suicide is a lot neater than all round murder. Means we don't have to keep looking for a murderer, doesn't it?'

Jairus gave an empty laugh as his head began to pound and his hands started shaking. He wasn't sure if it was the fury building up in his chest or the need for a drink that was making him tremble. 'Yeah, I suppose it is neater. That's how it works down here, is it?'

Davies' face went from smirking to slow seething anger. 'Listen, I do my job, all right? I take my orders and I go home and watch TV, play with the kids. That's all I care about. What did you do? Worry about it all? Yeah, you look the sort. Did they let you go because you started on the booze? I can smell it on you.'

'One too many murder charges got me the sack.' Jairus sat back, watched the detective's disbelief gather on his face before he added, 'The name's Jairus. J-A-I-R-U-S. Look me up online.'

'I don't have to. I've heard of you. I thought you looked familiar. Was it really self-defence?'

'You keep wondering that. I meant what I said, help me or I'll rip your world apart.' Jairus stared into the copper's eyes, until Davies looked away.

'All right,' he said. 'If you want the truth, I wasn't happy with the conclusion.'

'Yeah? Why not?'

'For one thing, the pathologist they sent down from London to oversee the post-mortems was a weirdo. There was something not right about him. The whole thing was too neat and tied up too quickly, but orders came from above to make sure it was wrapped up quickly. But anyway, it's all done and dusted now.'

Jairus huffed out a laugh. 'Yeah, nice and neat. That's the way they like it. You didn't find anything at all that would point to an assassination, rather than murder suicide?'

Davies raised his eyebrows. 'What, you think they were all knocked off to keep them quiet? Why? Far as I know they were just an ordinary family.'

'What about any computers they had?'

'We found one laptop which belonged to Steven Pinder. There was work stuff on there and a load of stuff that had been wiped off pretty professionally, but we figured that wasn't unusual. Probably porn he'd downloaded.'

'Nice to know you lot are thorough. Where's this laptop now?'

'Safely locked up in the evidence locker. Why?'

Jairus smiled. 'I need to have a look at it.'

Davies shook his head. 'Are you actually being serious?'

'Yeah, I am.'

'You want me to walk into the station, go to the evidence locker, get the laptop and give it to you?'

'Yeah, I do. You better hurry up.'

'Fuck off. I can't do that.'

'You can. Sign it out. I'll get it back to you before you start work in the morning. You haven't much choice, have you? Unless you want your wife to know what you've been up to?'

Davies stared at him, seething, then looked down at his bacon sandwich. 'You're a fucking arsehole. Do you know that?'

'Yeah. Hurry up and get the laptop. I'll meet you back here.'

Davies pushed the bacon sandwich towards Jairus. 'You might as well eat that. I don't fancy it anymore.'

The police detective got up heavily and trudged out of the cafe.

When he was gone, Jairus took out his mobile and dialled Rich. It took quite a few rings before he heard coughing on the other end, a groaning sound and a gruff voice say, 'Jay? Do you know what fucking time it is?'

'Yeah. I do. Nearly half past nine. Don't tell me you're still in bed.'

'Of course I'm in bed.' Then Rich lowered his voice. 'I'm not alone either.'

'Good for you. What you doing for the rest of the day?'

'Hopefully more of what I did last night and a bit of PlayStation action. Why?'

'I've got a job for you. I need a laptop decrypting. I'll make it worth your while.'

There was a groan on the other end. 'I'm lying next to a woman who let me...look, find someone else this time...'

'I would, but apparently not even the IT boys down here could unravel it. It'd be a personal challenge to you, wouldn't it?'

'Shit. Bring it back up here. I'll be waiting.'

'I can't. It's got to be back by the morning. Just get on the next train to Plymouth. If she likes you, she'll wait for you. Don't you want to piss all over the IT boys down this end?'

There was more coughing. 'Shit. You're a bastard.'

'Yeah, that's what people keep telling me. Text me when you're on your way.'

Cathy had been waiting for half an hour for Douglas Burdock to show his smug face, while sitting in a battered leather armchair and facing the almost ecclesiastical windows of his library. Beyond the windows were the mossy steps that led down to the miniature maze and the boating pond on the edge of the woods.

When she moved, she creaked. The skin-tight leather catsuit she was wearing made moving or even just sitting, a very noisy affair. The only part of her torso that enjoyed the stifling air of the room was her breasts. They were merely cupped by the leather outfit, allowing the top half of her nipples to be visible.

She had never been much of a snob, and had even shown scorn when she witnessed the emotion in others, but even she found it distasteful that a family like the Burdocks owned one of England's grandest and prettiest estates. She was not in the least bit naive, and was quite aware of the debauchery that would have been performed within the ancient walls. It excited her that such pain and pleasure would have been heard echoing around its high ceilings, ecstatic by the thought that her cries of pleasure would join the others that long since faded into history.

Even so, when she thought of Robert Burdock, the common, foul-mouthed, greedy and racist old man, enjoying the magnificent views in front of her, she felt disappointment and quite sad.

The door to the library clicked open and Douglas stood there for a moment, staring at her, dressed in another of his tailored suits. He smiled, then crossed the room.

'Don't move,' he said and looked her over. 'You look...radiant.'

She said nothing, and didn't even smile. She was not allowed to show any emotion or even speak without his say so.

'Did you visit your friend, Jairus?' he asked, then sat at his desk. 'You may speak.'

'I did.'

'What has he discovered so far?' Douglas smiled and raised his eyebrows.

'Very little. It's early days.'

Douglas laughed. 'Oh, come on. This doesn't sound like the man you described to me, Cat. Don't tell me I pulled you out of the fire for nothing.'

She crossed her legs and listened to the creak of the leather as it cut into itself. She moved because she knew the sound excited him. He didn't take drugs, smoke or even drink. His only stimulation was through sex and pain. The pain had to be given and never received.

'He'll do what you ask. He'll see it through to the

end, so don't worry.'

He stood up and leaned over the desk. 'I'm not worried, my darling. Do I look worried?'

She had to admit that he did not look worried, but she also noticed that there was a change in him, as if there was a part of him showing that she had not witnessed before. Even during the sadistic sexual games she had endured at his hands, she saw nothing in his eyes that suggested he had more darkness in his heart than any other man she had met. But now she could see darkness as if it was the blackest dot at the end of a tunnel of light.

She could think of only one man who had exhibited such darkness beyond his eyes, but that man didn't scare her in the way Douglas Burdock did.

'You can answer.' Douglas stepped closer, the smile becoming wider.

'You don't look worried,' she said. 'Not in the least bit.'

'I'm glad you can see it. If my father, the disgusting bastard, taught me one thing of usefulness, it was to never show worry or weakness. Not to anybody.'

'He certainly taught you well. Can I ask you something? Is it allowed?'

His smile was turned down a little. 'I'll allow it.'

'Thank you. Why did you put Jairus on to this whole thing?'

'That's a difficult question to answer. There's the main reason, of course. The prize at the end of his investigation. My prize, not his. But there's also the curiosity of seeing what he does, how far he'll go for the truth.'

'He'll go to the ends of the earth. I told you that.'

He nodded. 'I know. But I wanted to see it. I suppose I admire him in a way.'

There was a knock at the door. Cathy turned towards the door, then back to Douglas. His eyes had not strayed from her, and he did not blink as he said, 'Enter.'

The door opened and another suit, probably one of his bodyguards, she surmised, stood there looking around the room. In his hand, he held a mobile phone which he held out to Douglas.

'Speak to me,' Douglas said.

'Important call for you,' the guard said, then shut the door after himself.

Douglas lifted the phone to his ear. 'Sorry, Cat, but I'll be with you in a moment. Perhaps then we can play. Yes, Douglas Burdock here.'

Cathy watched on as a silent voice whispered something in his ear. Whatever was being said to him sent little reaction to his face. There was no way of knowing whether what was being said was happy or sad. Even his grunts of confirmation gave nothing away.

Cathy's mind turned back to Jairus, and the reason that she had dragged him into her dark world. The truth was she had no choice. When Douglas had appeared on the scene, promising to rescue her from the consequences of her actions, she'd known then that all wasn't what it seemed. In her world, they never were, she had learnt that in the most horrendous ways. The faces that showed the kindest of expressions usually hid a well of an almost inhuman appetite for cruelty.

Jairus was her insurance policy, the one person she knew who could save her if she ever needed saving. Even so, she hated herself for dragging him into it all.

'Good,' Douglas said to whoever was on the other end of the phone, then headed to the door and handed it back to the suit waiting outside it.

When the door was closed again, Douglas walked over to his desk, his face blank, and unlocked the top drawer. She heard the metallic rattle and knew even before she saw them what he had taken out.

'Turn around,' he said, standing and looking down at her.

She stood up and faced the windows. Immediately he grasped her wrists in one hand and clamped the handcuffs on her.

She found herself being turned around and then Douglas' hand landed firmly on her head, forcing her to her knees.

As she looked towards his crotch, she wondered what would happen next, but it turned out not to be what she expected at all. He stepped back, smiled down at her.

'You are a real piece of...art,' he said. 'You're too perfect too touch. Not in the way I really want to.'

Then she watched him turn towards the door and open it again. The guard was still stood there.

'Bring up one of the young ladies,' he said. 'Actually, bring up the skinny blonde one with the fake tits.'

The door was shut again, and Douglas grabbed a chair and placed it before Cathy. He sat down as he looked her over. 'I don't want you to speak. In fact, I forbid it. The young woman they're bringing up here, is a prostitute. A common whore. Worthless. They found her working the back streets of Kings Cross. Now you're wondering what she's doing here, aren't you? Yes, of course you are. I'll explain. The things I've done with you, the little games we've played don't really do it for me. I just wanted you to think that it does. I just needed you around to hook your friend, the big fish, Jairus. Thing is, the phone call I just received... Well, turns out that I don't need him anymore.'

She saw it then, the glint in his eye, the dot of darkness coming closer, eclipsing the light. She moved her hands. The clatter of metal filled the room.

Douglas laughed. 'You shouldn't have let me handcuff you, should you? You know what you are? You're a child that just climbed into a car with a strange man after he promised to show you some puppies. You are that silly child.'

There came a knock on the door. Douglas smiled, then answered the door. He opened it wide when he saw the young, skinny blonde woman adorned in a pink flowery dress. She could only be in her twenties, Cathy estimated, as her stomach clenched and twisted. She couldn't remember the last time her heart truly raced with fear. It was almost a shock to feel her chest pounding as she watched the bony woman step inside. Her big blue eyes were peering around the room, obviously impressed by the wealth and thinly veiled culture.

Douglas held up a finger to his lips as he stared at Cathy. 'What did you say your name was?'

The woman looked at Cathy for a moment, confusion crossing her face. 'Er...Gemma...'

'Oh, don't worry about her, Gemma. She's just here to watch.'

'Watch?' Gemma looked annoyed. 'You said this wasn't a sex thing! You promised me.'

'It's not, Gemma,' he said and put a hand on her shoulder. 'Not in the sense you think.'

'Go! Run!' The words had burst out of Cathy's mouth before she could think about what she was doing.

The girl just stared at her, wide-eyed, then spun her head to Douglas. But he was staring at her and shaking his head.

'Don't go anywhere, Gemma. Cat, I didn't give you permission to speak. That will cost you.'

Gemma had taken a couple of steps backwards, her eyes on Douglas.

Then he spun round, his suit flapping, as he lurched towards her. He drew his fist back and threw it at the young woman, who spun round as the blow cracked into her face. She toppled backwards as her legs gave way. She skidded along the floor then lay silent, her blonde hair covering her face.

Cathy watched her, saw her augmented breasts still rising and falling. Her eyes drifted up as Douglas straightened his suit, his chest rising and falling. As he sat in front of Cathy, examining his fist, she could see the burning flickering in his eyes and fear poisoned her system.

He was breathing hard as he said, 'That's better than sex. Why would I screw a whore, when I can just punch her? You can speak if you like. Have you got anything to say?'

She stared back at him.

He nodded. 'Speechless. Guess what? That phone call that came through telling me I no longer need your boyfriend...well, it means I'll have to have him killed, doesn't it? Which means I don't really need you. So, I'm going to leave now and run my father's media empire and then when I come back, you can begin begging for your life. Or...or I just may torture you for a while before I kill you.'

She screamed at herself in her own head, shouting for herself to keep calm, not to show any emotion.

He smiled, stood up and walked to the door. 'You can scream now if you want.'

CHAPTER 12

Tom was being chased in his sleep by someone or something. It was a person, then it morphed into a serpent or something...

His eyes opened, and then fixed on the yellow stained ceiling. There was noise somewhere, perhaps outside.

There was a moment where he was calm, trying to gather himself together and understand where he was, in the same poky room as always.

He recalled a snippet of the dream that was rapidly disintegrating, the faintest image of men standing round as he lay naked.

Tom turned over and pulled his knees up to his chest and muffled his mouth as he screamed into his palm.

He stopped when he heard something smash downstairs. He swung his legs over the bed and stood up and staggered for a moment, listening to the shouting downstairs and the pounding of feet spreading through the old house.

He grabbed his jeans, his hoody and coat and pulled them all on, his ears still fixed on the shouting coming from the rest of the house.

The footsteps came hard up the stairs but passed his room, and the next thing he heard was screaming. Linda was screeching at the top of her lungs.

Tom gripped the door handle and edged it open in time to see the half-naked skeletal shape of Linda being manhandled and dragged kicking and screaming across the landing by two policemen.

He retreated inside, his mind crawling with imagined insects, scurrying through his brain as he tried to work out how THEY knew where he was.

His thoughts scattered when there was a loud knock on his door. He turned towards the window, then ran to it and looked down at the driveway. Two police cars were parked across the drive while several uniforms stood guard. One of them looked up and raised his finger up towards the window to point at him, but he ducked away and squatted on the carpet.

The knock came again. Why were they even bothering to knock?

The door handle moved, the door creaked and Tom looked over the bed to see a man dressed in a pair of jeans and a shirt, standing in the doorway.

He looked up at the familiar face above the shirt and saw the disdain in the eyes of the driver, Joe.

He walked across the room and sat on the bed, and looked down on Tom, shaking his head.

'Is that it, Tom?' he said, then looked around the room. 'You're Just going to hide and hope it all goes away? Is that your tactic? Because I'm here to tell you that it will go away. We can make it go away.'

Tom looked up at him and saw the dark eyes staring down at him, the mock friendliness that did little to hide the sadistic nature of the driver.

'Yes, Tom, I can make it all go away. That poor girl that just got taken downstairs...Linda...isn't it? I mean, you know her as Linda...well, where she's going...well, it's not a very nice place. It's just to teach her a lesson. Keep her mouth shut. It's a simple lesson. Now, the question is, Tom, do you want to go with her?'

'Yes.'

Joe still had his mouth open. He shut it and bent closer to Tom. 'I don't think you understand what I'm saying...'

'I want to go with her. Wherever she goes, I want to go.' Tom found his eyes turning towards the cupboard, his mind buzzing with what he knew was hidden there. He looked down.

DON'T LOOK THERE! Don't look at it.

'Tom?'

Joe was now standing up, looking down at him. 'Are you sure? There's still time to change your mind.'

Tom stood up. 'How did you find me?'

'That I cannot tell you. Official secrets act and all that bureaucracy. But I can tell you that it wasn't you. You didn't give yourself away.'

Joe took hold of his arm at the wrist, ready to twist if he needed to. Tom stopped and turned his face towards Joe. 'Why are you pretending to be my friend? You're not my friend.'

'No, I'm not your friend, Tom. You're nothing to me. If they say you have to go, then you have to go. I won't bat an eyelid. Don't make a mistake of thinking I'll spare you a thought after.'

Tom carried on down the stairs as Joe put a hand on his back and pushed him forwards.

As they reached the bottom of the stairs, more shouting echoed through the house as two more policemen dragged Derek across the dusty floor. He was fighting, his teeth gritted, his arms struggling, pulling away from the grip they had on him.

Then his eyes fixed on Tom. 'Tim? What's happening Tim? How did they know we were here?'

'Come on, Tom,' Joe said, looking at the ex-soldier

with a little pity. 'Let's get you out of here.'

He couldn't bring himself to look at the old soldier who had kept them safe, had been kind to them, so let himself be taken to the unmarked car parked up the street.

'Get in,' Joe said and opened the back door for him.

'I want to go where Linda went.'

Joe rubbed his face and nose, huffed then looked him in the eye. 'I'm going to be honest with you, Tom...I don't know where they took her. I know it's not a good place...I know that much. Quite frankly, I don't care what they do with her. Just forget about Linda. Get in.'

Tom nodded, bent himself as if to climb in the car.

Then without knowing that it had happened, he'd thrown his fist and all his weight into Joe's face, then spun round and started running. People looked at him, and turned to look at the man running after him.

'Call the police!' Tom shouted at anyone listening. 'He's trying to kill me!'

When Tom managed to look back, Joe was standing still, bent over, panting, shaking his head.

Rich didn't look the slightest bit happy when Jairus picked him up from the train station. He threw his massive rucksack on the back seat then climbed in next to Jairus, but didn't say anything for a while.

He started driving from the station, heading towards the concrete monstrosity they called a hotel, pushing his way into the mid-morning traffic.

'She'll be there when you get back,' Jairus said, smiling at him.

'I don't know about that.'

'Yeah, she will. How did you meet her?'

Rich seemed to thaw a little as he said, 'She's a bit

of a groupie. You should see her, Jay. She's kind of a bit Goth, but not full on. She's so hot. God knows what she's doing with me!'

Jairus had the feeling he was supposed to say something comforting, to help boost his ego, but he looked into himself and found his well of human kindness had run dry. 'She'll be there. Got a real challenge for you this time. The Devon and Cornwall lot couldn't crack it.'

'They're a bunch of pussies.' Rich gave a slight smile. 'How the hell did you persuade the copper to hand it over?'

'I used the info you gave me.' Jairus drove the car into the dark underground car park beneath the hotel.

'Jesus. You blackmailed a police officer?'

'Yeah, sort of.'

Rich shrugged, then looked at him again. 'There could've been a perfectly reasonable reason why the hotels and the purchases were there.'

'But there never is, is there?'

Jairus slipped the card in the slot, then opened the door and let Rich enter his room. The IT man went straight to the laptop that was sat on the bed wrapped in an evidence bag.

'Better wear gloves,' Jairus said and threw some on the bed. 'We don't want our prints all over it. Just in case.'

Rich pulled on a pair, then took the laptop from the bag, and took it over to Jairus' desk. He opened it and booted it up. 'Let's see what your man has done.'

'How long do you think it'll take?'

Rich frowned up at him. 'You know better than to ask that.'

'We've only got until tomorrow morning.'

'Keep your pants on, Jay. I'll get it done by then.'

There was a light knock at the door. As Jairus went towards the door, Rich said, 'Please tell me that's room service with a bacon sandwich for me.'

'I don't think it is, but I'll order you one.' Jairus opened the door and found Helen leaning on the doorframe, smiling, dressed in a tight-fitting navy blue dress and wine-coloured blazer.

'There you are,' she said and walked into his room. 'I knocked earlier but you had vanished. Thought we could spend some time together.'

She stopped talking when she saw Rich tapping away at the laptop. Jairus got between them and said, 'This is Rich Vincent. Rich this is Helen Chara.'

Rich nodded and smiled knowingly. 'Oh, right. Got it. Hello, Helen.'

'Hi,' she said, then looked up at Jairus. 'You're up to something. What's going on? I take it this is your computer whizz you've dragged into your business... and seeing as there's an evidence bag on your bed, I take it that laptop is part of a criminal investigation? Am I right?'

'I think it's best you keep out of this.'

She half closed her eyes, scowling at him. 'So, even after last night, you're going to keep me at arm's length? I thought you might trust me by now.'

'How can I trust a journalist?' Jairus put on his overcoat, picked up his car keys and got ready to head out of the room.

'Granted. I'll give you that, but...where are you going now?'

'I need to go somewhere.'

She grabbed his arm. 'Have you had a drink today?'

'A little one.'

She sighed, then knelt down and opened the mini-bar and took out the vodka. She slipped it into her bag.

'You can have a drink, while I drive you to wherever you're going. How's that? I don't think you want to add drink driving to all the other dodgy things you've done, do you?'

Jairus rubbed his face, then caught Rich looking at him with a multitude of questions lining up in his eyes. He sighed, realising she had a valid point. 'Yeah, OK. But you only drive me. You stay in the car.'

Jairus looked at the small half-drunk bottle of vodka in his hand as Helen drove them along the A38 towards Looe. His hand was trembling, his whole body screaming out for him to take a drink.

Helen kept turning her head, watching him, taking her eyes off the road. 'You better take your medicine.'

'Yeah, I know. Just seems wrong.'

'I know. When this is over you can go to rehab or whatever, but right now you need to do what you need to do. Right?'

He nodded, and unscrewed the bottle top and took a long swig. When he looked up he could see the turning they needed. 'Turn left here.'

She slowed, signalled, and turned into the overgrown and darkened lane where the Pinder family lived. 'I take it we're heading for one of these houses?'

'The last one,' he said and put the bottle on the floor as she pulled into the driveway under the house and parked.

He took out the little kit he always kept with him, which included his lock-picking equipment. It would have been easier for him to persuade the policeman to have let him have the key to the house, but he decided he didn't want him knowing what he was up to today. It was bad enough he had a journalist with him, a fact that had caused his old headache friend to start knocking on the back of his skull.

He looked at her and saw she was tapping away at her phone. 'What're you doing?'

She looked at him. 'So, this is where the Pinder family lived? Steven Pinder, who shot his family dead, then turned the gun on himself. Let me guess, you don't think he did it?'

Jairus pressed his head into his hands and let out a groan. 'I don't know what I think. I'm just going to have a look around.'

'I'm coming too then.' She started to open her door, so Jairus grabbed her arm and said, 'No, you're not.'

She glared at him. 'I either come along, or I write a story about an alcoholic ex-police officer who's looking into a murder suicide. I'm guessing you don't want this splashed over the papers?'

'I see. Now the real journalist's rearing her...'

'I hope you're not about to say ugly!' Helen yanked her arm away and climbed out of the car.

Jairus followed her as she headed towards the concrete steps that led up to the house. 'You don't touch anything. In fact, keep your manicured fingers in your pockets, got it?'

Helen smiled before letting herself in the gate, then headed up towards the front of the house. Jairus sighed, looking around the overgrown lane. Only the occasional car passed through. Nobody seemed to be watching, so he joined Helen on the concrete veranda and took out his lock-picking set.

'How long is this going to take?' Helen asked, leaning over him as he approached the lock.

'You can sit in the car, if you want.'

'Sorry.'

He was a little rusty and his hands were shaky as he inserted the tools into the lock. In the old days, it would've taken him a matter of seconds to get the door open, but his trembling fingers and the fact that the lock was a specialist and foreign kind was making the job a lot more difficult.

At last he heard the click he was praying for, then pushed the glass door open. Immediately he saw the alarm sensor boxes placed in the corners of the large tiled kitchen that he was about to step into. He waved his hand, but nothing happened. He looked to his left and saw the keypad for the alarm. It was off. He stepped into the room and walked through the clinical and spotless space. Everything was minimal, someone had designed an uncluttered, but cold house. Immediately he got the sense that something was not quite right about the room but could not put his finger on what it was.

Jairus ignored the feeling and walked through a frosted glass hallway, noting more sensor boxes plastered everywhere. There were pressure pads by the doors to the bedrooms too.

Helen's heels echoed behind him as she said, 'Seems they were very security conscious.'

Jairus nodded. 'Yeah, seems that way. The alarm system covers the whole house. I'd say Steven Pinder was hiding away. Look at where this house is situated. In the middle of nowhere, with every security precaution he could afford.'

'So, he was scared of something?'

'Yeah.' Jairus stepped into the enormous master bedroom, which was clean and clinical like the rest of the house. There was no longer a bed, but blood stains were still present on the back wall.

'Oh God,' Helen said as she stood next him. 'What do you think really happened here?'

'I don't know. But something's not right, is it? A

man so desperate to protect his family gets up in the night to kill them and then himself. It just doesn't sit right with me.'

'If he was that terrified and paranoid, who knows what was going on in his mind.'

Jairus recalled the strange feeling he had when he first entered the house and walked back into the enormous kitchen and stood at the centre of the room. His eyes took in every inch, not allowing anything to escape his attention. Lastly, as Helen joined him and stood at his side, he examined all the sensor boxes. His eyes jumped to each small white box, then quickly back to the one positioned at the centre of the back wall. 'What's that one for?'

'It's a sensor like the rest. What are you getting at?'

He stepped closer to it, staring up at the box, seeing that it was positioned to take in most of the kitchen. But he looked at the other two sensors positioned on either side of it. 'That centre one is surplus to requirement.'

Helen joined him. 'Could be a camera.'

'Yeah, maybe. Let's have a closer look.' Jairus grabbed a stool from the breakfast bar near the window, then climbed up on it. He tapped the box. Something rattled inside. 'There's something in here. Something loose. Can you see if you can find a tool kit with a Philips screwdriver.'

'Oh, ok, I'll have a look around.'

Jairus stood there, trying to peer into the thin slits cut into the box, while listening to Helen's heels fading off somewhere. He heard her opening a cupboard somewhere, then her heels coming back towards him.

'Here,' she said and handed him a screwdriver.

'Thanks. Let's take a look at what's in here.'

DS Simon Davies shut the door of his boss' office, taking advantage of his holiday leave, and sat as his desk and looked at the lunch he'd bought himself.

He pushed it away as his hunger had deserted him around the same time his back had been put up by the ex-Met detective that had come strutting in, thinking he was the bee's knees.

'Fucking...cunt.' Davies took the lid off the coffee he'd also purchased and blew on it. He looked over at the mountain of paperwork he had yet to get through, then turned away and stared at the computer screen facing him. A photo of his boss' family floated across the screen, followed by another.

He shook the mouse, getting rid of the smiling faces and typed in the name: Jairus. Quite a few news articles appeared in the search which told him everything he needed to know.

The fucker was dirty. His bosses had obviously cottoned on to his game and kicked his arse out of the force. There was still a question bugging him though and that's how exactly he knew about Sue. He knew about the hotels and the shopping trips, which pointed to him having accessed his financial records, so he had someone on the force still feeding him information.

'Fucking...' Davies rested his elbows on the desk and rubbed his face, thinking about what to do, how to kick the dirty bastard right back in his balls.

He sat back and let his eyes dart over to his boss' top drawer. He knew it was unlocked, and was quite aware that he kept useless bits of paper or scraps of information in there in case they ever did come in useful. Davies opened the drawer, lifted a couple of memos and found the small business card.

There was little written on the card, just a name and phone number. Andrew Smith was printed on the card. He recalled the suited man arriving in the middle of the Pinder investigation to oversee things, and announcing he was from MI5 and that the deaths were linked to an issue of national security. There was an air about the man that Davies had disliked, the way he strutted about and gave orders as if he was the most important person in the room. But still, he resented Jairus even more than that self-important dickhead.

While the angry blood was still pounding through his veins, Davies put the card in front of him and picked up the landline phone. He hesitated, then quickly dialled the number.

There were only two rings and then a clear and well-spoken woman's voice said, 'Andrew Smith's office, can I help you?'

'Hello, yes, I'm Detective Sergeant Simon Davies. I met Mr Smith some time ago and he left me this number in case there were any developments in an investigation he was part of...'

'Can you tell me what the case was?'

'Yes, it was in regards to the murder suicide of Steven Pinder. He...'

'Can you hang on for a moment?'

The line seemed to go dead for a few minutes, and Davies considered hanging up just as the woman's voice came back.

'Sorry, Mr Davies, I'm putting you through to Mr Smith now.'

The phone was ringing again and Davies rubbed his face, waiting. When the sound came back, he could hear wind and the noise of cars racing past.

'This is Andrew Smith,' the man said, sounding as if his concentration was elsewhere.

'This is Detective Serg...'

'I know who you are. You were calling about the

Pinder murder suicide. Is that correct?'

'Yes, it's just that...well...'

'Can you please speed this up. I haven't got a lot of time.'

Davies fought the urge to slam down the phone. 'OK. An ex-DCI Jairus came to see me today, asking questions about the Pinder investigation. You wanted us to contact you if...'

'Thank you. Yes, I'm quite aware of Mr Jairus' interest in the case. I'll come by and see you this afternoon.'

'You're in Plymouth?' Davies sat up.

'Actually, I'm in Cornwall. I have a little matter to deal with then I'll come and pay you a visit.'

CHAPTER 13

DS Wood stood outside the door where the prison visitors entered and lined up to witness the guilty faces of their loved ones and have stilted, self-conscious conversations.

Brenton took another puff of his cigarette and pretended not to see her waving, or make threatening gestures so he would hurry up. He was taking his time, enjoying the fresh air while he still could. He shuddered at his mind's inappropriate imaginings as he pictured a prisoner stabbing him with a homemade knife.

He took another puff then stamped on his fag and walked slowly towards Wood, while his eyes rose to the barred windows, and the rotting, decrepit exterior of the Victorian prison. No amount of modern extensions could take away its rotten heart.

He waved his hand as Wood moaned at him all the way through the security check and into the private visiting area. A room had been set aside. A guard would be nearby in case of any trouble.

'Are you listening to me?'

Brenton turned when he realised Wood was addressing him, her eyebrows raised, her mouth tight like an impatient school teacher. 'Yes, of course I am.'

'What did I say then?'

'How good looking I am when I'm about to vomit?'

Wood managed a reluctant smile. 'No, I said I can't go in there with you.'

'What? You said you were...'

'I know. But he won't talk to me. You know that. He won't even open his mouth if I'm there. You know what he's like around women. He hates us. Scared of us, I reckon. You'll be fine. He's not Hannibal Lecter. He's just a sick and twisted and evil man. He's just a man.'

Brenton nodded. He was quite aware that Foreman was human like the rest of them – well, barely – but what was really bothering him was the fact that he was human too, with fear and hate and rage in veins. He'd seen police officers turned into potential murderers when faced with people like Foreman. He breathed deeply and reminded himself that all he wanted was information and to witness Foreman's reaction when he mentioned the murder of Mandy Rose.

'You ready?' Wood gripped his shoulder and gave it a squeeze.

'I could do with another fag.' He smiled.

'Shut up and get in there.'

He nodded, then pushed open the door and entered the visiting room. Most of the desks had been pushed to the side, leaving only one at the centre, and two chairs facing each other across it.

Brenton sat and waited, staring at the door, listening to the prison sounds echoing down to him. Then there were the heavy stamp of boots coming down the corridor.

The thick, reinforced glassed security door opened and the guard stood to the side to let the tall and well-built man into the room. Foreman looked a little withered and his thick and oiled short hair was a lot greyer. He was in his fifties, but looked much older.

As he approached the desk, Brenton saw the same old glimmer in his eye, the joy that had risen in him as he knew he was going to get to talk about his favourite subject: himself.

Foreman sat in the chair and crossed his legs, then gave a thin smile. 'Good afternoon, Jake.'

Jairus slipped off the cover of the sensor box and handed it down to Helen. He looked inside and nodded to himself. Somehow, he knew what he would find secreted inside the surplus box.

'What is it?' Helen said, stepping back and trying to get a look. 'What's in there?'

He reached in and took hold of the small, and cheap looking mobile phone. 'A phone.'

'Oh dear,' Helen said. 'If a man's hiding a second mobile phone in his house, it usually means he's having an affair.'

At the back of the box there was a small plastic bag that had several SIM cards inside it. 'Yeah, normally I'd agree with you, but look at this.'

Helen took the bag from him as he stepped down off the chair and handed it to her. 'SIM cards?'

'Yeah. In my experience, someone who's got a second phone and a lot of SIM cards is probably hiding a lot more than an affair.'

'Like what?'

'I don't know. Let's see what the phone says.' Jairus turned it on and watched as it rebooted, then took notice when he saw Helen's face turn toward the window. She was frowning. 'What is it?'

'Thought I heard a car slowing down.' Helen walked over to the window. 'I can't really see anything.'

'Open the door.'

Helen slid open the door and the chilled wind

came rushing in and toyed with her dark hair. A car door shut down below them, then the sound of a gate closing reached Jairus' ears.

'Someone's coming up,' Helen said, turning to Jairus and gripping his arm.

'Yeah, I know. Can you see who it is?'

Helen went to walk across the balcony, but Jairus grabbed her arm. 'Take off your heels.'

She nodded, slipped them off and rushed to the edge and poked her head over. She came back and slid the door shut. 'Two men in suits. They look like they can handle themselves.'

'Right, let's pack this up and try the back way.' Jairus jumped up on the stool and put the sensor box together, then put the stool back and took Helen by the arm. He started hurrying through the large empty house, his eyes jumping everywhere, trying find the best way to exit from.

'What've you got me involved in?' Helen said and pulled her arm away from him as they reached the wall of tall French doors that surrounded the back of the house.

'Don't worry, I'll get us out of this.' Beyond the glass was a wide and long stretch of lawn that at one time would have been neat and tidy but was now overgrown. The lawn rolled downwards and beyond the high fence at the far end of the garden, there was woodland.

He didn't know for sure who was coming up the steps to the house, but he had a pretty good idea. The two suited men who'd entered the pub that night and warned him off sprang to mind, which meant he and Helen could be up to their necks in trouble. He looked at her worried face and saw one more person he'd dragged into his own personal hell.

'We need to get to the woods,' Jairus said, slid open the glass door and stormed towards the fence. He jumped up, tried to get a grip of the fence but fell back down again. On his second go, he gritted his teeth and heaved his weight up so he could just about see down the field behind the house.

He sighed.

Three men were heading towards the house, spread out, cutting off their escape. One was suited, the other two dressed casually, but they all had hungry looks in their eyes and the lean bodies of highly trained men.

'What is it?' Helen asked him when he faced her.

'There are more of them coming.'

'More? What're we going to do?'

Jairus was about to reply when he heard his mobile beep. He looked at Helen, took his phone out and saw that he'd received a text message from a private number. He opened it and read, 'We did try and warn you.'

He showed the message to Helen.

'Who the bloody hell are they?'

'The same people who threatened me before. We need to get away now. If they killed Pinder and his family, then they won't hesitate with us.'

'Detective Inspector Brenton,' Brenton said, looking into the hollow, empty grey eyes that stared back at him. 'That's what you can call me.'

'If you want to keep a friendly air to these proceedings, you'll let me call you Jake.' Foreman smiled briefly, then put his long, and thick hands on the table. 'It's only polite.'

Brenton nodded, trying not to imagine the terrible things those hands had done. 'Polite? What do you know about being polite?'

'Everything. My mother brought me up to always be polite and kind.'

Brenton held in the disgusted laugh, even though the adrenalin fuelled by loathing tried to force it out. 'You like to think of yourself as kind?'

'Of course. Everybody likes to think the best of themselves. I've always tried to show kindness.'

'Even to your victims?'

Foreman's whole body seemed to prick into life. 'Excuse me? My victims? That is a word I loathe. They were not my victims. They were my lovers.'

'Your lovers? All of them? All those young girls you raped, tortured and strangled?'

'I have no recollection of strangling any girls. I had lovers who...yes, your society seems to deem them unable to take responsibility for their own sexual actions, but I know differently.'

'You do?' Brenton's mouth became dry and sticky, while his heart began to pound in his ears.

'Yes, I do. Those girls wanted it as much as I did. They knew what they wanted and they took it from me.'

'How did they end up strangled?'

'That I cannot answer. As I've said before, I've been set up.'

Brenton swallowed, tried to wet his mouth, while his fingers screamed out for a cigarette. 'But you had sex with them?'

'Consensual sex.'

The huff left Brenton before he even had a chance to stop it.

Foreman stared at him as his fingers curled up. 'That's a pity. We were having a nice conversation. Now I can see you think I'm guilty, like all the rest. Your problem and their problem is that their minds are closed off.'

Brenton calmed himself, tried to rise above it all. 'Closed off?'

'Yes.' Foreman leaned in, smiled. 'You won't even try to understand that a girl like Mandy Rose, a pretty young thing like her, can want a man like me.'

Brenton couldn't trust himself to open his mouth.

'I'll let you into a little secret...' Foreman leaned in closer. 'It was her and all the other girls that seduced me. I don't expect you to believe that. If you think about it, they're just a bunch of sluts...'

Brenton gripped his seat. 'OK, let's talk about Mandy Rose.'

Foreman sat back, smiling, showing his long, slightly crooked teeth. 'Let's. Do you want to know how she tasted?'

'No, I don't. You see, Edward, I'm not convinced you actually did what you said you did to her.'

'What are you getting at, Jake? Do you mean strangle her? If you do, then you're correct.'

'That's only part of it. I'm starting to doubt you ever met Mandy Rose.'

'Oh, we met. I assure you. It was love at first sight.'

Brenton sat back and shook his head. 'I think you're a pretender. One of those messed up individuals who feels compelled to confess to every murder that they read about.'

'Oh dear oh dear. You're trying to trick me, Jake. Are you secretly taping this? Let me speak clearly. I did not murder anyone. I had consensual sex...'

'Yes, I know what you said. No, no one's listening to this. I'm not even supposed to be here. How do you explain us finding evidence that suggests someone else...' he swallowed down his bile, 'enjoyed their time with Mandy Rose?'

'What evidence?'

'Now, I can't tell you that...'

'Because you're lying. Mandy gave herself to me...'

'Well, you're sure there wasn't someone else involved? Perhaps you had a friend? I know how you...well, sometimes you like to share, don't you?'

Foreman lost his smile, then rested his chin on his hand. 'I know what you mean. I know who you're referring to.'

'Do you? I think maybe you're the one lying...'

Foreman laughed briefly. 'You mean Leo. Leo the liar, the thief.'

'Leo? Who's Leo?' Brenton leaned forward, pushing away his repulsion.

Foreman smiled again. 'I don't know if I should tell you. What if Leo finds out that I've been telling tales?'

'If Leo is who I think he is...he won't be in a position to judge anyone.'

'Then he's dead, is that what you're telling me, Jake?'

'Maybe.'

'Good. I'm glad he's dead. He didn't care for them the way I did. He was a cruel beast. A sadist.'

Brenton breathed all the bad stuff down. 'Who is Leo?'

Foreman leaned in again. 'You have a daughter, don't you?'

'Who's Leo?'

'How old is she?'

'Don't even...who's Leo? Is his real name Leonard?'

'I bet your daughter's barely legal. She could make a nice bit of money on the side.'

He almost flinched as he bit into his own lip and dug his fingers into his legs. 'Tell me who Leo is or I tell every copper I know, then talk to all the papers and start telling everyone that you never ever touched Mandy Rose...'

'Perhaps, during the time you were chasing me, I was secretly meeting your daughter. Perhaps we were in love.'

Brenton began to shake as the blood gushed through his heart and made his hands turn into white furious fists. 'Shut up, tell me...'

'Maybe I did or maybe I didn't...it's in your head now, isn't it? It'll always be in there now, Jake. Me and your little girl, so sweet and innocent...'

Brenton stood up, unsure whether his trembling, hate-filled body would get him to the door or not as the unwanted images penetrated his brain. He tried to switch them off, but they kept coming. He grabbed the handle of the door to keep himself from turning back and attacking the evil bastard sat at the table. He knew he'd be smiling. He could feel it burning into his back.

'Jake.'

Brenton stood there, breathing hard. 'What?'

'Leonard Jameson. The politician. That's who Leo is… was. But I'm curious, because I haven't heard anything about him dying, so...'

Brenton faced him. 'Was it just you and Leonard?'

'Is he dead?' There was that smile again.

'You know the answer to that. Who else is involved?'

'Just Leonard.' The smile stretched.

'You're lying, Edward.'

'Maybe. But you will never know what I know, or how I think. But I know you. I know you'll always imagine your daughter in my arms with a smile on her pretty young face. That's the last thing I'll ever say to you, Jake. Goodbye.'

Brenton pulled open the door and hurried down the corridor to throw up.

'We need to climb over that wall.' Jairus pointed to the whitewashed wall to their right that acted as boundary to the next property.

Helen looked at him, then back towards the house. 'Maybe they just want to talk to you.'

'Trust me, they're not here for a chat. Come on.' Jairus leaped up, grasped the top of wall, found a foothold, and pushed himself up. He swung his left leg over and sat astride the wall looking down at Helen.

'Wait for me,' she said, holding out her heels.

'You'll have to leave those behind.' He reached out his hand to her. 'Hurry up.'

'Do you know how much these cost?'

'I don't care. Fucking hurry up!'

She threw her shoes over the wall, then took his hand and he pulled her up, letting out a deep groan. He helped her onto the wall, then jumped down into the overgrown passageway between the two properties. He froze, half listening to the desperate pants and swearing of Helen as she tried to lower herself down, half listening for the sound of the men who were coming for them.

He held out his arms and let Helen fall into him. He lowered her to the grass, then grabbed her hand as he started jogging towards the woods. He was bent over, his eyes watching out for the men.

A bush creaked, leaves pushed aside. A twig snapped.

Jairus stopped dead, turned to Helen who was wide-eyed and held a finger to his lips. He let go of her hand, then reached into his pocket and found his roll of trusty pound coins and gripped them tightly in his fist.

He hunched over again and made his way to the end of the passageway, where the bushes became wide open lawn until they reached the woods a few hundred yards away. He could now see the shape of a man standing half covered by the trees. The other two must have gone into the house, he decided as his iron-toothed headache bit into his skull and his heart began to pump hot and fast blood around his body.

He tightened his fist around the coins.

Then he rushed out, his teeth gritted, focusing on the shape of the man as he spun round, hearing the broken twigs under Jairus' shoes.

Jairus launched his fist at the man's face, but the man swivelled and grasped Jairus' wrist and somehow yanked him and sent him hurtling towards the fence.

At the last second, Jairus got his balance and raced for him again, this time throwing his whole bodyweight at him. He blasted his fist into his nose, sending the man toppling backwards. Now he had him pinned by his weight, sat over him. He pulled back his fist and smashed it into the man's jaw. Hands expertly grasped at Jairus eyes, then throat, but two more punches laid the man quietly down into the grass.

Jairus stayed there for a moment, breathing, looking down at the plain looking man who had short brown hair, and his nose smashed over his face. He searched the man's jacket and found only a hundred pounds in cash and no identification.

'Who is he?' Helen said, standing behind him.

'I don't know. They told me they worked for the government. He's got no ID. They don't carry ID. We need to go.'

'Where? My car's out the front.'

'Yeah, but you'll have to leave that.' Jairus grabbed

her by her arm and started running across the field, forcing her to run too. She kept looking back, panting, her eyes wide, desperate.

Up ahead was the woods where he knew they stood a better chance of escaping. Unless...he tried not to think the worst, that perhaps more men were waiting for them in the trees.

CHAPTER 14

Jairus and Helen ran through the trees, leaping over fallen branches and bracken, both breathing hard, both aware that the men would not be far behind them. Jairus stopped and grabbed Helen's arm. 'Wait.'

Helen doubled over, panting, looking up at him as she caught her breath. 'What...what's...wrong?'

'There could be more of them.' Then he turned to face the house again as he heard someone call out followed by the sound of running. 'They're coming. Run.'

He ran on, grabbing trees as he went, turning to check Helen was running behind him. She was, but now he could see silhouetted figures speedily entering the woods. There was four of them and they were gaining on them. Snapping twigs and the rustle of leaves found Jairus' ears, competing with the heavy beat of his heart.

'I don't...think...I can...' Helen said, slowing down.

'Yeah, you can,' he said, grabbing her hand and pulling her behind him. 'The road's up ahead. Maybe someone will stop.'

As they approached the end of the trees and heard the roar of cars passing by, he saw a parked car and a figure standing by it. He stopped and pushed Helen behind a thick tree. 'There's someone waiting there. Probably for us.'

'Oh shit. What do we do?'

He looked down at her. 'You go to him.'

'What? Fuck off! He'll kill me!'

'No, he won't. It's me they're after. I promise you, I'm not going to let anything happen to you.'

She kept looking up at him, breathing hard, then turned to stare at the car nearby. 'Oh God. What do I say?'

'Ask him for help. Say someone's after you.'

'Oh...shit...shit.'

'Go on!'

'Ok, all right.'

Jairus watched her walk away, slip on her shoes, then look back at him. He waved her on, then buried his hand in his pocket and gripped the roll of pound coins. Then he ran off to the right and circled round so he could sneak up on the car from behind. He hit the road as he heard Helen speaking to the man, telling him she was being chased.

Jairus watched the man, dressed in jeans and a leather jacket, turn his head back and forth and then smile at her.

'Don't worry, I can help you,' the man said. 'My car's here. Is anyone with you?'

'No, no one. It's just me.'

Jairus ducked down behind the car and began making his way along it.

'Why don't you get in the back of my car?' the man's voice had changed, had become commanding.

'I don't want any trouble,' Helen said.

'Where is he?' the man said.

Jairus leapt up and reached his arm round the man's neck, pulling him backwards. But the man fought back, launching himself back against the car, crushing Jairus against it. Then the man spun around, forcing his hand, palm open against Jairus' throat. He was choking, fighting for breath, pulling his fist up, getting ready to launch a punch. He jabbed his fist into the man's jaw, knocking his head to the side. His grip was still hard, pushing into his windpipe. Jairus smashed his fist into his face again and again.

Helen was watching, just a blur in the background, her hands held to her face.

Jairus grabbed the hand on his throat with his free hand and yanked it away, giving him time to smash his fist into the man's face again. He used his weight and all his strength to smash it again into his nose. The man's legs wobbled, his eyes blank. Jairus punched him again, sending him collapsing to the ground.

He looked down at him as the man laid there, still breathing, and moaning. He bent down, searched his clothes until he found his car keys, then opened the driver's side door. He realised Helen was still staring down at the man in a frozen state of shock.

'Hey! Helen!' he shouted.

She gradually looked up at him.

'Come on! They're coming!'

He could hear them coming through the trees, calling out to each other. 'Helen! Come on!'

She seemed to realise what was happening and climbed into the passenger seat.

He started the engine, put it into gear and joined the road. They reached the next junction, and Jairus turned onto the A38, heading towards Plymouth.

'What're we going to do?' Helen was staring ahead, her voice weak.

A couple of hundred yards ahead he saw a brightly painted art deco style building. It was an American style diner. He signalled and turned into the car park.

Cathy saw a glimmer of light far off in front of her. She blinked as more light spasmed and flickered across the ceiling. Her first instinct was to cover her eyes as the strip of blue light flickered above her, but her hands were cuffed behind her as she lay on her back, prostrate on some kind of hard bed.

When she bent her head back she could see a square of glowing light at the end of the room. A door was open and a man stepped in. He was suited, quite broad, and looked about the room, then left again.

Cathy turned herself over, a manoeuvre that seemed to take all of her strength and burned her joints. The inside of her head was coated in cotton wall, her mouth was dry. She moved and a burning pain roared through her back and arms. She swallowed down a scream as she heard the man come back into the room.

Douglas had beaten her, before she fell unconscious, and probably afterwards. Her next thought was for the young woman he'd punched into unconsciousness. What had become of her?

The man brought someone with him. Whoever they were, they were limp, carried over the shoulder of the man and laid upon another bed near the door. The woman was all bone, looking as if someone had merely inserted bamboo sticks into skin. Her hands were cuffed together. Cathy watched helplessly as the man ran a chain through the cuffs, then locked it to a metal bar attached to the wall. When Cathy looked at the wall behind her own bed, she found that she too had been secured in the same manner.

Then her eyes fixed on the far corner of the room. She squinted into the darkness and thought she could make out metal bars running from floor to the ceiling. A corner of the room had been turned into a small holding cell. Inside she thought she could make out human shapes, perhaps even eyes staring back at her.

She pushed herself up and then swung her legs onto the cold, tiled floor. This was a part of Douglas' home that she'd never been to, the rough games they had played having taken part in sound-proofed bedrooms. She walked towards the bed that had the newcomer lying comatose diagonally across it, stopping when the chain restraining her pulled tight, and was flooded with an emotion that she'd managed to keep at arms and cat and nine tails length for quite a long time. Embarrassment and shame burned inside her.

The young woman lying on the bed was pale, milky white and her veins were blue and squirming beneath her tightly drawn skin. She was covered in bruises, probably from when she had been manhandled and brought from wherever they had taken her.

Her eyes popped open. Big blue eyes flickered and she let out a howling scream.

Cathy started whispering words of comfort as if she was a child waking from a nightmare. Her scream was replaced by sobs that made her body tremble. The woman's crying seemed to set off more crying across the room in the cell.

'What's your name?' Cathy asked.

The girl breathed back her aching sobs, then looked up at her. She seemed to hesitate for a second before she said, 'Linda. Where am I?'

'In the cellar of a house in Hertfordshire. Why did they bring you here?'

She wiped her eyes. 'To keep me quiet. I think...I think they're going to kill me.'

'Kill you? Why would they want to kill you?'

'So I don't talk about what I know.' Linda looked around the room.

'What do you know?'

'I...I know we're not going to get out of here alive.'

'What're you doing?' Helen turned to look through the back window as Jairus parked the car in front of the diner. 'They'll be behind us! Keep going!'

'They won't expect us to stop.' He turned the engine off then looked towards an elderly couple who were heading towards their car. He had a thought, then took out his mobile. He climbed out and said, 'Give me your phone.'

'What? Why?'

He looked at her, saw all the fear and confusion in her dark eyes. She looked much older suddenly. 'They'll track us by our phones. Hurry up.'

She took out her phone quickly, then looked at it as if she was about to hand over her first-born child. Jairus grabbed it, then headed over to the car which the elderly couple were about to climb into.

'Excuse me,' he said, smiling at them. 'Could you direct me to Plymouth?'

The old man smiled then started to point up the road, talking in a Bristol accent. While the elderly woman looked away, and the old man stared off, pointing his withered arm towards the horizon, Jairus slipped both phones into the back of their car.

'Thanks, really appreciate that,' Jairus said as the old man stopped talking.

'You're welcome,' the old man said as Jairus turned and walked towards a confused looking Helen.

'Did you put our phones in their car?' she asked as Jairus took her arm and directed her into the diner.

'Yeah, I did. Let's get a table.'

A young, redheaded and very freckly woman, decked out like a 1950s waitress, gave them menus and took them to a booth that overlooked the car park.

'What happens to them when those men find them?' Helen stared at him across the table.

'Nothing. They'll see they're not us and leave them alone. Look at the menu. You need to eat.' Jairus took out the mobile phone he'd found at the Pinder home and started looking through it. There were no text messages, no calls made. He went into the contacts and found only four numbers, no names.

Helen looked up from the menu. 'What's on it?'

'Just some numbers.' Jairus slid out of the booth, his mind racing back to Plymouth, and Rich, who was sitting like a duck with Pinder's laptop in front of him. He recalled seeing a pay phone on the way in, so found some change in his pocket. 'Order me a black coffee. I'll be back in a minute.'

Helen nodded, gave a weak smile, and he headed off back towards the entrance, passing customers coming in and families sitting at the other booths enjoying enormous plates of American style food. He would have happily swapped lives with any of them at that precise moment, anything to not being hunted by several men who were probably trained killers.

He found the pay phone and got the operator to put him through to his hotel, then to his room.

The phone kept ringing for a while, then it was picked up and Rich said, tentatively, 'Hello?'

'Rich, it's me, Jairus. Listen to me, you need to get out of there, dump the laptop and get on the next train out of there. Got it?'

'Yeah, I'm hearing you. What the fuck's going on? What's this all about?'

'I'm not sure, but some people are tracking me down. Get out of there now.'

'Don't hang up. Don't you want to know what I found?'

'Yeah, of course. Tell me.'

'Well, I found another list of names. Two columns again. Ten names.'

'OK. That'll give me something to look into. I've got a mobile that I'll need you to take a look at.'

'Alright. Look, there's a name on the list that jumped out at me.'

Jairus stiffened, while his stomach knotted. 'Go on.'

'I'm just letting you know. I don't know what it means.'

'Spit it out, Rich.'

'Karine. Karine Skilton.'

Jairus didn't say anything, he couldn't. His mind was sprawling backwards and forwards in time, expanding and swirling all at once.

'Jay? You still there? That is your ex's name, isn't it? I mean, it's probably just a coincidence.'

Jairus took out the mobile he'd taken from Pinder's house and opened up the contacts list again. He ran through the few numbers as his iron fist headache smashed against the inside of his skull. He stopped at the third number. It was one of the few numbers he'd ever memorised. It was Karine's old mobile number. 'You need to get out of there, Rich.'

'I found a couple of deleted j-pegs too. Shall I email you them and the list of names?'

'No. Put them somewhere safe, and I'll come see you. Get out now. Wipe the laptop and dump it.' Jairus hung up and turned to look out the glass of the door. He had to close down his mind. Images of Karine were coming back to him, snapshots of their life before her death, all the times she'd been acting strangely. In the back of his mind he'd feared she was having an affair, but now he didn't know what to think.

He cleared his thoughts, brought back the

immediate danger they were in and hurried back to the booth where Helen was sat. He slipped back in and saw that his black coffee had arrived. He picked it up and sipped it as Helen watched him, seeming to examine his every movement. 'We have to go.'

Helen looked down at the table as she said in a quiet voice, 'I'm not going with you.'

'What? You can't stay here.'

She looked up and he saw determination in her dark eyes. 'It's you they're after. Not me. Someone I know's going to pick me up. You better take care of yourself.'

It was the fear that he knew was coursing through her body that made her act the way she was. He didn't blame her. Fear was beginning to poison his system too, even though he had to try and rise above it and not let it cloud his judgement. 'You sure?'

She nodded. 'I've made up my mind. I'm sorry.'

'Don't be sorry.' He got up, drank the rest of his coffee, then stared at her. 'Take care, Helen. Stay in public. Don't trust anyone. Good luck.'

'You too.'

He saw the smile she tried to raise, and then hurried out of the restaurant.

It was Tom's turn and so he got up off the waiting room chair and sat in the barber's chair. The man who asked how he wanted his hair to look, was a greying Italian. He had a sagging body and a bulging belly.

Tom told him to cut it all off and to leave a nice neat short haircut, then the Italian barber put a sheet round him like they always do and raised the chair. He started snipping, then running the vibrating clippers tightly up the back of his neck.

As the man worked his magic, Tom felt the eyes

opposite him calling to him, begging him to look forward and stare into the two pools of darkness, the portals to unimaginable horrors. He couldn't remember the last time he'd looked at himself in a mirror and now they surrounded him, pleaded for him to look at his own reflection and see what had become of the little boy.

He refused to turn his head towards the mirror, but instead focused his eyes on the bag he'd left by the chair. Inside was a suit that he'd bought with the money he'd saved up. He knew it had been a wise move to put plenty away and stash it for a rainy day. Not a rainy day, he corrected himself, but judgement day. Judgement day was coming.

The haircut was soon over and Tom put a screwed up ten-pound note into the barber's chubby hand and told him to keep the change, then retrieved the bag and headed up Wood Green high street. He turned right when he got the tube station and turned left when he reached a narrow road filled with terrace houses and one three-storey block of flats.

He'd paid his cash deposit to the Turkish landlord, or at least he assumed he was Turkish. He couldn't remember why he assumed he was Turkish. He mentally shrugged and took his bag up to the second floor, walking across the threadbare red and yellow flowery carpet.

He got inside the tiny studio flat, put the bag by his mattress and sleeping bag. He ran his hand over his jaw, feeling the harsh bristle of his beard. In the cramped grotty bathroom, he took out the pack of disposal razors and turned on the hot tap. With hand soap massaged into his beard, he began the careful and slow process of removing his beard.

When his beard was gone, he lifted his neck and

stared at the scarlet blushes around his windpipe. He looked at himself, but not in his eyes, never in his eyes.

He showered quickly, splashed on expensive aftershave, then dressed in his new dark blue suit and dark red tie.

Before heading out of the flat, he took the large manila envelope from under his mattress and walked to the front door. There was a mirror by the door, and it was screaming out to him like all the rest, pleading with him to stare into those lost eyes. He closed his eyelids tight, found the door handle by feeling around and then pulled open the door and left.

He walked down the alleyway beside the house and into a lane that ran behind the main road. There were lockups, five of them, further down and they were shadowed by trees. There were also two large garages, both owned by his landlord. A small amount of cash placed in his landlord's hand allowed Tom to use the one on the right.

He took out the key to the padlock and opened the door, pushed it up and listened to the un-oiled squeak. He stood looking at the ten-year-old black Ford KA that he'd paid cash for, no questions asked.

His mind had been muddled for so long, had had drugs and booze hurtling along his veins, poisoning his soul way longer than he needed. Now he was free. Yes, his brain was somehow damaged and he sometimes couldn't think straight, and it was sometimes hard to even move and get his body to do what he wanted. But not today – today it was working, and the only drug he needed was the cigarettes which calmed him and stopped him wanting to tear away at the ants and worms that sometimes crawled under his skin.

He climbed in the car, shakily lit a cigarette, and watched the red glow of it in the shadow of the garage.

He smoked it calmly, breathing in the smoke and the resolution he'd made. He was going to fulfil the plan he'd put in place. It wasn't much of a plan, in fact it could hardly be called a plan at all.

It was revenge. Not just for himself but for all the others.

He started the engine, then drove slowly out of the garage and down the bushy lane and towards his bloody destiny.

Jairus hurried away and left the restaurant and walked towards another building that was across the other side of the road. It was a department store that was advertising bargain clothes and other items. There was a scattering of cars in the surrounding car park.

He spotted a silver Compact Ford car right at the edge of the car park, then ducked down by the side of it. He took out his lock-picking equipment and started work on breaking into the car, even though his hands were trembling. He needed a drink badly, but this wasn't the time.

Eventually the door unlocked and he slipped inside and managed to start the engine. The words – if not a policeman, then a thief – came to mind as he reversed the stolen car and headed onto the road towards Plymouth. He planned on dumping the car the first chance he got and grabbing another. When he was in Plymouth, he'd get the train back to London.

He joined the A38, watching the traffic all around him, solitary people at the wheel or families off somewhere, excited kids in the back. He felt exhausted suddenly and he seemed to be trembling more and more. He needed a drink as the symptoms of alcohol withdrawal seemed to be overtaking him. His eyelids seemed heavy and his vision was going in and out of focus.

It was a couple of miles later that he began to feel even more lethargic and groggy. He'd started considering pulling off the road for a rest or even trying to find a motel when he noticed a car in the rearview mirror that was gaining on him. There were two men sat in the front. He kept watching them getting closer, until eventually the dark Audi they were driving was right behind him.

Then he looked to his left where a white van was parallel with him. The driver kept turning to look at him.

Jairus started to put his foot down, speeding up and getting closer to the car in front. The car ahead remained at the same speed even though Jairus was roaring his engine and nearly bumper to bumper with them.

Any normal driver would have made rude gestures or got out of the way, but whoever was behind the wheel was calm and in perfect control of the vehicle.

His head started to pound at the same time as his stomach knotted and his heart began to try and break through his rib cage.

He swung the wheel to his left, swerving his car towards the van, but the driver kept steady, keeping his cool. The car behind was gaining, closing the gap and boxing him in.

As he felt himself sinking with a sudden wave of exhaustion and nausea, the car in front braked hard.

He slammed on the brakes, while the white van swerved towards him, giving him no choice but to drive across the central reservation and into the traffic coming the other way.

His vision blurred as he saw the flash of cars roaring towards him, then the blast of car horns and the scream of tyres.

Then he was spinning, the steering wheel tearing itself from his grip. He tried to react, but everything was moving slowly. He could see that he was going to crash, that the car would be hit by another vehicle, but he couldn't do anything about it. His limbs and his mind no longer seemed to work.

It was like bumper cars. The other vehicles hit him, and he span and then flipped over sideways, rolling towards the concrete covered bank.

He flailed as the car rocked and rocked, and his head pounded against the headrest.

Then there was silence.

He was hanging upside down, unable to move, or see very well. Something was gushing down his face, and when the liquid entered his mouth and filled it with its iron sting, he felt himself falling backwards into an endless darkness.

CHAPTER 15

Kate Wood pulled the car up at the end of the bricked driveway and the farm-style gates at the bottom of it. Brenton turned his head and stared towards the large three-storey building that must have cost a bomb. It must have been a wreck at one time, maybe the remnants of an old stone barn, now converted into a house fit for a king, or just an arse-licking Commander.

The thoughts flashed into his mind again, the horrific images of Foreman with his...no, they weren't real. It was all just mind games. Still, ever since leaving the prison, Brenton hadn't been alone. He'd felt haunted by something, or rather had a terrible sense of foreboding that laid heavy in his stomach.

'You alright?' Wood said, and when he looked at her, he saw she was looking at him strangely.

'Yes, I'm fine.'

'You've hardly said anything since I found you throwing up in the prison toilets. What the bloody hell did Foreman say to you?'

'The usual fucked-up… stuff. Listen, he said that Leonard Jameson was party to it.'

'Party to what? Mandy-Rose's murder?'

'No, everything else. He still denies he murdered her.'

Wood slapped the steering wheel. 'The... shitty piece of... that fucker raped her... made that poor little girl's last moments on earth a living nightmare...'

'Don't...please don't talk about it.'

'Jesus, Jake, he really got inside your head, didn't he? Alright, let's talk about something else...like, why the bloody hell are we outside Swanson's bloody house?'

Brenton took out his cigarettes, then his lighter, hoping that a fag might take away the bad taste in his mouth. 'I don't know. He called me and told me to come over and bring the piece of paper with me.'

'He wants it back? Jesus, fucking... you know what they're about to do, don't you?'

'I've got a pretty good idea.'

'They're going to shut it down.'

Brenton took out the evidence bag and the piece of paper inside. 'We don't know that.'

'Don't we?' Wood raised her eyebrows.

'Why would they put us on it, then shut it down?'

'I don't know. Anyway, why the bloody hell am I here?'

Brenton opened the car door. 'Because if it's really bad news, you're driving us to the pub so we can get pissed up. See you in a bit.'

He didn't bother to listen to her annoyed reply, just walked through the garden gate and up the long driveway to the house and rang the bell.

He had to ring the bell a couple of times before he heard heels tapping along a wood floor.

An attractive, but tired-looking curvy woman in roughly her late forties opened the door. She had mousey brown hair and a glass of wine in her hand. 'You must be here to see my wonderful husband. Or are you here to see me? I've got plenty of wine.'

'Thanks, but I am here to see Commander Swanson.'

The woman awkwardly moved back to let him

through. 'Come in then, don't be shy. Sorry, can you tell I've had a few too many?'

'Not at all.' He stepped in and waited to be shown to wherever he was meant to be going.

Swanson's wife leaned into his ear, flooding his face with wine fumes and whispered, 'I had orders not to talk to you. Just let you in and try not to embarrass him, he said. How am I doing?'

Brenton did his best to smile, ignoring his sober hatred of drunk people. 'You're doing very well.'

'I'm Kim, by the way.'

'Nice to meet you, Kim. Jake Brenton.'

She smiled, then her eyes darted into the house and back again. She leaned in to whisper, 'He's not alone back there.'

'He's not?'

She shook her head. 'No, some suited wanker turned up a little while ago. Didn't even say who he was. Rude sod.'

'I see.' Brenton took out his cigarettes. 'Do you mind?'

'My darling husband hates the things. He'd go ballistic if he knew. So help yourself.'

'Thanks.' Brenton lit one and took a steadying puff. 'You seen this wanker in a suit before?'

'You know, yeah, he has been here before... or it could've been another wanker in a suit... anyway, he was here a while back.'

'Really? About a week ago?'

The wife closed one eye, then staggered on her heels as if the planet had just lost some gravity. 'Yes, about then. Something had obviously happened, because my darling husband looked like he was going to have kittens. Hey, you've got too much information out of me already.'

'I won't tell.'

She winked. 'Me neither. Our little secret. Fuck him. And the fucking wanker in the suit.'

Brenton laughed. 'Mind if I use your toilet?'

'I don't mind. Keep going towards the back of the house, first right. The games room, where you'll find the arseholes, is up a little further.' She smiled, then staggered off into another room.

Brenton hurried on and found the enormous and sparkling white bathroom and locked the door behind him and dropped his fag into the toilet bowl. He took out the evidence bag with the note inside it, then slipped it out carefully. He held it up to the light and saw that there was a watermark at the very edge of the piece of paper. He folded it just before the water mark, then carefully tore off that piece and slipped it inside his jacket. He put the note back in the evidence bag, and headed out of the bathroom.

He followed the sound of snooker balls being knocked across a table and found the enormous room at the end of the house. French doors lined the back wall, while dartboards, a snooker table and a skittles set filled the rest of the room.

Commander Swanson was standing over the table holding a snooker cue, dressed in a casual shirt, his sleeves rolled up. Brenton's eyes jumped to the suited man sitting at a table near the snooker table. The suited man was staring at him.

'Here he is,' Swanson said and laid the cue on the table then put out his hand for Brenton to shake.

He reluctantly took the hand and nodded to the suited man. 'Who's this?'

'A colleague,' Swanson said, his voice losing any friendliness. 'Never mind about him. Sit down and have a drink.'

'No thanks.'

Swanson stared at him as if he'd insulted his mother. 'What's wrong with you now, Brenton? Your boss said you were OK. I'm starting to think he was pulling my chain. I thought you liked a drink.'

'I do. I'm just worried about what your friend might slip into it.'

The suit kept staring at him emotionlessly, while his boss said, 'What the fuck are you talking about?'

Brenton said, 'Well, you see, I get the feeling that I'm about to get fucked whether I want to or not.'

'Bloody hell, Jake. Pull yourself together.' Swanson picked up a glass of what looked like scotch and took a gulp.

'He has a point,' the suited man suddenly said.

'Oh, you do talk?' Brenton walked closer, folded his arms.

The suit kept his emotionless state. 'I'm the man who's about to fuck you. I'm here to tell you that your investigation has come to an end. All your files will be boxed up and handed over, along with any evidence. I believe you have a letter?'

Brenton stared at him for a moment, while the piece of paper he'd torn off burned inside his jacket pocket. He took out the evidence bag and slapped it down on the table. 'There you go. You can go and burn it or whatever you're going to do. Tell me something though, what about Leonard Jameson's murder? Does that just go away?'

The suited man sat back. 'Sometimes cases go unsolved. You know that.'

'Yes, I do. Not usually the murders of MPs. Especially not when they're found with hairs on their bodies that used to belong to a murdered girl.'

'Shut your mouth!' Swanson was staring at him,

looking horrified, his eyes burning out to him. 'You keep that fucking mouth of yours shut, you got it?'

'You should listen to Commander Swanson.' The suit stood up. 'He's a wise man. If you tell anyone else about what you found, the evidence you discovered, then... you remember the trouble that your governor helped you out of about two years ago?'

The world seemed to alter, change colour and slow down. Brenton felt like collapsing, but stayed solid, staring at the suit, trying not to show weakness.

'Yes, he knows,' the suit said, smiling. 'She's a beautiful woman, isn't she? You should never get involved with fellow officers. Especially when you're married with kids. But even more so when that fellow officer persuades you to partake in drugs. We have the whole incident on film. You see, we like to keep a close eye on our best officers.'

Brenton looked at Swanson, but the Commander was staring down at his drink, refusing to look up. 'That's the way it is, is it?'

'Yes, it is.' The suit smiled. 'Get used to it. Then forget about it. Go and work on another case, and get a result and you'll feel better. The sting will fade in time.'

Brenton looked them over one more time, his mind becoming crammed with all the things he wanted to say, all the truths that would get him suspended or much worse. He thought logically, persuaded himself that he needed to be a policeman, to be able to do some good. He buried his anger in a shallow grave and headed back out of the house, lighting a cigarette as he went.

Tom parked the car under an umbrella of trees, tucked in where the country lane widened for a few feet. Everything was black, silent, just the ticking of the cooling engine. He lit a cigarette, then got out of the car and listened to the eerie sounds of the woodland, a crow squawking somewhere high above. There were miles of woods and the mansion at the centre of it. The country estate was visible when he scrambled onto the bonnet of the car, his fag hanging from his mouth.

There were glowing squares of light in the darkness, formed into the large rectangular expanse of house. Somewhere along the wide road that led to the main house, there were big black iron gates. A guard would be there, probably armed. Probably an ex-police officer or soldier. They always kept themselves protected, whatever the political climate was. It didn't matter if terrorists were threatening to bomb the UK or not, they always maintained a wall of bodies to keep the prols away from them.

It would never work, Tom knew that. It was like trying to keep water in a tightened fist.

He jumped down from the car, finished his cigarette, then started walking along the country lane, patting the envelope in his jacket pocket as he went. He turned right when he reached the wide road that wound all the way to the house.

It took him fifteen minutes to reach the big iron gates and the sentry-style army box beside it. As expected and right on time the guard stepped out and walked towards him.

Tom put his hand in his other pocket and felt the taser he carried there.

'Stay where you are and state your business,' the guard said in a northern accent. He was big, broad, definitely ex-army.

'Sorry, mate, I've just broke down up the road,' Tom said pointing a thumb behind him. 'My phone's flat too. Fucking thing.'

The guard was watching, reading him, judging him in case he was a threat. 'You're better off going back up where you came from, then turn right. There's a village...'

'You're joking?' Tom stepped closer. 'I'm supposed to be meeting a bird tonight. You ain't got a phone I can borrow?'

'Sorry.'

Tom shook his head. 'She's fucking hot too. I just want to send a text.'

The guard was staring at him, but Tom could see there was a decision being made behind his stupid, ignorant eyes.

'Real sort, is she?' the guard said, his cold stare melting a little.

'You wouldn't believe the legs on her.'

The guard smiled, then walked into his booth for a moment and came back carrying something in his hand. A mobile phone. He wasn't a bright soldier, just a follow your orders sort.

Tom smiled and walked towards him as he said, 'You've literally saved my life, mate.'

The guard held out the phone to him. Tom walked towards him, one hand in his pocket, gripped around the taser. He reached out for the phone with his right hand, while he pulled out the taser from his pocket and jabbed it into the guard's chest.

The crackle of electricity and the guard's cry of pain became one as Tom leaped back and watched the big man crumple to the ground, rolling and letting out a deep groan. He knelt beside him and jabbed the taser into him again. He took his phone and radio, then stepped over the convulsing guard.

Tom went into the booth and found a handgun,

put it in his jacket and started on the next part of his journey as he stared towards the orange squares of light in the distance.

They'd brought food and water and dumped it in the middle of the dark room. Cathy had taken it upon herself to take some to Linda and the young women in the cell in the corner. There were three of them, all staring at her with horror dug into their skin. One of them had reached out a small hand towards her and took the bottles of water and the fast food burgers that had been left. When the young woman stepped back, the light caught her body and Cathy could see her, and the other two women, who began to eat hungrily, were all heavily pregnant. Cathy stepped back, sickened at the thought of why the women were also being held captive.

When she woke Linda, she screamed until she seemed to come out of her nightmare and realised where she was. She shook her head when Cathy offered her a cheeseburger and a bottle of water.

'You going to starve yourself?' Cathy asked.

The woman looked at her with empty, beaten eyes. 'They're going to kill me anyway, why take their food?'

'If they were going to kill you, why haven't they done it already?' Cathy sat at the end of the bed.

'Because they want to know what I know.'

Cathy nodded and took a swig of water. 'What do you know?'

Linda glared at her. 'No offence, but I don't know you, love. You could be one of them. Look at the way you're dressed.'

Cathy looked down at the black outfit she was wearing and her almost bare breasts. She nodded. 'OK then, what about the girls in the corner?'

Linda looked over briefly, then down at the bed. 'I don't know... probably the same sort of thing they did to me when I was young.'

Cathy was about to ask her more questions when she felt strange. Her vision clouded and she shook her head. She recognised the sensation, the grey clouds coming in from the far corner of her eyes. She tried to stand up, but her legs were already crumbling. She turned her head when she heard moaning from the cell and then saw the girls doubling over and falling to the floor.

Linda was watching her, staring, saying something to her, but she was deaf to everything but the panicked beating of her heart as she collapsed to the cold ground.

She knew what it would be like when she woke up, the rolling fog and the queasiness. She felt like she had travelled, had been pulled far from where she had been, but her mind was taking its time to join her body.

Her eyes were open and she was looking up at the grand white ceiling, a stretch of pure white snow or icing on a cake.

She looked down to see she was sitting in a chair. Her arms were strapped to the chair by thin plastic straps. Same with her ankles.

She looked round the room once the mist had vaporised and found another room that could have easily been part of a museum of antiquities. Old vases, heavy pieces of furniture, enormous portraits of people long-dead surrounded her.

Then her eyes jumped to a chair at the far end of the room. A bearded man in a suit stared back at her. His face cracked into a smile as he pushed himself to his feet.

He came closer, his squinted eyes running all over her body. She knew his face, but it took her a few seconds to connect his face in her fractured mind.

James Howard. He was the creator of Britain's first mobile phone company. There had been many interviews on TV where he had offered his financial advice, whether it was desired or not, to the government.

'I was starting to think you'd never wake up,' Howard said and then turned and approached a highly polished antique cabinet. He opened a door and Cathy could see there were rows of various decanters filled with alcohol. He grabbed one filled with a light brown liquid inside. Whiskey, she surmised and watched him pour himself a glass and neck it. He looked at her, smiled, then poured another large glass.

He brought the glass over, still smiling. 'You shouldn't have eaten the food. Junk food will kill you.'

'Is that what you're planning to do to me?'

'Maybe... well, not me. I don't like to do the messy stuff. That's why I have employees. I point my finger, they do what I say.'

'Then why am I here? I'm guessing I'm not in Douglas Burdock's house.'

The businessman looked around his surroundings as he slipped off his suit jacket and rolled up the sleeves of his shirt. 'No, you're not. This is my place. Bought it about ten years ago. Not bad for an East End lad that had fuck all when he was spat into the world. My old mum said I wasn't breathing when I popped out... they slapped me on the arse, and now look at me! A fucking fighter!'

'Seems wrong somehow that you should own it.' She moved her hands and feet, trying to test how secure the restraints were. They were solid, which meant there was no way she was going to escape, and the room was probably the last she'd see. Her heart began to rocket in her chest.

'Wrong? What do you mean, darling?' Howard stepped closer, narrowing his eyes.

'Well, it's just that this house... there's a great deal of culture here... then there's you... you see what I mean?'

He disguised his anger by laughing, but she could see his fists tighten. 'Douglas warned me about you. He said you had quite a twisted mind in that delicate skull. He gave you to me without batting an eyelid, did you know that? Thing is, you're not my usual type.'

'No? Let me guess, you like them young and defenceless?'

He drank the rest of his drink. 'Young? Yes, definitely young. Pure, is the word I'd choose. Defenceless? No, they have to have some fight in them. But I know what you're thinking... why are you here? I'm mean, it's been a long time since you were pure. You're basically a whore.'

She pushed a smile to her lips, which she found very difficult, but she wanted to confuse him. She also made a mental note to cut off his testicles if she ever got free.

He stepped closer and grabbed her face in his big smooth hand. 'I'll tell you. It gets hard to get what you want, especially these days. You never know who's watching you. Thanks to the Internet, people have their suspicions. When it was just the TV and newspapers that people gleaned their information from, it was easy to feed them what you wanted them to know. Hiding the truth was easier. Freedom of Information, that's the disease now. One day we'll find a cure, until then, darling, we have to get our kicks elsewhere. You... well, you're just an appetiser.'

Howard crouched down. 'You're going to be passed around... and we're going to screw you and beat the living shit out of you. How do you feel about that, darling?'

She didn't say anything, kept the screams inside her head.

He was about to turn away, then playfully slapped his forehead. 'I nearly forgot. Douglas gave me a message for you. He wanted you to know that your boyfriend... Jairus, is it? He's been in a terrible car accident. Apparently, he's in hospital, and not in a good way. I don't think they planned for him to survive at all, but I'm sure Douglas' people can remedy that. Now, shall we begin the fun, darling?'

CHAPTER 16

There were spotlights along the gravel driveway, as well as those dotted among the grounds that surrounded the moss-covered house. There were also suited men standing by the stone steps that led to a large arched doorway at the top of them. They would probably be armed, Tom decided as he crept along and hid by a large bush that had been cut into a huge sphere.

He looked round the ground near him and saw a few lumps of stone piled up beside him. He took out the gun he'd taken from the guard and placed it on the ground while he dug a shallow hole in the soil. After placing the gun in the hole, he put a large stone on top, concealing it. He took out the mobile phone he'd taken from the guard and retrieved the phone's number and programmed it into his own pay-as-you-go phone. He left the phone half hidden by the stone, along with his taser, then stood up, straightened his clothes and walked towards the steps.

The men reacted immediately by approaching and surrounding him.

'You're trespassing,' one of the guards said. He looked very much like the one he'd incapacitated at the gates.

'How did you get past the gate?' another guard asked.

Tom made a drama of looking back the way he'd come, staring off into the darkness. 'I just walked through.'

The guard came closer, squaring up to him, giving him the dead eye. 'That's bollocks. Roger, call Nathan. Find out what the fuck's going on. Who are you?'

'Tom.' He pulled the envelope from his pocket and held it out to the guard, who snatched it and said, 'What's this?'

'It's a message for Mr Howard,' Tom said and smiled.

'Put your hands up,' the first guard ordered.

Tom did as he was told and stood motionless, staring up at the house as the guard frisked him. The only thing he found was Tom's mobile phone which he examined momentarily. Satisfied, the guard said, 'Right, you, come inside.'

Tom obediently followed him into the house and stopped in the massive hollow hallway, surrounded by hanging tapestries and giant old paintings.

'You wait right there,' the guard said. 'Sir James doesn't like time-wasters, so you better not be fucking around. What is it?'

Tom turned around when he realised the guard was now addressing someone behind him. Another of the guards, another stocky man with short dark hair, was standing there holding a mobile phone close to his ear. 'No answer.'

The first guard said a few vulgar words then, 'Go and see what he's playing at.'

Tom watched the first guard heading for the wooden staircase at the end of the hallway, then bounding upwards, taking two steps at a time.

He was alone, listening to his own blood as it noisily beat about his body. This had been his plan, to get this close to James Howard, but a big part of him never really believed he would succeed. He expected at any moment to be dragged out and beaten up, or worse. He steadied his breath, staring at the staircase, waiting in fear for the sound of the guard's footsteps to come back.

It seemed like hours. It was a cliché, but true. The few minutes he waited, strung out between his terrible past and his possible future revenge, were agonising. He was a boy again, waiting outside the door that he had stared at for so long, he could still recall every defect in the wood.

Even though he knew very well what lay beyond that door, and understood very well it could no longer harm him, he could still feel the terror echoing through his mind and body.

He stiffened, his heart racing as the heavy steps came back towards him, getting louder and louder until he caught sight of the guard's legs, then the rest of his frame. His eyes seemed blank as he walked calmly towards Tom.

He stopped uncomfortably close, staring down at him. 'Come with me.'

Tom started following the guard, then stopped when he turned around and pressed his hand to his chest.

'Wait,' the guard said. 'Put your hands up.'

Tom raised his arms as the guard slowly and carefully patted him down, all the time staring into his eyes. Eventually he seemed happy that Tom had no concealed weapons, and signalled for him to follow him up to the next floor.

The next floor seemed to stretch onwards, far along the massive house. Tom followed the guard along the checkered stone floor, past several grand doors with stained-glass decoration at their tops.

The guard turned at the penultimate door and faced Tom. 'Knock and go in. Behave yourself, got it? I'm not far away.'

Tom turned towards the door and knocked. The gruff voice commanded him to enter, and the familiar sound of it sent a blade of ice through his spine. He wanted to vomit as he began to shake. He gripped the handle, but he didn't turn it.

'Go on,' the guard growled, making Tom jump. 'Don't keep the man waiting.'

Tom rallied himself, sealed the memories behind a steel door in his mind and forced himself into the room.

He hadn't expected to find himself in such a big room, and stared towards a large antique desk that had some kind of PC sitting on top of it, but no one behind it.

Slowly, he became aware of heavy breathing coming from his right. He shuddered as he turned slowly towards the sound and saw the businessman sat heavily on a bulky green leather sofa. He had a white shirt on, the sleeves rolled up, sweat marks under his armpits. He was breathing hard as he wiped the sweat from his brow. He hardly looked up as his eyes were fixed on the envelope that Tom had delivered earlier. The eyes lifted gradually, seeking him out across the vast expanse of room.

The eyes showed only a little concern at first, mixed with slight shock. But as they rose and took in Tom, they morphed into something far uglier.

'What the fucking hell are you trying to do with this?' Howard was up, storming towards him, waving the envelope. 'Is this blackmail? Where the fuck did you get this?'

Tom remained still, watching the brutal man who now stood aggressively in front of him. The man was used to threatening people, ordering and bullying his staff.

'It doesn't matter where I got it, does it?' Tom said, his voice hardly audible. He cleared his throat.

'Son, you better start talking, and fucking fast. Who fucking gave you this shit? Who photoshopped this shit? You give me their name and I'll see you get a nice bonus out of it and you don't get carried out of this room in a body bag.'

Tom found himself smiling as a rush of an emotion he hardly recognised rippled through his body and stilled his raging, fearful heart. He didn't quite believe it at first, but then he searched his feelings and came to the conclusion that it was true. He no longer feared the bearded businessman standing in front of him. He wanted to laugh but he suppressed it.

'What the fucking hell are you smiling at?' Howard's face prickled with scarlet rage. 'Do you realise who you're fucking talking to? I'm Sir James Howard, you cocky little cunt.'

'I know who you are. You're the man in those photographs. You're the man sodomising those children.'

Howard's mouth fell open for a moment. 'I don't know who, but some bastard doctored those photos...'

'No, they didn't. I know they didn't.'

'How do you know that, you little shit?'

Tom smiled as he felt his body tremble with triumph. 'Because... because one of the boys in the photographs... is me.'

He almost didn't realise at first, but Tom had doubled over and vomited onto the rug they were both standing on. When he wiped his mouth, he looked up into the pale, numb face that stared at him.

After a moment, the steel gate of anger was back in place.

'You lying little shit,' Howard shouted. 'You want money, that it? Fuck you! Do you know that I can make you disappear?'

'Like you and the others made some of those kids disappear?'

The big hands were a blur as they grabbed him by the lapels and wrenched him forward, dragging him towards the big businessman's snarling face.

Tom was so close that he could smell the fumes of whisky on his breath, the stench of stale sweat. The smell was too much. It brought back those nights, all those years ago when he'd been drinking whisky then.

Tom threw up again, splattering Howard's trousers and shoes.

The businessman jumped back, his face and eyes blazing. 'Jesus... fucking hell!'

A booming noise came from the door and Tom stared towards it as he wiped his mouth again.

'Sir James?' the guard's muffled voice called through the door. 'Is everything all right?'

Howard rushed towards the door, and stood by it, his eyes fixed on Tom, the anger and disgust clear in his eyes. 'Yes. Everything is fine.'

'Are you sure?'

'Yes, I'm fucking well sure. Stay out there. Whatever you hear, just stay away. You got that?'

'Yes, sir.'

Howard nodded to himself, then rubbed his face. His eyes, now bloodshot and confused, stared at Tom, who realised that the businessman was in the thralls of panic, and his mind was racing to find a solution to the difficult situation he found himself in.

Tom already knew that there was only one remaining solution to both their problems. He watched as the businessman rushed towards his desk and began looking for something, perhaps tissues to wipe the puke from his expensive suit. He seemed to find some on the desk and began wiping at his trousers, swearing to himself, occasionally staring back at Tom.

Tom knew what the man was considering. No, it wasn't even a consideration anymore – it would have already gone beyond the decision-making process, and would have moved on to the logistics of how to kill him and dispose of his body.

Tom looked around the room and saw a large sculpture on a stand a few feet away. He went to it and picked it up, weighing it in his hands. It was heavy enough.

He carried it in both hands towards the wide back of the businessman, the sadistic child abuser, the evil bastard, and lifted it above his own head, feeling the weight of it pushing downwards, making the muscles in his arms work harder than they had in a long time.

He waited.

And while he waited, he willed the bastard to turn around, and let the memories flood to his mind, let them burst forth through the dam he'd carefully constructed as the fury poisoned his blood stream. His arms and hands trembled.

Then there was a terrible sound in the room, a strange kind of scream that filled Tom's ears. It was only when Howard spun around, his eyes wide, his skin white with horror, that Tom knew the sound was coming from his own mouth.

'What...' Howard said, then made a groaning noise as Tom smashed the ornament onto his skull.

The businessman tripped backwards, landing

against the desk as streams of blood cascaded over his forehead and eyes, squirting from the gash in his scalp.

Tom lifted the sculpture again and brought it down, listening to the wet thump it made as it pounded against Howard's forehead.

His eyes rolled, then his knees gave way as he fell to the floor. He stayed upright for a moment, fighting to stay conscious. His eyes seemed to almost close for a moment, and then he looked up at Tom accusingly.

Tom smashed the sculpture onto his head several times until the evil businessman was lying bleeding on the floor.

Tom slumped to his knees and let go of the ornament. He stared at the still figure lying a foot away from him, no movement coming from him, his eyes half closed, looking past Tom. There was some kind of noise coming from the hallway, shouting, but he could only really hear the beat of his own heart and the whispering voice in his head that told him that he had done it, he had slayed the beast, the demonic creature that had haunted him since he was a boy.

They were trying to open the door. It was the guards, shouting through the door, asking for their Lord and master to open it, making sure he was all right after all the screaming. It wouldn't be long before they got through the door. He sighed and looked at his hands. There was still so much to do, but he had done all he could, and he had to admit that he had not really planned a way out. They would kill him and he would not show fear.

He turned his head towards the far wood-panelled wall. He thought he heard something, a voice saying something, sort of muffled. Yes, he heard it again, a woman calling out.

He stood up and stared at the wall for a while, listening to the desperate calls for help.

Linda?

He ran to the wall, pressed his ear against the centre panel and shouted, 'Linda?'

'Help me!' the woman's voice screamed out. It wasn't Linda, but probably another poor woman he was torturing.

'I can't leave this room,' he shouted, his face pressed against the wall. 'They'll kill me if I do.'

'There's a door hidden in the wall.'

'Where?' He stood back, his eyes flickering all over the wooden panels that made up the wall.

'Somewhere there. You have to press the wall to open it!'

Tom started pressing his palms against the wall, but nothing was happening.

'What happened? Is he dead?'

Tom turned and looked towards the body that was still lying in a lump across the floor, a small pool of blood around his head. 'I think so.'

Tom looked up when the thumping began again on the door to the room and the guards' collective voices shouted out to him and the dead man. It would only be a matter of minutes, if not seconds before they got through the door. He stepped backwards, traced his hands over the framework of the wall, concentrating on the joins. Then he caught sight of something. A little square of light just to his right. He moved over and started pressing his hands all around the area he'd picked out.

Then he heard a click and a small door swung gently towards him.

The room beyond was lit by scarlet light which shone down from spotlights in the ceiling.

'Over here!'

Tom looked over to the far right corner, went to move, but stopped. He was staring at the woman who was naked, face down on some kind of metal bed, her wrists and ankles chained to it. Her back was deeply red, with welts and cuts covering her skin. When he looked at her face in the glow of the red light, the bruises on her cheeks looked almost black.

'Get me off this!' the woman screamed at him, so Tom rushed to her and started pulling at the cable ties that were holding her to the bed.

'There's a knife,' she said. 'He's got a small knife in his pocket.'

He looked back into the room he'd just left, where the dead businessman was still lying. There was a thudding coming from the door where the guards were trying to break in.

'Hurry up!' she shouted. 'Get the knife! Then shut the door.'

He nodded, then ran into the room and knelt by the body. He hesitated, his hand reaching out to the body, trembling, expecting the big man to suddenly spring up, screaming.

He shook his head, told himself to stop being so weak.

There came a cracking noise from the door as the guards pounded against it. He put his hands into the dead man's trouser pockets and found the small penknife.

The door crashed open and one of the guards stumbled into the room, his eyes jumping to Tom and the body.

Tom opened the knife, pointing it at the guard who was now slowly coming towards him. 'Stay there!'

He turned and ran as hard as he could, staring

towards the opening in the wall. He slid through and shut the door behind him, panting and looking down at the blade in his hand. He heard the noise behind him. The guard was bashing the wall, trying to open the concealed doorway.

'Hurry up! Cut these straps off me!' The woman's eyes were pleading with him.

Tom rushed to the woman and started cutting the plastic straps from her wrists.

'What's your name?' she asked.

'Tom,' he said, his eyes jumping up towards the wall that was now vibrating with the blows being hammered at it from the other side.

'Thank you, Tom. He would've killed me if you hadn't killed him. My name's Cathy.'

He nodded, cut the ties from her hands and then started on her ankles. 'They'll kill both of us if they get in here.'

When he cut the last tie, she got up off the table and grabbed some leather clothing from the floor and put it on. Her breasts were hardly covered. Tom took off his suit jacket and handed it to her. She took it, smiled and put it on and buttoned it up.

'Thanks,' she said, then looked around the room. 'Give me the knife.' He handed it over, but she was still looking around room. 'We need some more weapons.'

'There's a gun outside,' Tom said. 'I've hidden it.'

'That's no good to us in here.' She walked over to a cabinet on the wall, then started jamming the knife in between the doors. Eventually, she yanked open the cabinet and put a hand in. She pulled out some kind of baton, and patted it in her other hand. 'Luckily for us he was a sadistic bastard and loved beating up defenceless women.'

'And children.'

She stared at him for a moment, then turned to look towards the secret door where the sound of the men trying to break into the room was echoing around them. 'They'll be in here soon.'

'We're going to die.'

'No, we're not.' She held the baton in her hand, lifting it to his face. 'This can do some damage. You wait there. Just stand right there.'

Tom did as he was told and watched her storm towards the wall and stand beside the hidden door. She was staring at him, nodding while the guards were smashing away at the wall. He looked down at Cathy's hands and saw she was holding the baton and penknife tightly in them, her knuckles glaringly white.

The door smashed open, springing out and hitting the wall. There was room for one guard to come through at a time. The one who'd brought Tom into the house came through first, his fury-filled eyes fixed on him as he stomped towards him, pointing a thumb behind him.

'Did you do that, you fucking...'

Cathy lifted the baton and swung it, hammering it down at the back of his legs. He let out a shout, then collapsed to his knees. He fought to grab her as he scrambled to get up, but Cathy cracked the baton down on the side of his head. Tom watched him buckle and fall back down as another guard came through the doorway, making a grab for her.

He managed to clutch the baton and tried to wrench it from her hand, but Cathy stabbed the penknife into his thigh. The guard let out a howl as blood poured from his leg. His hand lost grip of the baton, so she swung it hard at his head. He stumbled backwards, one hand clamped to the wound on his leg. Cathy brought down the baton onto his skull, knocking him against the wall. He slumped down to the floor, groaning and shaking his head.

'Come on!' Cathy said, grabbed Tom and dragged him through the doorway and back into the other room.

The room was empty, so Tom followed Cathy to the door which was hanging on its hinges. She poked her head out, the two weapons still in her hands. 'There's no one here. We can go.'

Tom froze to the spot, knowing that they had to be nearby. 'They'll be waiting for us.'

'We can't just wait for them!' She grabbed his arm and pulled him into the corridor and back the way he'd come in.

They reached the main stairway, but Cathy stopped and gripped his arm. There were voices coming from below, then the sound of boots coming towards them, pounding the stairs. She looked back along the corridor, then pointed back where they had come from. 'There'll be a back staircase, the one the servants would have used.'

Tom began running, copying Cathy as she jogged to the very end of the hallway. She was right, there was a narrow staircase which they crept down, listening for anyone coming up.

'Seeing as they knew it was only you that had gone into see him,' Cathy whispered, 'they must have decided only to send a couple of people up to see what had happened. We were lucky.'

'We haven't got out yet.' Tom followed her down the narrow staircase, which led them past small cramped servants' quarters and a large kitchen. There was a fire door at the very end of the staircase which looked as if it was alarmed.

Cathy passed him the baton, then took hold of the

metal bar that would open the door and set off the alarm. She looked him in the eyes as she said, 'The alarm's going to go off. Where's the gun?'

'Nearby.' He took out his phone and brought up the number of the guard's mobile. 'I can find it with this.'

'Ready?'

He nodded then felt his heart begin to pound so fast as she pushed the bar. A high-pitched alarm started pulsing overhead, stabbing Tom's ears as they rushed through the doorway into the floodlit grounds.

Out of the corner of his eye as he ran after Cathy, he saw figures rushing towards them, shouting for them to stop.

Tom overtook her, pumping his arms, feeling his heart pulsating, threatening to explode, as he made for the spherical bush. He pressed the dial button on his phone and heard the ringing of the phone begin.

The glow of it was getting closer. He dived down, flipped the rock over and grabbed the gun.

'Give me that!' Cathy snatched it from his hand and swung around just in time to stop the guards in their tracks.

The nearest guard raised his hands up to his chest. 'All right, darling. Just calm down. We just want to talk to you both about what happened upstairs.'

'Call the police,' she said. 'Go on. Or will there be too much to explain?'

'Put the fucking gun down!' the guard said.

'Either call the police or back off. I will shoot the first person who comes anywhere near us.'

'Just stop playing around...' was all the guard managed to say before the blast of the gun made him shudder and grip his ears.

Tom had closed his eyes, and only the high-pitched

whine remained to confirm that Cathy had fired a warning shot close to the guard.

He opened his eyes to see the two men backing off. Whatever had happened to their employer, they had obviously decided it wasn't worth their lives to stop his attacker.

'Have you got a car?' Cathy said, backing up towards him, her eyes still fixed on the two guards.

'Yes, but it's at the end of the road.'

'Let's start moving,' she said. 'You two, call the police or whatever you're going to do. Do not follow us.'

Tom directed her along the dark path using the torchlight of his mobile to find their way. All the time they walked, he wondered what the men would do. They would have to eventually report his death, but what Cathy said was also true – if the police started digging, there would be a lot to explain.

They kept walking in silence, Cathy occasionally looking back at the big house for a moment before walking on. He could tell that something was weighing on her mind but he somehow felt it was not what had happened to her in that room. She was tough, he felt, and she could handle much more than what she had been dealt out by Howard and his sadistic kind.

He wanted to ask her what her story was, and why, when she climbed in the car and looked at her face in the rearview mirror, a single tear travelled down her cheek. But he didn't, he just wound down the window and lit a shaky cigarette.

'Hurry up and drive,' she said.

He started the engine. 'Where are we going?'

'Cornwall. I have a friend who lives there. I think he might help me save another friend of mine, if he's not dead already.'

CHAPTER 17

They came out of the darkness. Thin strips of glowing white light that came dancing forward. Then everything was eerily white, and the light became dancing figures that surrounded him. He didn't know who he was, didn't understand if he was a person, a separate entity from everything that surrounded him, just as a newborn child doesn't comprehend their uniqueness.

The figures were not just dancing. They were performing a ritual, waving some kind of sticks above their heads as a skeletal figure was brought into the room on a white bed. The dancers encircled the bed as they all came nearer and nearer.

Somehow, he understood it was the dance of the dead.

Their faces were ghostly, almost skull-like, but he recognised each one as they bounced past.

Carl Murphy, the man he'd stabbed to death, came laughing by, followed by the strangled man found in his flat. Then there was the woman who lived next door to the Pinders, her eyes empty, her skin flaking off. Why was she dancing the dance of the dead?

The last one came towards him, but she wasn't dancing, she was merely moving, almost floating, her cloudy eyes fixed on him.

Karine.

She lifted her hand as if to touch him, but he

was moving backwards, sinking into a grey fog that seemed to swallow him. It became a thick soupy liquid that he was drowning in. He tried to push himself up to the surface, but something kept dragging him back down. He looked down into the darkness beneath to see what creature had the strength to keep pulling him further down.

Now she was below him, Karine's hand, as slender and delicate as it always was, gripped on his ankle. Her face was tilted up towards him, a deathly smile on her face.

When Jairus surfaced from his nightmare, a kind of queasiness came with him as he looked up and tried to focus on the human-shaped dark blue blur that was hovering close to him. He was lying on a hospital bed. He put his hand down and felt the starched sheets rough against his palm.

He looked towards his left arm, which was being held in place in a plastic sleeve.

The blue human shape came closer and at last he could see that with the shape came a round, smiling face. A nurse looked down at him, then took out a small pen torch and waved it across his eyes.

'Looks like the morphine's wearing off,' the nurse said. She had mousey brown hair tied back. She was full figured, quite pretty. 'Glad you're still with us, Jay.'

'Jay?' he said.

She started putting a blood pressure cuff around his arm. 'That's what you told me to call you. I did try calling you by your first name, but that seemed to upset you. You probably don't remember.'

He shook his head. There was a drill burrowing into the front of his skull, which was joining together into some grotesque partnership with the same old headache he got every time he was under massive stress.

Images began to flicker before his eyes, jagged pieces of memory inserting themselves into his consciousness. The cars boxing him in, forcing him off the road. He could see the driver of the van staring at him just before he swerved.

Then nothing. His brain rebelled against the forced memory and made the pain in his skull ten times worse.

'They ran me off the road,' he said.

The nurse looked at him, her eyebrows raised as she pumped up the blood pressure cuff. 'You're saying someone purposely ran you off the road? It wasn't an accident?'

'Yeah, that's what I'm saying.'

'You've been through a traumatic event. Your foot's badly broken, so is your left hand and wrist. You also have several broken ribs. You've been on morphine for the last couple of days since the accident. You were lucky really that you didn't have a severe head injury.'

'You think my memory might be playing tricks?'

'I don't know to be honest, but all you can do is talk to the police.' She looked at his blood pressure reading. 'Well, your blood pressure is returning to normal. That's good.'

Jairus smiled, but suddenly grimaced when he felt the spikes of pain dig into his arm and foot. He looked around him, absorbing his new environment and saw a patient, a young man lying opposite him, and an old man asleep in the bed to his right. The television in the corner was playing to no one in particular, the volume turned down low.

His eyes flickered over to the open double doors,

where he saw a suited man leaning against the wall. Their eyes met, but the man in the suit smirked, shook his head and walked back out into the corridor.

'Who was that?'

The nurse looked to where Jairus was nodding. 'Who?'

'There was a man in a suit staring at me. Is he a policeman?'

'No, I don't think so. The police have been by a couple of times. I know their faces. You probably mean the couple of suspicious men who've been hanging round. They seem to be keeping an eye on you.'

Jairus tried to sit up but found his body screamed at him to stay where it was. 'I need to get out of here.'

'You're not going anywhere!' The nurse rolled her eyes. 'Look at the state of you. If you don't mind, I need to carry out my obs. You stay where you are.'

His eyes jumped to the doorway again as another bunch of memories stampeded into his already painful brain. Karine led the charge, reminding him of the fact that her phone number had been on Pinder's phone and her full name had been on his laptop. Why? His brain scrambled in every direction to make sense of what had happened so far, but he could not make it all connect to the murder of the journalist David Coulson.

Then his mind returned to the men who he knew were keeping an eye on him, hanging around the ward. He looked down towards his elevated foot that was also held securely in a plastic cast. He was stuck where he was, a sitting duck, waiting for either the police or the men who wanted to kill him to turn up.

Brenton was driving with Wood beside him sipping a takeaway coffee and reading a file on her lap. He hadn't said a word in twenty minutes, was gripping the wheel and replaying his meeting with the Commander and the fuckwit in the suit with the smug grin.

'So, how did we end up with this case?' Wood sat back and put away the file.

'It's an honour killing,' he said and pulled up at the traffic lights. 'Just because we happened to be in North London, they thought they'd give us this case to look into. Probably thought it'd keep us out of trouble for a while.'

'Yeah, because it's an honour killing! It'll go on and on! This is bloody punishment!'

'This is my fault.' He put his foot down, feeling the burn of anger pulsing through him.

Wood flicked his shoulder. 'No, it's not. You were doing your job, unlike most of the arseholes who're supposed to be in charge of us. The bastards have really pissed me off. I can't believe they've just shut us down. Bastards.'

Brenton swept his eyes over to her, saw the irritation turning her neck and cheeks scarlet. He briefly touched his shirt's breast pocket, then reached down to change gear. 'What can we do though?'

'There's not much we can do, is there? Unless you want to get the IPCC involved and really put a bullet into your career. We haven't got any evidence to examine.'

He looked at her. 'What if we did?'

'What do you mean?'

'I mean, if we still had some tangible evidence to examine, would you follow wherever it took you?'

She was staring at him, obviously trying to read him. 'And what if I did follow the evidence? Where would it get me? With no job, but with a nice warm feeling that I did the right thing?'

'Something like that. Yes.'

She looked forward. 'Honour killings are complicated cases.'

'They take a long time.' He took the next left, and headed down a narrow road.

'But it's still a case. It's somebody's daughter.'

He nodded, then saw the turning that would take them into the car park of the supermarket. 'I know.'

He parked up, then turned to face her as she said, 'Are we going shopping?'

'Very bloody funny. Listen, I need to know if you're with me on this.'

'On what?' Wood tried to look innocent but failed terribly.

Brenton put his hand in his pocket and gripped the small piece of paper then brought it out and handed it to her.

She examined it then looked at him as if he'd handed her a puppy's head. 'Oh Jesus! I don't believe you! You tampered with evidence?'

'How can it be evidence if there's no case? That bit of paper doesn't even exist.'

She rubbed her face, then looked up, then slowly faced him. 'All right. Then what do we do?'

'Hold up it up to the light.' He nodded to the piece of paper. 'Go on, hold it up.'

She sighed but held it up. 'It's a watermark. So?'

'What's it meant to be?'

She shrugged. 'Looks like... I don't know.'

'It looks like an island to me. I checked out the paper mills near here to see if any of them had produced that. They said they hadn't. I described the paper, and a couple of the people I talked to said it sounded like a kind of paper produced near Wookey Hole at a small paper mill nearby. I contacted them, but they said they didn't discuss their work. Wouldn't even confirm if they produced it or not.'

'So, they've got something to hide?'

He nodded. 'Looks that way.'

'So, why don't you start the engine and take us to this paper mill?'

He looked at her for a while, then started the engine. 'You sure?'

'No, but I can see you're not going to be happy until we look into this. So, let's go and get into trouble.'

Jairus had been lying on his left, half staring at the TV, then out the window at the dull grey sky. Winter had come knocking early and he hoped nobody would let it in. But it would come, cold and hard, beating at his door.

He'd fallen asleep, snoozing, and woke to find his left arm, the one encased in plastic, tingling and numb. He wanted to move his fingers, to make a fist, but he'd been told he couldn't. He couldn't even sit up straight. He was burning all over with anxiousness, his skin crawling with frustration at being cooped up in the swelteringly hot room. Why were hospitals always so hot? Didn't heat breed disease? Doesn't cold eradicate it?

He fought to lie on his back and lifted his head up on the pillows. With his head tilted upwards, he sat and stared at the other patients. They were half asleep too. But they probably weren't beginning to tremble all over, he thought as he raised his right hand and saw it vibrating. His heart also began to throb madly in his chest, while a cold sweat dripped down his armpits.

What he really needed was a drink, but he knew the hospital staff weren't about to crack open a bottle of vodka for him.

Then when he turned to look again at the other poor bastards imprisoned with him, he caught sight of a figure standing in the doorway. His eyes jumped to the same suit that had been peering at him before. But this time he didn't stay on the threshold of the doorway, he came striding in and stood at the foot of his bed. He looked Jairus over, clinically, as if he was trying to work out the logistics of something that had him a little baffled.

'You here to kill me?' Jairus asked, his teeth gritted, ready to fight for his life. Already the pulse of his stress headache was slamming against his skull.

The man looked at him only briefly, then turned towards the doorway, where another man in a suit was standing with his hands in his pockets.

'Is it clear?' the first suit asked.

The second stepped backwards into the corridor and looked both ways, then nodded. 'Clear.'

Jairus tried to push himself up, grasping for the bed, knowing that this was it, the fight of his life. The pain dug like knives into his chest, while his leg screamed out for him to stop moving. He bit down, gritted his teeth and screamed through the agony as he tried to wrench himself over.

'Don't move,' the first suit said. 'Don't be an idiot.'

'Yeah, right, fuck you!' Jairus said and screamed again as he got himself sitting up.

Now the other suit came rushing into the room and grabbed him, pushing him backwards.

'Get your fucking hands off me!' Jairus managed to grab the man's hand and twist his wrist the wrong way.

The suit pulled his hand away with a yelp. 'Fuck! Fuck you!'

Then there were footsteps coming into the room

and Jairus looked around to see a man in jeans and a brown blazer, short reddish-brown hair. He was holding something behind his back as he stood by the bed.

'Are you going to hold him down or what?' the blazer man said, looking at the two men as if they were idiots.

Both men leapt to it, grabbing Jairus and trying to force him back to the mattress, quite expertly moving his arms so that he had little choice to do what they wanted unless he wanted his arms broken.

The red-haired man came forward, pulling his arm from behind his back and revealing the syringe his was holding in his right hand.

'You're not coming anywhere fucking near me with that!' Jairus tried to tear himself away from the arms that pinned him down, kicking out with his one free leg.

'Jairus!' a female voice called out and the sound of it rang in his ears and sent a shockwave to his chest.

He looked towards the doorway and his eyes took in the female shape that was standing there. His eyes allowed his brain to understand what he was seeing, that Cathy was stood there, looking at him with pity. Beside her was another man, almost pressed against her. Maybe he had a knife of gun pressed into her back, he wondered.

'Cathy?' he said.

'Sorry, Jay, this was the only way.' She smiled sadly.

He jumped when he felt the prick of the needle as it burned into his skin. He looked down in time to see the drug being pushed down the syringe and entering his bloodstream. He counted as his mind raced to work out what was going on, counted like he had done when he was a kid about to have an operation.

They told him to count backwards at the hospital. And just like then, the clouds of darkness came into his vision, swallowing the light in the room and sending him down into the dark earth beneath him.

The last thing he heard was the voice of the nurse demanding to know what was happening, and then his eyes closed.

CHAPTER 18

He wasn't convinced his eyes would ever open again, but when they did and took in the glare of whiteness blazing back at him, Jairus wished they'd remained shut forever. With the bright light came something similar to a migraine, or a blade of ice cold steel being driven into his right eye.

When the blur of light cooled and shapes began to form, he realised he was in a huge, high ceilinged room with large ecclesiastical windows. He was lying on a hospital bed, but there was little else in the way of furniture in the room. There was a white wooden chair next to the bed and nothing more.

It was only when he turned his head towards the archway to his right, he saw Cathy standing there watching him in silence, adorned in a flowing white dress. She smiled and stepped further into the room. 'You're alive then?' she said, a little sadly.

'Yeah, I am. I think. You sound disappointed.'

She shook her head. 'Of course I'm not. You'll never know how glad I am that you're alive. I'm sorry about all the drama at the hospital, but we needed to get you out of there pretty quick.'

'It's OK. I forgive you. I hope I didn't hurt anyone.'

Cathy came closer to the bed. 'They'll live. It's what they get paid for anyway. Risking injury, I mean.'

'Yeah, that's what mercenaries do all right. I saw an

army tattoo on one of their arms. Who do they work for?'

Cathy looked towards the windows, then around the room. 'They work for the man who owns this house.'

Jairus' stomach sank as he wondered which rich man she had become a plaything for now. 'Please tell me Douglas Burdock doesn't own this house.'

She gave a slight huff, but he could see the bright burn of anger in her eyes as she said, 'Seeing as Burdock sold me out, I don't think I'll ever be visiting one of his houses again, unless it's with a knife in my hand.'

'This house belongs to me, Mr Jairus,' a quite high, but well-spoken voice said from the doorway.

A slender and tall man dressed in a lilac robe and grey jogging bottoms and a black t-shirt entered the room. He had wavy platinum blonde hair, a pale chiselled face and pink lips. He carried a cup and saucer in his delicate fingers and stood close to Cathy and smiled.

'I'm grateful for you letting me stay here,' Jairus began, 'but who the bloody hell are you?'

'This is Toby,' Cathy said.

'Toby Besnier,' the man said. 'You've probably seen me on the news.'

Jairus did recall the blonde man from the news and the Internet company he had set up that thrived to bring the secrets of the world's government out into the open. 'Yeah, I've heard about you. You've been living very dangerously.'

'As have you.' Besnier smiled and sipped his drink. 'Cathy told me the kind of trouble you were in and the people who you've upset. I felt I had to intervene.'

'It's much appreciated, but I would've been fine.'

Jairus tried to sit up again and managed to rest on his good arm.

'They arranged a car accident so they could kill you,' Cathy said. 'It nearly worked.'

'Yeah, nearly. But nearly isn't good enough.'

Besnier gave a dry laugh. 'I like your spirit, Mr Jairus. You're quite like me. They tried to crush me and my website, but it didn't work. I fought back. They cannot keep us down, can they?'

Jairus looked at him and his smiling pale face. 'Yeah, that's right. But aren't you having to hide away?'

Besnier examined his surroundings. 'I don't consider this hiding away. I built this house within an old castle deep in the woods because I like isolation, I always have. Even as a child, I liked to play on my own. I'm living on my terms, not theirs. You're welcome to stay as long as you want, Mr Jairus.'

Besnier smiled at them both, then quietly padded out of the room.

Once alone, Cathy said, 'You could have been nicer to him. Without him, you'd still be stuck in that hospital like a sitting duck. You've pissed them off, Jay, which means they'll try to kill you again.'

'Yeah, I know. So, who exactly are these people trying to kill me? One of them is Douglas Burdock, but who're the others?'

Cathy sighed. 'Look, let's get you out of here. I've got a wheelchair outside.'

Jairus watched her leave the room and listened as he heard the squeaky wheels being pushed along the floor and back into the room. Flashes of the crash kept entering into his mind, sending his heart booming again. But another feeling kept rolling over him and that was the comfort and pleasure at seeing Cathy again. Even though alarm bells rang loudly in his head every time they were near each other, he refused to listen to their warning this time.

As Cathy pushed the chair close to the bed, she said, 'You'll be glad to know Toby's had a medical team working on you. They've even got you Diazepam for the alcohol withdrawal. The rest of the painkillers they've got you on should allow you to move a bit more freely without all the agony.'

He tested her theory by pushing himself up with his good arm and found that only a soft blade of pain inserted itself into his ribcage. His foot throbbed as he sat upright, but the pain was definitely being kept at a distance.

Cathy helped him into the chair, and when he was safely in, started pushing him out of the room. They left through the giant archway and moved up a broad cream tiled corridor. Everything was painted white. There was a uniformity about everything, even the large glass windows that lined the very top of the corridor that allowed massive doses of light to shine down. Jairus also noticed that the glass was extra thick, probably bullet proof. He also spotted metal shutters that were ready to come down at a moment's notice. Toby Besnier was certainly in fear of his life, and Jairus decided that he was probably right to be scared.

Jairus turned his head to see Cathy's hand gripped tightly to the handles as the memory of the dance of the dead came into his brain.

'When I was out of it in the hospital,' he said. 'I had this weird dream or hallucination... I saw dead people dancing round my bed...'

'That'll be the drugs.'

'Yeah... I know... but I saw Carl Murphy and Karine... and I saw the woman living next door to the Pinder family.'

Cathy stopped the chair halfway down the hallway, then walked round and faced him. Her face said everything he needed to know and his stomach squeezed itself and twisted into a knot.

'It's not your fault,' she said. 'Just like Karine wasn't your fault. You can't hold yourself responsible for everyone who dies. They chose to kill her to keep her quiet.'

Jairus looked down at his hands and didn't hear anything else she was saying.

They parked into the wide-open space of the nearby empty car park. In front of them sat the big fat stone building that looked like something out of pre-industrial England. Beyond it were the steel and glass and modern homes that seemed to swamp what was left of the green land. Brenton hated seeing the new world eating everything up and was pleased to be looking at a chapter of the past. He wondered how long the building would stand before it was one day turned into apartments. He at least hoped the building was protected.

'Doesn't look much,' Wood said and climbed out.

Brenton joined her and lit a cigarette, preparing himself for the walk to the old building, and setting his mind to the task in hand. 'Looks a bloody sight better than most buildings you see being built these days.'

Wood smirked at him. 'You're stuck in the past, that's your problem. Look at you, smoking away... nobody smokes anymore.'

'They must do, or how do the fag companies make all their money?'

'From you!' She shook her head and walked ahead, and climbed the steps that took them up to the entrance on the second floor.

By the time they reached the wooden arched door, which had a smaller door cut into it, a straggle of adults and kids were lining up and paying an entrance fee to have a tour of the factory.

'Looks like we're going to have to pay nearly a tenner each,' Brenton said, stubbing his cigarette out on the metal handrail.

'You must be bloody joking,' Wood said, pulled out her warrant card and pushed it towards the face of a spotty young woman who was sat behind a desk and taking the money. 'Police business. We're coming in.'

Brenton followed her into a broad and high hallway that was echoing with the loud clunking sound of the machinery beyond. A young man was handing out protective grey coats to the visitors and tried the same with Brenton, but he showed his warrant card and said, 'Where's the boss?'

The young man, who had emo hair and rings in his ears, shrugged. 'I don't know. I just hand out the coats.'

Wood strode to the centre of the hallway and shouted, 'Does anyone know where the manager of this place is?'

A large woman with permed red hair, squeezed into a dark grey trouser suit, came walking towards them, taking her time. She looked annoyed, her face scarlet as she stood before them and gave a very unconvincing smile. 'Carol Mason. Can I help you?'

Brenton showed his ID, then took out the piece of paper that he'd slipped into a small polythene bag. 'We think you manufactured this paper. We'd like to know who you made it for.'

The woman looked at the piece of paper briefly, then back up to Brenton. 'I couldn't possibly tell you if we did or didn't make it. We make a lot of paper here.'

'Who can tell us?' Wood asked.

The woman looked at her watch. 'You're best off talking to Mr Chase. But he's not here at the moment.'

'Where is he?' Brenton said.

'He's off at a meeting, I think. He's always busy. He's involved in development too. What's this got to do with?'

'None of your business,' Wood said. 'Get Chase on the phone. Tell him to get his backside down here because the police are here. Tell him he's in a lot of trouble.'

The woman looked them both over, then at her watch, then huffed.

'Go on,' Wood said, waving her hand. 'Get on with it.'

When the woman had stormed off, Brenton turned to Wood. 'You pissed her right off.'

'Good. Did you see her face? She looked like a slapped arse.'

'That's what I missed about you. Your beautiful turn of phrase. Let's hope Mr Chase gets down here sharpish.'

'Hang on,' Wood grabbed his arm then pointed to a young man in one of the tour coats. 'Let's get ourselves a tour.'

Brenton followed her over to the young man and watched her giving him a big smile as she said, 'Hello, gorgeous. Fancy giving me and my mate a tour?'

The man blushed a little, then smiled awkwardly. 'Well, I think the next tour is at...'

'Come on, don't give me that.' Wood put a hand on his back and directed him towards the big metal doors that led to the main factory. 'You're supposed to show us around, so you're showing us around!'

The young man nodded, then walked towards the big factory doors, where he opened a smaller door within them. He let Wood and Brenton go first, sending them into a vast room that was filled with the almost painful hammering of machinery.

Every corner of the room was filled with giant machines that were doing their job, clattering away while a few factory workers stood around overseeing things.

The young man started to shout at them above the racket, trying to tell them about the history of the paper mill.

Brenton ignored what he was shouting, pulled out the plastic bag and the piece of paper and held it up to his face as he shouted, 'What do you know about this?!'

The young man looked at the bag and shrugged. 'I don't know anything! I just show people around!'

'Have you ever seen this sort of paper being made?!'
'I don't know. Maybe.'

As Brenton lowered the bag he caught sight of a tall suited middle-aged man storming towards them. His face was set in a scowl as he tapped the young man on the shoulder and said something in his ear which made him slope off looking uncomfortable. The man then squared up to Brenton, staring at him, and occasionally looking over at Wood.

'What the fuck are you doing in my building?' the suit said, the growl thick in his voice.

Brenton showed his ID, but the suit said, 'I know who you are. I'm asking what you think you're doing here?'

'We need to ask you a few questions,' Wood said. 'You are Mr Chase?'

He looked over at her as if she was covered in filth.

'Yes, I'm Chase. Come to my office. Hurry up. I'm busy.'

They followed Chase up a flight of iron stairs to the next floor and into a medium sized office. It all seemed old-fashioned to Brenton, not part of the present at all, apart from the PC on the desk. A window allowed Chase to look down on the shop floor from his big antique desk.

Chase didn't sit down at the desk, just rested his fists on it and stared up at Brenton, the scowl turned down a few notches. 'You going to tell me what you're doing here?' Chase said.

'Investigating a murder,' Brenton said, standing close to the desk, staring into Chase's eyes. 'Actually, it's possibly two murders. An MP and a young girl. You ever met Leonard Jameson MP?'

Chase looked away. 'No, I don't think I have. Look, you'll find that I have contacts. I can reach pretty far, you'll find that out too.'

'I'm shaking all over.' Brenton smirked.

'You should be scared. You really should be.' Chase stood up, folded his arms, kept staring.

Brenton took out the piece of paper and placed it on the desk, pushed it towards Chase. 'You made this. Who did you make it for?'

Chase didn't even look at it. 'I don't discuss my clients. Now, why don't you fuck off?'

'This piece of paper was part of another piece that had a murdered man's name it. Sent before he was murdered. I repeat, who did you make it for?'

'I repeat... fuck off.'

Brenton looked down at his jacket as his phone started to ring in his pocket.

'That'll be your boss,' Chase said, smiling, showing his teeth. 'You're in a big pile of shit.'

Brenton took out his phone and saw that a private number was calling. He answered the call. 'DI Jake Brenton.'

'What the fucking hell do you think you're doing?' Swanson's voice was full of bile and fury.

'My job.' Brenton turned and made eye contact with Wood, who was questioning him with her eyes.

'You took some of that paper, didn't you? You fucking... did I not make it plain? This is over! Are you listening to me?!'

'We don't know who killed Leonard Jameson. We don't know what really happened to Mandy-Rose.'

'Yes, we do. She was murdered by a paedophile. He's in prison. Just let it rest at that.'

'Sir...'

'Brenton... Jake. I'm not having this conversation over the phone. Come back. I'll meet you at the station. We'll talk.'

The phone went dead, so Brenton looked up at the still questioning eyes of Wood. 'We have to go.'

'In trouble, are we?' Chase said, a laugh rising in his voice.

Brenton turned and pointed at him. 'Don't go leaving the country. I'll be back to talk to you. Come on, Wood. Let's go.'

Jairus was sitting in his wheelchair, facing a set of huge ornate windows that covered one wall of the room. The room was about the size of a ballroom, but had only a few sticks of furniture and a white grand piano in the far right corner. The old damaged stone walls of the castle cut off half the view of the forest that surrounded the house.

But Jairus hardly saw anything that was really in front of his eyes. He saw only the dead parading before him with accusing looks. Karine was different, the manifestation of her looked at him with sympathy. He couldn't stand any of it and gripped his face, burying himself in darkness. He saw her name on the list and her number on Pinder's phone.

When he removed his hands from his face, he jumped a little to see Cathy staring down at him blankly, her arms folded. 'How long have you been standing there?'

'Not long,' she said. 'How long have you been torturing yourself?'

'Forever. Rich found a list on Pinder's computer. Karine's name was on that list along with two other names. I also found a pay-as-you-go phone hidden in his house. Karine's number was on his phone.'

Cathy crouched down. 'So, she's haunting you now, instead of you haunting her?'

'Yeah, seems that way, doesn't it? So, I keep asking myself why her name was on that list. I don't even know what the lists are for. There's two lists. The first list I found at David Coulson's house on his wife's laptop. He'd tried to delete the names.'

'Do you remember the names?'

'Yeah, I memorised them. The first list had the names Neil Grant, Matthew Pinder, and Ben Samuels on one side. On the right was printed Arthur Davidson, James Howard, and Leonard Jameson.'

Jairus watched Cathy straighten up, her face changing, thoughts rushing into her mind. 'What's wrong?'

'James Howard. That's the sadistic bastard who Douglas gave me to. He's dead. There was a man in the house, he said his name was Tom… he helped me escape. He killed Howard out of revenge.'

'Revenge for what?'

Cathy sighed. 'I'm not sure. From what he said to me, I think Howard had abused him. There's someone else... Leonard Jameson's dead too. Someone murdered him, but the police haven't said much more.'

Jairus rubbed his face as his brain scrambled to make sense of it all. 'So, chances are your friend Tom killed both of them.'

'More than likely. There's something that's been haunting me...when I was locked up, I saw three pregnant women being kept in a cell. Why would they be holding pregnant women captive?'

Jairus' mind ached. 'I don't know...I wish I knew what they were planning. The whole thing's messed up.'

Jairus heard soft padded steps and saw Toby Besnier walking across the room. He stopped close to Jairus and looked him in the eye as he said, 'I might be able to shed some light on your mystery. But I don't think you're going to like it very much.'

CHAPTER 19

Commander Swanson was waiting for Brenton when he reached the grubby incident room. He had his broad back to him, decked out in only his white shirt and pips, facing the whiteboard. Even with his back to him, Brenton could see the brass was under a great deal of stress. He was considering slipping back out when Commander Swanson turned around and looked straight at him.

'Brenton,' the Commander said and looked around the room at the smattering of bodies that had been brought in to deal with the honour killing case. 'Let's go in there.'

Brenton nodded and followed Swanson into the last of the interview rooms where a thick metal desk and three plastic chairs faced each other.

Swanson shut the door, then gestured to the table. 'Sit down.'

'Is this going to take long?'

Swanson's eyes bubbled with rage as he bounded to the table and slapped his hand down on it. 'I won't have any more of your... shit... do you understand? I'm in charge here! You fucking well got that?'

Brenton said nothing, just stared into eyes that were filled with so much more than the stress of the job... and it dawned on him. 'That note, with Jameson's name printed on it... it was sent to you, wasn't it? That's what's got you so riled up, isn't it?'

Swanson glared at him. 'You think you're so fucking clever, don't you, Brenton? Think you've got it all figured out, don't you? But do you know what you know?'

Brenton shrugged.

'Fuck all!' His boss turned away, scratched at his head, then took out and checked his mobile. After a few seconds, he turned and looked at Brenton again. 'Yes. It was sent to me. But it wasn't just meant for me... don't look at me like you're in judgement. Just remember that you've done plenty of stupid things in your career. That's exactly why you're going to drop this. You have to drop this before it all goes tits up. Just leave it alone. Walk away.'

Brenton was filled with nausea all of a sudden. 'What about Mandy-Rose? There's more to her murder than meets the eye. It looks like Leonard Jameson was involved in it.'

The Commander spun around and looked through the glass door to see who was in the incident room. 'Shut up, for fuck's sake. Jameson's dead. If he was involved, then he got his just deserts, didn't he? Be happy with that.'

'What about her family?'

Swanson closed his eyes. 'They have closure. A man's in prison. Don't go fucking with all that. It's over.'

'Where's that piece of paper from?'

'For fuck... you want to know too much. It doesn't matter. It's just some paper. You have to let this go. I'm warning you. Let it go before your career goes down the toilet. And they can make that happen really fucking quickly. Trust me.'

'So you expect me to forget about all this? What about DS Wood?'

'You dragged her into. You convince her to keep in line. If you both play nice, then you'll find yourself in a far better position in the near future. I guarantee it.'

'I'll give it some thought,' Brenton said.

Swanson stared at him. 'There's not much for you to think about, is there, Jake? It's the good life or they send you to hell. Don't take too long deciding. They need to know you're going to keep quiet.'

Brenton stared at him, feeling the sickness and anger reach through every part of him until he could no longer look at Swanson. He opened the door and left.

Besnier turned away after making his dramatic statement and walked across to the grand piano in the far corner and started filling the room with some light tune that Jairus didn't recognise. He wheeled himself over and sat staring at the thin, blonde-haired piano man. 'Are you going to tell us what you know?'

The pianist nodded. 'Certainly. In the last ten years of my illustrious career I have found myself in a duel with the forces of darkness. They've tried every trick in the book to discredit me after I began revealing the truth about the illegal wars they've been raging, and all the other evils they've committed in the name of democracy. But the fake democracy they have built is just a flimsy veil that hides something much more sinister.'

Jairus huffed. Besnier paused but then carried on playing the piano. 'Yeah, and?'

Besnier stopped playing and faced him. 'What I'm about to say, you will find hard to believe.'

'You'd be surprised what I'd believe right now,' Jairus said. 'Spit it out.'

'This great country of ours,' Besnier said and turned to face the window. 'This country is not what it seems. The people who govern us, who are supposed to carry out the bidding of the people, answer to another voice. They follow another agenda put forth by the people who have the real power. The banking and oil families, the rich people who have slowly taken ownership of this once great nation and enslaved everyone in debt.'

Jairus nodded. 'Yeah, I pretty much buy that. The system's corrupt. We all know that.'

Besnier faced him. 'How do you make absolutely sure that your politicians do exactly as you wish?'

'You buy them. Bribe them.'

'You've already done that. You've promised them a lucrative job after their term in government. But that's not security. There's always the risk they might disobey your orders. You have to know everything about them, every dirty little secret. You have to blackmail them. You want to invade some little country across the globe that happens to have huge pockets of oil, then you better make sure your prime minister signs the orders. You better have something on him that would destroy him if it was ever made public.'

'Paedophilia,' Cathy said and Besnier looked at her and nodded.

Jairus put his face in his hands and then scratched at his beard. He looked up. 'You're telling me that the British government are made up of paedophiles? Where's your proof?'

Besnier shrugged. 'I have none. Just stories. Information passed down to me from sources I trust. I've tried to get the proof I needed to run the story on my website, but... well, here I am living, not hiding in the ruins of a castle, in a house that no one officially knows exists. There is no modern technology here, Jairus. No mobiles. No laptops. Nothing. I'm safe from them here. I can see you don't believe me.'

'Yeah, well, I tend to need some evidence.'

Cathy moved closer to Besnier and touched his arm. 'Jairus was hired to look into the death of David Coulson, the journalist.'

Jairus watched Besnier as he sat back down at the piano and stared at the keys. 'Do you know anything about his murder?'

'A little.' Besnier pressed a key several times. 'A source in the security services told me he was killed by the British government. I've heard he secured evidence of a secret organisation within the British government that have been blackmailing the same paedophile MPs for their own agenda, whatever that may be. What have you uncovered?'

'I found a list of names on Coulson's wife's laptop.

Two of the names are dead. An MP and a businessman named Howard. Murdered by Tom, whoever he is.'

'If Tom was abused by them as a child,' Besnier said, 'then more than likely they were part of a paedophile ring made up of MPs, lords and other important people that were rumoured to be abusing children at private sex parties throughout the eighties and nineties. They've been allowed to get away with it, so the powers that be could collect their blackmail material. Children from children's homes, others abducted from the streets so that the ring could have their sick pleasures.'

Jairus looked up at Cathy and saw the sympathetic look in her eye. He'd been trying not to think about the fact that Karine's name was on the list he'd found on Pinder's laptop. Her past had always been a mystery to him as she would never go into too much detail. He knew she'd spent time in a children's home before being adopted. His stomach churned at the thought of what he may find out about her past, but there was no way he was going to stop digging. They'd tried to kill him, and he'd taken it very personally.

'Where's Tom now?' Jairus asked Cathy.

'I don't know,' she said. 'He was here, then he left. Said he didn't feel safe staying in one place.'

'Shit!' Jairus closed his eyes, clenched his fists. 'That's great. The one person who could tell me what the bloody hell's going on.'

'I'm sorry, but what were we supposed to do? Tie him up?'

'Yeah, it's what you're used to doing, isn't it?' Jairus said the words before he even registered the spite that they contained.

Cathy turned and walked across the room and left.

'She pretends to be a lot tougher than she really

is,' Besnier said as he stared towards the door she left through. 'You have to wonder what sort of life she's had that led her to the one she's living now.'

'Yeah. How do you know her?'

'Through research. I had people visiting sex clubs and the private parties of the rich and famous. She's a legend in those circles, you know. I arranged to meet her, more out of curiosity than anything else. The more I talked to her, the more I realised I liked her. Which is a rare situation for me, as I hardly like anyone. We've grown quite close.'

Besnier's words cut into him, so Jairus turned his chair towards the door and pushed his jealously away. 'Can you get me a car?'

'Of course. I can get you a clean car, and a driving licence under a different name. So, you're leaving us?'

'Yeah. I need to get to the bottom of all this.'

Besnier nodded. 'She knew you would leave. Let me warn you, Mr Jairus, for Cathy's sake. They will try and kill you again. You've caused them disruption, which means you were on the right track. Through my years looking into the murky world of politics, I've come to realise that the elite group I mentioned does exist and that they have become quite powerful within the British government. They've helped paedophiles reach positions of power so they can use them to help push their own agenda. Douglas Burdock and his father are part of it, and have used their media empire to sway public opinion and destroy any political threat to the agenda of the group. But they're only a small part of it. There are many others involved. Powerful people. There's a leader of the group, but I've never been able to find out who he is. That's who you need to find and bring him to justice.'

The dark clouds were crowding in, swallowing the top of his building, spitting out rain. Burdock watched the constant stream of it cascading down the glass, making it impossible to get a good clear view of his city. It was all just a blur, a brightly coloured blur.

His city. He still thought like that, still believed in what his father told him all those years ago as they stood in a smaller skyscraper looking out at the same city. The city belonged to them, they owned it because they told the people what to think. Want to win a war? Then you have to have the media in your pocket. That's what his father, the racist, pervert used to say.

Now he was standing in the tallest building in London, staring towards the great, green serpent and the old world around it and the new world that swallows it all up.

His mind flickered with a thought, a truth that brought anger into his chest.

Jairus was alive. The security services hadn't done a sufficient job of executing him. How difficult could it be? But it really didn't matter in the grand scheme of things. Jairus had no power, he was a lone wolf, a small voice in an angry storm.

Burdock heard his office door open and listened to the high heels getting closer. He turned and looked into the bright blue eyes of Olivia Henman, the chief editor of The Day, their flagship paper. Her red hair tumbled around her pale, beautiful face as she stared at him without a single drop of joy.

'He's here again,' she said.

'I've been expecting him,' Douglas said and smiled, a smile which completely hid his great annoyance.

'Why do you even entertain him?' Olivia rested herself on his desk.

'Because, my darling, he's an important cog in the

whole machine. An annoying cog, but still... where is he?'

'Same room as always.'

He nodded, smiled and moved quickly across the room and into the wide open space of the floor. His eyes took in the hive of activity, the numerous computer screens, the men and women sat behind the glass partitions that separated their desks as they spoke to the world and listened to it also.

He turned left and headed for the door to the main meeting room and entered.

The man with the dark receding hair and the steel eyes was sitting in the front row of chairs that were always lined up by the back window. He was reading a paper, and didn't raise his eyes when Douglas entered.

'I didn't think you'd be back for a while,' Douglas said, and leaned against the large wooden desk at the centre.

'Didn't you?' the man folded the paper and put it down, took out his mobile phone and put it back in his pocket. 'What with all that's been happening lately? I find that hard to believe.'

'Where's Jairus?' Douglas smiled.

The man looked up. 'I can tell you take great pleasure in unsheathing that knife and sticking it in. Remember, Mr Burdock, I'm here to clean up your mess. You and the others.'

'Yes, I know. But without us, where would you be? With a great deal of politicians thinking for themselves, and not doing exactly what you want them to do.'

'It's not the way I'd be running the show.'

'How would you run it?' Douglas raised his eyebrows.

'Jairus has disappeared. Gone to ground. He's not

in great shape. It'll take him a while to recover. But someone helped him escape from the hospital. Have you any idea who that might be?'

'I thought you were supposed to be the intelligence officer. How is it that you don't know?'

The man stood up and rubbed his hands together. 'Where's Cathy Durbridge?'

Douglas huffed. He was expecting the spy to bring that up, but not quite so soon. 'She was taken to Howard's house. He was meant to have his fun, then dispose of her.'

'But now Howard's dead and Tom is out there somewhere. Is he coming for you next? Because it would be very convenient if he was, then we could scoop him up.'

Douglas clenched his fists. 'I am not one of the men that abused him as a child. I'm not a paedophile. Don't you ever suggest that I am. Anyway, I was nothing more than a kid myself back then. It wasn't my plan to control our government this way. This is your people's doing. You put the paedophiles and psychos in charge so you could control them, and now you've got a group doing exactly what they want to whomever they want. Your people should've seen this coming.'

The man stayed quiet for a moment, but Douglas could see his mind was working overtime. 'Let's forget all that. Let's focus on the major problem we do have right now.'

'And what is that?'

'The stupid policeman that your people decided to use to clear away Leonard Jameson's murder.'

'What about him?'

The man sat down and crossed his legs. 'He's not doing what he's supposed to do. He's supposed to stop digging, but he keeps on pushing. Your people have something on him, something in his past. Isn't that right?'

'Yes. But that's not always a guarantee people will do what they're told. They're unpredictable.'

'Don't tell me about people. I know all about people and their motivations. Their desires. They all want the same thing. To be desired, to get more than they have. And everyone thinks they're better than they are, but they're not. Like you. You think you're so much better than your father...'

'I am better.' Douglas pushed a smile to his face, painfully squeezing it between the thorns that twisted into his facial muscles. 'My father is a bigot, a racist, a pervert who has used the power of the media to bend the world for his own purposes.'

'What about you? And your group? What's your motivation? Why do you help the most detestable and weak men and women into the highest positions of power?'

'To keep the status quo. To stop the rot, to keep the people where they need to be.'

The man laughed and shook his head. 'You keep telling that lie. I believe I know the truth. I think I know what you believe in.'

Douglas stared at him for a moment, wondering how much he really knew or even how much he cared. 'So, the policeman isn't doing what he's supposed to do. What do you expect me to do?'

'That's up to you. Commander Swanson's heart doesn't seem to be in it. I'm just warning you that if the police detective concerned doesn't get brought into line, we'll have to intervene like we did with Jairus.'

'Spell it out. What are you really telling me?'

The man stood up again, straightening his clothes, getting ready to leave, much to the delight of Douglas.

He then looked straight into Douglas' eyes and said, 'I'm telling you so you can tell your leader, that if he's not made to behave, then he's dead.'

CHAPTER 20

Jairus wheeled himself closer to the window and looked beyond the crumbling castle walls, where the forest surrounded them, the floor of it masked by myriad red and golden leaves. 'You really believe there's a secret group, or whatever you call them, orchestrating politics in this country?'

'Who do you think tried to kill you?' Besnier said, and swept his blond hair from his brow. 'What confuses me, is why did Burdock hire you to investigate Coulson's murder?'

'Yeah, that's what I keep wondering. I'll let you know when I find out.' Jairus looked towards the door again. 'I'm sorry, but I need to talk to Cathy.'

Besnier smiled. 'Good. Her room is across the hall. I'll get the car and your new identity ready. I just need to contact my people.'

Jairus began to wheel himself across the room but stopped when a thought occurred to him. 'How do you communicate with the outside world when you don't have any modern technology?'

'I have a man who keeps pigeons on the roof.'

Jairus stared up at Besnier, waiting for him to crack a smile. 'You're joking?'

'I never make jokes. The world is too serious for jokes.'

'OK.' Jairus found himself breaking out in a sweat

as he wheeled his chair across the massive room. His shoulders and arms began to ache with the effort and he was relieved when he reached Cathy's room. He leaned forward and knocked on the door a few times before she opened it.

She stood in the doorway, her right arm resting on the frame. She was dressed only in black bra and knickers, so Jairus fought to keep his eyes from taking in her now more toned body. He also caught sight of the bruises and scratches on her arms and the tops of her shoulders.

'Did Burdock do that?' Jairus asked.

'He did some of it. James Howard did a lot worse.' She turned and walked back into the room.

Fury bit into Jairus as he saw her back and the bandages that covered most of it. There were dark purple, almost black bruises covering her hips.

Her room was much like the rest of the grand house, enormous, painted in pastel colours, and the floor was tiled. Cathy walked to the giant bed and sat on it and crossed her legs.

'I'm sorry about what I said.' Jairus wheeled himself into the room.

'Are you? You shouldn't be. It was the truth. The truth has never really bothered me. It's lies that tend to destroy relationships.'

'Is that what we have? A relationship?'

Cathy stared at him. 'We did. Until you disappeared on me.'

'Yeah, I know what I did. I've said I'm sorry. I just wasn't in a good place.'

He saw the beginnings of a smile on her lips as she said, 'You don't look like you're in a very good place right now. Look at you. You look like you stepped on a landmine.'

'Yeah, but look at you, all black and blue.' He smiled.

'We're a right pair, aren't we? Some would say we're made for each other.' Her smiled faded.

'Yeah, but those people are probably crazy.'

'What are you going to do now? I get the feeling you won't be sticking around for long.'

The sadness in her voice sent a spike of regret through his chest. 'I've asked your new boyfriend to get me a car and a new identity.'

'Toby Besnier is not my boyfriend.' Cathy laughed as if he'd said something absurd.

'Why not? Not your type?'

'He's not anyone's type. He's asexual.'

'That explains a lot.'

Cathy stood up and slowly walked towards him. For a while she stared at him, took him apart. 'You're in no shape to go after them, but I know you well enough to know that you're going to anyway.'

'Yeah, and I know you well enough to know that you'd be disappointed if I didn't.'

'True. I would.' He helplessly watched as she bent down and gently touched his hand, her eyes finding his. 'I know we've been apart, me doing my sex thing, you doing your drinking, self-pity thing, but it doesn't feel like anything's changed between us. Or am I wrong?'

'You're not wrong.' The same old mixture of desire and fear entwined themselves in his heart and mind as she gripped his hand tighter. 'We're still both incendiary.'

She gave a quiet smile, that told him she agreed but that she no longer cared about the consequences. She began to pull him upwards. 'Can you make it to my bed?'

His eyebrows rose automatically, then his eyes jumped to the large bed. 'I'm supposed to be getting ready to leave.'

'You're not going anywhere trussed up like you are. I'll ask Toby to get one of those leg casts you can walk on and something less bulky for your arm.'

He nodded, not knowing what else to say as Cathy helped him up out of the wheelchair. She got under his arm and helped him hobble over to the bed. She turned him round and lowered him to the bed.

She stood before him, her hands on her hips, looking him over. Then her hands pushed him backwards to the bed. The pain killers allowed only a light cry from his ribs as he laid back on the bed. Cathy climbed over him, and slipped off her bra, allowing him to take in her naked breasts.

'I know you're not in any fit state for this sort of business,' she said, smiling. 'So I'll do all the work.'

He laid back, watching her do her thing, helpless, feeling the stress and the pain leaving his body and mind.

He listened to the sound of the whisky filling his glass, looking down to the brown liquid shining in the light of the kitchen. Brenton was staring out of the window of the flat he was now renting. He hadn't thought he'd be in North London long, so he grabbed the first reasonable place he laid eyes on. Two bedrooms, not badly decorated, small kitchen. He didn't care where he lived – it wasn't like the old days when he had to think about the wife and kids, and trying to keep a nice and pleasant environment around them all. All he really needed was a bed and chair, which he'd purchased from a second-hand shop, a small TV bought cheap from a local electrical shop. There was an oven included, but he didn't have time to cook and didn't really enjoy it anyway.

He looked down at the big brown, grease-stained paper bag that contained his Chinese takeaway and sighed as he took out his phone. He had the urge to hear a friendly voice, and just about the only person he knew who understood what he was going through was Wood. But he didn't want her dragged deeper into whatever was going on. He rubbed his face, scratched his beard and stared out into the street. It was a main road and a lot of cars were still coming past, even though it was nearly ten o'clock.

He couldn't get Swanson's desperate voice and eyes out of his head. There was a cover-up in process and Commander Swanson was up to his eyeballs in it. The taste of puke hadn't left his mouth since his conversation with the brass had ended, same as the image of a lifeless, raped, beaten Mandy-Rose stayed with him, nestled uncomfortably with all the other horrors he carried with him. He'd made the mistake of looking up the crime scene photographs and now they had burrowed deep inside him. A little girl's voice was speaking to him, asking him why the terrible things she'd endured had been done to her.

He pushed the voice away, deafened himself to it.

It was over. If he kept digging around he would be finished, with no job, no power to catch the next evil bastard that decided to take a young child, abuse them and…

He'd catch the next bastard for Mandy-Rose, in her name. A man was in prison for her murder anyway.

Yes, a man who said he hadn't killed her.

'Shit!' Brenton slapped his hands down on the work surface, bent over, gritting his teeth. 'Fuck!'

He stood up again, rubbing his face, as he heard his

mobile ringing in his jacket pocket. He took it out and saw that Wood was calling him. He laughed sadly for a moment, listening to the chime, trying to think of a way to tell her that they had to back off. He knew the words would stick in his throat, threaten to choke him.

He took a deep breath and answered the call. 'Hey, you all right?'

'Yes, I'm fine,' she said, but she sounded a little distant.

'Are you sure?'

She let out a harsh breath. 'What the fuck are we doing?'

'I wish I knew.' He moved to the window and saw a car pull up opposite.

'What did Swanson say?'

His stomach tightened. Here it was, the moment of truth. 'He wants us to drop it.'

'Jesus... that fucking... what did you tell him?'

Brenton didn't answer, he was still staring at the car parked across the street. Then his eyes jumped to a blonde woman who appeared in his field of vision who was heading to the car. The driver peered out and smiled at her as she walked round and climbed into the passenger seat. He let out a breath as the car took off.

'What's wrong?' Wood said.

'Nothing. I'm getting paranoid.'

'I know what you mean. There's something heavy going down. I mean, who can put the pressure on to get this shelved?'

'I hate to think.' Brenton turned to his takeaway bag and prodded it a little, but the sickness filling his stomach removed his appetite. 'Listen...'

'You sound serious all of a sudden.'

'Do I?'

There was a pause, the longest pause and he waited for her voice to come back as if it was the guillotine coming for his neck.

'Please don't tell me that you're going to do as you're told like a good little boy?' she said.

He closed his eyes, knowing that he was about to lose her respect for ever. How could he explain that it would mean the end of their careers, their reputations if they kept on going, and all the dirt they would have on him would come flooding out? He wanted to cry as he said, 'What choice do we have?'

'What did they promise you to keep you quiet? For fuck's sake, it was you who kept pushing me into this. What about Mandy-Rose, and her family?'

'They didn't promise me...'

'Really? Prove it to me. Keep digging. For instance, this watermark on the paper... it looked like an island, didn't it?'

He rubbed his eyes. 'Yes, but it's just a watermark. It doesn't...'

'Look it up. Knowing you, you probably traced the outline of the image. Yeah?'

Brenton walked to his solitary second-hand chair and slumped into it, then he took out his notebook and flipped through the pages until he found the sketch he'd drawn of the watermark. 'Yes. But what good will it do?'

'Look it up. Find that island. It must have some relevance to the person who had the paper made. Why else would it be there?'

Brenton stared at the drawing for a while, listening to her breathing, and his own. He got up and fetched his laptop and rested it on his lap as he turned it on and waited for it to boot up. 'What if we find such an island exists? What then?'

'That's up to you.' She stifled a yawn. 'But in all bleeding honesty, can you really walk away from this when you know there's a chance that others might be involved in Mandy-Rose's murder?'

He didn't say anything; he didn't have to because she already knew the answer.

When his laptop was ready, he put his fingers on the keyboard and said, 'This Island could be anywhere.'

'Then start at home and spread out. We could get lucky. Look, I'm tired and I'm going to get some sleep. Let me know what you find.'

He put his mobile down and thought for a moment, trying to figure out how he was going to find the right island without searching through every island in the entire world. Then he had an idea.

He fetched a black marker pen and drew another version of the island, took a snap of it on his mobile and uploaded it to his laptop. He then searched for photo and shape recognition apps and found one called FindIt.

He had to enter a few lines of information, which was what he was looking for: an island, and where it might be in the world. He started close to home entered the British Isles, then got himself another glass of whisky and sat back down, expecting the search to take a while.

His eyes widened when he was back in the seat. The software had found four islands that looked similar to the watermark, but only one of them was a close match. It was called Tebel Island, and was situated close to the Isles Of Scilly, off the coast of Cornwall. There wasn't much there according to the Google search he did on the island, apart from a large exclusive hotel and a few apartments situated right on the beach front.

He sipped his drink, wondering if the paper belonged to the hotel. But why would that fact be guarded in so much secrecy?

He spun his head towards the window when the sound of a woman shouting and screaming filled his ears. He pulled himself up, still with his drink in his hand and headed to the window. He looked down and saw a couple, probably in their thirties, tussling in the street. The man was grasping her arm as she was trying to get away from him. He sighed as he saw the young woman punching his chest, shouting for him to get off.

Brenton looked about the dark empty street, hoping for some bystander to intervene, but there was no one listening apart from him. Also, he knew that even if there was someone passing by, the chances are they would ignore the woman's plight. Nobody in London wants any trouble.

Then he started listening to his paranoia, the troubled voice telling him this could be a set-up to get him outside.

The woman broke away and started along the street, still screaming over her shoulder. The man stood there for a moment, staring. Then he was running suddenly, shouting, grabbing her. He turned her round and grabbed her by the throat.

'Shit.' Brenton grabbed his ID, pulled open the door and hammered his feet down the stairwell, headed through the main door and out onto the street.

He was breathing hard, standing watching the couple walking off drunkenly across the road, heading off into the sunset.

He shook his head, half relieved to see them disappear, half annoyed to be dragged out into the cold night air. He found his cigarettes and lighter in his jacket pocket and lit one. He took a few puffs, as he thought about the island and wondered what it was all about, what the connection could possibly be.

He dropped the cigarette as he shivered, then hurried back into the building and let himself into his flat. He walked to the kitchen, his eyes fixing on the takeaway bag, then he stopped as a feeling of unease washed over him.

It was movement that made his heart pump harder. Behind him a figure came from the kitchen doorway. He jerked round, his heart pounding, his hands clenched into fists. The man was stocky, staring at him with neither anger or any emotion he recognised.

'What the fuck are you doing in my flat?' Brenton shouted as the man kept heading for him. He looked round and saw the kitchen table and grabbed for it, pushing it between them.

But the man stopped it with his hands and hurled it out of the way.

Another man, slimmer, just as nonchalant as the first, came into the small kitchen. Like the first, he had nothing in his hands, and was armed only with a look of concentration.

Brenton dived to the wall as the first man made a grab for him, his eyes looking around for a weapon. He had no sharp knives and damned himself for not bothering to get any.

A hand grabbed his wrist and twisted his arm at the same time as there was sudden jab of pain to his leg. His knees crumpled as his right arm was almost torn out of its socket and jerked backwards. His hand was twisted and the pain stabbed through his arm and shoulder.

'Don't struggle,' the first man said, pushing Brenton down further.

He tried to pull himself away, but the pressure made it feel as his arm might snap.

'Fuck you!' Brenton bellowed. 'Get the fuck off me! I'm a policeman, you arsehole! I'm a fucking policeman!'

The second man brought his square, pale face and light blue eyes closer to Brenton as he crouched down. 'We know who you are. We're sorry as hell. But these are orders.'

'Orders?' Brenton felt his whole body shaking with anger and fear. 'Whose orders? Go and tell them to come and see me themselves. Fuck you!'

As he watched the second man reach into his pocket and take out a strip of tablets, it started to dawn on Brenton what was happening and how much trouble he was really in. He saw the man pop the pill from the strip then look up at him.

'Open your mouth,' the man said.

'Fuck off!' Brenton tried to break free again, but he was held tight, unable to move without the blades of pain attacking his arm.

Then he was hit in the throat. A jab had been landed in his neck and his mouth burst open as he coughed and fought for breath. A hand gripped his mouth and squeezed his jaw, while fingers penetrated his mouth. The pill was pushed into his throat, making him gag and choke, a hand then clamped down over his nose and mouth.

'Swallow!' the man gripping him shouted.

Brenton fought for breath, jerking his head side to side, trying to pull himself up. He wanted to spit, anything to stop the pill going down his throat. Already he could taste its chemical flavour as it began to dissolve on his tongue.

The boom of his heart filled his ears as he began to

struggle to take a breath.

Then he swallowed.

He had no choice. As soon as he'd swallowed, the man released his nose so he could breath again.

'Fuck you!' Brenton shouted against his hand. 'What the fuck was that?'

No one answered him, both men simply kept hold of him, their eyes finding each other, or the rest of the room. The second man checked his watch.

Brenton let out a harsh breath when the first painful tingle shot through his left arm. His heart hammered even more in his chest, his ribs and flesh becoming tight. He gritted his teeth when a red-hot poker seemed to burn straight through his chest.

He could feel the blood pounding, flooding through him.

Then he couldn't take anymore, and he let himself go, falling backwards into the nothingness, his mind focusing on Wood as the night seemed to swallow him.

CHAPTER 21

They had to wait two days before the doctor could arrive to check Jairus' injuries and see if he was OK to travel. But his mind was set anyway; he'd decided that whatever the quack said, he'd be hobbling out of the fucked-up prison that Besnier had constructed around himself.

He waited patiently in his room, sitting on the bed, waiting for the doctor to come in while his whole body was ready to burst with angst, and his mind battled an army of demons. There was part of him that wanted to curl up and hide somewhere, the fearful part of him that still wanted the comfort of his mother when death seemed to be close. The rest of him was alive, heating his blood, filling him full of hate and fury, desperate to get his hands on the bastards that had tried to kill him and murdered the Pinders and their neighbour.

Jairus looked up when he heard the slap of shoes coming towards his room and watched the floor beneath the archway, waiting for the shadow.

A middle-aged woman with reddish brown, greying hair, tied back in a ponytail entered the room. She wore grey trousers and a white blouse under a long black wool coat. She carried a doctor's bag and put it down by the bed, and looked at Jairus, examining him head to foot.

As she took off her coat and put on some latex

gloves, she said, 'You look in pretty good shape for a man who ended up in the middle of a pile up.'

'Yeah, luck was on my side.'

She smiled slightly. 'That's one way of looking at it. On the other hand, the reason I'm here treating you and you're not at a hospital tells me a great deal. Take off your shirt.'

Jairus did as he was told and sat upright as the doctor pressed her fingers against his strapped-up torso.

'Someone wanted me dead,' Jairus said and she looked up into his eyes.

'I don't want to know. Mr Besnier pays me quite well to mind my own business. You've broken several ribs, but if you keep them strapped up, they should heal OK. None of them are out of place.'

'What about my foot?'

She knelt down and looked his foot over, and gently prodded the cast and his bare, bruised flesh. She got up, opened her bag and took out a pair of long silver scissors and began cutting away at the cast at the back of his foot.

Soon his foot was free of the cast and he could see the black, red and blue bruising that covered his foot.

'It's no longer swollen,' the doctor said and stood up. 'That's a good sign.'

'Yeah, I guess. What happens to it now?'

'Well, we've got a new treatment for broken feet.'

'Yeah, and what's that?'

She smiled. 'Walking on them. That's what we advise. Have a go.'

Jairus pushed himself off the bed and onto his good foot, keeping the broken one up and tucked in. He tentatively put the broken foot on the ground and automatically flinched.

'Don't be afraid if you hear a cracking sound,' the doctor said. 'That's just the bones snapping back into place.'

Jairus took a couple of hobbling steps forward and raised his broken arm. 'What about this?'

'That I'd keep on for a couple more weeks if you can. Right, I've got pain killers, and all the other medication I was asked to bring. I'm afraid you'll be a limping pharmacy for a while. By the way, you might want to think about booking yourself into rehab when you have time.'

'Yeah, I will. When I have time. Thanks.'

The doctor smiled a little sadly and watched him as he took a few more careful steps. 'That's it. Put some weight on it. I'd wish you good luck with whatever you're doing, but seeing as you're still in once piece so far tells me all I need to know. You're a survivor.'

'Yeah, I hope so. Thanks again.'

The doctor picked up her bag and headed to the archway, then stopped and turned around. 'You know, Toby Besnier is a survivor too.'

'Yeah, because he hides away.'

The doctor nodded. 'Think about that.'

No sooner had the doctor left, Cathy came in carrying a large rucksack on her back and pulling a suitcase on wheels behind her. She was dressed in tight black jeans, boots and a dark red jumper. She dumped the bags down and looked him over. 'You set? Doctor give you the all clear?'

'Yeah, she did. We leaving already?'

'I figured you'd want to get on the road as quickly as possible. The car's here. Looks like it rolled off Ford's first production line, but that's the point, isn't it?'

He laughed. 'Yeah. Driving licences?'

'All the IDs are here. I picked up a couple of disposable mobiles too and a bunch of SIM cards.'

'Good. Don't suppose you've got a suit for me to wear?'

She smiled, held up a finger, then headed out of the room for a minute before coming back with a suit bag which she placed on the bed. 'Dark suit. Black tie. Light blue shirt. OK?'

He nodded. 'Perfect. Let's get going.'

'What are you going to do?'

He stared into her eyes. 'What I always do. Raise bloody hell.'

DS Wood was sitting in a chair behind one of the battered desks in Southgate police station's incident room. A man in overalls was drilling away, taking the computers away, closing down the operation. She kept watching the glass door, waiting, her skin crawling with hate, fear and every different emotion that seemed to be rampaging through her since she'd learnt of DI Brenton's death. She put her face in her hands and breathed out, held back the tears, swallowed it all down. Her mind hadn't quite accepted he was gone. Like in every cliché about death she expected him to walk in smelling of cigarettes, unshaven, but smiling.

She turned when she heard the doors squeak open and saw Commander Swanson practically marching towards his temporary office. She'd made some calls and managed to find out that he was coming over to pick up some files he'd locked in his desk.

She got up and headed towards him. 'Sir? Commander Swanson?'

He had his hand on the door handle when he stopped and looked at her. Automatically his face fell into sympathy mode as he said, 'DS Wood. It's good to see you. I was knocked for six...'

'Can I have a word, sir?'

Swanson looked round the office. 'We're talking now.'

'In there?' She gestured to the office.

He lost all pretence of politeness and quickly opened the door and held it open for her. 'Sit down.'

She did, and kept herself in check, keeping the suspicions and anxiousness from her face, her body. She fought her natural urge to bite her nails. It was a childish habit that she despised in herself.

'I take it this is about DI Brenton?' he said as he sat in the chair opposite. 'We're all in shock. Bloody hell, a heart attack. Jesus, could happen to any of us.'

'Is that definite? I didn't think the post mortem had been done yet.'

Swanson sat back, staring at her, his eyes peeling back her skull. 'It hasn't. But the paramedics said that's what it looked like. Remember, that he didn't live a very healthy life style. Heavy smoking. Drinking. Takeaway food. I believe he'd ordered a Chinese that evening. It takes its toll.'

Wood ran through the speech she'd written in her head, but little seemed relevant and most of it ridiculous. 'He was under a lot of pressure and stress.'

Swanson pointed at her briefly. 'Good point. He was.'

Wood prepared her words, but they clung to her lips for a few seconds. 'His lifestyle... his general lack of fitness, the smoking... if... if someone wanted to see the back of him, then making it look like he had a heart attack wouldn't be difficult, would it?'

Swanson stared at her, anger slowly emerging in his eyes. 'I'm going to pretend that I didn't hear that ridiculous notion.'

'Do you want me to repeat it?' Wood felt herself shaking all over.

'No! I do not. Let me make myself clear, DS Wood. If you want to keep your job, you will never mention that theory of yours again. Do you understand me?'

'Understood. When's the post mortem?'

Swanson looked at his bulky silver watch. 'Round about now actually. It's taking place at the morgue in Edmonton Police Station. We should get answers soon.'

'Good.' She swore in her own head, dug her fingers into her palms.

'I'm going to send flowers to his wife.' Swanson looked solemn.

'His ex-wife. Quite frankly, I don't think she could give a shit about him.'

'Still...'

Wood stood up, unable to keep her anger in check for much longer. 'I better get back to my former station... the workload's building up.'

Swanson nodded. 'That's it. Get stuck in. It helps.'

She stopped in the doorway as a thought occurred to her about the post mortem. 'I take it the post mortem's being performed by Dr Jeremy Garrett?'

Swanson sat back. 'Actually, it's not. They're getting another pathologist in.'

She walked back to his desk, her suspicions multiplying, swarming her entire body. 'What? What's wrong with Garrett?'

'I don't know. I guess they wanted someone they trust, who they've worked with before. Look, you'll be told the results, same as everybody else.'

Wood took out her phone, looked at the time. 'When did you say it was being carried out?'

'Anytime now...'

Wood stormed towards the door, pulled it open and slammed it shut behind her.

Jairus' memory of actually leaving the castle home of Toby Besnier was only hazy as the drugs formed a nest of cotton wool and dough around his brain. He had a sense that Cathy was driving as vertical strips of brown and clouds of green raced past. Puddles of golden brown and red covered the ground.

He shut his eyes again and when he opened them, the autumnal colours had been ripped away and replaced by the noisy silver and grey of London. He watched a red double decker bus screech, hiss and overtake them, and sat up to take a look at the city he felt like he hadn't laid eyes on in years.

'Welcome back to the real world,' Cathy said with a gentle smile that seemed touched with sadness.

'Yeah, beats castles and forests.' He rubbed his face and eyes.

'Where first?'

He looked round, read the road signs, grasped hold of his bearings. 'Join the North Circular, get off at Edmonton, then head for Ponders End. I've got a lock-up there.'

She looked at him. 'Is that where you keep your darkest secrets?'

'Some. But mostly it's where I keep my past.'

She huffed, then drove them to their destination and carefully crawled the car down the narrow alleyways and parked close to a set of battered lock-ups.

Jairus climbed out and stared at the familiar metal door, mentally preparing himself for the ghosts that waited for him inside. He fished the key out of his pocket, unlocked the door, hitched it open.

Cathy joined him as he slipped under the door

and switched on the fluorescent light that flickered, burning his eyes. He limped towards the shelves of books and the piles of cardboard boxes.

'What are we looking for?' Cathy said, and picked up one of the books and flicked through it.

Jairus looked over everything that belonged to Karine and everything it represented. He didn't believe in ghosts, but a big part of him wanted to speak to the walls, to the memories, and ask her who she really had been. Slowly but surely the realisation was growing inside him that he hadn't really known her at all. In the last weeks together, he had sensed she had a secret, but typically he'd suspected infidelity.

He enclosed his face in his hands, sighed, then looked around the small brick room again. 'Her phone's here somewhere. We need it. We also need to find any addresses of old friends, family, anyone she might've talked to before she died.'

Cathy nodded. 'OK. I'm not usually the sensitive type, but I can't help feeling a bit weird about going through your ex's stuff.'

'Don't be. It needs to be done. Forget sentiment, it doesn't do anyone any good.' Jairus headed over to the boxes and started ripping them open and sorting through the piles of photos and paperwork he found, while he sensed Cathy watching before she dared to join in.

There wasn't much in the first few boxes, just lots of bank statements, old bills, and more photographs. He found a smaller box, ripped it open and found three mobile phones. They predated the smart phones, and looked like small grey bricks. 'Which one of these is the later model?'

Cathy came over, looked them over and pointed to the smaller silver phone. 'That one.'

'Yeah, I thought so. If I turn this on, they could get a track on it. They probably have her old number in the system.'

'Who? You're talking about MI5?'

Jairus shrugged. 'Whoever tried to kill me. That was well executed. No one questions a car crash. But let's say it is the secret service, then as soon as I turn this on, they'll have our location.'

'Then what do we do?'

Jairus put the phones into his pockets. 'We go and see Rich Vincent. If anyone can get the info off these devices without setting off the alarm bells, it's him.'

'OK. Where is he?' Cathy turned to another box and started opening it.

'I've no idea. Probably shacked up with his new girlfriend if he's got any sense. Far away from this shit.'

Cathy huffed. 'But you're going to drag him back into it?'

'Yeah, it's what I do. What's in that box?'

'More photos. Oh, and a quite a number of postcards.' Cathy held out a bundle of postcards held together by an elastic band.

Jairus took them and read through them. 'That's weird. Several postcards sent from the same female to Karine dating back roughly two years before she died. Janine Latch.'

'Did Karine ever mention her?'

'Never.'

'No offence, but a lot of the time you men don't hear what we're saying. Even when you do listen, you don't hear what we're really saying.'

'That's because you talk in code.' Jairus flipped through the cards again. 'They all say the same things basically. Having a nice time. Having a lovely time.'

'That's what people write on postcards.' Cathy went on to the next box.

'Yeah, I know. But these were all sent from the same place every week over two years. Who does that?'

'What do you think?'

Jairus peeled back the stamp. Underneath was a series of numbers and letters printed carefully in biro. Each card had similar numbers and letters. 'It's a code. Fuck. What were they scared of?'

'We have to find her.'

Jairus held up the first postcard. 'She's in Great Yarmouth. Let's go and find Rich first though.'

DS Wood gained entry to Edmonton Police Station, and then got directions from a passing female constable to the morgue which was in the basement not far from the cells and the IT department. She hurried down the stairs, her anger entwined with self-loathing. Why hadn't she gone over to see him that night?

Tiredness and the draw of her warm bed had been too strong and now Brenton was dead.

Was he even killed? It was a ridiculous notion and easily put down to paranoia, but there was the cold feeling in her stomach that kept echoing her suspicions.

She came to a sudden stop a hundred yards from the large doors of the morgue when she saw a thickset, blond-haired PC on the door.

She approached as casually as possible and produced her ID. 'DS Kate Wood. Hi, is that DI Brenton's post mortem going on in there?'

The PC looked over his shoulder then nodded. 'It is. Bloody terrible business. You never know when your time's up.'

'You mind if I take a look?'

The PC sighed, then slowly shook his head. 'Sorry, boss, but orders. I'm not allowed to let anyone in, not even the Queen.'

'Fuck.' She ran her hands through her hair, now feeling the swell of fury taking over. She swung round and slapped the wall. 'The fucking... bastards!'

'You all right, boss?' The PC looked sympathetically at her.

'Yes, I'm fine. Can you tell me if Dr Garrett is in there?'

'No, boss, he was in there in the beginning, but left in a bit of a huff. Think he's in his office back down the corridor.'

Wood turned on the spot, found the pathologist's office and hammered her fist on the door. 'Dr. Garrett?!'

The door opened and the lanky, bespectacled figure of Dr Garrett, dressed in light blue scrubs, stood looking down at her. 'Hello. You want to join me in drowning my sorrows?'

Wood watched as his bony white hand produced a metal cup from a flask. 'It's whisky.'

'No thanks, doctor.' Wood gestured to the post mortem room. 'How come you're not in there?'

'Come in,' he said and stepped back, revealing his pokey cluttered office that was filled with books, a large antique desk and a small stereo. The quiet music coming from the stereo seemed to be Johnny Cash, but she couldn't be sure.

She entered and watched him shut the door behind her then take a sip of his drink.

'Firstly,' he said, looking gravely at her. 'Let me give my condolences. I know I only met your partner once, but he seemed...'

'I've always hated that term. Partner. Sounds American... and a bit like we were sleeping together or something.'

Garrett raised his drink. 'Hear, hear. But I am sorry.'

'So, why aren't you in there?'

Garrett sat at his desk. 'Because they've shipped in another pathologist. If you can call him that.'

'What do you mean? You know him?'

Garrett nodded sagely. 'I'm afraid I do. Dr Henry Wilson. The man barely made it through medical school, and since then he's been involved in numerous potential medical scandals. Thing is, he's always managed to dig himself out of the hole he's found himself in. Or I should say his very expensive lawyers have. He's also an alcoholic drug addict.'

'Jesus... what the fuck is he doing in there? Have you told them what you know?'

He took another drink. 'It wouldn't make a blind bit of difference. The reason Wilson is in there and I'm not, is because he'll do as he's told. He's the man they bring in when there's big money or reputations at stake. They tell him what they want in the post mortem results and he signs on the dotted.'

Wood pulled out a chair and slumped into it and put her face in her hands. When she looked up, Garrett was pouring himself another drink. 'What are we going to do?'

'You tell me what exactly we can do. By the time an investigation does get started into Brenton's death, if you can convince anyone that he was killed... I take it that's what you believe... and why Wilson's in there... well, by the time you get an exhumation order, the body will be too degraded to tell you anything useful. Not forgetting that if Wilson is here because of the reason you believe, then someone high up has arranged it. They won't make it easy for you. I'll tell you this, Wood, in my early days I carried out post mortems in connection with airline crashes or involving manslaughter caused by large corporations... and they play dirty. Very dirty. I'm here now because I wanted to get away from all that. Murder seemed a lot simpler. Now here I am again. I haven't drunk whisky in years.'

'Are you saying I'm stuffed? There's nothing I can do? They've won? My friend's possibly been murdered and I've got to smile and... fucking... suck it up?'

He put down his drink and leaned forward and lowered his voice. 'No, I'm not saying there's nothing you can do. What I'm actually saying, is that if you go down the official route, then you'll find yourself at a dead end.'

Wood sat back and stared at him, trying to read him. 'What if you could get a look at the post mortem report?'

'A look at his body would be better.' He took another drink. 'But they'll want to bury or cremate him as soon as possible. It doesn't give us a lot of time.'

'No, not very long at all.' She smiled.

CHAPTER 22

Cathy parked the car in the quiet little street, opposite the row of twelve identical and neat redbrick houses that Jairus knew had been sold very cheaply in the last five years. They were part of the development that had been built in the middle of the wasteland between Ponders End and Edmonton, where the old factories had been long since pulled down. The reason the houses had been sold off cheap was because nobody in their right mind wanted to put up with the smell from the nearby sewerage works that made the place stink like a pig farm.

As Cathy climbed out and held her nose, she said, 'Who the hell would live here?'

'Someone who wants cheap housing,' Jairus said, getting out and limping towards number six. They'd managed to track down a couple of Rich's band members and found his new girlfriend was presently living with the pungent stench.

Cathy rang the doorbell, and looked Jairus over. 'Perhaps you should keep out of sight. The sight of you will probably give her nightmares.'

'I don't think so. She's a goth by all accounts.'

'I hate goths.'

'Yeah? Why's that?'

'They pretend to enjoy living in a world full of dark feelings and emotions. If they really came face to face with true darkness they'd suck their thumbs and scream for their mummies.'

The door was opened by a slender, porcelain-skinned young woman. Her hair was crow black, as was her skirt and punk style t-shirt.

Her green eyes flickered between them. 'Er... hello? If you're here to talk about God...'

'No, we're all out of bibles,' Jairus said, limping closer. 'Rich home?'

A look of realisation took hold of her pale skin. 'You must be the legendary Jairus.'

'He is,' Cathy said. 'I'm Cathy. Is he home?'

A screech of electric guitar echoed from within the house, and they all looked towards it. The girl looked back at them. 'He's been playing guitar all morning. Maybe you can get him to give it a rest.'

The girl let them in, and told them to head to the lounge on the right. Jairus hobbled beside her, giving her the once over. 'I didn't catch your name.'

'Ivy,' she said and looked down at his leg. 'You look like you were in a car crash.'

'Yeah, I was.'

'Sorry. Got a mouth on me.' She directed him and Cathy into the small, messy lounge.

The walls were dark purple, the dark wood shelves filled with vinyl. Rich was kneeling by a huge amp, resting his electric guitar on one leg. He looked over, saw Jairus and clambered to his feet, a big smile of relief spreading across his face.

'Jesus... fuck me,' Rich said, breaking out into a laugh. 'Look at the state of you! I'm glad to see you're alive though, mate. The bastards can't keep you down for long.'

'No, they can't.' Jairus slumped onto a brown leather sofa. 'That's what I want to talk to you about.'

Rich lost his mirth, looked at Cathy, Ivy, then back at Jairus. 'What do you mean?'

Jairus took out the three mobile phones and put them on the floor by Rich's feet. 'I need another favour. Look, thing is, these people mean business... I've upset the apple cart... well, actually, I've pretty much pissed all over their apples... and now they want to kill me.'

Rich smiled. 'You're warning me off?'

'Perhaps you should listen to him,' Ivy said, a hardness clear in her voice.

Jairus looked at her. 'Yeah, perhaps you should this time.'

Rich looked at Ivy, then down at the phones. 'Who else is going to help you? I'm sorry, Ivy, but I have to help. I can't just sit back...'

'All right,' she said, then headed out of the room.

The guilt dug into Jairus, but he ignored it and pushed himself to his feet. 'I'm sorry, mate, but I've got no one else to turn to.'

Rich picked up the phones and shrugged. 'Fuck it, mate. Fuck it. What are friends for?'

'Not messing up your love life.' Jairus gripped his shoulder. 'Thanks though.'

'I've got my gear set up in the spare room.' Rich walked out into the hall, his eyes on the mobiles.

'You can stay down here,' Jairus said to Cathy as he followed Rich out of the room and up the beige carpeted stairs. Cathy didn't say anything, just nodded and sat down.

Rich took him into a box room that had a small window, a black battered desk, a leather office chair, and a monster of a PC and three monitors attached to it sat on the desk.

Rich sat in the office chair and put the mobiles on the desk. 'I take it we can't turn these mobiles on?'

'Yeah, you got it. No doubt that's what they're waiting for.'

Rich started opening up the phones and taking out the SIM cards. 'Any idea who they are?'

'Not really, nothing for certain. Looks like Leonard Jameson and James Howard were into child abuse and were killed by one of their victims. Thing is, Burdock put me on to this case, but turns out he was in league with Howard.'

'What? Then why would he get you to look into Coulson's murder?'

'I'm beginning to think I was used to get to someone. They knew I'd do a thorough job of looking into Coulson's murder, and end up leading them where they needed to go. Makes me sick to think of it, but maybe I helped them cover something up. Pinder's neighbour is dead because of me. Maybe others have been targeted because of what I found out.'

'You didn't kill them. They did. Sounds like Coulson must've have stumbled onto something too.'

Jairus nodded and watched Rich load up the information from the SIM cards.

Rich looked at him, his brow creased up. 'These are Karine's phones?'

'Yeah. I need to know what she was up to before she died. She was keeping secrets from me and her name was on that list you found on Pinder's laptop.'

Rich nodded and started tapping away at the keyboard, scrolling through reams of information that Jairus couldn't make head nor tail of.

'Want to give me something to look for?' Rich said.

Jairus rubbed his beard and eyes, thinking back to the weeks and months before the terrible, haunting day that he found her lying on the bathroom floor. The memory grasped his heart and squeezed his stomach as if he was standing in the hollow, echoing bathroom again, looking down at himself, listening to his voice shouting her name as he shook her still body. He pushed backwards, his mind reaching further to a few weekends when she had gone to visit friends while he'd been working solidly. She'd gone and come back without him even noticing.

'Look for any periods when the phone left London,' he said, looking over Rich's shoulder.

'OK.' Rich started scrolling again. 'Right, she left London on a few weekends.... went to... Great Yarmouth it looks like. Can't see any other trips away.'

Jairus took out the pack of postcards Cathy had found in the lock up. 'Can you pinpoint an address?'

'Yep. Dickens Avenue, not far from the beach. Could be just a mate she was visiting, nothing else.'

Jairus showed him the postcards. 'Someone sent her these every week for two years before she died. There's a code under the stamp.'

Rich pulled out a postcard and peeled back the stamp. 'He let out a laugh.'

'What is it?'

'Well, I might be wrong, but the numbers and letters look like a library serial number. Each of these could refer to a book. I'd check the local library, maybe? Your woman here, the one who sent these, may have been leaving a message in those books.'

Jairus patted him on the back. 'See, that's why I need you, Rich. Apart from the fact that you're about the only friend I've got left.'

'Don't, you'll have me crying in a minute. Oh, and I thought I'd better keep those j-pegs handy. You know, the ones I found on Pinder's laptop. I printed them out for you.'

Jairus watched him look under the desk and open

up a folder. He handed him two small photographs. One seemed to be of a large hotel that was set back from a beach. The other was a shot of a kebab shop in a busy high street. 'Any idea where these were taken?'

'Yes, I do.' Rich took the beach front photograph from him and held it up. 'This is of the beach on Tebel island. The same island that Coulson had photos of on his computer. Coincidence? I don't think so. And the kebab shop is in Balham High Street. Why the hell would anyone want a pic of a kebab shop?'

'Yeah, that is a mystery. What about the island? Find out anything about it?'

'Well, that's the weird thing. As hard as I've looked, I can't find much at all. To book any of the hotel rooms, you have to be loaded. That's about it. When there's not much about a place or person online, makes me feel like someone has worked extremely hard to hide something.'

Jairus examined the photographs again. 'Yeah, does make me curious. But what does an island and a kebab shop have to do with Coulson's murder, or the Pinders for that matter?'

'Search me. What're you going to do next?'

Jairus picked up one of the postcards. 'I'm going to go and visit this person and see if they know what the hell's going on.'

DS Wood was sitting in a dusty corridor, looking down at the myriad slats of wood that made up the polished floor, counting them and losing count. They had the same floors in schools, and the whole place smelt like a school. She was actually seated in a corridor in an old building in the grounds of Highlands Hospital, trying to organise her thoughts, and build a plan of action.

Down the other end of the corridor was a door that she'd watched all the other people enter one by one and then leave. She waited, watching for the last patient to come out so she could go in there and say what she needed to say.

She looked up when she heard the door open and an old, hunched-up man came out coughing into his handkerchief. The door shut again and so Wood hurried down the hallway and knocked on the door. Anger inspired questions and accusations that fought for supremacy in her brain as she read the name on the door.

Dr Teresa Brenton.

A cold voice from within told her to enter. She opened the door and walked in, but stood in the doorway of the small but neat doctor's office for a moment, waiting for the slightly plump, dark-haired and smartly-dressed woman to look up.

'Do you have an appointment?' Dr Brenton said without any sign of warmth in her dark eyes.

'You don't recognise me?' Wood said, and looked round the office, which she realised was devoid of any character, much like the woman sitting at the desk looking at her with a blank expression.

'No... do I know you?'

'Not really. We only met once. It was at a works do a while back.'

The doctor shook her head ever so slightly. 'I'm a bit lost.'

Wood took out her ID and slipped it across the desk, then watched as the doctor looked at it and the realisation made only the slightest change to her composure. She looked up. 'I remember now. It's been a long time. I'm sorry...'

Wood waved a hand, then took back her ID. 'Save

it. How're you coping?'

'It's a shock... I can't...'

'You hadn't really been together for long... had you?'

There was a glimmer of anger as Dr Brenton got to her feet. 'No, we hadn't. That doesn't mean...'

'What does it mean? Did you know anything about his life? His work?'

'What is this exactly? You come here, show me your warrant card... is this official police business?'

Wood stared at her, the fury ebbing away. 'No, it's not official. But there's questions I have. Doubts...'

'Questions you have? What about his bosses? I've talked to them, and they didn't mention any questions, or any doubts.'

'No, they wouldn't. Have they told you the outcome of the post mortem?'

'No, but they don't have to. I know his lifestyle, the amount of stress he suffered. It was a heart attack. I've lost count of the times I had...'

Wood moved closer, chose her words. 'I'm going to say something now. And I'm going to be direct. Unemotional, because I think you can appreciate it.'

The doctor sat down, folded her arms. 'Go on.'

'We don't like each other, do we?'

After a pause, the doctor said, 'We don't really know each other that well, but... no, I guess we don't. What's your point?'

'Well, I'm going to say something else, and it has nothing to do with us, or how we feel about each other...' Wood took in a deep breath then exhaled. 'I think Jake was killed.'

The doctor stared up at her, seeming to wait for more. 'Killed? Is this a joke... I don't believe this...'

'I'm serious. We were looking into a murder... an

MP... the more we dug, the more we were told to drop it.'

The doctor rubbed her nose, let out a huff. 'What? So, because you were looking into some case, you think... what? That someone had him killed? He had a heart attack! He smoked heavily! He drank. He ate... pardon my language... but he ate shit.'

'I know. I warned him about it. Did you know that they brought in a different pathologist? A pathologist whose background is shady, to say the least?'

'I know they brought in a pathologist, but because it's one of their own. They said that's what they do. Who says he's shady?'

'The pathologist who was meant to be carrying out the post mortem.'

The doctor rubbed her nose again and shook her head and looked up at her. 'Professional rivalry? Could that be a factor? His nose was obviously put out of joint.'

Wood felt the build up of anger that almost pushed a series of venomous words from her mouth. She controlled herself, aware what she was sounding like. 'OK. I know what this sounds like. But trust me... we were looking into some dark areas, digging up things that someone high up was trying to keep quiet. The post mortem they've just carried out will undoubtedly say he died of a heart attack. Maybe he did. But don't you want to be sure? You weren't divorced. You're still his wife, his next of kin. Which means you can push for this. You could get them to let Dr Garrett take a look and get a second opinion.'

The doctor looked at her for a moment before saying, 'You're not expecting there to be a second post mortem. You believe that if I do push for a second post mortem, they'll make an excuse not to have one.

And therefore, I'll be convinced that there is indeed something amiss.'

'I know I'm not going to be able to convince you of anything. You need to find out for yourself. Think about it.'

The doctor gave a pretend smile. 'Oh, I will. Now, I have a meeting to go to, so if you don't mind.'

Wood nodded, smiled politely and left the office. When she got to the end of the corridor, she said, 'Bitch!' and kept on walking out into the car park.

She found her hire car parked a couple of streets away and climbed into it and sat for a moment. She looked up into the rearview mirror and caught a glimpse of her hastily packed suitcase on the backseat. She closed her eyes, gently head-butted the steering wheel and then huffed and started the engine.

Jairus walked down the stairs to find Cathy leaning at the bottom of them, her arms folded, waiting. He walked past her, opened the front door and headed towards the car. Cathy was behind him all the way, which wasn't hard because of his awkward limp.

As he reached the car, he turned and put out his good hand. 'Keys.'

She stared at him. 'Where do you think you're going?'

'Great Yarmouth. I need the keys.'

'You're going to drive yourself, are you?' She looked him over, then raised her eyebrows.

'Yeah, that's the idea. Are you going to give me the keys or do I have to take them off you?'

She smiled. 'I'd have fun letting you try... but I'd like to know how you're going to drive with your hand like that.'

Jairus looked at the plastic cast that covered his

forearm and most of his hand. He looked up at Cathy. 'Open the boot.'

Cathy took out the keys and pressed the button on the fob to release the boot.

Jairus went round the back of the car and opened the boot and looked at all the equipment and supplies they'd taken from Besnier's castle house. Among the gear there was a small hunting knife, which Jairus found and began cutting away at the part of the cast that covered his hand.

'What the hell are you doing?' Cathy moaned and let out a sigh. 'Just let me drive.'

'I have to do this alone. OK?' He cut the last part of the cast and ripped it away, then clenched and unclenched his hand. He had full movement, even though there was still a small amount of stiffness and pain in his wrist.

'You're ignoring the other leads to delve back into your past,' Cathy said. 'I was listening to you upstairs. There are other more advantageous leads you could follow, but once again you're choosing to haunt your ex.'

Jairus chose not to say a thing, even though his inner, deeper anger, threatened to drown him. He was angry with himself and with Cathy because he knew she was right, and that his weakness was taking over.

His hand was shaking as he lifted it and held out his palm.

Cathy put the keys in his hand, and stepped back as he climbed in.

He started the engine, reversed, then stopped as a thought occurred to him.

'Find somewhere to stay,' he said. 'Don't stay with family or anyone you know.'

'I'm not an idiot,' she said and nodded towards the

end of the road. 'Go on, do what you have to do.'

He nodded and put the car into gear, but his stomach twisted and the iron fist smashed into the top of his skull. It was the fact that he was going to be entering Karine's world, her murky past, digging up her dark secrets that was beginning to poison his mind.

He closed off his fears and drove on towards his fate.

CHAPTER 23

The library looked like a wonky pyramid made up of white metal and glass that had been plonked beside the rows of shops and council offices. It was situated a few streets from the sea front, and so Jairus parked close by and hobbled in its direction, carrying a folded piece of paper in his hand that had all the stamp codes scribbled on it.

His heart was acting like a kind of emotional metal detector, pounding harder the closer he seemed to get to Karine's murky past.

In the large arched doorway of the library, he leaned against the wall as he felt himself go lightheaded. His hands were trembling when he lifted them, so he fished around in his pocket for that day's pills and swallowed them all down followed by a gulp from the bottle of water he'd purchased on the way.

He unfolded the piece of paper as he headed for the main desk, where a tall young man was talking to a much shorter pretty young woman with lots of curly blonde hair.

Jairus slapped the piece of paper on the desk, making them both flinch. 'Could you get these books for me?' he said, then added, 'Please.'

The tall young man looked down at the piece of paper, frowning, running his fingers over the list. 'Ok... do you know the titles of these books?'

'No, I don't. But they should be the numbers of the books.'

The young man nodded, then went over to a computer, taking the piece of paper with him. He typed away, then looked up at Jairus. 'The first book is Pride and Prejudice. The second is Anne Frank's' Diary. Gemma, could you start noting these down?'

Gemma, the girl with the bush of blonde hair, grabbed a pad and pen and started writing them down. Then she looked over at Jairus. 'If you find somewhere to sit, I can bring them over.'

'Yeah, OK,' Jairus said and limped over to an empty table and slumped into one of the plastic chairs that surrounded it.

He had to sit down. His legs couldn't take standing up anymore, not with the tremor of excitement and uncontainable fear twitching through them. Even as he was sat watching the bush of blonde hair fetch the relevant books, his right leg was vibrating, the toe of his shoe tapping at the ground.

Eventually she came over with a trolley full and pushed them to his desk. 'These are all of them. Quite an eclectic collection.'

'Yeah, I know, I'm an eclectic kind of guy,' was all Jairus could bring himself to say.

The young woman stayed for a moment, watching him pull the books closer to him, until she looked at him closely and more than likely saw the bruises and the uncontrollable shakes that had overtaken him.

When she had gone, he opened Pride and Prejudice and began flicking through the pages, the lines of black words neatly printed on the yellowing paper.

He stopped, a page between his fingers. The words 'come soon' were neatly written in tiny writing in the right-hand margin.

He put the book down and made a note of the message. The next book he grabbed was Raymond Chandler's Farewell My Lovely. He flipped through the pages as his eyes jumped around the pages, scanning every space, while his heart beat on.

He was almost at the end of the book when he saw the words, 'Tesco Metro' in the same tiny writing.

He made a note and grabbed Anne Frank's Diary. He found the number '114' written in the same hand. In Fahrenheit 451 he noted down 'Filby' and went on to Wuthering Heights. Halfway through the book, he found the words 'Tyler Road', noted it down and then sat back, trying to catch his breath as he could almost feel Karine's past reaching towards him.

He gathered himself, pulled himself up to his full height. Dizziness enclosed his head and he had to make a grab for the desk in case he toppled over. When he looked up, the librarians were watching him suspiciously.

He rushed away, headed for the door, as an ants' nest of fears and dark thoughts crawled across his mind.

Wood drove slowly along the street, past the line of boutiques on Muswell Hill High Street, looking out for Dr Garrett. She slammed on the brake when she caught sight of him standing outside an old church that had now become part of a chain of pubs. Sacrilege, she thought, even though there wasn't an ounce of religion in her body, and parked up in a side street. It was getting darker and the maroon sky was getting deeper, sinking behind the neat little row of shops that were filled with extremely early Christmas shoppers.

She'd almost not recognised the skinny frame of the pathologist as he was now decked out in black cords, a light blue shirt and brown blazer.

He climbed into the passenger seat, and briskly rubbed his hands together as he said, 'Winter's arrived. I hate the winter.'

'What're we doing here?'

Garrett examined the interior of the car for a moment before he said, 'This is a very immaculate car. I don't take you for the obsessive type, so I presume this is not your usual vehicle.'

'It's not.'

He nodded. 'What about your mobile?'

'I left it at home, and I left it turned on. Do you think I'm paranoid?'

He took off his round-rimmed glasses and wiped them on his shirt. 'No, I don't. I think you're being very sensible. How did it go with the ex-wife?'

'As expected. The cow's being very difficult.'

'Thought as much. That's why we need to pop into this pub. It's a trendy little place called Jimmy's. In there we'll find Dr Henry Wilson. It's still early, so he'll still be speaking English and won't have pissed himself yet.'

'Seriously?' Wood started the engine and pulled away from the pavement.

'We're a strange bunch, we pathologists. It's the nature of our work, spending all that time in conversation with the dead. It can send you a bit loopy.'

'I can understand that.' Wood saw the pub and pulled into the street beside it.

The pub was a large building, bulky even, built in the 1800s, now painted blue and white. Wood followed Garrett through double doors that had a stained glass window above them, and found herself in a big and airy room filled with wooden tables, uneven wood floors, which bustled with bodies and their conversations. Garrett pointed towards the back of the pub, and so they squeezed through the crowd and headed into the more private alcoves towards the back.

In the far corner, they found a middle-aged balding man sitting on a black leather sofa, nursing a pint of Guinness and a glass of whisky.

Wood went and stood by the table in front of him, while Garrett sat down at the other end of the sofa.

Dr Wilson, who picked up his pint, looked up at Wood with raised eyebrows, and then looked over at Garrett. He shuffled his body round to face Garrett, and pointed a finger at him. 'I know you, don't I?'

'Yes, Henry, you do,' Garrett said, as if he was talking to a small child.

Wilson's eyes returned to Wood. 'I don't know you.'

'I'm Detective Sergeant Kate Wood,' she said and showed her ID. 'You performed an autopsy on my former partner today. Do you remember?'

He huffed, scowled, and took a sip of his pint. 'Of course I remember. Believe it or not, young woman, but I'm dry when I work.'

'But what about the other stuff, Henry?' Garrett asked.

Henry smiled at him. 'Actually, I kicked that little habit a while back. I'm clean.'

'Really?' Garrett said. 'Too little too late, though, isn't it? The damage has been done.'

Henry wiped his lip. 'What's that supposed to mean?'

Wood grabbed a stool and sat on it. 'It means at some point in your outstanding career, you fucked up. And you must have fucked up royally, because they've got your balls in their pocket, haven't they?'

Henry stared at her, then looked at Garrett. 'You've really started bumming around, haven't you, Jeremy?'

'She's right,' Garrett said. 'This afternoon proved it. What did they tell you to write on that post mortem? Heart attack?'

Wilson took another sip of his pint and Wood noticed he was suddenly calmer as he said, 'My mind may not be as sharp as my scalpel, but I'm not so blunt as to realise that if you're asking questions like that one, then you don't have any answers. If say, I had been coerced into putting a very different cause of death to the one that in reality took your colleague's life, then my orders would have come from far above your rank, wouldn't they, DS Wood?'

'What did you give as cause of death?' Wood asked, fighting to keep herself calm.

Wilson shrugged. 'I don't suppose it matters. Have you heard of the term atherosclerosis? I know Jeremy has.'

Wood looked at Garrett.

'Atherosclerosis, is the build up of plaque in the heart's arteries. The plaque hardens and narrows the arteries and deprives the flow of oxygen-rich blood. This can lead to coronary heart disease and of course a potentially fatal heart attack.'

Wilson sat forward, his bloodshot eyes fixing on Wood. 'Your colleague was a heavy smoker, a moderate drinker, with a very unhealthy diet. His cholesterol was through the roof. His blood pressure would have been also. It was untreated. I found a severe build-up of plaque and a narrowing of his heart's arteries. Now, you police officers like to boast that you're human lie detectors, so please be kind enough to tell me whether I'm lying or not.'

Wood had to admit he was right on that score. So many of her colleagues believed they could spend half an hour with a suspect and come out of the interview room knowing whether they did it or not. She was not from that old-school world of policing, but even so, she knew a few of the telltale signs. Also, she knew that Brenton's lifestyle was much as Wilson had described. She'd hit a brick wall, but tried to hide her depressed state from both pathologists.

'There,' Wilson said, looking at Garrett. 'There was a look in her eye that told me I'd hit the nail perfectly on the head. Defeat is a hard emotion to mask. Now, if you don't mind, I plan on getting very drunk.'

Wood stood up. 'We're going to push for a second autopsy.'

Wilson laughed. 'You won't get it. They like things neat and tidy. Garrett has probably told you as much.'

Garrett moved closer to Wilson. 'I believe you when you say he died of a heart attack, Henry.'

'So you should.' Wilson sipped his Guinness.

'I haven't finished, Henry. You see, a heart attack can be induced. There are lots of undetectable compounds that will bring on a coronary incident. But if you know what to look for, then you can easily tell if the heart attack was natural or artificial.'

Wood thought she saw a flash of something across the old drunk's face and a twitch along his jaw as he said, 'Yes, if you know what you're looking for and you can get to the body in time. Before cremation.'

Garrett stood up and squeezed Wilson's shoulder. 'We will, my old friend. I can guarantee that. The wife, who is a doctor, is about to ask for a second post mortem. If they try and put her off, which of course they will, then her suspicions will be raised. She won't want the body cremated just yet, will she?'

Wood watched as Garrett walked away, passing her by, and heading into the crowd. She remained and looked down at the bent pathologist as he put his hand on the whisky glass. He looked up at her, but there was none of his self-assured cockiness left in his eyes.

'You might want to drink a lot more of those, mate. You've got a whole pile of shit coming for you, so being drunk might be your best bet.' Wood followed Garrett's path through the crowd and met him out in the now icy air.

As Garrett rubbed his bony hands together he said, 'Now we have to convince his wife to keep pushing for a second post mortem. Can you do that?'

'Even if I have to put a bloody gun to her head.'

Jairus booked himself into a bed and breakfast a street away from the promenade, then parked outside the small Tesco Metro and looked into the glowing interior, making everything around it seem shrouded in blackness. There were only a few late-night shoppers inside.

Jairus climbed out, and headed into the warmth of the interior and the harsh light that burned at his eyes. There were two servers on the tills. One was a bearded, slightly overweight young man and the other was a blonde stick of a woman, probably in her mid-thirties.

When the bearded young man left the tills to head into the office, Jairus walked over to the counter and stood in front of the woman. He read her name badge: Janine. Same as the name as on the postcards. She was almost skeletal, which made her head look far too big for her body. The way her skin was stuck tight to her skull, and the dark lines beneath her big fearful eyes made Jairus suspect years of drug abuse.

'Can I help?' the woman said in a quiet, whisper of a voice.

'Yeah, Janine, you can,' he said, and smiled. 'You can tell me if you've worked here long. More than five years say?'

Janine's face tightened into uncomfortableness. 'I'm sorry... why do you want...?'

'Ever have a friend called Karine Skilton?'

The woman's face became flushed. 'Er... no. What's this about?'

'I think you did have a friend called Karine. Is your name Latch? Yeah, I can tell by your reaction that it is. You just didn't expect anyone to come here apart from her.'

The woman stood frozen, but her eyes jumped around the room. Fight or flight mode had been triggered.

'I knew Karine,' he said, and smiled, trying to put her at ease. 'We lived together.'

The woman seemed to examine him closer, to really look at him. 'Are you... are you Jay?'

He nodded as a wave of sadness washed over him. It was almost as if Karine was saying his name one last time from beyond the grave. 'Yeah, I'm Jay.'

The woman's anxiousness washed away, and some light returned to her eyes. 'She talked about you... a lot.'

'Really? That's nice to know.'

Janine looked towards the office door as it opened and the male member of staff came back.

'Eddie,' Janine said, smiling, 'Is it all right if I take my fag break now?'

'Sure,' Eddie said, and took her place as she grabbed her coat.

'I'll meet you round the back,' Janine said as she

stepped round the counter. 'There's a metal gate. I'll let you in.'

Jairus nodded and watched her head through the office door, then went back out into the chilled night air. He limped round to the alleyway that ran behind the shop and found the tall metal fence and gate.

Janine was already unlocking it when he reached the gate, and let him into the delivery area. He shoved his hands into his pockets as Janine took out pack of cigarettes and lit one. She let out a sigh filled with satisfaction then smiled awkwardly at him as if she was trying hard to find anything to say.

Jairus was the opposite; his words were queuing up, fighting for supremacy, forming questions that he was desperate to ask and afraid to at the same time. He thought he'd start small.

'Have you lived here all your life?' he asked.

She nodded. 'Most of it.'

'What about Karine?'

She looked at him strangely, so he added, 'There's a lot about Karine's life that... well, she wouldn't talk about.'

Janine nodded, as if she understood what he meant. 'She had her secrets.'

'Yeah, she did. Thing is, Janine... I need to know everything.'

'She told me you were a policeman.'

'Yeah, I was. Not now.'

Janine took a drag of her cigarette. 'What's this then? You just decided you wanted to know more about her?'

'I was asked to look into a case. Privately. Thing is, it seems to link back to Karine. I found the postcards you sent and the codes you left under the stamps.'

She blushed. 'I thought I was being clever.

Should've known. Mitch is right, I'm useless.'

'No, Mitch is wrong. That was clever. Who's Mitch? Boyfriend? You're not wearing a ring.'

She laughed awkwardly. 'No, he doesn't believe in all that. I don't think he gives a shit really. Sorry, shouldn't be telling you all this.'

He smiled, observing her flushed cheeks, she way she took too many rapid puffs of her cigarette and hardly looked him in the eye. He recognised the telltale signs of a woman who had suffered years of mental and possible physical abuse. His hands gripped into fists as a spark of fury flickered deep inside him. 'It's fine. You can tell me what you want.'

She looked at him briefly. 'But you want to know about Karine?'

'Yeah.'

Janine finished her cigarette and stubbed it out against the wall. 'All right. Well, I can meet you tomorrow morning, if that's any good?'

'Yeah, that would be great. Should I meet you here?'

'Here'll be fine. About nine. I'll let you out.'

When she unlocked the gate and opened it for him, he stepped through and faced her as she locked it back up.

'I'll see you in the morning then.' He smiled.

She nodded, then hesitated as she went to walk away.

'What is it, Janine?' he asked.

'It's just... me and Karine... things... I mean, back then when we were...'

'Are you trying to tell me there are things I'm going to learn that maybe I don't want to know about?'

She nodded, then looked at her hands.

'Let's talk tomorrow.'

CHAPTER 24

'You've managed not to fuck it all up then?' Robert Burdock said in his usual spiteful tone, saliva splashing the air.

Douglas as usual ignored his father's manner and turned his head towards the magnificent glowing London horizon beyond the wall of glass. His father was tucked up in his wheelchair, his pasty, scrawny legs poking out from the thick blanket that was wrapped around him. 'All is well in the Burdock empire.'

'I don't really give a shit. What happened with the slut?'

'The slut?' Douglas could hardly comprehend his father, as his mind was elsewhere. He'd noticed with a large amount of regret that Nurse Wright had not been at her usual post, waiting for him in the same way a dog waits for its master. He wanted to ask his father, but then he would be highlighting a weakness to the old bastard and it would only prove to be a bruised point that he could keep prodding at.

'Yes, the sex worker slut, you know!'

'You mean Cat?'

'Yes! That's the slut.'

'She's gone. I let her go.' Douglas got up, walked towards the window.

'You let her go?!' His father's voice became almost

a screech. 'Did you get sick of her sucking your cock like a vacuum cleaner? Jesus Christ, son, what the fuck's wrong with you?'

He turned and faced his old man, allowed himself to be reminded what a weak and feeble creature the once mighty media mogul had become. 'Sometimes, Father, things have to end. Our relationship had run its course.'

'Relationship?! Fuck me!'

Douglas had had enough. His nightly visits to his father to tell of all his latest sordid activities were becoming draining, and it didn't help that Nurse Wright's absence was weighing heavily on his mind.

He heard one of the automatic doors click open back along towards the glowing lights of the kitchen. A flicker of shadow let him know she was back.

'That fucking nurse is back,' his father said. 'I better go back to my retard routine.'

'I'll go and talk to her.' Douglas didn't wait for his reply, just headed straight into the kitchen area where Nurse Wright had her back to him, putting something on the table.

Her head turned, her eyes taking him in with a slight jump. 'Oh, sorry, you made me jump.'

'No, I'm sorry,' he said, his eyes following her figure, imagining her without the tunic. 'I shouldn't have sneaked up on you.'

She smiled, and he could see that her nervousness had taken hold again. Then his eyes fell upon the small iced bun she had put on the table. 'Bought yourself a little late-night treat?'

She blushed, looked at it and shrugged. 'Yep. Well, thing is... it's actually my birthday...'

'Your birthday? And you're here looking after my father? You should be out enjoying yourself.'

'I don't really get to go out much, not with Megan to look after.'

He gave her his best heart-warming smile. His mind reached back then towards his father and the great annoyance he had given him when he kept digging around the slut issue. There was also the memory of his order to keep his hands off his nurse all those months back.

'You can say no to this, but why don't you let me take you out for dinner once you've finished here?'

Her face transformed from quietly shy to terrified. Then he watched the happiness and surprise wash over her.

'You... you don't have to do that.' Her face grew red, and he watched her chest rise and fall with her panicked breaths.

'I don't have to. I want to.' He smiled again. 'You finish at ten, don't you?'

'Yes... yes I do. Everywhere will be closed anyway.'

'I know somewhere that will be open. If you want to go?'

'Yes... of course I do.' She blushed again.

'Good. I'll send a car to pick you up at quarter past ten.' He smiled at her, taking great pleasure in her confusion and happiness that seemed to have wrapped around her, making her glow. He turned around and headed back out of the hospital apartment without looking back.

Anne Wright looked at herself in the small mirror in the hospital toilet and sighed. She looked a mess, she thought, and swore under her breath that she hadn't told him she needed to go home first. It was a little fortunate that she kept a couple of dresses and some makeup in her locker just in case she ended up heading out with her friends. They liked to meet up and go up the West End.

Her hair didn't look too bad. Luckily, she had already washed and straightened it in the morning because she knew Douglas Burdock would be visiting the old man. It had been hard to get Robert Douglas into bed tonight and she felt a twinge of pain in her back. It was almost as if he somehow made it more difficult for her.

She looked towards the bedroom that he now lay silently in. She gave a shudder. That was the effect he had on her; even though she knew the man was an empty shell, she still felt the former tyrant and chauvinist was still hidden within him. Every time she was around him, the rumours about his sexual predatory nature came back to her, and she would start to imagine that his eyes were running all over her, his hands ready to reach out.

But Douglas Burdock was another matter, and she could only recall good things about him. It was an amazing piece of luck that she landed this job. An old doctor friend had heard of the position and recommended her, and she had thanked her lucky stars ever since.

But never had she actually expected Douglas Burdock to ask her out on a date.

Was it a date? He had asked to take her out on her birthday. Why would a busy man ask to do that unless he was attracted to her?

She looked at herself. She wasn't bad looking, and she did often get offers from men when she was out.

She finished putting on her makeup and a little perfume, then picked up her purse and headed through the security desk where she signed out and stepped into the lift.

All the way down, she checked the time on her

phone. She was ten minutes early to meet the car, but it was already parked outside the main entrance, the limo's engine rumbling, spewing fumes into the night.

She blushed again when she approached the car, and a stocky grey-haired man smiled briefly, then opened the door for her. She did her best to look elegant as she got inside the car, but she knew she had failed.

The car moved, quietly, easing out of the massive car park and joining the late-night traffic. All the way to her destination, while she could hear her heart hammering, she worried about how to get out of the car while still keeping her dignity.

The car came to a stop outside a large house in Chelsea. She leaned towards the glass, looking up at the front, the magnificent windows, the warm lights inside them. She was taken with nerves suddenly, realising that this was a world where she didn't belong, and as much as she told herself that class and money didn't matter when it came to love, her mind refused to accept it.

The door opened, and the chauffeur stood holding it, expressionless like one of the guardsmen outside Buckingham Palace.

He's just a man, she told herself. A human being like you, just with lots of money and power.

She needed to wee.

A man in a grey suit stepped out from the doorway of the house and opened the front door for her. She smiled, but he only nodded his head professionally. For some reason she felt invisible, as if they all knew that she was not meant to be there, and that this was all a mistake.

Panic almost took her and she nearly ran down the

road. Pull yourself together. Don't be a coward. He likes you! Why wouldn't he like you?

Your hair looks a mess. Your bum's too big. Your nose is wonky.

She shut off the voice in her head that sounded a lot like her mother, and smiled as a middle-aged woman in a trouser suit, holding a mobile phone greeted her.

There was little friendliness when the woman said, 'Please go up the stairs to Mr Burdock's apartment. He'll be waiting for you.'

Anne smiled and her face burned with sudden embarrassment for even being alive let alone being in a house that she had no business being in.

But she followed the woman's eyes towards the broad carpeted staircase that seemed to wind around deep into the building. She delicately took the first step, looked back at the woman, but she had already disappeared.

The rest of the staircase was in darkness but when she took another step the spotlights above her began to turn on and light the way.

The sound of a lock unlocking came from the solid red door at the very top of the staircase and then it opened slowly.

A silhouette stood at the top of the stairs, black against the glow of warm light behind.

It was when she reached the person that she saw with shuddering nervousness and excitement that it was Douglas himself, a smile cut deeply into his face. His cologne filled her nostrils, while her eyes fell upon the expensive suit he had changed into. He was clean-shaven, sharp, and she found herself thinking about what it would be like to kiss him.

She hid her thoughts, buried them, even though the glow of her cheeks gave her away.

'Welcome to my home,' he said, stepping aside and gesturing through to the hallway.

'It's beautiful,' she said, her voice fading slightly. Her mouth was suddenly dry.

'Thank you,' he said and walked behind her as she stepped into a wide and long hallway that had a deep red carpet that ran along the never-ending corridor. 'I'd like to say I decorated it myself, but that would be an awful lie. We save the lies for our newspapers.'

She looked at him, but saw he was smiling. She laughed and allowed him to escort her into a room halfway along the corridor.

She caught her breath when she stepped in and found herself in an expansive room that looked pretty much identical to one she remembered entering when she visited a stately home a couple of years before. There was a mammoth fire place, a huge portrait of some nobleman above it, a collection of expensive vases scattered about the room, and other works of art. Brown leather sofas and armchairs sat in each corner.

'This is where I like to relax,' he said and stepped around her and walked to the centre of the room. 'Come and sit down.'

She stood still for a moment, allowing enough time for the world to stop spinning quite so fast, but it didn't slow down. She tried to control her nerves, to not look like such a rookie in this world of the rich and famous, but she realised that she had already failed several minutes ago. She could feel her cheeks and chest glowing bright pink like they always did when she was nervous.

She tried to walk straight forward, to not lose her balance as she stepped onto the enormous rug and towards him as he sat on the leather sofa. She took several deep breaths, which seemed to help slow her heart down as she sat about a foot from him. She was stiff, upright, while he was laying back, his arm stretched out casually towards her, a soft smile on his face.

'I know how you feel,' he said, his smile stretching, his eyes smouldering. 'You're afraid you might break something. I can't blame you. See these vases? Each one is worth roughly twenty thousand pounds.'

'Oh my God,' she said. 'I think I'll stay away from them. I can be accident prone.'

He laughed, got to his feet and approached a small dark wood antique table which had five similar vases sitting upon it. He stared at her, still smiling, put his hand round one of the vases and lifted it in the air.

She watched on, feeling herself frown, thinking she knew what he might do, but also suspecting that he was only joking. Then she watched him turn and throw the expensive vase at the wall where it shattered into many pieces.

'Was that?' She put her hand over her mouth, suppressing her laughter. 'Was that a fake one?'

'No. That was real. It was Chinese. Very old. You should try it. And don't worry, I shall put the value of these vases into a charity of your choice. Come on. Have a go.'

She laughed again as he beckoned her over. She got to her feet and slowly made her way to his side. 'I can't...'

'Of course you can.'

She looked down at the vases. 'They're not real, are they?'

'Why would I have fake vases?' He raised his eyebrows.

She shrugged, then looked down at one of the smaller ones. She tentatively picked it up and looked it over, as if she knew how to judge a fake antique vase from a real one. When she looked up at him, he nodded, then gestured towards the wall where the pieces of the other vase still lay scattered.

'Do it!' he said, almost taunting her.

She laughed, held the vase as if she was about to throw it. Then she shook her head. 'I can't.'

'I shall put double its value into a charity of your choice. Now throw it.'

It happened without her thinking about it; her hand flew backwards, her body swinging with it, throwing the antique ornament towards the wall.

She shuddered and closed her eyes as the vase smashed to pieces. 'Oh... my God. Did I really just do that?'

He clapped his hands. 'Yes, you did. I'm very proud of you.'

'Oh my God.'

'By the way, I lied to you.' He grinned.

'They are fake?!'

'No, they're real. But they're worth about a hundred thousand each.'

Her mouth fell open, her eyes jumping to the broken pieces all over the floor. 'No! Oh my... I can't believe I just did that.'

'I shall put three hundred thousand pounds into the charity of your choice. Name it.'

'Cancer research.' She smiled.

'Have you had someone close to you suffer from cancer?' His face became serious, almost solemn.

She looked down at her hands as she fiddled with one of her rings. 'Yes... my brother. A few years ago. I looked after him most of the time.'

He put a hand on her shoulder and squeezed. 'That must have been tough. You must be a good person.

I mean, going into nursing and all. And looking after your brother. Do you consider yourself a good person?'

She felt her face burn again. 'I don't know... don't really think about it. I like to think I'm a good person. I try not to hurt people.'

He smiled, patted her arm and said, 'You are a good person. Now, we shall celebrate your birthday.'

He sat up and pressed a gold button, quite like a doorbell, on the table in front of them. There was no sound, but very soon a door opposite them opened and a dark-suited middle-aged man came into the room carrying a tray. On the tray was a bucket of ice with an opened bottle of champagne inside. The bucket was placed between them along with two champagne flutes.

'Thank you,' Douglas said to the man, who nodded and left the room.

Douglas lifted the champagne from the bucket, grabbed her glass and filled it.

She smiled brightly and took the cool glass and held it tightly as Douglas poured himself a drink. She felt her heart racing as he tapped his glass against hers. The fizz filled her ears as he moved closer, his leg touching hers.

'A toast,' he said, lifting his glass. 'To the future. Come what may.'

She smiled and tapped her glass against his, then put the champagne to her lips as he did so. She sipped it, feeling the bubbles burn her throat. It was obviously expensive stuff, but to her champagne all tasted the same. But she didn't want to look like a fool. 'Delicious.'

'It should be. Cost the earth.' He put his glass down on the table and seemed to watch her as she took another few sips.

She laughed and smiled at him.

He seemed to lose the friendliness from his face suddenly as if it had all drained from him, leaving only a blank stare.

'Are you all right?' she asked.

He nodded, but a blank, emotionless look remained. 'You're very pretty.'

'No, I'm really not.'

'Yes, you are,' he said firmly. 'And very good. Very, very kind.'

She felt herself blushing once again.

The glass seemed to slip from her hand. She wasn't sure how it had happened, but the glass had dropped from her fingers and fell to the floor.

'I'm sorry,' she said, and went to move to pick it up, but her head seemed to spin.

'You feeling OK?' he asked.

'Think I'm feeling a bit drunk, but I've only had a couple of sips.'

He nodded. 'It has that effect. You'll feel very tired in a moment. You won't fall unconscious straight away. At first, you'll be awake, but unable to move.'

She looked at him, his words hanging in the air like an early frost. She was waiting for him to smile, to laugh, but there was nothing in his eyes that said he was making a joke. She looked at the champagne glass, then up at him. 'You're joking?'

He shook his head.

She put the glass down on the table, felt anger and panic pulse through her. Her hands were shaking. 'I think I better go.'

He sat back, put out his open hand as if he was agreeing. She stood up, but her legs weren't really there. She slipped to one side. He didn't move. She could feel him watching her, as if he was observing an experiment.

Then somehow she was looking up at him as he was looking down at her from the sofa, his face still empty. He got up slowly as he removed his tie, unbuttoned the top buttons of his shirt. He stepped over her and walked out of view. When he came back, he grabbed her ankles and began dragging her across the floor, but she couldn't feel anything as her mind fogged up.

He dropped her for a few seconds and turned to the wall, and pressed his hand against it. She watched him open a hidden door and a dim light shone out towards her.

She fought to move, telling her arms and legs to start working, but nothing happened.

He came back out of the room, stood looking down at her for a moment, his eyes scanning her body. She moved her mouth to scream, but only a garbled sound came out.

Douglas crouched down over her, brought a finger to his lips and made a shushing noise before smiling.

He grabbed her ankles and dragged her into the next room where she could see there was a bed with only a mattress upon it. A blue bulb coldly illuminated the room as he dropped her to the floor.

She tried to focus on him as he moved away, but the room grew darker and darker, making her eyes lose him somewhere in the blurred corners of her vision.

Tiredness came eerily over her, her eyelids shutting as the greyness rushed towards her.

Her eyes did open again, somewhere during the night. She felt no material touching her body, her arms and legs spread out. Sleep absorbed her again, but not before she saw him walk in front of her as he removed his shirt, revealing his sinewy body. There was a tattoo over his heart. It was black and seemed to made up of slithering serpents with an animal's skull at the centre of it.

He laughed, manically.

She closed her tear-filled eyes, believing she would never open them again.

CHAPTER 25

Jairus stood outside the bed and breakfast, which was just a house like all the rest crammed beside it, but a little grander, with large rooms not very well decorated. He dug his hands into his overcoat, and felt the tug of the icy wind that rose off the cold sea. He looked out across the dark water, where it met the grey sky. Heavy rain was coming, heading inland.

He looked at his watch. She was late, and his body was alive with fear and nausea. He remembered the first time he was told to sit outside the headmaster's office at school, the way he was shaking, terrified of what punishment he would get… and the one waiting for him when he got home. He would have liked nothing more than to tell that boy that the fear he had then was nothing, was a spit in the sea compared to what he felt right now.

The rumble of a badly maintained engine came around the corner. It was a small green Renault that had collided with something at one time. Janine was behind the wheel, looking tired, her hands tightly gripping the wheel.

She parked up, so he climbed in, put his seat belt on, smiled politely at her. She smiled back, lit a cigarette, took a hungry puff, lowered the window and drove on.

'Where shall we go?' he asked, looking at the grey

streets, the old Victorian buildings that had been turned into amusement arcades lining their route.

'I thought you'd want to see where me and Karine met.'

'Is it far?'

'Half hour,' she said, never taking her eyes from the road. 'We don't have to go, not...'

'I have to go. I need to.'

She looked at him quickly, nodded, took another drag of her cigarette and kept driving.

They kept to a coastal road, passing the occasional car coming the other way, while the wild sea leapt up at them from below, spitting foam high over the rocks. The wind pushed the car, and Jairus watched Janine fighting with it, gripping the wheel.

The ashtray was filled with dog ends by the time the dark red gothic building merged above the rocks. It had been obviously designed as one long block, a multitude of thin chimneys poking from the roof. The many dark windows glistened at them as they grew closer.

'Is that it?' Jairus gestured to the ominous building.

She nodded. 'Yes. Horrible, isn't it?'

'Yeah. Bloody horrible.'

'Used to be a workhouse. I don't think they changed it much before we moved in.'

'You don't have to go there. You can drop me off here, I'll walk the rest of the way.'

She shook her head. 'No. I'll take you.'

Janine took them down a slip road that led towards the red monstrosity, which seemed to grow even more sinister as they approached. As they pulled up at a set of iron gates, Janine pointed towards the fence that surrounded the old building. 'There's a gap in the fence a couple of hundred yards up.'

'You've been inside lately?'

She avoided his gaze as she parked the car in front of the gates. 'Well... yeah, they're pulling the place down... building some flats or something... thought I'd have a look around... you know.'

'Yeah, I know.' He did know, he decided, as they both climbed out and headed back around the building parallel with the wire fencing. Digging around in his own dark past was becoming an obsession with him, so why would it be any different for anyone else who had suffered similar terrible events. There was something else though, something on her mind as she showed him the way to the small gap in the fence. He'd learned a long time ago how to read people quickly, to tell the difference between a mind troubled by the past or a mind troubled by the present.

He brushed it all away as he managed to just about squeeze through and stood still for a moment, taking in the whole atmosphere, getting a sense of everything bad that could have possibly happened. In his experience of institutions set up to protect the vulnerable and weak, seldom did he find good things happening inside their walls.

Douglas Burdock sat back in the limo, unfolded the paper and began to read the financial section as he always did. He need not read what the other papers said because he knew already what the other papers were saying. He had people to read through them, and scour the Internet for any libel or defamation they could find, and the rest was down to his excellent legal team.

He lowered the paper as he heard a soft moan from the seat opposite him. Anne Wright was lying on her side, now redressed in the clothes she had been wearing when she arrived at the apartment he'd rented for the evening. Her arms and legs were cuffed.

She looked pale and he could only imagine the amount of discomfort she would feel once she was fully awake.

Her eyelids fluttered.

He had been pleased by it all. More than pleased. He had been in ecstasy to see her lying unconscious across the bed, her slender pale arm dangling over the edge. He'd watched her for a long time before he allowed the pleasure to begin.

He allowed himself brief moments of controlled pleasure, but not too much, for the rest he liked to reserve for the one night he and all the others looked forward to.

She opened her eyes and shut them a few times before realisation seemed to come over her. Then her big, scared eyes jumped to him and the tears began.

'It's over now,' he said and started reading the paper again, or at least pretending to.

'What... did you do to me!' She fought to sit up, her eyes screaming out to him.

'Nothing you hadn't really wanted.' He smiled.

'You drugged me!' she looked down. 'It hurts. Oh... God... what did you...?'

He put a finger to his lips. 'Quiet now. You will never tell anyone what happened to you. Any evidence has been removed from your body. No one will believe you anyway. You will continue to work for my father...'

'You must be... sick... I'm not...'

'You will. For one thing, I know you desperately need the money. Think of your child's future. If that's not enough, I took photographs of you last night. How would you like those photographs to find their way to your child's school?'

'You... wouldn't dare! Don't even...'

'I would. You know now what I'm capable of. When you see me again, you will be polite. Courteous. I know you hate me now. Probably even want to kill me. But you're alive. Be thankful for that. And you will have money. A good life for your child. Think hard about that, Anne. If you go to the police, or try and sell your story, all those things will be taken away.'

She was staring at him, her eyes stabbing at him, killing him over and over. He wanted to laugh as she panted, her heart obviously pumping pure hatred all round her body. He always loved the way they looked in the cold hard daylight of the morning after, their world now ripped apart. He especially loved the exquisite moment where they realised they could have a good life afterwards if they kept it all to themselves. The look in their eyes was always the same, and he loved seeing it, and replaying it in his mind, like a beautiful melody that haunts the mind long after hearing a song.

'So?' He lost his smile, made his face business-like. 'What's it to be? A good life for you and your child, or...?'

She began crying again, her head turned away.

'You're doing the right thing. We're nearly outside your home.' He smiled as the car stopped, then watched as the driver walked round and opened the door for her.

Anne was wiping the tears from her face, sniffing, looking bewildered. He leaned towards her, released the cuffs from her arms and legs.

'Just remember that you're keeping quiet for your family. To keep them secure. Security is very important, isn't it? You need to keep them safe. Remember that. Now, I'm very busy. Off you go!'

She wiped her eyes, looked at the open car door, then at him, her eyes burning, her body trembling. She pulled herself awkwardly from the seat and stepped onto the pavement, still wiping away her tears.

The chauffeur climbed back into the car and drove him away from the pavement, and the horrid little suburban street.

He turned and watched her for a moment, still in shock, looking around her, then heading up her garden path.

He picked up his newspaper again, looking forward to the next time he would see her and the look of defeat he'd see in her eyes.

Janine took them along a cracked stone path that led to the double doors at the centre of the building, then pointed towards one of the windows. 'We can climb up there and get in through the window.'

Jairus stepped up and examined the chipped and battered blue doors and found they didn't look very secure. He raised his good foot and kicked at the lock several times before the doors gave in and flew open. 'Looks like I've found another way in.'

Jairus stepped into the wide open, foyer, and walked across the scuffed wood flooring. He stopped dead and grabbed Janine's thin arm as she was about to keep walking. 'Wait. Look.'

He pointed to the floor, where numerous needles had been discarded across the room. 'The junkies like to have somewhere private to get out of their skulls.'

He carefully cleared their way with his boot, then directed Janine onwards.

'I guess it's time we had a chat,' Jairus said.

Janine nodded, then pointed towards the stairs. 'There's a room up there... I sit in there sometimes... there's a table and chairs.'

'Yeah, all right. Let's go.' He followed her, even though something had started to bother him, a burning feeling in his stomach that told him things weren't quite right. Not only that, his stress headache – which sometimes acted like an early warning system – had turned up. But she was Karine's friend and he had to find out what had happened all those years ago, and why she had kept it from him.

Janine opened a dark red door and walked into a room covered in dust. A cold breeze rattled through a broken window. He watched her hug herself as she moved to the window and looked down on the car park.

'She was my best friend,' Janine said.

'Yeah, mine too.'

'She had a way of making you feel like you were the most important person in the world.'

He nodded, smiled at the familiar emotion. 'She did. She did.'

'She... she got me through all that... stuff. If it weren't for her... I would've...'

'Janine?'

She looked round at him, stared right into his eyes. 'They would come most weekends... sometimes during the week...'

'Who are they?'

She looked at her hands. 'The men. Men in suits... important men. We knew they must be important because the staff took orders from them, did whatever they asked. But... it wasn't until later on that we knew how important they were.'

Jairus' headache pounded deeply into his skull as

his stomach turned over and over, his fists clenching automatically. 'What happened? What did these men do?'

She turned away, looked out of the window again. 'They would have us picked up in a car. They usually took us to a house somewhere... the first time they told us they were taking us to a party... we were excited... until we realised what they wanted to do.'

Jairus clasped a hand tightly over his mouth, swallowed down the taste of vomit. He breathed in and out and found his voice. 'These men... these important men... they...'

'They made us... do things... to them. Sometimes they... would...' Janine's back began to heave, her body shaking as her hands rose to her face.

'Janine...?' He waited for a moment, waited patiently for her to gain control again while the blood turned to acid in his veins. 'Janine, I promise you I'm going to find the people that did those things to you.'

She turned around, found his eyes, and burst into tears again as she said, 'And Karine. They did those things to both of us, to us all. I'm sorry... I'm so sorry.'

Jairus looked down at his hands, saw them trembling, while feeling a blast of fury building inside his heart.

He caught sight of Janine's face, her eyes jumping to behind him, the flash of doubt in her eyes. He heard a sound, a step on the dusty floor, and swung around to see a man pointing a gun in his face.

CHAPTER 26

He saw the gun barrel long before the face of the man holding it out to him, jabbing it towards his face. Already the fear and anger and shock had taken over, pumping Jairus' blood, adding to the acid that Janine's words had churned up in his gut.

He focused in on the man's face, ignoring the gun. He was in his thirties, drawn, pale, short dark hair, lots of stubble. There was madness in his eyes, and that made Jairus' head begin to pound even more furiously. 'Don't point that fucking gun in my face!'

The gun wavered for a moment, the eyes behind it becoming more determined. 'He's one of them!'

'Don't talk to her, talk to me!' Jairus waved his hand. 'Why don't you start by explaining why you're pointing that gun in my face?'

'Who are you?' the man said, struggling to keep his voice from becoming a scream.

Jairus looked behind him at Janine. 'I'm a friend.'

'No, you're not!' The gun was closer, shaking. 'You're one of them!'

'One of who?' Jairus stared into the eyes beyond the barrel.

'The men... the men who did those things to us... you know what I'm talking about.'

'He's a policeman, Tom,' Janine said, her voice strained.

The man flashed his eyes at her then back at Jairus. The rage only seemed to grow as he stared. 'See... a policeman... one of them. Some of them were policemen! Judges! Politicians! You're all supposed to help us! Protect us! But it's all a fucking lie!'

Jairus held up his hand, the name Janine had spoken still echoing in his skull. 'Tom? That's your name, right? I was a policeman, Tom. I'm not now. You have to listen to me. I'm not one of them. I'm trying to get to the bottom of all this. You can help me...'

'You can't trust him!' Tom shouted at Janine.

'He was Karine's fella!' Janine shouted back. 'He's alright. She always said he was alright.'

Tom shook his head. 'How do you know they didn't send him to mess with you, to help find us all? They have to get rid of us. They'll stop at nothing to get rid of us all. Look at his wallet.'

Jairus closed his eyes, then rubbed his face. 'That's not going to help. My ID says I'm someone else. I'm in hiding.'

'You're lying!' Tom stepped closer. 'I'm going to kill you like I killed the others.'

Jairus nodded. 'Yeah, that's right. Leonard Jameson and James Howard. Yeah, I know about them. The news isn't telling the truth about their deaths, but I know. I know because you met a friend of mine. Cathy. In fact, you helped her escape from Howard's home. For which I'm grateful.'

Tom's face changed, lost the look of rage and confusion. 'She was good to me.'

'Yeah, she's good to me too. She's like that.'

Tom lowered the gun. 'You're Jairus... She said about you. Said you could help me. Tried to get me to stay at that house.'

'She's right. I can help.' Jairus pushed a smile to his

lips that hurt.

Tom gave a laugh full of sickness. 'How can you help? You're not even a policeman anymore. What can you do? These people are powerful. They'll crush you before you can even get close to them.'

'Yeah, they can certainly try. But I'm a bit like a cockroach, I just keep on going. They've tried to kill me once already.' Jairus lifted his arms out straight from his sides. 'Here I am. Still breathing.'

'I'm going to kill them all, or die trying.'

'Then you will die. Revenge will get you killed.'

Tom stepped even closer. 'If you were still a policeman, you'd try and arrest me, wouldn't you?'

Jairus nodded. 'Yeah, that's true. But I'm not a policeman. Not anymore. They saw to that.'

'If I stop what I'm doing... if I go along with you, they'll kill us all. Me, you, Janine... and the rest. I can't let that happen.' Tom lifted the gun, his hand trembling even more as he aimed it at Jairus' face.

'Tom, don't do this. I'm on your side. Think about this... don't pull that trigger.'

Tom shook his head and took out a pair of handcuffs and threw them over to Janine. 'Cuff him to the radiator over there. Do it, Janine! Do it!'

Janine scrambled to get the handcuffs, then looked up at Jairus. 'I'm sorry.'

'Don't be. Do as he says.' Jairus headed over to the radiator and sat cross-legged on the floor. He held up his wrists and allowed Janine to cuff him. 'You're making a big mistake, Tom.'

Tom lowered the gun as he walked backwards to the doorway. 'Maybe. Maybe not. You can release him in ten minutes. Goodbye, Janine.'

'Tom!' Janine called out. 'Wait!'

There was no reply and Jairus listened to his dusty

footsteps heading away from them as he watched Janine staring at the doorway. She rubbed her eyes, and turned around, looked at Jairus, and apologised with her eyes.

'He's been through a lot,' she said, sniffing.

'Yeah, but you all have.' Jairus rattled the handcuffs, which made Janine jump to life and take out the key. 'Who was Tom talking about when he said the rest?'

'All the others they took from all the children's homes and the ones they kidnapped from the streets. Tom told me there's a group of journalists that have been trying to uncover it all, and get at the truth of what they did to us. Thing is with Tom... well, you can't believe everything he says. They really messed him up.'

Janine took the cuff from around Jairus' wrists; he got to his feet and rubbed his arm. 'Have you heard him talk about someone called David Coulson?'

She shook her head. 'I don't think so. I don't remember him saying any names. He just told me they were trying to expose what's been going on for years... kids being abused like we were.'

'Have you heard the name Pinder before? Matthew Pinder?'

Jairus saw the flicker of recognition in her eyes before she said, 'I think Karine mentioned that name. Maybe. She'd been in touch with someone she thought might help us get justice. I told her I thought it was pointless... they'd never let the truth out about what happened to us. But she kept saying she'd met some people... I think she mentioned that name… Pinder.'

Jairus felt the stress headache arrive again, bringing with it a black, thunderous cloud over his skull. 'Did Karine ever mention her illness to you?'

Janine's face creased up, her eyes looking lost.

'Illness? No. What was wrong with her?'

'She had a weak heart. That's how she died.'

Janine's face changed, from expressing being lost, to deep thought.

'You all right?' he asked.

'Yes... I just think... well, if she had a heart condition, I would've thought she would've told me...'

'Yeah, me too.' His skin began to crawl with ants. 'During the last times you saw Karine... did she seem scared?'

'Shit...' Janine covered her mouth, her eyes growing. 'What? What's wrong?'

'The last time I heard from her... she came to my house... oh, no...'

Jairus grabbed her arm. 'What happened?'

'She turned up at my house... I was at work... she'd never come to my house before... Mitch was there. He told her to get lost. He doesn't like me to have friends... she'd never come to my house before. She wouldn't... said that it was too dangerous.'

'Did you hear from her after that?'

She shook her head, wrapped her arms around herself. 'No. I sent a few more postcards, but never got anything back... oh, God... do you think they found out what she was doing?'

Jairus swung around, a wave of pain washing over him as his heart began thumping, his mind racing back to the day they'd rowed and he'd left in a mood only to come back and find her lying on the bathroom floor. His guilt at leaving her alone to die was flooded, drowned by a tsunami of fury as he came to a sudden realisation.

His eyes fell on a chair and he grasped it up and swung it towards through the window as he let out a deep painful howl. Janine covered her face and cowered away as he upturned the table, smashing it against the floor, sending dust up around their feet.

He stopped, bent over, heaving, staring out the shattered remains of the window, feeling the cold air hitting his face.

'You okay?' Janine asked, slowly stepping towards him, her face stark with fear.

'No, I'm not okay. I think they murdered Karine. I was hired to look into all this by Douglas Burdock... and I'm pretty fucking sure he knew about Karine's murder... the sick bastard hired me, so he could fuck with my life.'

'Oh... God... what're you going to do?'

Jairus straightened up, looked at her, but saw only Karine on the day he rowed with her and left. 'I'm going to make sure I'm right... and if I am, then I'm going to find Douglas Burdock and kill him.'

DS Wood heard her work phone ringing and managed to pull it from her jacket as she drove towards Tottenham. She still had the honour killing case to look into, and the thought of it, the complexities of it all, and the hard-faced relatives that looked blankly at her and told lie after lie made her want to throw up.

And she missed him. Missed his unshaven face, his tired eyes, the smell of stale tobacco that clung to his clothes.

The number was private. She pulled over to take the call, in case it was Garrett trying to get hold of her.

When she answered and said, 'DS Kate Wood, hello?', she heard soft breathing on the other end.

'Hello?' she repeated. 'Who is this?'

'The ex-wife. The woman you hate.'

Wood sighed. 'I don't hate you. I don't even know you.'

There was a pause on the other end, then a deep breath. 'Well... you're going to really hate me now.'

'Why's that?'

'It's happening today. The cremation I mean.'

'What?' Wood's heart kicked into life, thumping hard as she blankly watched the traffic roaring past.

'You heard me. We're doing it today. It's just family.'

'Fuck! Who told you to do that? Who put the pressure on you?'

'No one.'

Wood heard the lie in her voice. 'They want him burned before anyone can re-examine the body, you do know that, don't you?'

'Jake died. Let us mourn in peace.'

The phone went dead. Wood sat there for a minute thinking, then called Garrett.

'They're having the funeral today!' she said, when she eventually got him on the line.

'So, they got to her?' Garrett said. 'Hardly surprising, is it?'

'The stupid bitch.'

'Don't be too hard on her. She's got plenty to lose. A family, her livelihood. She wouldn't have any choice but to go along with them.'

Wood shut her eyes for a moment, tried to push away the anger that was churning up her thought process. 'What do we do?'

'There's not much we can do. I know it's not what you want to hear.'

She buried half her face in her hand. 'Where would they be having it?'

'Enfield Crematorium, I would think. What are you thinking of doing?'

'I'm going to go there and try and talk sense to her.' Wood started the engine, and looked round at the heavy traffic, noticing the spits of rain that had started hitting the windscreen.

'I'm not sure that's such a good idea.'

'That's too bad,' she said and hung up the phone and headed for Enfield Crematorium.

She took the A10 then turned left through the black iron gates and up the long driveway towards the main redbrick building with the tall chimney rising from the centre of the roof.

She parked round the back and hurried to the main chapel. By the time she reached the arched doorway, people dressed in the appropriate dark colours were trickling out. A hymn was playing, something that Brenton wouldn't have wanted played at his funeral. This couldn't be it, she decided and slipped past an old lady that was being helped along by a spotty teenage boy.

She stopped just inside the doorway when she saw the bitch doctor talking in a hushed tone to another much larger woman with curly red hair. The doctor had an ill-fitting black trouser suit on, and a facial expression that seemed to match. As the large redhead said her goodbyes, Wood swept in and stood in front of the doctor.

'What're you doing here?' the doctor put her hands on her hips, her face growing scarlet.

'Well, I thought I deserved to see my best friend off.' Wood looked towards the red curtains that the coffin would have disappeared through before being taken off to be burnt. 'Do you know that they burn the body, but then they're left with the bones which they grind down to dust?'

'Jesus... what a thing to say...'

The doctor went to walk away, but Wood grabbed

her arm. 'I'm sorry, was that out of order... well, that's a bit like not inviting the ex-colleague and best friend of the deceased, isn't it?'

'It's family only. That's what we, his family, decided.'

'Who pushed you to get it over with as quickly as possible?'

'I've got people to talk to, so let go of me.'

Wood stepped leaned close to her ear. 'Come outside and have a quiet chat with me.'

'No, I haven't got...'

'Do you want me to start telling everyone what I know? How embarrassing and awkward would that be at the wake?'

Doctor Brenton stared at her for a few seconds, steam practically rising from her flushed skin. 'Fine. In the car park. Come on.'

Wood followed as Dr Brenton stormed out of the chapel, giving brief hellos to the fellow mourners offering their condolences.

They kept on going until Dr Brenton reached a large silver BMW and turned to face Wood, her arms tightly folded across her chest. 'Go on then.'

'Who put the pressure on you, so you'd get him gone before another post mortem could be carried out?'

'Jesus... he died of a heart attack! He lived a very unhealthy life!' Dr Brenton turned away, put her hands over her face as a sob caught in her throat. 'Oh Jesus... why? Why did you have to come here?'

'Why did you bother to tell me about the ceremony? You could've waited until tomorrow.'

She lowered her eyes to the ground. 'I just felt that you should know... I was going to keep it... well, you know... but guilt kicked in.'

'Maybe a cry for help?' Wood caught her eyes as she looked up.

The doctor looked around the car park for a moment before stepping closer and lowering her voice. 'Everyone will be gone from my place by ten. Come around then.'

Wood nodded, then watched as the doctor wiped her eyes, then stormed off back towards the chapel.

Jairus looked quietly at the wiry, fearful woman beside him as she parked the car outside a narrow house with an overgrown garden out front. All the houses looked the same in the estate, but some had broken bits of cars outside or piled bags of rubbish spilling everywhere. He knew the kind of estate it was – the international kind, where a mixture of hard-working, but poorly paid people rubbed shoulders with the plain idle who collected welfare and maybe committed petty crime on the side.

'I need to know where Tom might be headed next,' Jairus said. 'Who he might be after.'

Janine shrugged, looked at her lap. 'Could be anyone. There were a lot of people, important people that came to the parties.'

'Any you can name?'

She looked up, out of the windscreen, and took a heavy breath. 'I know... I mean, I recognised one of them... saw them on the TV, but no one would believe me... you wouldn't believe me.'

'I'll believe anything right about now.'

She looked at him and tried to smile, but it crumbled and her frown returned. 'Anthony Claire.'

Jairus had been looking ahead, but swung his head round to stare at her. 'Anthony... Tony Claire? You mean the Deputy Prime Minister?'

She gave a sad laugh. 'See, I knew you wouldn't believe me.'

'I didn't say I didn't believe you. You're sure he's one of the men who abused you?'

'I'd never forget his face. I can't. I wish I could. Oh, shit!'

Jairus saw that she was staring behind him, and turned to see that the front door of the house was open and a topless, muscular, bulldog of a young man was swaggering down the path, his face set into a death stare. He had tattoos all over his chest and arms.

'Janine!' The bulldog pointed a finger at her. 'Inside! Now!'

'I better go,' she said, flushed with fear. 'Can you get back to the hotel?'

'Yeah, don't worry about me.' He watched her get out, then watched the bulldog man come to his window and hammer his fist on the glass.

'Oi, cunt!' the bulldog said, stepping back, his fists balled up at his sides, the veins on his neck sticking out. 'You wanna get out my bird's fucking car?'

Jairus huffed, rubbed his beard and eyes, then climbed out of the car. 'I'm just leaving.'

The bulldog squared up to him, even though he was a foot short. 'Na, you're not, mate!'

Jairus stared down at him. 'Yeah, I am, and I'm not your mate.'

'Mitch, don't...' Janine pulled his arm, trying to get him back towards the house.

'Fuck you, bitch,' the bulldog said and spat onto the pavement, right by Jairus' shoe. 'I just caught you with this fucker. What do you think you're playing at, mate?'

Jairus looked at Janine and saw her head shake and her eyes plead with him. 'I'm not playing at anything.

I'm just leaving. I don't want any trouble. Janine knew my ex, that's all. See you, Janine.'

Jairus turned, stuffed his hands in his overcoat pockets and started walking. The bulldog walked behind him for a few feet, cursing, calling him out, trying to get him to turn around, and also to show his macho strutting to the neighbours. As much as he hated it, he kept on walking, not wanting to land Janine in more trouble, although all the time he walked he was seething.

He reached the hotel without even being conscious of it as his eyes and mind were masked by a red curtain of fury that was not just fuelled by the tattooed yob, but by the flashing images of what Karine and the other innocent children had had to endure.

Jairus walked up the steps to the bed and breakfast's front door, took out the key and stopped. His mind cleared a little and he was left with a haunting feeling of regret and guilt. He'd not been able to protect Karine and Janine back then, all those pain-filled years ago, and now he had walked away, leaving an abusive relationship.

'Shit!'

Jairus turned on the spot and headed towards his car, climbed in and started the engine.

He managed to find his way back and parked up outside Janine's house, got out and stood leaning on his car.

'Janine!' he shouted, and when she looked terrified between the grubby net curtains, he waved her over.

But the front door opened, and the bulldog swaggered out, swearing as he came.

'Mitch, please, don't!' Janine called after him.

'I want to ask Janine a question,' Jairus said, looking past him at Janine as she came to the door, looking soaked in fear. His eyes jumped to her left cheek and he saw that a bruise had already started to blossom.

'Talk to me, cunt, not that bitch.' Mitch eyed him, his fists balled at his sides again.

'Janine, I think you could be in danger,' Jairus said, looking into her eyes. 'These people will find you and could do you some harm… or even kill you.'

'What the fuck are you on?!' Mitch pushed Jairus backwards, but he still ignored the bulldog man flexing himself, giving him the dead stare.

'Is this the life you want?' Jairus said and saw her starting to cry. 'I can help you. Get you away from here, get you to safety.'

'Really?' she asked, wiping away her tears.

'Oi, shut up, you!' Mitch snapped his fingers and looked at Jairus again. 'She ain't going nowhere, mate.'

'I'm not your mate. Men like you make me sick. You like to bully, because it gives you some kind of power in the world. A world in which you feel lost and insecure. You strut around with your tattoos on display, giving it large, because inside you're scared. Janine, pack up your stuff.'

'Stay there!' the bulldog shouted, but she ran into the house. 'You fucking cunt!' the bulldog got even closer, his eyes burning, his muscles twitching.

'Yeah, that's me. Now, Janine's coming with me. That's the way it's going to be, got it?'

'Fuck you!' the yob's shoulder twisted, his arm firing forward, his fist heading for Jairus' face.

Jairus grabbed his fist, yanked his arm away and thrust his head forward, smashing his forehead on the bulldog's nose.

He let out a shout filled with pain and grasped his smashed nose that spewed blood into his mouth. Jairus kicked out, punted his foot into the man's shin, making him crumple to the floor, still shouting and swearing. To shut him up, he grasped him by his throat and squeezed his windpipe.

'You're going to forget she existed,' Jairus said, his teeth gritted. 'If you do ever meet another woman, then you're going to treat her like a queen. You got me? Because I'm going to be checking up on you. Nod your head if you understand.'

The yob nodded, and coughed, fighting for breath.

'Good.' Jairus looked up as Janine came out wheeling a small red suitcase behind her. He let go of the man and opened the boot and put her case inside. Then he opened the door for her and climbed in himself.

'Let's get you out of here,' he said and started the engine.

'What're you going to do?'

'Find out what the bloody hell's been going on and put a stop to it, even if it kills me.'

CHAPTER 27

Cathy closed the lid of the suitcase she'd borrowed from Rich's girlfriend and stood there for a moment, thinking. She barely recognised herself in the mirror, now dressed in a thick grey jumper, and black leggings.

Jairus had vanished on her and she almost hated him for it. He'd done his disappearing act on her once already and she swore she wouldn't let him get away with it again. But something had happened to her as Douglas Burdock inflicted pain on her and took his pleasure. Through the mist of red pain that had become so far removed from the pleasure she enjoyed, she saw his face. She pictured him and somehow it helped, as if his face, or the memory of it, was an anaesthetic against the horrors being inflicted upon her.

'You're not really leaving?' Rich said, poking his head round the bedroom door.

'I can't stay here any longer. I have to get away.'

Rich stepped inside, looking awkward, as if he was scrabbling around in his brain for the right words. 'He'll be back.'

'Maybe. But I need to find out what happened to those pregnant girls he had locked up with me.'

Rich nodded. 'Where are you going to start?'

She put the case on the floor. 'I've got a... I was going to say I've got a friend, but I don't think you'd call them a friend... anyway, they owe me a favour and I'm sure they'll point me in the right direction.'

'This person... are they... are they part of the world you used to belong to?'

She gave a laugh at the notion. 'A part? They invented that world. If Jairus comes back, tell him I couldn't wait.'

'Jay won't be pleased.'

She looked at him as she pulled out the handle of the case. 'He knows me. He'll understand.'

Cathy started the old car Rich had managed to get her, and drove, heading across London towards the little club that not many people knew existed. It was on the outskirts of the West End and from the outside it looked like a small wine bar. In fact, there was a small wine bar on the street level which few customers wandered into, and out again when they'd had one drink and found the place uninteresting. What they didn't realise, and Cathy knew very well, was that there was a staircase that led from the back of the men's toilets down into the basement. The expensive soundproofing prevented the heavy beat of music to reach the outside world, which in turn disguised the screams and moans that would accompany the fast rhythm.

Cathy managed to find a parking space after fifteen minutes and walked the rest of the way to the wine bar, where she bought a glass of white wine and sat at one of the round metal and glass tables at the back, so she could peer out at the passing world. Streams of black cabs and red buses and tourists, all padded out for the winter, flickered past while she waited.

She looked up at the CCTV camera positioned above the bar where hardly anyone bought a drink. How many people wandered in and questioned how it was possible for such a place to stay in business, she wondered.

She looked up when she saw the camera turn towards her and stop. She raised her glass and smiled.

Two minutes later, a dark-skinned man, his hair slicked back, wearing a pinstriped charcoal suit, came to her table and looked down at her.

He didn't say anything, just nodded towards the toilets, then walked over to the bar and sat at it.

Cathy finished her drink and headed into the toilets. She pushed open a door at the back of the toilet that was marked private and headed down the dark carpeted stairs that led to a massive equally dark room. She could make out the small bar that lined the wall to her right, and the hazy outline of the seating.

The few spotlights that beamed down allowed to her to see the figure sat at a booth near the back. A silhouetted hand beckoned her over, and she sat opposite the aging man who she hadn't laid eyes on for five years.

He hadn't changed. He was still thin, bony, with receding silver hair and grey sharp eyes that peered at her through thin slits in his face. He was dressed in black as always, silver rings covering his bony fingers. On both hands the nails of his index fingers were painted black.

'Cathy,' he said, saying her name as if he was tasting it. 'It's an absolute pleasure to see you after all these years.'

'That's a lie,' she said. 'I know how you derive your pleasure and to my knowledge I've never been involved.'

He smiled. 'Pleasure for me has always been a flexible affair. But I know you're not here to go over old times. You've found yourself in a little bother, haven't you, Cathy? I always knew you'd get out of your depth eventually.'

'How much do you know?' she asked and saw him give a little knowing smile as he examined his hand.

'You know I see all, Cathy. I still have my eyes and ears. Your mistake was getting involved with the Burdock family, but I guess that it was only a matter of time before you did. He helped you out of the trouble you were in, didn't he?'

She nodded, as she knew it was pointless to try and hide anything from him.

He sat back and nodded. 'I knew it. Of course, I knew it. That's what you get for playing too hard, Cathy. I did warn you. Someone was bound to get hurt. Heart attack, was it? You gave one man too much of a good time and his heart couldn't take it? A very prominent man. It's not easy to clean up something like that.'

'Yes, but let's talk about the trouble I'm in now. What do you know about that?'

'I know that they're looking for you... hunting would be a better word. Hunting you and this... Jairus person. Seems you've upset some very important and dangerous people. But you did a good job of disappearing for a few days, which means you've had help. But you didn't stay gone for long, which means you've now become the huntress. Am I right? Yes, I can see that I am. It would have been better if you'd vanished, got a new identity, perhaps left the country.'

'You're probably right. But I'm here. I need to ask you something.'

He smiled. 'Of course you do. Ask away.'

'I was being held at Sir James Howard's house. There were several pregnant young women there, so the question is... do you know where they might have taken them?'

He stared at her, unblinking for a moment, before he said, 'I'm afraid my knowledge doesn't extend to the desires of James Howard. I can only guess why they were there at all, but I fear the words would make us both sick to our stomachs.'

'Then can you tell me if the security services have been recruiting paedophiles for years and putting them in positions of power?'

The man's smile dropped. 'You of all people know the power of sexuality, Cathy... how it is controlled, used to get what one person wants. It's the oldest weapon there is.'

'That doesn't answer my question.'

He stared deep into her eyes. 'There's too much at risk for them. They need assurances in these dangerous times. There was a time when homosexuality, when it was illegal, would guarantee some kind of forced loyalty. Those days are long gone, thank God. Now, what is the darkest secret you can know about someone, and the fear of exposing that secret make that person commit any political act you wish?'

'Jesus...'

'But not just paedophiles, Cathy.' He sat back, watching her carefully.

'Go on.'

'There were certain things that needed to be done. Tasks carried out that the ordinary men and women involved in politics wouldn't be able to do. Not even the child abusers would be guaranteed to do what they asked, because the tasks were so barbaric. The child abusers would usually end their own lives when faced with such dark missions, and the video and photographic evidence of their own crimes. So, they needed to recruit more ruthless minds, the kind of people who would not think twice when asked to carry out a murder. But not only murder. Murder mixed with deviant sexual acts to destroy the victim's reputation. Or perhaps you need the target eliminated and his whole family into the bargain and you want it to look like the target killed them and then himself. Who do you ask to carry out such a mission?'

Cathy thought of the Pinder family, and then of Jairus who was out there somewhere trying to get to the bottom of it all. 'Are you telling me that they've been employing psychopaths to do their dirty work?'

'Who else? But can you see the obvious pitfall?'

'They would need to be intelligent. Psychopaths consider themselves higher in the food chain, and are usually narcissists, therefore they wouldn't take orders for long. They'd want to be in charge.'

He smiled. 'Exactly.'

'So, could these psychopaths be the individuals I've heard have formed a secret group within the British establishment?'

'It would certainly make sense for such a group to form eventually. It's a kind of evolution, if you think about. Survival of the most ruthless. You have to remember, Cathy, that politics isn't just one group of people with one agenda. It's not even three main political parties with three agendas. There are myriad groups with myriad agendas. It just so happens that a group made up of psychopaths have decided that they know what's best for this country and they won't let anyone stop them.'

'Who might their leader be?'

'In such an organisation there would be no identifiable leader. None of its members would know who was giving the orders.'

'That doesn't make...'

'Listen, countries have governments, have heads of state... why? They don't need leaders, not really. The civil servants, the machinery, keep it all going. Why have a leader? Because they make a good target. Let the terrorists take their best shot. Turn them into martyrs, then you've a better excuse to go to war against the country you decide carried out the assassination. You think the Prime Minister and the Queen have tight security? Think again. It's all for show.' He sat back, half closing his eyes, the remains of his smile vanishing. 'But the question really is... why did you come here? You see, I know you, Cathy. I know your almost psychic insights into the minds of anyone you spend enough time with, which means you more than likely know what sort of animal I am.'

She nodded. 'I do.'

'I guess that's my weakness. My lack of soul, of conscience. Our kind think of it as a strength, but it can definitely be both a strength and a weakness. So, the game's up. You know my secret, and I know yours. So why are you really here?'

She forced a smile to her lips. 'I'm here because I knew what you would do as soon as I showed my face. Are they on their way?'

He leaned forward, looked into her eyes. 'Do you think he'll come to your rescue?'

'No. He won't. I don't need to be rescued. I'm not a damsel in distress.'

'Good. No hard feelings, Cathy.'

She smiled. 'No hard feelings.'

Even though his hands were trembling around the mug of black coffee he was nursing, Jairus knew his face displayed nothing of the anger and pain and absolute fury that pounded in his booze deprived blood.

Not one customer in the greasy spoon knew that he'd reached boiling point, that his hands and arms were crammed with murderous intentions.

The truth was he'd been walking around for months in a kind of trance, held in place by booze and self-pity. Now he was having his moment of clarity, and could see everything around him in sharp focus, including the tall, bespectacled stick-like figure of Dr Jeremy Garrett who had just entered the cafe.

The doctor sat down opposite him in the booth, his eyes jumping around the room before landing on Jairus with a worried expression.

'You look how I feel,' Jairus said, trying to smile. It was almost a pleasure to see a familiar face.

'You look like I feel after a night on the sauce,' Garrett said and seemed to try and relax. 'It's good to see you, Jairus. Bloody good, in fact. Sorry, I'm still in shock from receiving your phone call. The last time I saw...'

Jairus lifted a hand, shook his head. 'Yeah, let's not talk about all that. I'm sorry, but I need to get down to business.'

The doctor nodded and cleaned his glasses. 'I understand. You asked me to find out about Karine's autopsy and the pathologist who carried it out.'

'Yeah.' Jairus took a sip of his coffee as he noted a strained look in his old friend's eyes. 'What is it, doctor? Something bothering you?'

'You asked me to find out who carried it out and, well, it seems that the person who performed it has also popped up on my radar recently.'

Jairus could feel it coming, the wave of bad news, the sudden, unexpected tide of doom. 'In relation to what?'

'The death of a police officer.' Garrett took off his

glasses, sighed, rubbed his eyes and replaced his glasses. 'It's a long story. But to cut that long story short, the police officer in question was looking into some delicate matters that he was warned away from several times... then he was on a mortuary slab... suspected heart failure.'

'You're about to tell me that the same person carried out the police officer's autopsy and Karine's?'

Garrett nodded and looked like he wanted to vomit.

'You think this police officer was murdered?'

'DI Jake Brenton was his name. Good man. I'm almost certain he was murdered. But they've cremated the body. We've got little chance of proving it. What about Karine?'

Jairus rubbed his face. 'I don't know. I need to talk to this pathologist. Do you know where I'd find him?'

'That depends on what you're going to do to him.'

'Just ask him a couple of questions. That's all.'

Garrett sighed. 'I thought that's what you might say. Listen, before you get ahead of yourself, I thought I better warn you that the police officer had a partner who's been helping me look into his death.'

'Yeah, and who's that?'

'DS Kate Wood. She's from out of town. She was brought in to look into the murder of Leonard Jameson MP.'

Jairus buried his head in his hands, and let out a tired groan. 'You've got to be kidding me. What I'm looking into, it's linked to Jameson's death.'

'Oh God. What the bloody hell's going on?'

Jairus pushed himself to his feet and felt his entire body screaming for him to drink a bottle of vodka and sleep it all off. 'I don't know. A cover-up, I think. One big fucking cover-up. This DS Kate Wood, am I going to get aggro from her or what?'

'She's just about ready to do anything to make all this right, I think.'

'Right, take me to this pathologist and get in contact with DS Wood and tell her to meet us there.'

Jairus almost parked his car on the pavement, but slammed on the brakes at the last moment, making Garrett lurch forward.

'You're not a happy bunny, are you?' Garrett said, rubbing his neck.

'No, I'm far from being any kind of bunny.' Jairus climbed out and started heading along the street, dodging through the straggle of late-night shoppers and partygoers. His eyes fixed on the tall and slender female adorned in a trouser suit on the corner, opposite the pub he was heading for.

'DS Wood?' he asked, looked her over then over to the pub. 'Is he in there?'

She stared at him, open-mouthed. 'Er... yeah, bloody hell. It is you! I'm sorry, I've heard stories...'

'Yeah? Well ignore them, I do. Where is he?'

'Always sits in the back. What're you going to do?'

Jairus clamped eyes on her. 'Whatever it takes to get to the truth. You got a problem with that?'

She shook her head. 'No, not at all. Glad to have you onboard. There's just things I can't be seen to be doing.'

'That's why I'm here.' Jairus took out his car keys and threw them to Wood. 'My car's the pile of rust parked badly up the street. Get it closer to the back of the pub. I take it there's a fire exit at the back?'

'Yes.'

'Good. I'll see you in a couple of minutes.' Jairus pushed the door open and entered the busy pub, his eyes sweeping the place. He shoved people out of the way, ignoring the names he got called and headed for the darker part of the pub at the back.

He stopped in front of a battered leather sofa where an ageing, dull-looking man was nursing a pint of Guinness.

The man's eyes slowly rose from the black liquid and found Jairus.

'Can I help you?'

'No, you can't help me. You can't help anyone. But I can help you.'

The pathologist's confusion filled his face as he said, 'I'm sorry, but I don't know you... if you don't mind...'

'I'm going to help you get a few things off your chest. Should take you about a minute to finish that pint. I'll give you thirty seconds.'

'Who do you think you are?'

'My name's Jairus. Does that ring any bells? Do you know who I am? If you don't, you're about to have a crash course. Finish your pint.'

The old man stared up at him, then shakily did as he was ordered.

'Good. Now get up, we're leaving.' Jairus grabbed him under the arm and lifted him to his feet, marched him to the fire exit and pushed him through. They stepped out into a tiny yard that was crowded with bin bags and fag ends.

Wood had parked his car in the road behind the pub and sat at the wheel looking nervous.

'Open the boot,' he said and pushed the pathologist round the back of the car.

'If you think I'm getting in there, you've got...' the pathologist started to say.

'Shut up,' Jairus said and opened the boot and started bundling the old man in. 'Now keep quiet.'

He shut the boot, and climbed onto the back seat and looked at Wood behind the wheel, watching him in the rearview mirror, and saw Garrett sitting in the passenger seat.

'Where are we going?' Wood said and started the engine.

'Somewhere where no one will hear him scream.' Jairus sat back, let his head fall back to headrest and closed his eyes.

CHAPTER 28

Jairus stood in the narrow, grimy kitchen, his arms folded, trying to calm himself, telling himself to take back control. The flashes kept coming; the intrusive imagined images of what Karine and the others had been subjected to.

He closed his eyes, covered his face, and let out a growl.

'How are you holding out?'

Jairus uncovered his face and saw Garrett staring at him while he cleaned his glasses.

'I've been better.'

'How did you find this place? We're so high up, might as well be in heaven.'

Jairus gave an empty laugh. 'Wherever we are, it's so far removed from heaven. So far removed.'

'He's in there, waiting, mostly complaining through the tape on his mouth.'

Jairus nodded, shoved his hands deep in his pockets and walked into the living room area. There was hardly any carpet left, and the wallpaper was peeling off the walls. A stained mattress lay in the corner, the pathologist sitting with his hands cuffed behind his back, the tape over his scarlet face.

DS Wood was sitting on the only other chair, quiet, arms folded.

Muffled complaints constantly poured from the

tape over the pathologist's mouth while his eyes grew and shrunk with every noise he made.

Jairus put a finger to his lips then ripped off the tape from the pathologist's mouth.

'You're in a whole world of trouble...'

Jairus clamped his hand over his mouth. 'I'm going to be asking you some questions, Dr Wilson. You answer them, or you die.'

Wilson laughed, full of vitriol. 'Do you think me an idiot? You're a policeman! You're not going to murder me in cold blood.'

Jairus moved in close, engaged his bloodshot eyes, let him see the bedlam beyond his own his eyes. 'Read my lips. I'm not a policeman anymore. Let me put it plainer. I once lived with the most beautiful, kind, clever, gentle woman that ever set foot on this hate-filled world. Thing is, before I met her, when she was just a child, some men did some evil... evil, things to her. So, you see... I couldn't save her back then... and I wasn't there for her when she died. But I am going to be here for her now. I will go to hell and back, and I will throttle the life out of you and feel no guilt whatsoever. Understand?'

'You're crazy!' Wilson looked towards Wood and Garrett with wide pleading eyes.

Jairus grabbed him by his throat. 'Yeah, I am crazy! I don't expect you to remember, but the woman I loved, who I believe they murdered to keep her quiet, ended up on your table. You signed her off as having a heart attack, because that's what they pay you to do. Just like they paid you to sign off on her partner, DI Jake Brenton. He was murdered, wasn't he?'

Wilson coughed and spat as he fought for breath when Jairus let go. 'What the fucking hell do you expect me to say? If I put heart attack, that's what they died of.'

Jairus clasped his hands round the doctor's throat and squeezed and watched his mouth open and gasps and spit burst from his lips as his skin slowly became red and then purple. 'How does that feel? Does that help you remember? Tell me, did DI Brenton really have a heart attack?'

'Oi!' Wood grasped his arm, tried to pull his hands away from Wilson's throat. 'Stop it! You're going to kill him!'

'That's the point, isn't it?' Jairus stared into her eyes, as his hands released from the doctor's throat.

The pathologist coughed uncontrollably for a couple of minutes, but his skin remained a red almost maroon hue. He eventually looked up, his eyes now clear of any mocking as Jairus knew they would be. 'You are mad!'

'Yeah, insane. So, you better start talking.'

Wilson coughed some more, looked at his bony trembling hands, then at everyone in the room. 'I know what you all think of me. You all despise me.'

'We pity you,' Jairus said.

'I hate you,' Wood said.

Wilson looked at her and nodded. 'Can't blame you for that. There are cigarettes in my pocket... can I have a smoke?'

'No, fucking way!' Wood shouted.

Jairus looked at her. 'What's the harm? Where can he go? Take off the cuffs.'

Wood shook her head, but trudged over and released him.

The doctor rubbed his wrists briefly, then fished around in his coat, still coughing and trying to control his breathing. He poked a cigarette between his lips and lit it with a shaky hand and looked up at Jairus.

'Thank you. That's very merciful of you.'

'That's the last merciful thing I'll do for you, so take advantage while you can.'

Wilson took a few deep puffs and sighed. 'They'll kill me. In fact, they won't kill me straight away. They'll destroy me... they'll tear me apart... then they'll kill me.'

'Yeah, and what do you think I'm going to do?'

'You'll just kill me. Maybe you'll make it quick. And I'd thank you for that. They'd kill me slowly and let me know that everyone I care about or have ever cared about will be raped and then murdered after I'm gone. And I'll know they mean it because these people have no conscience, no moral compass.'

'And your moral compass is working just fine, is it?' Wood snarled at him.

'I'm doing this because I have to! They've got me by my balls and they'll never let go. None of us might realise it, but we're all dead. You, him, me... all dead.'

Jairus took the cigarette from his hand and threw on the floor and stamped on it. 'We're not dead, not yet. Now talk to me. Did Brenton die of a heart attack?'

Wilson rubbed his face and eyes. 'Yes, he died of a heart attack...'

'You lying cunt,' Wood growled.

Wilson looked up at her. 'No, I'm not. That's what killed him, but the toxicology, if it hadn't been smudged, would have shown that something was given to him to bring on that heart attack.'

The old doctor looked up at Jairus almost with a look of sympathy in his eyes. 'This girlfriend of yours... was it a heart attack with her too?'

'Yeah.'

Wilson nodded and took out another cigarette and trembled as he lit it. 'Do you know about the island?'

'Yeah, well, I've heard something about it.'

'You don't know. But in for a penny, in for a pound. We're all dead anyway, all in limbo... it's off Cornwall, not far from the Isles of Scilly. It's an exclusive place to go and stay...'

'Tebel Island,' Jairus said and dug his hands into his pockets. 'I've heard of it.'

'So have I,' Wood said, shaking her head and looking exhausted. 'The watermark outline of an island was found on some paper that was used in a note used to threaten Leonard Jameson's life. That's what Brenton was looking into when he was murdered. What the bloody hell happens on this fucking island?'

Wilson took a long drag on his cigarette before he looked up at Jairus. 'You wouldn't believe me if I told you.'

'People keep trying to prejudge what I will and won't believe... just fucking tell me.'

'Yeah,' Wood said stepping closer, her face fixed in a scowl. 'Tell him so we can hurry up and get away from you.'

Wilson looked at her and huffed. 'Don't say I didn't warn you... human sacrifice. That's one of the many events that takes place there.'

Jairus rubbed his face and laughed, but it came out as a sound full of sickness. 'Come on, doctor, what are you trying to feed us?'

'See, that's what I knew your reaction would be. Fine. Don't believe me. You wanted to go down the rabbit hole, and now you're here.'

Jairus stepped over and clamped his hand round his throat again. 'So, we're talking Satanists? That the bollocks you're trying to sell us?'

'That's pretty much it, yes. A satanic cult. That's what they're about. And they recruit members from all sectors of the country. Like the Freemasons they move you up in rank. First thing you know is that you've joined a nice exclusive business club where you can make all kinds of connections. Slowly after that they introduce the different levels, where things gradually get more and more sinister. Of course, if you show you're not into what they want you to do, you rise no further. Only the most sadistic bastards rise to the top, and by that time they own your soul.'

'Commander Swanson?' Wood said, her eyes burning into the pathologist.

Wilson sucked on his cigarette. 'He told me what to put as your partner's cause of death, so what do you think?'

'I was told that James Howard had a few pregnant women locked up in his cellar,' Jairus said, as the ooze of sickness filled his stomach and made the ants crawl all over his skull.

Wilson let out a harsh breath, then dropped his cigarette and stamped on it. 'More than likely they were heavily pregnant, probably due around now.'

'You telling me what I think you're telling me?' The sickness spread through Jairus' body.

Wilson looked up, held his stare. 'Doesn't seem real, does it? Human sacrifice in this day and age? But what's one more atrocious act among all the many we read about every day?'

Wood hurried from the room, slammed a door along the hall. Probably the toilet, Jairus thought, and felt like joining her in excavating his stomach. Jairus looked back at Wilson. 'It doesn't surprise me. It still goes on. Some people still believe they need to appease their God or Satan or whatever. When does it take place?'

'It's October. When do you think?'

Jairus nodded.

Wilson pulled himself to his feet with a groan. 'Can I stretch my legs?'

'No.'

'Oh, come on, where am I going to go?' Wilson showed him his empty hands as he looked round the room.

'Yeah, OK. Don't try anything.' Jairus strode from the room and took out one of his pay-as-you-go mobile phones, then brought up the number he had for Rich.

'Rich Vincent, hello?' the gruff familiar voice said.

'It's me,' he said and headed to the battered front door and stood in the hallway.

'Jairus? For fuck's sake, thank God. I didn't know what had happened to you.'

'Yeah, I've been busy. That island, the one we found on Coulson's wife's laptop?'

'Tebel Island? What about it?' There was the creak of a leather sofa being sat upon.

'I want you to find out who's planning on going there, anyone in the public eye. I think those pregnant girls that Cathy saw are probably headed there too.'

'I doubt they'd be on any passenger list then.'

Jairus looked up as he saw Dr Wilson walk out into the hallway, still smoking, heading for the back bedroom. 'Yeah, probably right, but check for any heavily pregnant women heading there. I want to know everything about that island.'

'Jairus?'

'Yeah?'

'Cathy's gone. I thought you should know.'

'Gone? Gone where?' Jairus paced the hall, scratching at his beard.

'She said she had to find out what happened to those pregnant women she saw in Howard's house.'

'Jesus... did she say where she was going?'

'Only to see an old friend, someone who might have information for her...'

'That means someone that's part of her old world, the sordid world.'

'Sounds like it. Sorry.'

Jairus breathed out, rubbed his eyes. 'They'd be keeping an eye on her old contacts. They'll have her by now. Thing is, Cathy isn't stupid... she went there for a reason. I just don't know what that is.'

'Oh, Jay, there's something else... a Tony Fenton's been trying to get hold of you, called Edmonton nick in the end... says he needs to talk to you. He's at the Royal Free hospital Intensive Care Unit. That's all I know.'

'All right. I'll head over there at some point. Thanks.' Jairus ended the call, took out the SIM card, and threw it in the kitchen sink.

He heard the sound – the splinter of glass that filled the air – but he didn't take it in, didn't recognise it for what it was.

Then Garrett was rushing out the living room, his eyes searching for what had made the noise. Jairus followed him into the back bedroom. Wood was the last to enter the filthy room with the empty bed, the grubby net curtains being whipped and blown into the room.

The ice-cold air pushed and pulled at Jairus' face as he stared at the old doctor who stood at the centre of the large window, half turned, his watery eyes looking back behind him at the long drop.

'What're you doing, Dr Wilson?' Jairus asked.

The old man took his eyes away from the edge and stared emptily at him. 'It's over... it's over for me. I've got nothing left.'

'Don't do it,' Garrett said, holding out a hand. 'Henry. We can sort all this business out.'

Jairus put his hands in his pockets and stepped closer, the broken glass crunching beneath his shoes. He listened to the crackle of it as the wind whipped the curtains at his face. 'I can protect you.'

The doctor laughed, but it was hollow, and dry. 'No, no you can't. I'm dead. I think I've known that for a long time.'

'You can make this right, tell your story.'

The doctor shook his head, then turned to look down again. 'I'm going to hell. That's something else I'm sure of. I've done so much more than lie for them.'

Jairus took another step closer. 'Whatever you've done, we can sort it out...'

The doctor fixed his eyes on Jairus. 'You wouldn't be saying that if you knew.'

'I need to arrest him,' Wood whispered, stepping further into the room.

Jairus held up a hand. 'Wood, Garret... get out! Let me talk to the doctor alone.'

'If he's involved...' Wood started to say, then stopped and left the room. Garrett followed her after giving a last look at Jairus as he said, 'What are you going to do?'

'Try and talk him in, of course.' Jairus pushed the door shut, forcing Garrett out, then turned to watch the old doctor still standing in the window frame, his grey hair being tugged at by the wind.

'I'm not coming back in,' he said and Jairus saw tears in his eyes.

'I can understand that.' Jairus held up his hands and moved closer and saw the doctor watching with suspicion.

'Don't try anything.'

'Like what? You want to jump, so what difference does it make to me? I'm not a policeman, remember? I just want to talk.'

'I don't mind talking. They can't touch me now.'

Jairus stepped even closer. He was now within reach, and if he'd grasped out he would've been able to latch on. 'Did you ever visit the island?'

The doctor's jaw began to grind as he looked out at the grey windy sky. He nodded, but only slightly. 'That's how they get you. Tempt you. Suck you into their world. Then they know you'll do anything for them, because you've got no choice. You have to keep their lie going, because it's your lie too.'

'How do I get onto the island without them knowing?'

Wilson laughed. 'You can't, you idiot. You won't even get close.'

'Tell me something useful.' Jairus saw him shuffle backwards, closer to the edge, the wind blasting, a pigeon flapping past.

'I can't tell you anything more. Please don't try and save me.'

Jairus lurched towards him, pressing his hands out, pushing towards his chest.

The doctor opened his eyes wide as he rushed backwards into the grey, icy air, sucked downwards with only a harsh shocked breath.

Jairus stood in the empty window, looked down, but could only see the concrete lip of the building as the icy wind flicked up at his face.

The door behind him opened and he stepped backwards a few feet, still staring towards the broken glass.

'Oh Jesus...' Wood rushed past him, grabbed hold of the frame, trying to poke her head out. All Jairus could see was her hair being spun in the air as Garrett hurried across the room.

Then their eyes fell on him, their demands to know what happened arriving at his ears only as a muffled murmur.

'He jumped,' Jairus said and turned towards the door. 'We better get out of here. I think I can hear a siren already. Wipe everything down, then let's get out of here.'

CHAPTER 29

Death clung to Jairus all the way from the tower block to the Royal Free hospital, but it was only when he got deep inside its glaring white walls, that he begun to smell it on himself. He was moving slower too, as if some heavy creature had grasped hold of his back and dug its talons into his spine. In his mind's eye he could see it as an inhuman ape-like creature covered in some kind of razor wire instead of hair.

His mind was not right. His mind was not right.

It was a chant that kept on beating in his skull as he kept on moving, heading towards his destiny… or fate.

He kept seeing the doctor lying at the base of the tower block, his head a big red explosion of deep red. A community police officer and an actual PC were in the process of covering the body when they reached the ground floor.

Wood, looking ghostly, had driven them all away, and the unanswered questions were hanging in the air as if they were actually visible, like cigarette smoke.

Jairus dug his hands into his pocket and joined the horde of patients in their gowns, nurses chatting, and one very young looking Asian doctor at the bank of lifts.

They rose through the floors as the guilt kept on playing in his mind.

Tony Fenton was waiting for him in the corridor, staring at a notice board on the wall while the hospital staff rushed round him. He seemed oblivious to the horror of the Intensive Care Unit, but Jairus imagined the horrors that he would have witnessed inside the walls of Wandsworth Prison.

'Tony?' Jairus patted him on the back.

Fenton turned to him, his face relaxing, losing some of it pale tightness. 'Thank fuck you're here. He's in there.'

Jairus watched him thumb back towards the circus of nurses and doctors behind him, the constant soundtrack of orders being confirmed, and questions being asked while a phone kept ringing somewhere. 'Who?'

'Frank Saunders,' Fenton said and ushered Jairus away from all the chaos and towards a small waiting room. 'He was stabbed in the gut by one of the other inmates during a small riot.'

Jairus looked towards the bustle. 'How bad is it?'

'Looks like he's going to make it. Lost a bit of blood, but he's alright. Whoever stabbed him didn't do a good enough job if you ask me.'

'Yeah, you're right. Why am I here?'

The prison guard fished around in his pocket and brought out a plain brown envelope and held it out to Jairus. 'Saunders made me promise to give this to you if anything should happen to him.'

Jairus took the envelope, looked it over, and lifted his eyes to a curious looking Fenton. 'When did he give this to you?'

'A couple of days ago. He seemed more and more agitated lately, since you visited. He must've known he was in trouble. What the fuck's going on, mate?'

Jairus stared at Fenton, then looked at the envelope

again. He took a deep breath, then ripped it open.

It was a piece of tatty prison paper, with finger marks over it and doodles of flowers round the edges that only partly hid three naked female bodies. At the centre, written in neat, slightly slanted handwriting were a few names:

Tom Smith, Douglas Burdock, Toby Besnier, Anthony Claire, Stephen Hyde-White, James Swanson.

Underneath the neat printing was written in a more anxious hand:

One of them knows more than they are letting on. They give the orders. They cut up David Coulson with their own hands to keep him quiet. He was onto the leader. He knew who it was. Find them before they get you.

Yours, from Hell, Frank Saunders.

Jairus read the letter again, then lifted his eyes up to Fenton. 'Where have they got him?'

'Down the corridor. The room's being guarded. What're those names about?'

'Probably Saunders having a game with us before he shuffles off this mortal coil.' Jairus reread the note. 'But there could be something in it. Recognise any names?'

Fenton took the piece of paper and looked it over. 'Burdock. Anthony Claire? The fucking Deputy Prime Minister? For fu...'

Jairus lifted a finger to his lips. 'Let's not broadcast this.'

'Alright... Wasn't that Besnier the Internet traitor bloke?'

'Yeah. I think that was put in there to mess with my head. Same with Tom Smith. But who is Stephen

Hyde-White? I need to see Saunders.'

Jairus stormed out of the waiting room, stuffed his hands and the note into his pocket, and headed past the cacophony of noises that rose from the cubicles. He dodged between beds being ripped along the corridor and scrub-adorned people rushing in and out of the rooms.

'Can I help you?' a stocky male PC said as he stood in the doorway of the last private room.

'Yeah, just seen a man down the other end brandishing a knife.'

The PC looked past his shoulder. When his eyes flickered, Jairus lurched forward, pummelling his fist to the PC's solar plexus, blowing the air from his lungs and spinning him round. As the PC doubled over, Jairus walked into the small room where Saunders was lying still, his eyes shut, a tube running from his mouth to a machine next to him that beeped and flashed numbers.

Jairus took out the note, screwed it up in his fist, and stood by the bed. 'What's this, Frank? What the fuck is this?'

He heard the chatter of the police radio behind him and turned to see the PC pulling himself up to his feet, one hand clasped round the radio. 'Requesting...'

'Don't bother.' Jairus pushed past him and headed down the corridor.

As he drove across London, quite unsure of where he was heading next, Jairus called Rich. While he waited for the call to be answered, he stared at his own white knuckles as he gripped the wheel while red brake lights kept flashing in hordes of pairs all the way into the hazy, misty distance.

'Rich Vincent,' his friend said.

'Stephen Hyde-White?' Jairus said, then listened to his friend coughing for a moment before he replied, 'Stephen Hyde-White? That name's familiar. Hang on.'

Jairus waited, staring at the twinkling lights, the people under umbrellas and the harsh unforgiving rain now hammering the streets in sudden waves.

'Stephen Hyde-White,' Rich said and paused for irritating effect. 'QC.'

'Shit. Queen council. Bloody hell. Has he defended anyone of note?'

'The Burdock family on several occasions.'

'Why doesn't that surprise me?'

'He was also part of Toby Besnier's defence team, but seems there was a falling out and he got rid of him. What do you reckon?'

'I think someone's messing with my head. Where would I find this Stephen Hyde-White?'

'Hackney... looks like he...'

'Basement flat?'

'That's right, how did you know?'

Jairus' head began to pound. 'Did he live with a Julia Robins by any chance?'

'They were engaged for a while? What the fuck's going on, Jay? How's this all connected?'

'I'm not sure, but I think David Coulson might've been murdered in Hyde-White's flat. Do me a favour and text me the address and find Helen Chara for me, will you?'

'Her again? OK, whatever you want. What're you going to do about Cathy?'

The traffic seized up again and Jairus closed his eyes, feeling the exhaustion creeping up his body. He shook it off, and ignored the slither of self-loathing that snaked through his body as he imagined Cathy with Burdock. 'She can look after herself for the time being. She's a survivor. But at the same time, I'm sick of chatting with the monkeys. Talk to you later, Rich.'

Jairus walked across the open courtyard, his hands shoved into his pockets, the wind biting at his face. He stopped and looked up at the tall building as the low winter sun caught it and made it glimmer as if made from solid gold. He looked towards the security gate and started walking again, watching the two well-built men already stepping out to meet him. They could read him. It was part of their job, their expertise as mercenaries. Undoubtedly the Burdock family would have spared no expense to protect themselves.

'Do you have an appointment?' the first man, with short greying hair asked, his grey eyes fixed on Jairus.

'No, the truth is, I don't.' Jairus stared into his eyes, let him see what he was all about.

The guard stepped closer, lowered his voice to almost a whisper. 'Why don't you go home? Rethink whatever you're up to. Go home and have a nice drink.'

'Yeah, you'd like that, wouldn't you?' Jairus nodded towards the glass doors of the skyscraper. 'Why don't you make yourself useful and call up Douglas Burdock and tell him I'm here to talk to him?'

'You need an appointment,' the other, blond-haired man said. 'No one sees him without an appointment.'

Jairus faced him, met his eyes. 'Yeah, I know, but he'll want to see me. Just run along and tell him I'm here and that I've brought a shit load of trouble with me if he doesn't lower the drawer bridge.'

The first guard huffed out a laugh. 'Think you're tough, don't you?'

'Yeah, I do.'

The first guard nodded to the blond one. 'Call him. Hurry up.'

The guard strolled off after giving Jairus the dead stare. He listened to the long drawn out muffled call, then watched the blond guard amble back and face his partner.

'What did they say?' the first guard said.

'He can go up.' The blond guard looked at Jairus, then lifted a finger and pointed it at Jairus. 'You're going to get yourself in a fuck load of trouble with your mouth.'

Jairus shouldered past him, and headed for the glass doors across the courtyard. 'Yeah, I know. Not from you though.'

He stormed on, and headed into the reception area, where he was greeted by another uniformed guard with a hand-held metal detector.

'Hands up, please, sir,' the guard said.

Jairus did as instructed, lifted his arms and stood still as the guard swept the metal detector all over his body, then patted him down.

He was directed towards the lifts and sent up to the 41st floor, where he was met by a full-figured redheaded woman pushing forty.

'Welcome to Burdock Entertainments,' she said, but there seemed a distinct lack of pride as she spoke the words. Jairus said nothing, just put his hands in his pockets and watched as the woman gestured along the wide cream-carpeted corridor and followed her as she swayed her hips towards an expanse of crisscrossed glass.

She pointed to a glass door, which slid open automatically as Jairus approached.

Douglas Burdock was sitting at a wooden desk in the corner of the room, the hazy and jagged London skyline behind him. He smiled brightly, as if he was actually delighted to see Jairus.

He stood up and held out a hand, 'How's my investigation going?'

Jairus stood in front of the desk, his hands still deep in his pockets as he huffed. 'You mean my investigation into you?'

Burdock folded his arms across his chest. 'Is that what it is? Well, have you found any concrete evidence that I murdered David Coulson or had him murdered? Don't worry, nobody is listening, and I'm sure you're not wired for sound. Speak freely.'

'No, I haven't found any evidence. Nothing that would stand up in court.'

Burdock nodded. 'And if you did, I don't think you'd find the chain of evidence would find its way into any court in the land.'

'Yeah, or I'd end up dead, or any witnesses I might find would meet with an accident… or maybe even a heart attack.'

Burdock smiled then sat down. 'I'm so glad you came here, Jairus. I'm so, so happy you survived that terrible crash.'

'Yeah, I bet you are. You should've killed me. You missed your chance and you'll regret it.'

Burdock laughed. 'Will I? Really? Let's forget the fact that I have your girlfriend in my possession, what really can you do? We are deeply entrenched in this country, the government, it's industry. We're not going anywhere. We control the media too. If you control the media, you've won the war.'

Jairus pulled up one of the ornate antique looking chairs that sat opposite the desk. He sat down and stared at Burdock. 'Seeing as no one's earwigging this conversation, why don't you tell me what this has been about? Why did you hire me in the first place?'

Douglas sat back and put his hands behind his head. 'I only work with the best. After talking with Cat, and doing my own research on you, I knew you were the genuine article. I was certain that if I put you on the trail of David Coulson's murderers, then you would find the people I needed to be found. Which you did. Congratulations.'

Jairus' hands balled into fists. He saw himself grabbing Burdock by the throat, throttling him until he confessed and then throwing him out of the window. He breathed deeply, hid his anger. 'What's this all about? You and a bunch of like-minded psychopaths getting your jollies off, pretending to be Satanists?'

Burdock sat up. 'You don't believe in the battle between good and evil?'

'Not in terms of the devil and God and all that nonsense, no.'

'Can you prove that the devil doesn't exist?'

'You know I can't prove that. But we're adults, and we don't believe in goblins and ghosts, do we?'

'But many adults, as you put it, believe God exists. They believe it with every fibre of their being. What evidence is there to support their claim? Miracles? Jesus' face appearing on a slice of toast?'

Jairus turned towards the view. 'You're talking to the wrong person. I don't believe in God. If I did, then I'd also have to believe he was a nasty, spiteful piece of work.'

'Because you've seen all the terrible things that happen to people? You've endured it every day of your career, haven't you?'

'Yeah. I have.'

'Would you describe many of those acts as evil?'

Jairus didn't reply, just huffed out an empty laugh

and stared at Burdock.

The media mogul nodded. 'All those acts of evil, couldn't they be taken to be evidence that the devil exists?'

'You're making a huge leap.'

'Am I? Surely there's more evidence of evil in our world than there is of good. Remember, Satan was an angel thrown out of heaven just because he disagreed with God. Who's to say God was right and Lucifer was wrong?'

Jairus stood up again. 'Yeah, you're right. I have seen acts that I would happily label evil. So yeah, I know it exists. But I know that evil is part of a mental disorder, that results in a lack of empathy. Psychopathy, they call it. A certain percentage of the population suffer from it and a certain percentage of those sufferers are violent and wish harm on the rest of the population. Now, they can dress up their violent acts as religion, in the strange worship of a fallen angel, or whatever makes them happy, but I know it's just how they get their kicks, by manipulation and sadism. Well, I'm not going to stand by and let them get away with it.'

Burdock stared at him without emotion for a moment, then broke into a short-lived laugh. 'Now, comes the most amusing part for me. You see, I hear what you say, Jairus, and I believe you sincerely believe it all, but for you to wreak vengeance and bring these psychopaths to justice, then you'd need to be a policeman, wouldn't you?'

The wave of fury washed over Jairus, but he let it, felt the ripple all around, felt his heart hammering, telling him to kill the man before him for the greater good. But no good would come of it, as he knew there were more like him out there, still swimming the waters, searching for their prey. 'I've come to terms with the fact that that's not going to happen. But I'll find a way...'

'But will you? I stand by what I said. You did as I asked, and performed the task very well, therefore, I'm quite happy to have you reinstated as a policeman so you can punish the wicked.'

'Yeah? But then you know I'd be coming after you first, and your mysterious leader.'

Burdock smiled. 'Well, of course that's one of the stipulations. You come after me and my colleagues, and we'll destroy your career. You know we can do that. Oh, and don't forget I have Cat, or Cathy as you know her... and I don't have to tell you too much detail, but her death will be agonising and long. So, you take some time and think about what's important to you. Think of how many serial killers you can hunt once you're back on the force. Anyway, I'm very busy now, so call me on this secure number and tell me what you decide.'

Jairus watched him push the card across the desk, then slowly stood up and dragged it back towards him. He pocketed it and stood up, while doing an exceptional job of hiding the murderous rage building up in him.

He did not trust himself to utter a word without the venom leaking out from his tongue, so turned and opened the door and left.

All the way down in the lift, his brain crawled with a trillion insects that each carried a notion on their back. Each was poisoned with irrational thought, or a knee-jerk reaction. He wanted to kill Burdock, and with his bare hands. He wanted to see him on his knees as he begged for mercy, but he knew in reality that was unlikely to happen.

He then thought of Cathy, and how she would

be tortured to death if he turned down the offer. Eventually his mind thought of the lives he might be able to save if he swallowed his pride and his morals and took Burdock up on his deal.

By the time the lift reached the ground floor, Jairus had begun to laugh, but he didn't understand why. The security people looked at him strangely as he laughed to himself and walked through the building and across the courtyard.

He reached the street and took out his phone and dialled the number Burdock had given him.

It took a minute for Burdock to get on the line, but when he did, he said, 'That was quick. Made your decision already, Jairus?'

'Yeah, I have. I've decided you can stick the job up your arse.'

'That's not a very wise choice...'

'Yeah, you're probably right. But this is what I'm going to do... I'm going to come for you and the rest of the psychopaths and I'm going to stop you. I'm going to destroy your little psycho club, and I'm going to save Cathy as well. You know what else? I'm going to kill you. With my bare hands. So, Douglas, I'd start writing your last will and testament, because I'm coming for you.'

CHAPTER 30

Jairus parked a little way from the skyscraper, his arms and legs still pumping with adrenaline, almost blinded with anger. He tried to breathe in calming breaths, rubbed his face, tried to get some kind of grip.

He needed to formulate a plan of action, but his mind kept throwing images of bloody revenge at him. He shut them down, lowered his head and closed his eyes. The blackness encased him and soon the traffic seemed to fade away and he was left in an almost serene quietness.

His mind romped on, but not in any random direction it liked; it lit a path forwards as if a dark tunnel lay before him and was being lit a light at a time until he could see the end.

He opened his eyes, a grin appearing on his face, and he checked the date on the dashboard clock.

He took another disposable phone from the glovebox, put in a SIM and dialled Rich Vincent and waited, rubbing his beard, his leg tapping manically.

'Hello, Rich Vincent,' the familiar voice said, and he thought he could hear gunfire in the background.

'You playing a computer game?' Jairus asked.

'Yep, GTA five. What can I do you for today?'

'You can always say no, mate. Things are going to get messy and dangerous.'

There was a dry laugh. 'You mean things haven't

already got messy? Fuck me. What do you need?'

'I need you to locate Helen Chara, the journalist.'

'Your wish and all that. I'll text her whereabouts to that phone in a sec. Anything else?'

'Yeah, book me on a boat to the Isles of Scilly, will you? The day after next. Better book me a bed and breakfast too.'

'The Isles of... so you're heading to Tebel Island?'

'Yeah, that's where they'll all be at Halloween, so that's where I'll be too. Right, talk to you soon.'

'Hang on,' Rich said.

'What?'

'You visited the Ship pub on the Isle of Dogs a while back, yeah?'

'Yeah. Why?'

'Seems it burnt down a couple of days ago. No one was hurt, but thought it was strange. Maybe a coincidence.'

Jairus rubbed his eyes and sighed. 'Not likely. Get hold of the landlord, Terry Stephens. Get him to meet me at the remains of the pub. Talk to you later.'

A few hours later, when darkness had fallen, Jairus was sitting in his car, facing the charred remains of the Ship Inn. Warning signs and a tall fence surrounded the large car park. He heard the sound of an engine slow and begin to crawl behind him before his car was flooded with light.

The car's lights blacked out as it parked parallel with him on his right-hand side. In the quietness of the night, Jairus could hear the cooling fan of the other car, and the click of the car door as the driver climbed out.

Jairus recognised the large frame of the man, especially the overhanging belly as he walked round and climbed into the passenger seat.

Terry Stephens took a couple of minutes to adjust the seat to a comfortable position, then sat back and sighed.

'I'm sorry,' Jairus said, staring out at the silhouette of the pub.

Terry looked at him. 'Did you burn my fuckin' pub down?'

'You know I didn't.'

'Then why the fuck are you sorry?'

'If the people who set fire to your pub are the people I think they are, then it's my fault. I brought this to your door.'

'Why did they do it?'

Jairus scratched his head. 'The people I'm dealing with are a bunch of psychos. They get their kicks from inflicting pain and watching the agony it causes. It could've also been their way of drawing a line under Coulson's murder. No doubt developers will get hold of this wasteland and build a few posh apartments. So, Coulson's murder gets forgotten about.'

Terry huffed, then pulled out a tobacco pouch from his coat pocket. 'You mind?'

'No, knock yourself out.'

Terry rolled himself a fag, lit it and opened the window. 'These fuckers... these psychos that you're after... I take it they're after you too?'

'Yeah, especially since I just declared war on them.' Jairus laughed, and Terry laughed a deep gravelly laugh too.

'You're on your own then, mate?' Terry sucked on his cigarette.

'There's a couple of people helping me, but I'm pretty much on the frontline by myself. Which probably makes me insane.'

'Well, if you need any help... you know where I am.'

Jairus looked at him, watched his craggy profile and the smoke leaking from his mouth. 'That's a nice offer, but they've already taken away your pub, I don't want to be responsible...'

'Do you know how many fucking times I've found myself shit scared, wearing a uniform, walking up some street where every bleeding local hates me and wants me dead, and all I'm waiting for is a bullet or bomb to finish me the fuck off? You know what, mate? I realise now that I was happier then. Yes, I know now that when I thought I was helping protect people back home from terrorists, what I was actually doing was ensuring some fat cat fucker was getting fucking richer, but I was doing something. I felt alive. Know what I mean?'

'Yeah, I know.'

'Well, then what have I got to lose? Wife went years ago. Daughter doesn't like me, and God only knows where she is now. I've got a teenage son from another relationship to look after now. Just give me a bleeding chance to get back at the bastards who did this at least.'

Jairus found himself smiling, pleased to have an ally. He took out another disposable phone and SIM card and handed them to Terry. He also took out a notebook and wrote down Rich's number and tore it out. 'My friend will use that phone to contact you when the time is right. That's his number in case they come for you. This meeting alone could put a price on your head, so keep an eye out.'

'I always do. Make sure you call me, cause I get fucking bored sitting at home and golf has lost its fucking magic.'

Jairus smiled as Terry opened the door and pulled himself out. 'I will. Thanks. Watch your back, Terry.'

The man gave a quick salute, then ambled back to his car while Jairus started the engine and reversed out of the car park.

It was two hours later, as he sat outside a newly built set of apartments close to Victoria coach station that Jairus watched Helen Chara drive her car down into the car park beneath the building. He quickly climbed out and ran across the busy road, getting a toot from a passing driver for his troubles. He slipped past the barrier and ran down the slope and into the concrete parking area.

It was only one level of parking bays and he easily spotted the lights of Chara's new BMW at the far end. The lights went off, leaving the car in the dismal light above her.

Jairus shoved his hands into his pockets and hurried over as she climbed out. and stood staring at her, waiting for her to turn around.

She did, and her eyes flashed at him as she jumped out of her skin, her hand landing on her chest. 'Jesus! Oh my God, you scared the life out of me!'

'Yeah, well I ought to throttle the life out of you,' he said, and stepped closer.

'Why? What have I done now?' Her eyes flickered, avoiding his harsh stare.

'I remember the minutes before the crash. I remember feeling dizzy.'

'Well, you weren't well, were you? You've been suffering from alcohol withdrawal.'

Her hand went up to touch up her hair. Jairus snapped his hand around her wrist. 'You put something in my coffee. That's why you were there. They sent you to keep an eye on me, then drug me.'

'Get off me!'

She tried to wrench herself away, but Jairus pulled her arm and spun her around easily. He yanked her arm up her back. It was enough to make her yelp. 'Breaking your arm won't be enough for me, not for revenge. I wonder what else I can do. I've got a few scars on my body from all this, so perhaps I can give you a few.'

'I didn't go there to drug you...'

He yanked harder, making her scream. 'Yeah? Then why?'

'All right, OK! Jesus Christ, yes, you're right... I was there because Burdock told me to keep an eye on you! I had no choice!'

'He's got something on you? Yeah, evidence that you were up to no good in the whole phone hacking dirty business?' Jairus twisted her arm, and she screamed out again.

'Yes! Yes! OK? Yes... fuck you. I followed you because I had to.'

'When did they tell you to drug my coffee?'

'When we were in the diner place. I had another phone on me, so they could stay in contact. I didn't have any choice, did I? What was I supposed to do?'

'There's always a choice, Helen. But guess what? They'll know you talked to me, and you'll be another loose end now. You're already dead.' He let go of her arm, letting her collapse to her knees, and turned to walk away.

He heard her scrambling to get up, her heels scratching at the concrete, her voice calling out to him, begging him to wait.

He stopped. 'What?'

'You can't leave me. They'll kill me! Help me!'

'What do you expect me to do?'

'Protect me! Do something!'

Jairus smiled. 'You told me Coulson was friends with a woman. Was the woman involved with Stephen Hyde-White?'

There was no reply, so Jairus turned around and saw her looking down at the floor. 'Talk to me, Helen or you're on your own. If you think some moral itch will make me take pity on you, then you're wrong. That car accident took away that moral itch for good. I'll walk away and listen to the news report that tells me you died of an overdose or in a car accident and I won't feel an ounce of remorse.'

She looked up and he saw the tears in her eyes. 'I'm... sorry... I'm so sorry, I didn't want it...'

'Stop crying, pull yourself together and talk to me.'

She wiped her eyes, coughed, seemed to swallow down the fear. 'She was shacked up with Stephen Hyde-White at the time Coulson was murdered. Something went on between the three of them. I don't know what, but it was serious enough to get Coulson murdered.'

Jairus watched her for a moment, tried to judge her movements, the flicker of her eyes, then he nodded, happy that she was telling the truth. 'What time is it?'

She took out her phone. 'Nearly ten. Why?'

'Hyde-White lives alone in that same flat, doesn't he?'

'Yes. Why?'

'Well, he won't be expecting any visitors this late, will he?'

Jairus sat outside the plush basement flat situated on the corner of the Hackney street and watched Helen Chara heading down the steps. He wouldn't normally trust her, but he'd looked into her big watery eyes and seen the fear that gripped her. He was her only hope of survival and she knew it and was practically clinging onto him for dear life.

He waited for a few minutes, then heard the beep of his phone. He took it out and saw she'd sent a smiley face, so climbed out and headed across the quiet street and down the steps. The glow of warm light could be seen beyond the large black wooden door. He hammered his fist on the door, then shoved past Helen as she quickly opened it.

A tall, slightly overweight man in his mid-forties and wearing a pinstriped suit stood behind her, his face stamped with confusion. He raced towards Jairus, his anger building.

'What the bloody hell's going on?' he shouted, squaring up to Jairus. 'Who the fuck are you? This is my house...'

Jairus grabbed him by his lapels and smashed his back against the wall. 'Yeah, I know whose house this is. I also know what happened here.'

Hyde-White lost his look of anger, swallowed by sudden slow-burning horror. 'What... what are you talking about... I should call...'

'David Coulson? You recognise that name? Yeah, you do. I can tell because your skin's lost all its colour. Come on.' Jairus grabbed him by the scruff of his suit jacket and pushed him into the open plan flat, towards a leather corner sofa that sat next to the kitchen diner. After he pushed him face down onto the sofa, Hyde-White pulled himself up and sat awkwardly.

'Who are you? Police?' Hyde-White adjusted his tie, staring up at Jairus. 'No, you're not police. A policeman would know to keep their nose out of this.'

Jairus listened to Helen's heels tapping their way towards him before he heard her say, 'What're you going to do to him?'

'Torture him until he tells me the truth.' Jairus stepped closer to Hyde-White. 'You were right... well, partly right. I used to be a policeman. But now I've got no rules to follow, which makes me more dangerous. You will tell me everything before the night's out.'

Hyde-White was breathing hard, his face ashen. 'They'll kill me.'

'I keep hearing that a lot lately. I'm here, think about what I'm about to do.'

'It'll be worse with them... much worse... you cannot imagine how much worse.'

Jairus lurched forward, grabbed him by the throat and wrenched him to his feet. 'Death is death! Fear is fear. Look into my eyes so you know I mean it. I'm going to rip you to pieces unless you start talking.'

Hyde-White coughed and spluttered and managed to nod his head, so Jairus let him go and watched him stumble towards the kitchen.

'I've got a drink here somewhere,' he said, rubbing his neck and looking around the gleaming room. 'I need a drink.'

Jairus moved towards the kitchen, watching the suited man, who now looked terrified, shaking all over, pulling open the cupboards.

Then he stopped searching and straightened up, and Jairus froze where he was.

Hyde-White lifted his hand, which had a small black revolver clenched inside it. It was small, which meant it was only a 22.

'Don't be stupid, Stephen,' Jairus said, holding up his hands.

'Oh, God...' Helen said from behind Jairus, her voice breaking.

Hyde-White looked down at his hand and the gun within it, then up at Jairus. 'This... oh, this is not for you. This is for me...'

'Don't do it!'

'Why not? I'm finished. If you knew what they made me do for them, then you'd want me to pull the trigger. You'd want to pull it yourself.'

Jairus stepped closer. 'That may be true... but listen to me. You can get back at them. It's not too late...'

'It is too late.' Hyde-White raised the gun, his hand shaking, and closed his eyes.

'Listen to me!' Jairus shouted. 'Look at me. Hear me!'

Hyde-White opened his eyes, so Jairus said, 'Tell me about Coulson... he was murdered here, wasn't he?'

He looked at Jairus, then his eyes sprang over to the living room, to the centre of the floor. Jairus followed his eyes. 'Is that where he died?'

Hyde-White nodded, his eyes fixed and glassy as if he was caught in a nightmare. 'Right there... they held him down. They made me watch and filmed it... they always film stuff like that so they can watch it again... and again...'

'Who else was there?' Jairus took another small step closer, slowly making his way around the kitchen counter, his eyes on the gun that Hyde-White had now lowered.

'Mickey... Frank... Douglas and some other men... they brought Coulson over...'

'What men?'

'I don't know. Suited. They gave orders after it was over, told us how to clean up.'

'Was one balding, the other bigger, mean looking?'

Hyde-White shrugged. 'I think so.'

'Why did they kill him?'

'Because he'd found out too much... same old

reason. They had no choice... none of us did. That fucker... Coulson... I'm glad he's dead... do you know why? Because he was fucking my wife! But he was only using her to get to me and the others... he somehow got wind of what was going on, started sniffing around, finding the... kids.'

'So they killed him here then dumped him outside the pub? And Mickey goes down for it.'

'Mickey didn't care. All he was interested in was killing and he didn't like life on the outside anyway, so they used him for their dirty work. But they had him killed in prison because they knew they couldn't trust him to keep his mouth shut.'

Jairus took another step. 'This psycho club of theirs... who's the leader?'

'How the fuck should I know? Nobody knows. All I know is what I told you.'

'What about Toby Besnier?'

'Besnier? What about him?'

'Isn't he a member of their club?'

Hyde-White frowned. 'Besnier? No, he's made their lives hell. If they could find him, they'd kill him.'

Jairus reached out a hand and grabbed the bottle of whisky on the side. 'Good, then let's have a drink.'

'I don't want a drink.' Hyde-White lifted the gun again, his eyes filling with tears.

Jairus sent the bottle sliding towards him, forcing him to side step it and lower the gun. Then he lurched towards him and grasped his gun hand and twisted his wrist the wrong way, forcing him to open his hand. The gun clattered to the tiled floor, and Jairus kicked it away.

'Give me that!' Hyde-White screamed, more tears coming. 'Let me finish the job! Get off me!'

Jairus saw Helen walk towards the gun and start to

bend down. 'Don't touch it! Step back.'

The window blew out, sending glass spewing across the living room as Hyde-White flinched. A blossom of blood grew across his chest and he fell to the floor.

A second shot whizzed past Jairus, catching his jacket as he shouted, 'Get down!'

He dived to the floor and saw Helen do the same as she screamed and covered her head with her hands. Several shots were fired into the room, then there was nothing, just the cold breeze coming through the broken window.

Hyde-White was still, staring up towards the ceiling.

An engine started outside, roared and then the sound of a car tearing away from the pavement filled the night air. Jairus pushed himself to his feet and rushed out the front door and into the street but caught only the sight of the car's brake lights as it tore round the corner and vanished.

He walked back into the flat and saw Helen holding her face and staring at the body.

'I've got to go,' he said.

She looked at him with horror filing her face. 'What? You're going to leave me here?!'

'I can't stay. The police will be here soon. You came to interview him, but you found him in a state, talking about suicide. Then he got the gun out, but you talked him into putting it down. Then someone shot him through the window. That's all you know! I wasn't here! You got it? If you mention me...' Jairus stormed towards her and grabbed her by her jaw. 'I'll come for you, Helen. I'll come for you so fast and I'll bring hell with me. You got that?'

She nodded, so he let her go, stuck his hands into his

pockets and walked out of the house as he heard the distant sirens. He kept his head down as he walked, while his plan started to formulate in his head.

'Don't worry,' he said to himself, to Karine's ghost. 'Don't worry, darling, I'll get them for you. I won't let you down again.'

CHAPTER 31

It was a very different room she found herself in, and an even more different light source. There were glass tiles above them, allowing the streetlights to bathe the small cell.

No, not a cell, it was actually some kind of dungeon, and not of modern manufacture, but one that harked back to the Dark Ages.

But the grumbling of traffic allowed Cathy to know without doubt that she was still in London and under a busy main road.

Hidden in plain sight.

She looked down at the cell door, the only modern and well-built attachment to the old room.

Somewhere along the corridor a door opened, and footsteps came down. But they took their time, stopping occasionally.

Cathy sat back and folded her arms and tried to give the impression that she was perfectly relaxed. Even when the small square of light opened up in the door and a figure cut it out, she smiled and remained still.

The man stood there for a moment, watching her.

'Cathy...' he said, as if he was pleased to see her. 'My dear...'

'I thought you preferred Cat,' she said.

Douglas stepped into the room and the light from

the glass bathed his smiling face in grey light. 'That's when you were my pet. You've given yourself to him now. Even though you'll never lay eyes on him again. Of course, he'll lay eyes on you... I'll make sure of that... but it will be in a morgue. And it will take place not long before he dies.'

'He'll keep coming.' She stood up and stepped closer. 'You do know that, don't you?'

'You talk about him as if he's some kind of superman. He's not. He's just a stupid ex-policeman. He's not going to rescue you.'

'No, he's not. I know that. I don't want to be rescued.'

Douglas looked at her and she thought she saw a brief flicker of confusion in his eyes.

'You offered him his job back, didn't you?' she asked.

Douglas smiled. 'I did. He told me to shove it up my arse. I liked that. I'm so glad he didn't take me up on my offer. It's so boring when they do that.'

'What else did he say?'

'He said he was going to kill me. I believe he really meant it.'

Cathy smiled. 'He does. Now, Douglas, I want you to do me a favour.'

Douglas laughed, then backed himself up so he could lean against the door. 'Asking a psychopath for a favour. That's a good one. Go on, what's this favour?'

'I want to talk to the woman I met at James Howard's house. Linda, I think her name was.'

He stared at her, no sign of a smile. 'Linda? I don't recall a...'

'You know who she is. She's one of the young girls they abused all those years ago. You've been trying to find her to stop her from telling her story.'

'I haven't been trying to stop her, but yes, you're correct with the rest of your assumption. But she might be dead for all you know.'

'No, she's alive. Someone wants to make sure she doesn't ever talk to the papers or anyone with a sympathetic ear. That means she's worth something to you or your leader, whoever that maybe. So, you would've kept her alive.'

'I wish people wouldn't keep referring to him as my leader. He's not. We don't have leaders...'

'Someone always wants to be in charge. It must be much harder for a bunch of psychopaths.'

'Why do you want to talk to her, what good would it do you?'

Cathy moved closer to him, looked into his lifeless eyes. 'Did she know Jairus' girlfriend?'

'Yes, actually she did.'

'I want to know what happened to them. I want to know everything they went through.'

Burdock watched her for a while, scratched his cheek, then nodded his head. 'OK. I'll fetch her.'

'She's here?'

'Yes. You're all here. It's easier to transport you if you're all in one place. I'll send her along in a moment.'

Cathy sat down again and tried to make herself comfortable as she waited, listening to the grind of traffic far above her head.

Burdock opened the cell door, then looked her over. 'I'm curious. Why did you hand yourself back to me? You're not the depressive type... you don't seem suicidal, so why come back? You know you'll die, so why?'

Cathy looked up at him, pleased that his psychopathic mindset had no understanding of empathy or any kind of human emotion. 'You'll never know.'

Burdock studied her, half smiling, nodded and left.

It could have been only fifteen minutes later at the most when the woman was directed by a suited man towards Cathy's cell. He opened the door and pushed the scrawny blonde woman inside as she screamed and scratched at the air.

Cathy rushed to her, whispering calming words, promising that she meant her no harm. Eventually, Linda's big tired and red eyes seemed to absorb the fact that she was not about to be tortured or abused.

'Do you remember me?' Cathy asked, but Linda scratched her own arms and shook her head. 'I was locked up with you... never mind... I need to ask you something.'

Linda looked through her, then around at the dark, damp walls. 'They never ask me nothing. Just push me around. Sometimes they...'

'Do you remember a girl... she would've been slender, with dark hair and dark skin... very pretty... she would've been in one of the care homes with you...'

Linda looked at her. 'I knew a girl like that. Yeah, she was there back then... she was so pretty, so innocent looking... I think that's what they liked... oh, God...'

'They did evil things to the both of you, didn't they?'

Linda bit down on her bottom lip, scratched fiercely at her arm and nodded, shuddering.

Cathy sat closer, then lifted Linda's chin so she could look into her eyes. 'There's a man I know... he's a police... he was a policeman. He was involved with the girl you're talking about. He wants to know what happened to her, and when he finds you... which he will, he'll ask you about her and what she had to go through.'

Linda stared back. 'Alright...what...'

'Never tell him. Never utter a word. Just tell him you never knew a girl who fitted her description. If you tell him the truth, I promise you that I will kill you myself. Do you understand?'

Jairus stood at the window after he heard the engine rumble and come to a stop outside the apartment building. He looked down and saw the marked police car parked outside. He watched the female police constable open the back door for Helen Chara and help her out.

He looked up and saw that the black night had lightened to a kind of dark blue. The sun was somewhere behind the skyline and rising fast.

He sat down and let out a groan as his bones screamed out at him.

Helen let herself in and switched on the lights and jumped back and almost screamed when she saw him sitting in the armchair.

'You utter bastard!' she shouted, then pointed one of her manicured nails at him. 'You left me there with him! Then they turned up... I've been answering their questions for hours!'

'Yeah, I know. I'm sorry as hell.'

She stormed closer. 'No, you're not! You couldn't give a shit... you're as bad as them... psychos you're chasing... you have as much empathy as them!'

'Don't tar me with the same brush.' He stood up, his shadow falling over her.

She flinched a little. 'Oh, right, this where you give me a slap?'

'No, I don't do that. What did they ask you?'

'Everything. Wanted to know why I was there...

they kept asking me to tell my story over and over again. I stuck to it. I never mentioned you.'

'Did they mention me?'

'No.'

Jairus looked out the window. 'Was it just the police who talked to you?'

'Yes. Well... actually, this other man turned up, but they said he was just there to observe.'

'Suited? Receding dark hair?' He turned to her and saw the look of confusion on her face.

'Yes. Who is he?'

'British Secret Service. They have a stake in this, I just don't know why. Him being there means they know I was there. Chances are they knocked off Hyde-White. Question is, why didn't they kill him before I got to talk to him?'

Helen shrugged. 'I don't know... maybe they didn't think he was a risk...'

'No, that's not right. These people are always thinking ahead. They're insane, but they're not stupid... in fact, they're very intelligent. They've thought of every move I might make before I have. Hence how they knew I'd go and see Hyde-White. Killing him in front of me was probably their way of sticking their fingers up at me.'

Helen rubbed her eyes. 'You sound like you admire them.'

'Admire them? No, I hate them with everything they've got. They killed the woman I loved, even before I met her.'

'So, if they know every move you make, how're you going to win?'

'They'll let me live long enough to see what I do next. I think they think I'm going to lead them to someone or something.'

'Who?'

Jairus looked at her, saw that the fear had diminished, and now curiosity sparked in her large dark eyes. 'I don't know yet.'

Jairus walked towards the door and put his hand on the handle.

'You're not leaving me again?'

He turned the lock and slipped the bolts across. 'No, I'm staying here until the morning. I've got nowhere else to go.'

Then he walked over to her, got close and lowered his mouth to her ear. 'Why don't you want me to leave? What did they tell you to do this time? Drug me? Slit my throat when I'm asleep?'

Her big eyes were open, looking up at him. 'No! They didn't tell me to do anything! They just let me go. But I don't blame you for not trusting me...'

He looked at her, read her body language, watched her eyes. 'They didn't, did they? I don't think they need you anymore. So why don't you want me to leave?'

'Because I'm scared.' She looked down.

'No, you're not scared. You don't get scared. Not really.'

Her face changed, brightened a little as she looked up. There was another look in her eye and now he recognised it. Probably the same look a female praying mantis has before it kills its lover.

'I want you to stay, because I want you... to stay.' She tilted her head back, lifted her face closer to him.

'Maybe I don't want to stay.'

'Yes, you do. You already said you're staying right here... thing is, a man like you has probably got plenty of safe places to stay... But you chose here... somewhere dangerous. What does that say about you?'

'Probably that I'm a little suicidal?' He didn't flinch when her hand came up and gently touched his cheek. 'For all I know you're wearing a wire.'

She smiled. 'Why don't you check?'

He looked down at her black shirt, then slowly unbuttoned it, until he could see her full, tanned breasts held firmly in a lacy black bra. 'No wire.'

She smiled, then pushed his coat off his shoulders and let it fall to the floor as she loosened his tie. He watched as she unbuttoned his shirt, then pulled her to him suddenly, which made her gasp. He kissed her, closed his eyes and found the darkness slowed the runaway train of evil thoughts that seemed to continuously travel around his mind.

But somewhere in his skull, as he took her body, he could already see the dawn coming up and the next day begin. And the next day he knew would lead him onwards towards the island where he suspected he might face his darkest moment.

CHAPTER 32

The Scillonian ferry boat was jam-packed even though it was almost winter; the passengers filled most of the seating in the lower decks and all the seats on the upper deck. The rain hammered the top deck while the dark grey angry sea spat up tirelessly toward the sides of the boat.

Jairus stood at the stern, staring back the way they had come, his waterproof coat zipped up and his hood over his head. He watched intently, the waves battling each other, fighting for supremacy as the grey mist swallowed most of the view.

Some passengers clung to the sides, heaving their guts into the sea, or were sitting with green faces and paper bags held under their sallow chins.

Most of passengers were made up of men and women carrying expensive cameras and wearing green warm-hooded coats, he noticed.

'They're twitchers,' a man's voice said beside him, rising above the howl of the sea and rain.

Jairus turned and took in the man standing beside him. It was the man with the dark receding hair, the one from the Ship Inn, dressed in a dark suit and thick overcoat, rocking from side to side as he gripped one of rails.

'They come this time every year,' the man said and stepped closer.

'Yeah? They must be crazy,' Jairus said and looked towards the sea.

'It's the definition of insanity, isn't it? Doing the same thing over and over and expecting a different result?'

'Yeah, so I've heard. But I wouldn't know really, as this is the first time I've been here.'

The man stepped closer again. 'I've been here lots. They're beautiful islands, but there's only so many times you can keep coming back. And I come here for work, so it's different.'

'Is this where you warn me off again?' Jairus looked into his eyes, feeling the rain spitting into his face.

The man looked out to sea. 'That seems like it would be a pointless undertaking. We tried that once, and to warn you again... well, that way madness lies. I'm just here to show you that we know all, we see all.'

'You think you do. But everyone has a blind spot.'

'No, not us. We know everything. For instance, I know you're going to die on that island if you go there.'

'Yeah, I'll admit there's a chance... which means there's a chance I won't.'

'It's a slim chance. About as thin as a slice of ham, I'd say.' The man smiled, then lost any sign of pleasantness as he said, 'It might be me who finishes you off... or my partner. Perhaps we'll both be there. Anyway, I'm not saying I'll like it.'

'Yeah, I know. Nothing personal.'

'That's right. Anyway, won't be long before we arrive. I'm going to get a coffee. I'll see you when I see you.'

'On the day of reckoning.'

The man nodded, looked out at the waves, as if thinking deeply, then turned and made his way inside.

When the boat docked at St Mary's, the main island of Scilly, and the hordes of passengers had squeezed along the corridors, Jairus made his way out onto the gang plank and walked down to the long and narrow stone dock, his hands shoved into his pockets.

He looked out for the suited spy, but never saw him among the families and birdwatchers who carried their big cameras and heavy bags onto the dock. He kept on walking, feeling the light rain being blown towards him while the foam of the waves crashed upwards behind the tall barrier stone wall that ran all the way to the main road. Seagulls were gliding and squawking above him, diving towards the fishing boats moored along the dock.

Jairus took out the piece of paper that he'd scribbled the address on of the bed and breakfast that Rich had booked him into and saw that it was somewhere along Church Street, which was the main street that ran through the centre of the island.

His room turned out to be positioned halfway down a promenade of grand houses, a little way from a hotel and a church, and a narrow row of shops and restaurants.

The front door was open, and he found his bag sitting inside the door, delivered by the island's luggage company. He walked up the rickety stairs and found the key to his room in the lock and his door wide open. It was certainly a place far removed from the crime-riddled one he'd left behind in London.

He unpacked, locked the door and headed back down the stairs and into the harsh rain. He took the coastal road and turned his head to see the boats being churned and rocked by the wild sea. The police station was positioned a little way back from the centre of the town, and so he turned into a narrow passage by the tiny post office and followed it until its end then turned right.

He stopped, with his hood pulled up, and stood watching the small police station. There were two marked cars parked up the street.

Before he'd left, he'd contacted DS Wood and she'd told him about one of her old colleagues who had taken a position on the local force. She could be trusted, Wood had promised, and could possibly give him some insight into the comings and goings of anyone of note who might have recently arrived on the island.

He carried on across the street, headed into the police station, and walked up to the desk. A male PC, mid-thirties with receding short blonde hair was sitting at the desk.

He smiled as he stood up and said, 'Good afternoon, can I help you?'

'Yeah, I'm looking for Sergeant Sarah Webster.'

The man leaned back and folded his thick arms. 'She's out on a job at the moment. Should be back soon. Want me to give her a bell?'

'Yeah, that would be handy.'

The PC nodded and disappeared through a doorway, and Jairus tried to listen but he only heard distant mumbling.

When the PC lumbered back and sat down again, he said, 'Says she'll be about fifteen minutes. You know the Atlantic hotel and pub in town?'

'I'll find it.'

'She'll meet you there. Buy her a cappuccino, she loves them. Better wear a flower in your lapel, so she knows who you are.' The PC grinned.

'She'll know who I am.' Jairus turned on the spot

and headed out of the police station, watching the PC out of the corner of his eye. He'd got up again and headed through the doorway. Suspicion had begun to crawl all over Jairus like ants, burrowing into his skin, finding his soul.

As he headed back along the narrow passageway, listening to the wild wind whistling eerily all around him, it felt like everyone's eyes were on him, watching. The birdwatchers were the worst, always around, dressed up in their waterproofs, trudging along, carrying their big cameras with the long lenses.

The Atlantic pub was beside the busy Co-op shop, sat right on the road. Inside it felt like an old pub, with low ceilings and real fires burning in the crooks at either end. It was dark and only the dull light outside illuminated the place.

He sat near the doorway after getting a black coffee for himself and a cappuccino for Sergeant Webster.

He kept his eyes on the door, watching the occasional rain-spotted and windswept customers coming in looking for warmth.

It was twenty minutes before a bulky female PC with dark brown hair came in wrapped up in a rain coat. Her eyes jumped to Jairus straight away as she rubbed her hands together.

She pulled out a chair and sat down opposite him. 'You're Jairus?'

He nodded.

'Kate didn't say much, so I looked you up.' Webster's eyes fell to the coffee. 'Is that for me?'

'Yeah. Cappuccino.'

She laughed and shook her head. 'You've met PC Dave Philips. He's a piss taker. I can't stand coffee.'

'He's hilarious. I need your help.'

She pushed away the coffee, but kept looking at

him, her eyebrows knitting together. 'I figured you did. I trust Kate. She's a good judge of character. You though... you seem like a colourful character.'

'Yeah, that's me. What do you know about Tebel Island?'

'There's a leaflet in the tourist information office.'

'So now you're the comedian?' He sat back, sipped his coffee. 'Thing is, Sergeant Webster, you don't come across as the comedian type and I saw the look in your eye when I mentioned that island. So, I know that you know something.'

Webster sat forward and rested her arms on the table. 'I know enough to keep my nose out. You're looking for trouble and you'll find it there.'

'What happened?'

'My first year here. A big yacht comes and drops anchor not far from here. Thing is about the Isles of Scilly, there's no customs, so many boats come and go. You can easily sneak past the coastguard and smuggle in what you like. Well, I was informed by a vigilant islander that boats were coming and going from the yacht in the middle of the night. I was also told that the occupants were popping out to Tebel island, even though it was winter, and it was all shut up, like it's supposed to be now.'

'What did you do?'

'I waited for the next boat to leave the yacht in the middle of night and I brought the rower in for questioning. Thing is, they refused to say a word. They had no ID on them either. Then I get a call from the mainland police telling me release him or I'll lose my job.'

'Did you leave it there?' Jairus sipped his coffee.

'They didn't leave me much choice. But I did pay a visit to Tebel Island and saw there was a lot security there. I know the Freemasons take over the hotel towards the end of the summer sometimes, but never that late in the year. Something was definitely going on out there. What're you planning on doing?'

'I'm planning to pay a visit there maybe tomorrow night and see what's going on. Do you know anyone with a boat who'll take me out there?'

'I'm sure you'll find someone with a boat for the right price. Just ask around.'

'Yeah, don't worry I will.'

Webster sat upright, looking ready to leave. 'Right, I've got duties to see to. Domestic violence cases and all that juicy stuff. My advice to you is stay away. Forget about it all.'

'I can't.'

She nodded, looked around the pub and rubbed her hands briskly again. 'Right. Take care. Hope you stay out of trouble. I won't hold my breath. Give my love to Kate when you see her.'

Jairus watched her cross the darkened room and open the door. The wind and rain tried to fight inside, but she pushed onwards and shut the door.

He was alone again, trying to calculate his next move.

There was some little light beaming behind the skyline outside the glass walls of the hospital, even if it was being pushed away by the aggressive dark clouds that surrounded it.

Douglas Burdock turned his eyes away from the view and stared at the large hospital bed that had cost him thousands to put in the room. It was a drop of spit in all the oceans of the world combined.

His father's bony and weak body lay under the starched sheet. It was almost not there at all, and only his ugly, disproportionate head gave away that an actual human lay beneath it.

God, he was ugly, Douglas decided. He'd never thought about it before, but he had noted the comments made by the few journalists left that were not in his father's employ. But there was no getting away from the fact that the old man was unattractive, and it irked him suddenly that his model mother must have gone to the marital bed much like a prostitute. The only saving grace was that he had inherited her looks and not his.

Robert Burdock was not aware of it, but he was dying. Douglas smiled.

The stage was set for his complete takeover of the media empire, and the last arrangements for the offering were being made. There were several recruits yet to be initiated who had passed the many stages of the procedure.

Movement to his right caught his eye and he looked round to see Dr Jerry McCain looking at him through the small window in the door.

Douglas took another look at his sedated father and then left the room and joined the doctor in the large living area that cost thousands more than the bed.

McCain sat on the sofa, patting down his suit and trousers. 'Good evening, Douglas,' he said and gave a sympathetic smile.

'There's no need to pretend with me,' Douglas said and stood over the doctor. 'We're all friends here.'

'Force of habit. I've made arrangements as required.'

'Good. He's sedated at the moment, sleeping like a baby. He thinks I'm going to save him.'

The doctor laughed but it was devoid of emotion. 'They all think that. My father was of that opinion too.

When do you want it done?'

'Soon. I'll let you know. After the offering.'

McCain smiled. 'I'm looking forward to that. The babies are all healthy. The women are recovering nicely, but they obviously don't realise what's about to happen.'

'Of course not. It won't be just the babies and the young ladies that will be sacrificed.'

McCain looked up. 'Really? Who else?'

'Loose ends. It doesn't make any difference. It's easier to do it all together and easier then to dispose of them all. Less of a mess.'

McCain nodded. 'Makes perfect sense. Will he be there?'

'He will. Not that it makes any difference. People put too much faith in him as a leader. Want a drink?'

'I haven't got time.' McCain stood up as the door to the room opened and Nurse Wright stepped inside.

Her face flushed as soon her eyes took in Douglas and the doctor. He could see that venom filled her eyes as she carried on, mumbling an apology for disturbing them. It was time she looked in on Robert Burdock, she said.

'I better go,' McCain said, his eyes following Nurse Wright as she disappeared into the old man's room.

'I'll see you at the offering,' Burdock said, but didn't even make eye contact with the doctor as he left. His mind was on the nurse, thinking of her in the next room, trying to do her job, even though her whole body was beating with hatred and repulsion.

It aroused him, as of course he knew it would when he planned the seduction and the inevitable rape.

He walked towards the doorway and blocked it, leaving only enough room for her to slide past and he waited.

She finished her work on his father and turned and froze when she saw him. He smiled, but she avoided his gaze and walked towards him, already twisting her body to get past.

He moved into her way, made her stop dead, the anger now forming tears in her eyes.

'Please...' She looked down, her body trembling.

The word rang like a bell through his mind, the most perfect note. It resonated in his body and filled him full of pleasure.

He stepped aside and allowed her to walk through to the living area and towards the kitchen. He almost laughed when she stumbled on her way into the kitchen.

She stopped by the sink, frozen, and he could tell her mind was turning over and that words were trying to find her dry hate-soaked lips.

'Go on, say it,' he said and moved closer to her, merely a foot from her back.

She said something, but he didn't quite hear. 'Speak up.'

'I know...' she said, her voice breaking, dying away.

'You know what exactly?'

'What... what you're planning.'

He took her arm and turned her around and was a little surprised to see her startled, shy eyes meet his.

'And what am I planning?'

She looked down. 'I'm... I'm a nurse...'

'Yes, I know that... explain yourself.' He lifted her chin. 'Look at me and spit it out.'

'I'm a nurse, so I know what to look for... so... so I know your father hasn't got Alzheimer's or any of the conditions the doctors say he has. I know you pay them a lot of money to lie for you.'

He couldn't help but smile as he put his hand round

her throat and felt the pulse beating hard in her neck. 'What else?'

'I know... that... you're planning on killing him. You want to take over his empire...'

He tightened his grip around her throat. 'Do you know what I am? You must have some realisation of what sort of animal I am by now.'

'You're...'

'I'm what?'

'Evil.'

He laughed. 'That's such an overused word. Evil is what the normal people call that which they cannot explain. What I am is what the professionals call a psychopath. It took me a long time to come to understand what I am and my place in the world. But I know my place and it is at the top of the food chain. They used to lock us up and study us, but now they use us to do the things that they cannot do themselves. Trouble is, we can think for ourselves and we're tired of being used. There's a war going on, and we are going to win. There are no heroes... well, maybe there are some. There is a man that some thought was a hero, who might have tried to stop us, but he's about to be finished. He thinks he's on the right track, but he's not. So, you see, no one's going to help. The question is, who're you going to tell?'

She shook her head. 'No... no one. I can't. I just... I just want more money.'

He let go of her neck. 'That's more like it. You can have more money, if that's what you want. Good for you! Now, I have somewhere else to be.'

Thankfully the rain had let up a little as Jairus headed towards the harbour, but the wind had picked up and kept pushing him towards the wall. The sea was raging and filled his ears with its rampant noise.

He could see some of the boatmen mooring their vessels after a few passengers had disembarked. The weather was now too wild for anymore crossing, so most of the boatmen were heading off towards the warm lights of the nearest pub, the Mermaid which sat on the end of the harbour.

Jairus' first instinct was to join them in the warmth of the pub and down a few glasses of straight vodka. He looked back at the pub but kept moving towards the last of the tourist boats still being moored at the harbour. He spotted a man, approximately in his mid-thirties, with a young man's wiry beard, tying up the boat, wrapped up in waterproofs.

Jairus headed down the dank stone steps as the young boatman was stepping on to them. 'Can I have a word?'

The young boatman had already stopped to take a rolled-up cigarette from inside his coat and light it. He took a drag and shrugged as he scratched his beard. 'Sure. What do you want to know, mate?'

'I need to find someone who'll take me out to Tebel Island.'

The boatman raised his also wiry eyebrows. 'Tebel Island? This time of year? You won't get anyone to take you, not when the sea's spitting like she is.'

Jairus looked to where he pointed a thick and weathered thumb. 'Yeah, I can appreciate that. But I need to get out there and I'm willing to pay whatever it takes.'

The young man took a drag of his roll-up and scratched his beard again. 'You better have the price of a new boat in your pocket then, mate. Cause that's what any boatman is risking taking you out there. There's treacherous rocks on the way out. Few of these boys have got the experience to get past them.'

'Yeah, and who has?'

The young boatman looked back up the harbour, then pointed his cigarette towards the other boats. 'See the green and yellow boat? It's called The Sparrow. The fella who owns that one might be crazy enough to take your money. He's called Seth.'

'Where might I find him?'

'Try the Mermaid, if not there he lives in Anchor Cottage, just opposite the Co-op. Good luck.'

Jairus gave a brief smile then headed back up the steps, fighting with the wind that kept pushing and prodding him sideways. As he looked up towards the glowing lights of the Mermaid, he hoped Seth was sat in the warmth nursing a pint.

He pushed open the door and the wind battered his back and forced him on. Nearly everyone sitting around the small rectangular room, all at battered wood tables, looked up at him briefly.

There were old paintings on the wood-panelled walls and various kinds of sea knots in frames. Jairus walked to the bar, where a tall and balding middle-aged man asked him what he would like to drink.

'Black coffee, please,' Jairus said, and looked around at the weathered faces that drank and chattered to one another.

When the barman came back with his coffee, Jairus paid then said, 'Is there a boatman called Seth in here?'

'Seth's not here,' a thick Cornish voice said from the corner.

Jairus turned to see an old man with a grisly silver beard and denim cap gripping a hot cup of something between his thick hands. 'Do you know where he is?'

'Might be at home.'

'Anchor Cottage?' Jairus asked as he picked up his

coffee and sipped it.

'That's where you'll find him, son,' the old man said.

'Thanks,' Jairus said, drank down his coffee and went towards the door and battled with the wind and rain as he headed back to the harbour.

He walked through the centre of the town, past the supermarket and post office and then turned right up the narrow road that swung around to his left and was filled with whitewashed stone cottages. Everything looked grey and misty as he headed for the smallest one that seemed set back a little, and had a little courtyard out in front, which was gated off.

He stepped through, got under the shelter of the eaves and took down his hood and wiped the spots of rain from his face. He knocked and waited for a minute before knocking again.

He heard the sound of an old lock being undone and the creak of the door.

He didn't move when he saw the suited man with the receding hair sitting in an armchair opposite the door. He lowered his eyes and saw the small gun in his hand and the shiny black silencer attached to it.

'Come in,' the suited man said, beckoning him with his free hand. 'Or I can put you down from here if you want. It'll be inconvenient, but I'll do it.'

CHAPTER 33

Jairus, not being a fool, did as he was requested and shut the door behind him. Out of the corner of his eye he saw a large figure move and turned to see the bigger, harder looking man standing with his arms folded across his big chest.

'Inconvenient for who?' Jairus asked.

'Us of course.' The seated agent looked down at his gun. 'I thought this might happen later, or you might actually get to the island and you'd be disposed of there. But I decided it was pointless to drag this out. I don't suppose you thought it would end like this either, did you?'

Jairus forced a grin to his lips, tried hard to relax his hands and to calm the sudden racing of his heart. 'It's not over yet.'

The agent stood up. 'It is. We do this for a living. We've done this so many times before that's it's almost a bore now. You'd need a miracle to save you now, and we don't believe in those, do we?'

'No, we don't.' Jairus looked around the room, trying to find anything he could use as a weapon.

'We've cleaned the room,' the agent said. 'We've thought of everything.'

'Yeah, I know. So, you're doing the dirty work for a bunch of psychopaths?'

'Or maybe a bunch of psychopaths are doing our

dirty work?' The agent raised his eyebrows. 'People use each other to get the job done. It's how it works. It's how it's worked forever. We need Douglas Burdock and his group of crazy bastards because they've got so many politicians in their pockets that they have the ability to wield a lot of power. So, we work with them and keep them inline. Occasionally we have to clean up after them. It's unfortunate that you're the mess this time. You seem like a good guy and there are few of them left.'

'So help me stop them.'

The agent sighed. 'No can do I'm afraid. This is not just my job, it's my life. My death. What do you think would happen if I just started letting people off? You understand?'

'Yeah, actually I do.' Jairus looked around the room, his mind still trying find a way out, but he already knew there wasn't. He was going to die wherever they decided to take him, unless he fought for his life. He looked at the hard-looking, obviously ex-military in the corner who was keeping a sharp eye on him. They would be both highly trained.

'Stop trying to figure this out,' the agent with the gun said. 'Open the door.'

Jairus turned around and slowly opened the door, feeling the blast of wind and rain trying to push him back into the house. For a moment he wondered what had happened to the owner of the house, and quickly forgot as he stepped out into the courtyard and saw another man stood across the passageway, watching him. He was well built, dressed in a thick dark coat, with the same cold hard look in his eyes as the other two.

'That's right,' the agent said behind him, raising his voice above the wind. 'It's over. Keep walking and turn right.'

Jairus did as he was told, and found himself taking the narrow back streets all the way to the end of the town and towards the beach. All three of them kept their distance, setting themselves out so any of them could get a good shot off without endangering each other.

Jairus' mind was now crawling in every direction, scurrying for an idea and coming back empty. He knew where they were taking him, making him walk out past the beach, up the steep path that would lead close to the rocky cliffs.

Jairus reached the top of the cliffs as the roar of the sea filled his ears. He could make out the foam of the sea spitting high in the air as the men trudged up all around him, positioning themselves perfectly. There was just enough light so that he could make them all out as they stood watching him.

Their leader took out a bottle from inside his coat and lowered it to the ground just in front of Jairus and stepped back.

'What's this?' Jairus looked down and saw that it was a bottle of vodka. 'Never mind. I get it. I come up here and drink myself stupid and fall off the cliff?'

'It makes it easier for us that you have a problem with drink. Especially since you recently had a car crash that nearly killed you.'

'I was dry that day.'

'That's not what your blood will say.' Their leader raised his gun and stepped closer. 'Start drinking.'

Even though the sea was raging, and the rain had begun to beat hard on the muddy ground, splashing up at his trousers, the blood pounding in his ears blocked everything else out as he bent down and picked up the bottle. He looked at the label which he could hardly read in the dim light, his mind still searching for a way out.

A miracle.

He huffed out a laugh, unscrewed the top of the bottle and lifted it as if to make a toast. 'I've been dying for a drink.'

The man opposite him nodded. 'Drink it. Drink it all. It'll make it easier on all of us.'

Jairus lifted the bottle to his lips, then froze when he heard a voice behind him.

'Someone's coming,' said one of the agent's men.

The man holding the gun on Jairus, looked into the darkness. 'Where are they?'

Jairus turned and tried to make out whatever the man had observed, but only the bleak grey darkness and the hideous rain filled his vision. He turned towards the blurred outline of the other thick-set agent, who had something held to his face. Night vision, surmised Jairus, wondering also if the time was right to make his escape into the darkness.

'Don't move,' the first agent said from behind him. 'What's he dressed like?'

The spotter said, 'Green anorak. Flashy Camera in one hand, rucksack on his back.'

'It's a fucking birdwatcher,' the agent said behind Jairus.

The spotter lowered his night vision goggles. 'This late?'

'They set up in the middle of the night,' the gunman said. 'Catch the birds first thing. Wait until he's passed.'

All of them were silent, turned towards the blackness as slowly the sound of boots trudging up towards them came out from under the roar of the sea and the patter of rain.

Jairus could see him now, the green-shrouded figure coming in their direction, emerging from the murky darkness.

Jairus watched the birdwatcher as he seemed to turn and head inland before he seemed to merge with the rock formations that littered the rest of the cliff.

He was gone.

'Let's get on with this,' said the agent with the gun.

There came a whistle of sound, almost lost beneath the waves, ripping past Jairus. The agent with the gun jerked and shouted into the wind.

A voice yelled from out in the darkness for Jairus to get down. He dived down, burying his face into the grass and mud as he saw muzzle fire glow somewhere ahead of him in quick succession.

Tap, tap, the shots came and Jairus counted as blasts came and were answered by the agents around him.

Jairus lifted his head and saw the spotter firing a shot as he ran towards the birdwatcher. Then his chest popped and he stumbled and slumped to the ground.

Jairus took in the silence, now only the wild sea lashing at the rocks. He turned his head and saw the third man was lying still barely six feet away.

The sound of the trudging boots came again out of the night and Jairus lifted his muddy face to see the tall, well-built figure coming towards him. He still had a silenced pistol in his hand, the slight waft of smoke emanating from the end, being taken by the wind.

'I didn't have much bleeding choice, did I?' Terry Stephens said, looking over the dead men lying around him.

Jairus pushed himself to his knees with great effort, still feeling his heart pounding in his chest and ears, and got to his feet. 'No, not much choice. Help me roll their bodies over the edge.'

Terry got beside him, crouched down, and helped him push the agent down over the grass and rock until they had him perched on the edge. Jairus crawled out, blinking as the rain filled his eyes and mouth. He could see the sea roaring in, smashing against sharp rocks below. The sea retreated, then gathered itself for another attack.

'Now!' Jairus shouted and they both pushed the body off the edge and watched it plummet towards the rocks below. Jairus clambered to his feet and looked at Terry Stephens. 'Thanks for saving my life, by the way.'

'No worries, mate. You'd do the same.' Stephens looked at the gun he took from inside his jacket and lobbed it towards the sea.

'How the fuck did you know where to find me?'

'Your mate, Rich. Managed to get hold of him and persuaded him you could do with keeping an eye on. Bleeding good job I did.'

'Yeah.' Jairus turned towards the agent that had wielded the gun and stood over him. He somehow regretted that the man was dead but told himself there was no other way.

He grabbed hold under his arms and began dragging him towards the cliff until Terry lifted his feet and helped him drop him into the water.

After the third agent was delivered without ceremony to the wild grey water beneath them, Jairus buried his hands into his pockets and turned towards the town and began walking.

'What now?' Terry asked, as he caught up with Jairus.

'We hold up until tomorrow night, then we find a boat to take us to Tebel Island to finish this thing.'

'I've got a boat. It's how I got here.'

Jairus stopped and looked at him. 'You don't have to come. It's going to be a rough crossing and chances are they'll be waiting to kill me.'

Terry laughed. 'You think I'm going to fucking let you go there on your own, you're having a laugh.'

'Yeah, but you don't know me. You really going to follow me into hell?'

'Why not? I've been bored ever since I left the army, pissing about with that fucking pub. I need some bloody action. Anyway, you'll need some cover fire.'

Jairus nodded, then walked on. 'OK, let's get some rest before we go to war.'

Cathy woke up with a bolt of electricity surging through her. She thought it might have been a nightmare, but then she looked at the dank cell she was in and decided that nothing so mundane as a bad dream could make her fearful.

She looked over at Linda, who was lying on the mattress that had been unceremoniously thrown in the corner for her as if she was a dog. Now the skeletal woman lay like a baby, curled up, whimpering in her sleep.

The door opened above them; Cathy had become accustomed to the grinding sound of the door being unlocked and pushed open. She listened to the steps, the sound of expensive shoes slapping down the hardwood floor that came carefully towards their cell and knew for certain that Douglas was paying them a late visit. The armed guard's heavy steps followed and then the door was unlocked.

Cathy held a hand to her eyes to block out the sudden burn of light that flooded the dark room.

She blinked and focused and saw with disbelief, and a huge sickness filling her stomach, that Douglas was holding a small baby wrapped in a blanket. The child was asleep, and Douglas cradled it gently, rocking from side to side.

He smiled at Cathy, and suddenly she wanted to vomit.

'What are you doing with that baby?' she asked, unable to contain her concern and hatred.

'That's none of your concern,' he said as his eyes fell upon the sleeping Linda. 'Wake her up.'

'No!' Cathy found herself on her feet, her heart pounding, her hands balled into fists, unable to keep her eyes from the sleeping, defenceless baby in his arms. 'What the fucking hell are you doing with that baby, Douglas?'

Douglas ignored her and carried the baby closer to the figure on the mattress and began jabbing his shoe into her backside.

Linda groaned and yelped in her sleep, then sprang up, blinking back her tiredness and looking up with confusion stamped deep into her hollow face.

'Linda,' Douglas said, and gently tilted the baby, so Linda could get a good view. 'Look at this poor innocent child.'

Cathy watched as Linda lost her look of tiredness and panic and horror filled her big eyes. Immediately tears began to stream down her cheeks as her head shook from side to side.

'Don't... please... don't,' she said, her voice barely a whisper.

Douglas crouched down. 'It's not me, Linda... I would never harm a hair on any child's head... I could never... but the people I deal with... well, you know very well what they enjoy... you know what they would do with this child.'

'Douglas!' Cathy stormed towards Douglas and

got herself between him and Linda. 'Give me that baby. Please. Give it to me and I'll walk out of here...'

Douglas smiled. 'And you'll never speak of any of this? Don't make me laugh. Your hero, Jairus, is off to Tebel Island, to try and stop what's about to happen. But he can't. No one can. Jairus is going to die on that island. Get out of my way, you stupid bitch.'

Cathy stared at him, then turned when she saw the guard step in and point a gun at her. 'This... this group of yours... whatever you think you're doing or going to accomplish... it can't last... you'll all end up dead.'

Douglas lost his smile and stepped close to her, pressed his face to hers. 'Maybe. Probably. But it's been fun. Now, get the fuck out of my way.'

Cathy stepped away and watched Douglas crouch down and smile at Linda.

'Now, Linda,' he said. 'I can stop anything happening to this child and the others... I can stop them from being harmed if you do something for me. You don't want to see this baby harmed, do you?'

Linda let out a howl as her red, puffy eyes streamed more tears.

'Talk to me, Linda.'

Linda managed to shake her head.

'Good... do as I say, and no harm will come to this child or the others.'

'Don't listen to him,' Cathy said, ignoring the gun pointing at her head.

Douglas took a deep breath, closed his eyes, and said, 'Take her outside and get her ready for the journey.'

The guard told her to leave the room as he jabbed the gun at her, so she stepped towards the door with her eyes flickering over to Douglas and Linda. As she left the room and before the door closed, she glimpsed

Douglas whispering close to her ear and Linda nodding as if they were planning some terrible and grotesque conspiracy.

Cathy found herself, as she was led down the corridor, wanting to scream for Jairus to help her. It was a ridiculous and weak thing to want to do, and she would never give Douglas the pleasure in seeing her so defeated and helpless, but she hoped that Jairus was on his way.

CHAPTER 34

Rich Vincent stirred when he heard the door shut. He looked blearily up towards the ceiling, wiped his left eye and fought to sit up. He took a quick look beside him and saw that Ivy was lying there, breathing quietly, asleep, then jumped back up the bed when he fixed on the figure sitting by the window in a chair.

'Who the fuck are you?' Rich said, sitting up more. Ivy stirred a little.

'Tom,' a man's voice said quietly. Then he stood up and dragged the chair, which had been taken from the kitchen, closer to the bed and sat again.

Now Rich got a clear look at his haggard face, his patchy beard, and the craziness in his wide eyes and then down at the gun and knife he had rested on his lap. 'What do you want?'

'I wanted to look into the eyes of evil,' Tom said, lifting the gun a little.

'Evil? What're you talking...'

Tom leaned forward, his crazy eyes growing bigger. 'Be quiet. Let me think... yes, I wanted to look into the eyes of someone who will do anything they're asked, who doesn't give a shit about anyone else... they just follow orders like a lapdog.'

'Listen, I don't know what you think I've done...'

Tom shook his head. 'Not you. Not you! Her!'

Rich watched Tom point the gun towards Ivy as

he tapped it against her body under the duvet. She moaned and muttered something in her sleep, then let out a painful cry when Tom smacked the gun down on her leg.

Ivy jumped back, pulled her body back to the wall, looking ready to strike out like a terrified cat. Her eyes stayed mostly on Tom. 'What the fuck?!'

'You're a bitch,' Tom said.

Rich looked between them, saw the confusion on Ivy's face and the hatred on Tom's. 'There's obviously some kind of mistake. Listen Tom, I know...'

'You know nothing.' Tom turned the gun on him as it trembled and wavered. 'You probably think the sun shines out of her pretty little arse... but she works for them... she's helping them cover it all up.'

'You're wrong,' Rich put his feet to the floor, held up his hands. 'Please, calm down...'

'That's how I found you,' Tom said, putting his seething eyes back on Ivy. 'I followed you. I saw you at Burdock's tower in the sky, his castle. He thinks he's safe there but he's not. Not safe from me. He's been helping the child abusers get away with it... he's as guilty as them.'

Rich slowly turned towards Ivy and noticed she was looking intently at Tom, but not with fear and confusion anymore. It had sunk away quickly and had been replaced by cold hard calculation. Rich tapped her shoulder and said, 'You were at Burdock's place? Is that right?'

She turned and looked straight through him. 'What would I be doing at Burdock's?'

'I don't know. But he said he followed you to here. Talk to me... what's going on?'

Tom laughed. 'You know what's going on. She's been lying to you. She works for them.'

Rich looked at Tom and tried not to see the gun and the psychosis that had obviously overtaken him. Then he faced Ivy. 'Is this about Jairus?'

'Who?' Tom sprang forward. 'You know Jairus? Where is he?'

Rich shook his head. 'I don't know.'

Rich's head jerked, pushed sideways by the pressure of the gun muzzle that was being pressed into his temple.

Tom was snarling behind the gun, his eyes ablaze. 'Where is he?! I need to know! They're going to kill him!'

'Who?' Rich yanked his head from the gun.

'The psychos! They're planning on trading him and killing him! Where is he?'

'He went to Tebel Island. he'll be heading there tonight.'

Tom lowered the gun and grasped his face, shaking his head, muttering to himself. 'If he goes there... that's where they'll do it. Kill him there and dump his body. That can't happen. I know now... he's the only person I can trust to help me kill them... I can't do it on my own.'

'It's too late,' Ivy said, blankly. 'He'll be on his way now. They've made sure he gets there. He'll be dead soon.'

Rich stared at her, as fury made him want to slap her. He took a few breaths, telling himself he wasn't that kind of man. 'What're they going to do?'

She looked away. 'I don't know.'

Tom raised the gun and leant forward, bringing it closer to her face, making her move back. 'You do know. But what I really need to know is where they're taking the babies and the others they plan to sacrifice.'

Rich looked at her as he felt the sickness rising

through him. 'Babies? They're going... to... no, I don't...'

'It's fucking true!' Tom was snarling at her. 'It's how they get their kicks and how they find others to initiate into their pack... others fucked-up like them. So, they'll grow and grow and one day take over and evil will be good and good will be evil. That's the plan, isn't it?'

She looked up, her brow creased. 'You're crazy! Sacrificing...'

He pushed the gun into her forehead, forcing her head back to the headboard. 'Tell me...'

'Wait!' Rich held up his hands as his heart beat erratically, his head pounding. 'We need to help Jairus. If he's heading into some kind of ambush, we need to stop him. He'll know what to do, how to stop this human sacrifice thing.'

Tom turned and looked at him and seemed to blink himself out of his rage. 'Yes... OK... can you get hold of him?'

Rich closed his eyes, then gripped his face with both hands. 'No... shit... fuck! No... I can't.'

'Then we torture her until she tells us how to stop what's going to happen to him.'

Ivy huffed out a sickening laugh. 'You morons... there's no way to stop it. Jairus is heading to an island that's cut off from the rest of the world. Even if you could call him, you'd be lucky to get a signal. So, basically you're fucked.'

Tom swept the gun into the air, ready to slam it down, but Rich grabbed his wrist. 'Don't! We need her. There must be a way of contacting him. There's a hotel there. There must be a way of communicating with the island.'

Ivy laughed. 'It's all been shut down. They've

thought of everything.'

'What do we do?' Tom stared at him, waiting, looking desperate, and almost completely crazy.

Rich tried to clear his mind, to make sense of the insanity that now surrounded him. He pictured Jairus heading towards the island, not knowing the terrible things that awaited him. He turned and looked at Ivy, who stared at the walls, realising that she was a stranger who had fooled him. He sat down on the bed and said, 'Ivy...'

'That's not my name,' she said, looking down at her hands.

'What's your name?'

'Does it matter?'

He sighed. 'It matters to me. What's your name? Please.'

'Julie.'

'Is it? Really?'

She shook her head.

'For fuck's sake. Who are you? Come on, my friend's going to die... don't you care?'

She looked straight into his eyes. 'No. I had a job to do. I did it. End of conversation. I'm not saying another word.'

Rich stood up, stared at her for a moment, and the sudden realisation came over him that she was a complete bitch and as heartless as the people she was serving.

And then it hit him. He sat down again, put his head in his hands. 'There's nothing we can do. They're going to kill Jairus, and there's nothing I can do. He's dead! That's it, he's dead.'

The night was black and so was the sea, and only grey foam spat into the air as the waves crashed against the boat's hull, rocking it violently side to side.

Jairus beamed the boat's spotlight into the dark waters, as they tried to spot the treacherous rocks that lay somewhere between the island and the enormous Bishop Rock lighthouse that was silhouetted on the horizon. The rain hammered down onto the deck and Jairus could taste it and the salty seawater in his mouth.

It was madness, he thought, his entire body alive with fear and adrenaline, thinking about what was happening on the island, imagining strange rituals and satanic human sacrifice.

He turned and looked through the windscreen at Terry Stephens as he steered the boat, a solemn look upon his face.

The water was clear of hazards, but he could see rough waters ahead at the point where the boat would get closer to the small island that had appeared on the horizon. They were now only minutes away from reaching their destination and almost on call, Jairus' raging headache began to beat at the top of his skull.

He left his post, satisfied that the really rocky waters lay far ahead, and headed into the cabin and stood shoulder to shoulder with Terry Stephens.

'What have we got in terms of firepower?' Jairus asked.

'Look in the kit bag behind me,' Terry said and nodded to the floor.

Jairus looked behind him and saw the long green bag and knelt by it. He unzipped it and found an automatic rifle that had a telescopic sight attached. There was also a semi-automatic handgun beside it – and ammunition.

'We're getting close now,' Terry said.

Jairus stood up and looked out across the violent

sea to the island that rocked back and forth in his vision. He was suddenly gripped with coldness and dug his hands into his pockets.

'They'll know we're coming,' Jairus said.

'Of course.'

'Thanks for coming.'

Terry flashed him a look then stared straight ahead. 'Don't thank me. Just think about what you're going to do when we get there.'

'I don't even know what to expect. The people I'm dealing with are psychopaths. Anything could be waiting for me.'

'I'm sure you're up to the task, mate. I've got faith in you. Your friends do too.'

Jairus laughed. 'Yeah? Well, I wish I had some sort of faith in myself. Truth is... everything I touch seems to... well, it doesn't usually end well.'

'That's life. Here we go. Better get on that spotlight.'

Jairus headed out, grabbed the spotlight and beamed it out towards the island. Straight away he could make out the foam and spit of the waves that exploded upwards as they smashed against the rocks.

'Starboard!' Jairus shouted above the waves and Terry took the boat around the set of rocks that seemed to jut out from the island like a knife. There were more to their left, but not as sharp and widespread, so Terry swiftly got around them and headed into a little bay, then shut the engine.

As they bobbed in the water, lifted again and again by the waves, Terry fetched the sniper rifle and Jairus watched him attach a silencer to the barrel.

'Are we killing this morning?' Terry asked as he loaded a magazine into the rifle.

Jairus looked towards the island. 'These people... they won't hesitate to put us down... so...'

'Put them down first?' Terry nodded. 'Right then. Now, usually for a sniping job you would use a bolt action rifle, but we haven't got time for fucking around, have we?'

'No.'

'Needs fucking must then.'

Jairus watched on as Terry rested the rifle on the bow of the rocking boat, aiming towards the island, closing one eye and breathing steadily.

'There's a stone dock that sticks out of the bay just in front of us,' Terry said. 'I can see two men, stood looking like they're guarding the road. Yep, fuckers have definitely got sidearms and a radio. Your call, mate.'

Jairus focused on the island, thinking, taking deep breaths, imagining the horror that was probably taking place beneath the hotel. He rubbed his eyes, scratched his beard as an image came to him. He saw an innocent baby lying on some kind of altar, Burdock holding a knife in his hand. 'Do it. Take them out.'

Terry focused again, breathing, putting his finger round the trigger. Jairus watched him take a long breath and hold it, moving his body slightly to deal with the movements of the boat.

Then his finger was squeezing.

There was a sound like air being sucked in and a sharp whistling noise. Terry moved, switching his view, taking a deep breath, and again pulling the trigger.

Terry stood up, staring towards the island, and swung the rifle over his shoulder. 'Two down. Now we can moor the boat.'

The boat banged against the stone dock as Terry moored the boat. Jairus hopped onto the deck and looked round as Terry followed him and joined him as he headed up the path towards the hotel.

The two guards lay strewn across the concrete path, half their skulls missing.

Jairus looked away and stuck his hands in his pockets as he stormed along the road they joined that would take them around to the front entrance of the hotel.

Terry took the rifle from his shoulder and walked ahead, sweeping the terrain as he would have done as a professional soldier.

There was the sound of gravel crunching up ahead, making Terry hunch down near the bushes that lined the narrow path. Jairus ducked in too and watched as a suited figure stepped onto the road and headed towards them.

'Don't shoot him, unless you have to,' Jairus whispered, feeling that he was tired of the death that constantly surrounded him. He stepped out with his hands raised.

The man saw him and pulled out a gun from a holster positioned on his hip. 'Stop right there! State your name and business.'

Jairus flinched when an explosion of blood ripped open the guard's chest, sending him thudding the ground. He turned and watched Terry moving towards him, his eyes on the dead man. The ex-soldier took the guard's sidearm and then searched him.

'I told you not to shoot him...' Jairus began.

'I had to,' Terry said and walked towards the front entrance of the hotel that jutted out from the main building. It was one long canopy of glass and steel protruding towards the beach, ending in an enormous set of arched glass doors.

Jairus joined him at the doors and saw themselves reflected in the glass as he held out his hand. 'You better give me that gun.'

Terry looked at him, staring at him, breathing hard, lowered his weapon and walked over towards the beach.

'What is it?' Jairus said, his skull beginning fill with the same old tension headache.

Terry turned and looked him in the eye, silent for a moment, some dark thought obviously hovering beyond his hard-man eyes. 'I never told you, but I have a boy... he's sixteen years old now...'

Jairus closed his eyes, sure of what Terry was about to say, listening to the icy cold waters hitting the sea defences all around them. He opened his eyes again. 'They have him, don't they?'

Terry nodded. 'I'm sorry... but what could I do?'

Jairus looked around him, nodding, the realisation of what had been really happening spreading all over him. 'Yeah, I'm getting the picture now... what a fucking fool I've been. Now, let me see if I've got this right. Your job was to get me here?'

'Yeah.'

'So, what was with the agents who looked very much like they were going to kill me?'

'They were meant to kill you. Look I'm not part of all this... all I know was what I was told, mate. There's some kind of civil war going on in this country... between the secret service and the psychos you're after. Believe it or not I think they're trying to keep them in line. Thing is none of them want to risk having you walking round. The secret service told Burdock and the rest that you were going to be taken out. I was sent to stop that from happening and make sure you got into that hotel.'

Jairus turned and faced the building, the blood down pounding in his veins, his brain throbbing with pain. He breathed in, tried to take hold of himself. 'Any idea what's awaiting me in there?'

'No. But you'll find a way through it. Cause if not we're all dead.'

Jairus faced him again. 'They're psychos, Terry. Do you really think you can trust them?'

Terry gritted teeth and looked almost close to tears as he said, 'What fucking choice do I have? Right, enough of this... when you step into this building we'll have one hour to do whatever it is.'

'One fucking hour for what?'

Terry pointed the rifle at him. 'I don't know. Just open the door. It's not locked.'

Jairus turned back around, breathed hard, cleared away the flock of panicked black birds that had flown into his mind. He reached out and pulled open the door and stepped into the dark foyer. It was a grandiose long strip of wood floors and glass that let the moonlight flood in.

He kept walking across the wood flooring, listening to the echo of his and Terry's shoes as they reached the long crescent-shaped reception desk.

'Behind the reception desk,' Terry said, jabbing the rifle through the air. 'There's an office behind it.'

Jairus carried on around the desk and examined the door, then looked at Terry. 'What's in there? Someone waiting to slit my throat?'

'You know I don't know. There's a hidden door behind a fake wall at the back of the office.'

Jairus went in, checking the corners, his blood now hot with fear and adrenalin, and his hands balled into fists. He stepped up to the wall at the back of the office.

'You pull it away...' Terry started to say, but Jairus pulled back his fist and slammed It through the thin layer of paint and plasterboard. He ripped the rest away, allowing a good view of a large stone archway that led to an ancient set of stone steps that would have belonged to the castle hundreds of years ago.

'You want to go first?' Jairus asked, gesturing towards the steps.

'Afraid not, mate.'

Jairus nodded, then headed slowly down into the darkness, taking each worn away step carefully, staring into the abyss, waiting for one of the psychos to come out of the shadows. He stole himself, his fists ready, going down and down with Terry on his heels.

At last he arrived at a modern, metal door that had been fitted to the low medieval archway.

Jairus put a hand on the door for a moment, trying to sense what was waiting behind it.

He pushed it open and shuddered to a stop, staring at the figures that sat and stood in the small stone-floored, damp room.

There was a skinny blonde, wild-eyed woman holding a gun, pointing it at the heads of a man and woman who were manacled to the chairs they were sat on.

The man was the deputy prime minister. The woman was Cathy Durbridge.

CHAPTER 35

There was silence for a moment before the terrible sobbing came from the woman holding the gun. Jairus broke out of his stare, his state of shock, stepped further into the room and tried to absorb all that was before his eyes.

He cut out the woman's sobs and focused on the two tied-up figures, trying to ignore what the manacled woman meant to him, and stared at the man in the pinstripe suit, his tanned jowls hanging over his shirt and tie. His mouth was taped, but his eyes were wide, watching Jairus.

It took the anger a while to arrive, but when it did, it spread through his body like swarming locusts, eating away at the little mercy and sympathy he had left.

'What the fuck do they expect me to do?' Jairus shouted.

'Suffer,' Terry said. 'I think that's the idea. See that woman who's holding the gun? Well, mate, her name's Linda. Back when she was a kid, a ring of paedophiles made up of important men abused her. Now, that's left Linda in a bad way upstairs, if you know what I mean?'

'Yeah, I do,' Jairus said, and looked into the streaming and crazed eyes of the woman. 'What else?'

'They know her mind, all the stuff she's done in the past, her criminal record... basically, they know she'll pull that trigger and shoot your friend when the time's up.'

Jairus turned to face Terry. 'How?'

'Because if she doesn't, they'll slaughter several babies.'

Jairus put his head in his hands. 'What am I meant to do to stop that?'

'There's a knife by the deputy prime minister's chair. You have to stab him, cut his throat, whatever it takes to kill him. If you look up in the corner behind me, you'll see a camera... it's feeding live to a computer somewhere. You have less than an hour now.'

Jairus looked up and saw a small camera in the far corner, its tiny black eye peering down at them all. 'So, if I don't kill him in that time, Linda shoots Cathy, and you kill me?'

'And everyone else in this room.'

Jairus closed his eyes, then turned and faced Linda, who was staring at him, her eyes still red, bulging with tears and madness. 'Linda... listen to me... these people... they're psychopaths and they will murder those children, no matter what I do and no matter what you do.'

She let out a scream, the gun trembling in her hand as she convulsed with each sob as she tried to form a sentence. 'How... how can I take that... risk?'

'She's right,' Terry said. 'How can you?'

Even though Jairus had told himself not to, he found his eyes landing on Cathy, finding her eyes. He didn't find panic there, just as he thought he wouldn't. She was calm, and her eyes were telling him to do whatever he had to do.

He laughed suddenly. He heard it coming from his own mouth, the laugh of a madman. 'This is an impossible situation. They know we'll not walk out of here alive. None of us. You're right... they just want to see me suffer before I die. Just because they get off on it.'

'Maybe,' Terry said. 'Maybe not. Maybe they want to film you killing the deputy prime minister... that's some serious blackmail material to have over someone.'

Jairus took in the man in the suit, feeling the pain and agony and hatred infecting him again. The deputy prime minister began to talk, muffled words, probably pleading, coming from behind the tape.

'You, shut up!' Jairus jabbed a finger at him. 'You don't get to talk. You understand. You say one thing to me... one thing... and I'll pick up that knife and do what they want. So shut the fuck up! Let me fucking think.'

'There's no way out, Jairus.' Terry sounded defeated. 'They've thought of everything.'

'No, there's always a way. Do I have to stay in this room? Is there anything in the fucked-up rules that says I have to stay here the whole time?'

'No, but what good will it do? What're you going to do out there?'

Jairus shoved his hands into his pockets and headed through the door. 'Think.'

DS Wood parked up outside the newly-built houses that were situated not far from the old sewage works. The sewage smell was still thick in the air as she climbed out and headed towards the house the man had asked her to come to.

He was called Rich Vincent and was a close friend of Jairus, or so he said. She wasn't taking any chances and had a Taser in one of her coat pockets and a Casco baton in the other.

She rang the doorbell and waited, her head close to the door, listening out for the sound of someone coming. She could hear someone, the faint sound of footsteps coming down the stairs, then a pause. Hesitation.

The footsteps started again and then the door began to open, revealing a man with long brown hair, with subtle streaks of grey, who was wearing an Iron Maiden sweatshirt. He looked tired, serious, and worried.

'Rich Vincent?' she said and stepped into the house. 'She took out her ID as she looked round the hallway and showed it to him. 'DS Kate Wood.'

'Thanks for coming,' Vincent said shutting the front door. 'You're about the only person I think I can trust. Jairus mentioned you... basically, he said I should try and get hold of you if I found myself in the shit.'

Wood huffed out a laugh. 'So, you're in the shit then?'

'My back teeth are floating in it.' Vincent pointed a thumb towards the stairs and Wood's eyes followed it, climbing the stairs until she saw the bearded man in the green army coat standing at the top, holding a gun.

The man stepped down towards her, his eyes fixed on her as if he was looking beyond her, maybe into another crazy dimension where he might come from.

'Who's this?' Wood said.

'My name's Tom,' the man said, scratching his beard.

'And who are you, Tom? And why are you pointing a fucking gun at me?'

Rich stepped between them and said, 'It's all right. I know it looks bad, but he's on our side. Thing is, we've just found out that Jairus is heading into a trap.

He's heading to Tebel Island, but they're waiting for him. Looks like they've led him there to kill him.'

Wood looked blankly at both men. 'What do you expect me to do? If you're right, and he's on his way there, then he's dead.'

Rich let out an angry sigh. 'Can't you call someone? Send the Cavalry? Do fucking something.'

Tom stepped down the stairs, still staring at Wood. 'They're going to slaughter the babies tonight.'

'What? Who is? What babies?'

Tom looked down at the floor. 'It's what they do. They find new psycho recruits, make them do terrible things, so they know they're willing to do anything... And so they have blackmail material on them.'

'We need to find out where they are taking the babies,' Rich said. 'If we can't save Jairus, then maybe can salvage something from this mess.'

Wood shook her head, then looked at them again, noting the conviction and madness in their eyes. 'OK... I've been through some crazy stuff lately... I know there's something very sinister going on... so, OK, I buy it. How do we find this place where they're taking them to?'

Tom pointed his gun towards the ceiling. 'We ask the evil bitch we've got tied up upstairs.'

Jairus walked back up the stone steps, into the hotel, and out through the glass doors where he stood looking out at the raging sea. He realised he had as much chance of winning as he had of changing the tides.

He felt like walking straight on, submerging himself in the icy waters. It would be justice, payment for all the mayhem and death that he had caused over the years. Maybe this was his Judgement Day.

No.

He shook himself out of his dark place, and saw the light on the horizon, the dancing moonlight that tiptoed along the ragged water. With darkness there came light. He was the light. The psychos were shrouded in darkness and evil.

He was kidding himself, but he gripped hold of the idea and refused to let go. Then his eyes fell upon the boat moored on the stone dock.

'So, what now?' Terry asked behind him.

Jairus turned. 'I figure a way out of this.'

Terry huffed out a sickened laugh. 'There's no way out. Don't you get that?'

'No, I don't. If I did, I might as well be dead already. How old's your boy?'

'Don't. Don't even talk...'

'Chances are they have him with all the others they plan to... look, I think I can do this... but I need you to help me.'

'Go on.'

'Is there a radio on that boat?'

Terry's eyes flickered over towards the boat. 'Actually, yes there is. What're you suggesting?'

'I need to make contact with a friend of mine. If I can get a message through to him, then we might have a chance.'

Terry stared at him for a while. 'You can save my boy?'

'I can try, Terry. I'll do my best.'

Tears filled the ex-army man's eyes. 'You swear? You swear on your life?'

Jairus nodded. 'I swear. We have about forty minutes. There'll be a signal sending the images from that camera to wherever they're watching from. If my mate can locate and track the signal, then we'll have a chance of finding your boy and saving those kids.'

Terry lowered the gun. 'Come on then. We haven't got long. If we're gone too long they'll get suspicious.'

DS Wood entered the bedroom and stopped, swore loudly, then looked around at Rich. He looked ashamed, while Tom looked crazy as ever. When she looked into the room again, she made eye contact with the goth girl tied to the chair with the duct tape over her mouth.

'Fucking hell,' she said, almost letting out a scream. 'What the fuck are you two doing? What's your plan? Torture her? Jesus...'

'Yes, that's what we were planning,' Tom said, walking in, pointing the gun at her and pulling out a big carving knife.

'Put that away!' Wood shouted. 'You start cutting her up and she'll tell you any fucking bollocks that comes into her head.'

Wood pulled the tape off her mouth. 'Right, luv, whoever the fuck you are, you're about five seconds from having yourself cut open, so I'd start talking if I was you.'

The woman looked up, calmly, as if she'd been simply reading a book before she was interrupted. 'You're a cop, yeah?'

'DS Wood. Nice to meet you, woman tied to a chair. So?'

The woman smirked. 'So I know you're not going to let them torture me. Which means I'm keeping my mouth shut. Arrest me or let me go.'

Wood listened to her, feeling a little like she'd like to torture her herself. 'I don't suppose it'll do any good appealing to your sense of decency?'

'No.'

'She'll tell us,' Tom said and pressed the gun to her

head.

'Put that away, you crazy bastard,' Wood growled.

Tom took the gun away, though his eyes still burned into the woman.

The room fell quiet as everyone seemed to be thinking, looking at each other, waiting for something to happen or be said.

A phone started ringing somewhere, a muffled ringtone calling out and breaking the spell.

'Shit,' Rich said, 'that's my phone.'

Wood and the rest watched as he began lifting clothes and electronic equipment and guitars until he found his mobile and answered it.

'Rich Vincent,' he said, slowly pacing the room. 'Yes, that's right. What? You're joking. OK, how... OK, I'll write it down. Pen? Someone, I need a pen.'

Wood pulled out her notebook pen and laid it before him on the bedside table. He picked up the pen and started scribbling something down. 'Thank you. Thank you very much.'

Wood watched him end the call, rip out the piece of paper and rush out of the room. She followed him into a narrow office crammed with giant computer screens and keyboards and several gizmos she couldn't identify. 'Who was that?'

Rich sat in front of what looked to be a large radio set and began fiddling with buttons and a tuner as he said, 'That was someone from the coastguard with a message from Jairus.'

Wood sensed someone behind her and looked round to see Tom standing there listening. 'The coastguard? Has his boat fucking sunk or what?'

Rich picked up a small microphone and held it to his lips. 'I have no idea. We'll find out in a minute.'

Wood waited, her feet balled up in her shoes,

wanting to bite her fingers as Rich kept fiddling with the radio and static screeched out into the room.

'Jairus?' Rich kept saying into the mic. 'Jairus? You there? Jairus? For fuck's sake, man!'

'There's radio etiquette, and procedure, you know?'

'I know, but quite frankly it can kiss my arse right now. Jairus. Talk to me!'

'Rich?!' Jairus' voice crackled weakly into the room. 'Thank God. Can you hear me?'

'Just about, mate. You're alive then?'

'Yeah, for another thirty-five minutes at least.'

'What? What does that mean?'

'Nothing. Listen, I'm on Tebel Island. There's a live feed being sent from the hotel. Can you interrupt it? Make it seem like a technical glitch?'

'No worries, I'll do my best. In the next thirty-five minutes, I'm guessing?'

'Yeah. We need to trace where the signal's coming from too. Can you try and do that?'

Wood watched Rich huff out and breath and rub his eyes. 'I can try, mate... but that signal could be bounced off God knows where. The servers could be in Outer Mongolia.'

'Yeah, but isn't there's always a trail?'

'Usually.'

'Try, mate. We have to try, Rich. We have to stop them killing those children.'

Rich nodded and looked at Wood. 'I know. I'll do all I can. Thing is, Jay, turns out Ivy... well, she's not who I thought she was... she's working for them.'

'OK... sorry, mate... but maybe she can tell us something, then.'

'That's what I hoped... but she's not talking to us.'

'Who's us?'

Rich looked up at Wood. 'DS wood, and a man

called Tom. He has a gun.'

Tom pushed past Wood and stood over Rich. 'Jairus?'

'Hello, Tom,' Jairus said, sounding tired.

'I'm sorry about what I did last time we...'

'Forget it, Tom,' Jairus said. 'We need to pull together and find out where they're planning to carry out their ritual. You need to get Ivy, or whoever she is to talk.'

Tom raised his knife. 'We have to torture her! Make her talk.'

'Nobody's going to be torturing me!' a voice shouted from across the landing.

'Was that her?' Jairus asked.

'Yes.' Rich rubbed his eyes. 'She's hard as nails that one.'

'Yeah, well, she needs to see the light,' Jairus said. 'Do whatever it takes. We're talking about the lives of children. Innocent children. Tom, do what you have to.'

'I will,' Tom said and looked towards the bedroom, smiling.

'Fuck off!' Ivy's voice screamed. 'You're all bluffing! You won't let that… that crazy fucker torture me!'

'Rich, bring her closer, so she can hear me,' Jairus said.

'I can hear you just fine from here!' Ivy shouted.

'Good,' Jairus said. 'Then you must know all about me. The things I've done, or at least been suspected of doing, like murdering a suspect. Two suspects, actually. Well, Ivy or whoever the fuck you are, it's all true. Every fucking rumour. You know what else. They abused the woman I loved when she was a child, so don't try and say I'm bluffing. I will let them do whatever they have to do to you to find out where those kids are! You hear me now?'

Wood took in the agony of silence that poisoned the atmosphere. 'I think she got the message.'

'Yeah, I think so too,' Jairus said. 'Rich, I've got a disposable phone on me, so try and call me on this number...'

Rich scrawled down the number he read out, then said, 'Got it, Jay, but doubt I'll get through. You're in the middle nowhere and I know the signal's crap out there.'

'Yeah, I know, but I'd like to try and keep in contact. Do what you have to do and call me as soon as you have something. You got it?'

'Yes, mate. Listen...'

'I've got to go. Over and out.'

'Jairus? Jay?' Rich shouted into the mic, but his voice didn't return.

'What was that about?' Wood asked, noting Rich's sudden look of despair.

Rich looked up at her as he dropped the mic. 'The giving him a call business? Yeah, I thought that was strange. He knows I probably won't be able to get through to him. He would've tried to call me if there was a chance...'

'Which means?'

Rich gave an empty laugh. 'Fucked if I know.'

Wood had a feeling of dread pour through her, melting away the little hope she'd been harbouring. 'I think it was pretence... not meant for us, but for someone who might've been listening.'

'For what reason?' Rich stood up.

'I don't know, but I think your friend is in serious trouble.'

CHAPTER 36

Jairus stood up after putting away the radio and took out the disposable phone in his pocket. He put in a SIM card and turned it on. After a few seconds the phone booted up, but there was no signal.

Of course, he knew there wouldn't be.

Terry cradled the rifle at the stern of the boat, watching with a little hope shining in his eyes.

'Anything?' Terry asked.

Jairus looked over at him, picturing the scene down beneath the hotel, his heart beginning to rage once again. 'A weak signal.'

'So there's a chance he might be able to get through?' Terry stepped closer.

Jairus lifted the phone in the air, staring up at it, doing his best to act hopeful. 'Do you know much about mobiles and technology in general, Terry?'

'I can't say I do.'

'Well, the man I just talked to on the radio does. He knows everything there is to know and then some, and he can pull off technological miracles. If anyone can get a call through to here, it'll be him. I've just set him a challenge, so he'll want to rise to it.'

Terry looked back towards the hotel. 'We better get back in there. Linda's pretty fucked up in the head... I can't blame her really. What those fucking bastards did to her... I can't... I don't want...'

Jairus put the phone in his pocket. 'She'll pull that trigger when the time comes. They know she will, just like they know what I really want to do right now is take that knife and plunge it into that fucking evil bastard in there.'

'Maybe it won't come down to that.'

Jairus nodded, then climbed up on the side of the boat and jumped down onto the dock. He shoved his hands into his pockets and headed into the hotel with Terry right behind him.

'How long we got left?' Jairus asked hammering down the stone steps.

'Jesus... twenty-five minutes... we're fucked.'

Jairus stopped dead and faced him. 'No, we're not. Have faith. I'm not going to let them win.'

Inside the room, the silence was broken by the constant sobs of Linda, who had sunk to the floor, still cradling the gun.

Linda scrambled to her feet when she saw Jairus and pointed the gun at the deputy prime minister and Cathy.

'Where the bloody hell have you been?' Linda screamed at Jairus. 'You going to leave us in the lurch? Walk out on the babies?!'

'Calm down, Linda,' Jairus said, looking her in the eyes, trying to make himself sound calm. He turned and stared up at the camera and the tiny red light by the one shiny eye staring down at them all. 'I'm not going anywhere. I'm here to the end.'

Linda gave a sickening laugh. 'I've made a... I've a made a choice.'

'What choice, Linda?' Jairus asked. 'What are you talking about?'

'They want him dead.' Linda jabbed the gun into the deputy. 'I can't blame them... it's evil scum like him that did those things to me and all the others! They've got away with it for far too long!'

'Linda!' Jairus stepped closer. 'Look at me, Linda. Don't do anything that we'd all regret...'

'If I kill him...'

'Don't! They want me to kill him! That's the whole point of this! If you kill him, then they'll sacrifice those children and Terry's boy. That's not going to happen. Trust me!'

'Trust you?! Trust you! You think they're already dead! You said so.'

Jairus felt the nausea attack his stomach and throat, and the skull-crushing headache knock at the top of his skull. Tiredness tried to pull him to the floor, but he shook it away. 'There's a chance, Linda. These people, they like to play games with people's lives. Killing those hostages now would spoil their fun. I know people like them, I've arrested quite a few.'

'We're running out of time, Jairus,' Terry said, his voice strained.

'Yeah, I know.' Jairus turned and looked up at the camera. The red light was still glowing. He slipped his hand in his pocket and grasped the mobile phone. He lit it up, but kept it hidden in his pocket and saw that there was no signal. He brought up the ringtone menu and found the default setting, and hovered his thumb over the button.

He looked round the room, stared into the wide and terrified eyes of the deputy prime minister and felt the poisonous hate invade every cell of his body. Cathy's eyes watched him, engaged him, told him that whatever he needed to do was OK with her. Then he saw her eyes jump from him to the corner of the room. He turned and saw the camera's red light had gone out.

Jairus swept round and hurried towards the door, past Terry, who stared at him.

'Where the fuck are you going?' Terry shouted, hurrying after him as he took the stone stairway back up to the hotel.

'The camera's down,' Jairus shouted over his shoulder. 'I don't know how long for. I'm going to try and phone Rich and see what's going on.'

As Jairus headed across the reception area of the hotel with Terry following after, pointing the rifle at him, he played the ringtone.

'Is that your phone?' Terry asked, his eyebrows raised.

Jairus pulled it out and put it to his ear and heard only his thumping pulse beating into his skull. 'Rich, that you? I can hardly hear you! What? What's happened? You're joking? Jesus... thank fuck! Who's there now?'

'What's happened?' Terry came closer, lowering the gun.

'Rich?' Jairus called into the phone. 'Rich? Fuck! He's gone. They've done it, Terry. They've found where they were holding them all.'

Terry stared at him for a while, looked at the phone in his hand. 'You're having me on? You're telling me they found my lad?'

Jairus smiled. 'He's safe, Terry. So are the other children they had with them.'

'How's my boy? They haven't harmed...'

Jairus walked up to him. 'He's fine. Now we need to get in there and sort out this fucking mess!'

Terry looked beyond him, nodded, slung the rifle over his shoulder and headed towards the cellar. Jairus followed, his lie still in his throat, threatening to choke him as he followed the ex-soldier down the stone steps into the dank room. Somewhere the psychos had Terry's boy and the babies, but Jairus forced the image out of his skull and concentrated on the room he was entering and the possible deaths that could still occur.

Rich looked at DS Wood and saw that she looked ready to throw up. He stepped close to her and said, 'You all right?'

She looked at him as if he'd asked her for a sexual favour. 'No, I'm not bloody all right! We're talking about letting that... man, go in there and...'

'Torture her,' Rich said, nodding, feeling just as nauseous as he guessed she did. 'I know... and it goes against every principal I have, but I don't know what else we can do? We haven't got long left. I've managed to break the broadcast for a little while, but it'll be back on soon.'

Footsteps came slowly up the stairs and they both turned to see Tom coming up them, still carrying the gun at his side. He looked at them both, then said, 'I'm ready. I'll get it out of her.'

'No, you fucking won't!' Ivy shouted.

Her shouting went right through Rich and he found it hard to recognise her as the same woman he had accidentally met in his local, on one of the nights before his band played. But it wasn't an accident at all; whoever Jairus was up against had been playing the long game and knew enough about him to know who he'd go running to for IT assistance. They were always one step ahead.

'Where's the cop?' Ivy shouted, sounding desperate.

Wood walked into the bedroom, and Rich followed and watched the two women face each other.

'You going to plead to my sisterly side?' Wood asked, setting her face into rock.

'No, I want to remind you of what the right thing to do is...'

Wood sprang forward, pointing a finger at Ivy's face. 'The right thing?! You of all fucking people... Jesus. I've been doing the right thing all my bleeding life, love! What have you been doing?! Did they tell you that you were doing it all for the greater good? Well, I've got news for you, you stupid... bitch... they lied to you. They're about to sacrifice babies... Babies! You hear me?'

'You're deranged!' Ivy shook her head, looked away.

Tom stormed in, the gun aimed at Ivy, his teeth showing, his eyes as mad as ever. 'You're going to talk! I'm going to cut off a piece of you for every lie you tell me! You lot get out!'

Rich stepped into the room and looked Into Ivy's eyes. 'If you don't tell us where they've taken those babies, then I can't help you. I'm sorry, but I'd rather save those kids than you. Goodbye.'

He turned and headed out of the room, his fists clenched, his stomach turning over. A voice was telling him to turn back and stop Tom from whatever he was going to do, but he kept on going. He went into the bathroom, shut the door, locked it, and slid to the floor, ready to clamp his hands over his ears.

'Wait!' Ivy cried out. 'Wait! Don't let him!'

Rich scrambled to his feet, battling with the door, fumbling to unlock it as Ivy began to scream the house down. He pulled open the door and ran into bedroom to find Tom with the knife in his hand as he was going towards her.

Ivy was panting, sobbing, trying to push herself backwards away from the blade.

'You got something to say?' Rich said, looking into

her crying eyes.

'I... I didn't know about the babies... I work for MI5. I was just told to keep an eye on things. Report back what Burdock and that lot were up to.'

Rich nodded. 'OK... what are they up to?'

'I'm not sure,' she said, sniffing, 'but they've got something organised at Hatfield House tonight. They've got a lot of security around the place. You wouldn't even get close.'

Wood looked at her watch. 'What time is all this supposed to start?'

'She's lying,' Tom said, staring at her.

'No, I'm not!' Ivy said.

Tom looked at Rich, burned his eyes into his. 'They wouldn't sacrifice them there. It's too high profile. I know these people, I've watched them for a long time, I know how they think.'

'Then where?' Wood asked.

'Somewhere smaller, low key,' Tom said, then pointed his gun at Ivy. 'Isn't that right?'

'I wouldn't know!' she screamed. 'I really don't know. You're all crazy.'

'Then we go ahead as planned and torture you.' Tom dug the gun into her cheek, while she clenched her eyes shut, the tears beginning to stream down her face.

Rich grabbed the barrel of the gun and pulled it away from her cheek. 'Stop it! Can't you see she doesn't know! She's telling us anything we want to hear!'

'What about the signal from the camera?' Wood asked.

Rich shook his head. 'Like I thought, it's being bounced round the place... by the time I tracked the original source again... it'll be too late.'

'What are you saying?' Wood grabbed his arm, turned him round to face her. 'We've lost? Those children are going to die?'

Rich looked at her. 'Yep, that's what I'm saying.'

'It's all over, Linda,' Jairus said, holding up his hands, hoping that she would buy the lie as well as Terry had. He was banking on them all wanting to believe him, giving in to their own desperation.

Linda stared at him, open-mouthed. 'What do you mean it's all over?'

'They've found the babies, and they're safe now.' Jairus came closer, made himself smile, even though the effort made him want to throw up.

Linda's eyes jumped to Terry and back to Jairus. 'Who says? You could be lying.'

'Why would I lie?' Jairus' skull began to beat with blood.

'To stop me from shooting them! You don't want me to shoot your friend, do you? You'll tell any lie as long as I don't shoot your friend, isn't that right?'

'Linda?' Terry said, coming towards her. 'Put the gun down. It's all over now. They're safe. I trust this man. He wouldn't lie about a thing like that.'

She looked between them, then down at the deputy prime minister and Cathy. 'How can I be sure? If I shoot them, then it won't matter... will it? The babies will be safe, won't they?'

'Linda!' Jairus shouted. 'Listen to me, Linda... don't do this! You don't want to kill them! You don't...'

'He's abused children!' Linda shouted, waving the trembling gun at the politician. 'He's evil! It'll be justice for the terrible things he's done.'

'What about Cathy? She's an innocent...'

'Innocent?!' Linda stared at him, her eyes more

crazy than ever. 'They told me all about her... told me about all the depraved things she'd done for them. She's part of their sick... gang! If I kill them, then I'll know...'

There was a loud oily, clicking sound that echoed in the room. Jairus spun his head round to see Terry pointing his rifle at Linda, his finger around the trigger.

'Put that fucking gun down, Linda!' Terry said, his voice shaking.

'Terry, don't,' Jairus said, the sickness filling his stomach as his heart pounded. 'It'll be OK. She won't... she has to listen to...'

'I don't care!' Linda screamed. 'Kill me if you want! I'll kill them first and the children will be safe!'

'Linda!' Jairus stepped closer. 'Don't do this... please... I'm begging you...'

Linda looked at him, seeming to calm down and think. Her eyes went back to the deputy prime minister. Then she seemed to take a breath and her finger tightened on the trigger as her arm stretched out.

The gunshots echoed in the room, booming into Jairus' ears as he fell to his knees. He gripped his face as his ears were filled with the high-pitched winning.

He looked up slowly and saw Linda slumped by the wall, blood covering her chest and shoulder. He closed his eyes again, holding in the puke that wanted to pour out of him. He breathed in, struggling to his feet, grabbing at the wall.

'She's not dead,' Terry said somewhere over him.

Jairus heard Linda sobbing again and felt like crying himself, but held it all in and breathed in, cleared his thoughts and looked at the deputy prime minister. He was lying on the ground, the chair tipped up under him. There was blood coming down his shirt and jacket.

'Help me,' Jairus said, kicked away Linda's gun and started untying the politician until he could roll him onto his back.

He pulled the tape from his mouth and listened to the groans and venomous stream of abuse that poured from his well-educated mouth. Jairus made eye contact with him and pointed into his face.

'You keep your mouth shut,' Jairus growled. 'You hear me?! I don't want to hear anything you've got to say right now.'

'That crazy bitch shot me!' the politician spat, before clenching his teeth.

Jairus grabbed him by his lapels. 'That woman, her name is Linda by the way... was going to kill you. That man over there saved your pathetic life. You should be thankful he didn't kill her... because if he had, then we'd have to dump her body out at sea and you along with her! You hear me? Now shut the fuck up!'

Jairus clambered up and looked at Terry. 'I don't think the wound's too bad. See if you can find some bandages or something.'

After Terry left the room, Jairus untied Cathy and took the gag from around her mouth. He watched her as she ran to Linda and saw to her wound.

'There's no signal out here,' Cathy said, not looking up from Linda's arm.

'Yeah, I know.'

'You're playing a dangerous game. If he finds out...'

'Then let's make sure he doesn't find out. OK?'

She looked up and nodded. 'It's good to see you, by the way. But you know this isn't a rescue.'

'Yeah, I know. I just happen to be here anyway.'

'What about the babies? You really think this is about human sacrifice?'

'Yeah, I think it is. Whoever's behind all this and this group believes in evil. Pure evil and Satan and all that shit. They've basically created a very powerful cult and their members are politicians and bankers and media moguls and God knows what else! They will slaughter those children, if they haven't already.'

'He's coming back,' Cathy said.

'Not another word about it then.' Jairus looked towards the door and saw Terry arrive with a first aid box and no rifle. He breathed a sigh of relief as the ex-soldier began patching up the deputy PM's wound.

'You really going let this bastard live?' Terry asked. 'I'd finish the job.'

Jairus looked down at the wounded man. 'Yeah, I'm going to let him live. There's nothing I'd like more than to take that knife and cut him open... but I'm not done with him yet.'

'Right,' Terry said, and stood up. 'That should stop the bleeding... so, are we going to get the fuck out of here, or what?'

Jairus nodded. 'Yeah, let's get this lot on the boat and get back to London. We've got work to do.'

CHAPTER 37

It was another six hours before Jairus, Cathy and Terry arrived at Ivy's house after dropping Linda and the deputy prime minister at Toby Besnier's house in the woods to be treated by his medical team.

Rich let them all in, and watched in silence as they all solemnly came in from the cold and stood in the front room.

'I thought you lot would be happy to be alive,' Rich said.

Jairus looked at him. 'Yeah we are. Ecstatic. Have you got spare cuffs hanging round?'

'Spare cuffs? What sort of perv do you think I am?'

Jairus stared at him. 'Just get them.'

Rich went off, headed upstairs and came down with a pair of black cuffs in his hands. 'Here you go.'

Jairus swung round as he pulled out the gun he'd taken from Linda and pointed it at Terry. 'Sorry, Terry, but I need you to kneel down.'

Terry stared up at him, lost for a few seconds. 'We're not going to meet up with my boy, are we? You fucking... you lying...'

Jairus pointed the gun firmer. 'On your knees, Terry. Now.'

Terry shook his head, the anger setting his eyes into thin slits as he turned and kneeled down. 'I tell you what, Jairus... if anything's happened to him... if they've... you're dead, you know that, right?'

'Yeah, I know, Terry. Rich, cuff him.'

Rich huffed, then went over to Terry and started putting the handcuffs on Terry's wrists as his hands were outstretched from his body.

'No,' Jairus said. 'Not like that. Come on, Rich, you know the first rule of cuffing a suspect is you never cuff them with their hands in front of their body, not unless you want them to be able to use the cuffs as a weapon. Let's not forget Terry is an ex-army hardman.'

Rich put on the handcuffs behind Terry's back, then stepped away as Jairus crouched down in front of him and looked into Terry's eyes. 'I know you want to kick the shit out of me right now, Terry, but believe me when I tell you that if anything's happened to your boy, then I'll destroy the people who did it.'

Terry didn't say anything, just stared up at Jairus.

'Right, let's step into your office, Rich,' Jairus said, and signalled for Cathy and Rich to follow him.

When Jairus closed the door after them, he said, 'Where did you leave Ivy?'

Rich rubbed his eyes, looked at Cathy then back at Jairus. 'Where you said. They'll find her. Why the hell did we let her go?'

'She doesn't know anything.' Jairus rubbed his beard. 'She's just a drone to them. Where's Tom?'

'I don't know and I don't care. He left. What was I supposed to do?'

Cathy touched his arm. 'Nothing. He's severely damaged. He needs help now, not vengeance.'

'Yeah, but vengeance is more satisfying,' Jairus said. 'Thing is, we've got no way of knowing if they've carried out their human sacrifice or not. I doubt any bodies will turn up. They'll leave no evidence.'

Rich nodded and sat at his computer. 'Oh, yeah,

after you called me on your way back here, I started looking into this whole cult thing. You ever heard of a journalist called Morie Terry?'

Jairus leaned over Rich's shoulder. 'Yeah, wasn't he an American investigative journalist who looked into the series of murders committed by David Berkowitz?'

'That's right. He dug around for years, then wrote a book about what he found. He reckoned that satanic cults had burrowed their way into America and Britain and were twisting governments for their own sick and evil desires, like human sacrifice and child abuse. What if he's right? What if it's all true?'

Jairus rubbed his eyes. 'I'm starting to believe it is.'

Rich nodded. 'Me too. But I've been looking into satanic rituals and their whole fucked-up holiday system. There are a few days on the way to Halloween that are earmarked for human sacrifice, but the 1st of November, tonight, is the main event. It's called Satanist High. The person to be sacrificed could be of any age, of either sex.'

Jairus pulled out a chair, sat down and pressed his face into his hands. 'That's it. It's tonight. Last night was meant to fuck with me, to make me kill that bastard politician or to watch me suffer. They get their kicks from all this.'

'But how do we find where they're going to carry out this sacrifice?' Cathy asked.

Jairus sat up. 'You know, something's been bothering me all this time. When we looked at Pinder's laptop, he had all those photos of all those expensive properties... and that one photo of that kebab shop in Balham. Why?'

Rich shrugged. 'Could be lots of reasons.'

Jairus nodded. 'Yeah, true, but it's the one small thing that keeps scratching at the back of my mind.'

Cathy smiled. 'And the Jairus I know and love is back in the room.'

Jairus laughed. 'Right, Rich, you dig around and see if you can find any properties Burdock owns or even the deputy prime minister.'

'They wouldn't use anywhere they actually own,' Cathy said.

'You're probably right, but I'm clutching at straws. You two look into that, I'm going to check out this kebab place.'

Shops and people flashed past, sandwich shops and cafes and arcades and electrical places that made up the long Balham high street. A wider road off of it had a busy market filling every inch of it, with crowds bustling through. He took the next turning and parked up near a small garage that advertised MOTs.

The sun was sinking behind the houses, giving way to the growing rush hour traffic and the blue darkness that came slowly with it. Jairus climbed out, sunk his hands into his coat pockets and took the littered lane that ran behind the high street. It grew narrower until it was barely an alleyway. Directly behind the kebab shop, he found big overflowing metal bins and the small backyard that led to the kitchen.

He hid behind the bins for a minute as he saw a skinny, hooked-nosed young man smoking as someone shouted at him from inside. Jairus kept watching as the young man put out his fag, spat on the ground then went inside.

The stench of some kind of meat being burnt alive on the grill filled his nostrils as he went around the bins and looked up at the windows above the shop. They were curtained off, a fact that made his skin crawl.

Jairus looked down at the ground and saw that the lad hadn't quite put out his cigarette, so he picked it up and blew on it until it was glowing bright red in the dismal light.

He pressed the butt to the overflowing boxes and bags hanging out of the bins and stood back as the flames rippled up and at speed ate away at everything they got hold of. Grey and black smoke started to fill the small yard and alerted the kebab staff that there was a problem to panic about.

An alarm started somewhere, and the staff started exiting the building and bringing buckets of water with them.

While resting against the wall, Jairus calmly watched the whole conflagration and the flustered bodies that came out. It was a couple of minutes later that a tall, dark-haired man in a shirt and tie came out of the shop, his face set into confusion. Behind him came a short but stocky man with greying red hair who looked furious. His angry eyes seemed to hunt the ground around him until they found Jairus.

He stormed over to Jairus and pointed a thick finger in his face. 'Did you do this? Is this your doing, mate?'

Jairus grinned at the man with the lowland Scots accent. He recognised a fellow policeman when he met one. 'Yeah, I did it. I did it to smoke you out and it worked. My name's Jairus. I'm guessing you knew Pinder and Coulson?'

The Scotsman half closed his eyes and frowned. 'Jairus? I've heard of you. Aye, you've made a lot of noise over the years. I should've heard you coming, but I'm getting old, getting deaf. I knew those two and I'm still mourning them. They were brave people trying to help an impossible situation.'

Jairus nodded and dug his hands into his pockets.

'Let me guess. You've been operating out of here, trying to bring down the paedophile and psycho VIPs, and Pinder and Coulson were going to testify?'

'That's right, son. They helped us find more victims and hide them away, what good it did in the end. They've murdered or at least disappeared every person who's helped us. I'll tell you what though, they hadn't reckoned on me! I will not stop until every last bastard of them is rotting in prison!'

'Yeah, that's good to hear. But who exactly are you?'

The Scot patted down his jacket until he found a pack of cigarettes and a lighter and lit one. 'DSU Dudley Black. I was on my way out of the force when they pulled me back in for this.'

'Yeah, I've heard of you. You're a legend.'

Black coughed out a laugh. 'Some fucking legend. Someone above me wanted me on this... there's a civil war going on in the force... some of them are in the pockets of those VIP bastards, the rest are trying to get justice. I'm stuck in between, right in the firing line! You are too, son!'

'I know. It's the way I like it. So, how's this work, this setup?'

'I look after a bunch of investigative journalists and dig up what they can, including witnesses if they can.'

Jairus watched the kebab staff putting out the fire. 'David Coulson?'

Black's face was drained of light suddenly. 'Aye... Dave was a good man and he died because I got him involved. Same with Stephen Pinder and his whole family. Those sick bastards will get what's coming, believe me.'

'I do. Does the name Karine Skilton mean anything to you?'

Black narrowed his eyes. 'Aye. Coulson found her.

She was going to tell us... Jesus Christ... she died of a heart attack, didn't she?'

'That's what they told me at the time. But I know different now. I think they murdered her and made it look like a heart attack.'

Black threw his cigarette to the floor and stamped it out. 'The bastards. How did you get dragged into all this?'

'Douglas Burdock hired me to investigate Coulson's murder, but turns out it was a sick game. For whatever reason, he likes messing with my life. Listen, do you have any idea who their leader is?'

'I'm not sure they have a leader, I'm not sure they operate like that.'

'There's always a leader. Someone's always in charge and I need to find who it is, so I can end this.'

Black scratched his head. 'Well, I haven't got a clue who's giving the orders, but I've been keeping an eye on Douglas Burdock and his father. They've got the media sewn up and have been using its power for their own ends for years. Problem is, no one can get anything on them, they're too shrewd.'

Jairus rubbed his hands together. 'There'll be something, there always is.'

'Maybe, but all I know for sure about Douglas Burdock is he visits his dying father most nights during the week. When the old evil bastard kicks the bucket, he'll be in charge of the world's biggest media empire. That's the last thing we need.'

Jairus nodded, taking it all in, imagining the old man dying in a hospital somewhere, picturing the old pervert would have wanted a nice view. 'Who looks after him?'

'Well, he's living in a private hospital overlooking the Thames. There's a nurse they've hired to look after him.'

'Attractive?'

'Yeah. And not that well qualified. We can't find anything on her.'

Jairus dug his hands into his pockets and turned to walk away. 'You won't. She'll be an innocent, the sort of person they like to treat like dirt. I'll need to talk to her. Set it up as soon as possible and maybe we can find a way of at least pissing off Douglas Burdock's old man.'

'I'll try and get hold of her.'

'Make it happen and do it now. We think they're planning some big ritual tonight involving human sacrifice and she might have some idea where it might be happening.'

'You think they're actually Satanists?'

'Yeah, don't you?'

Black huffed. 'I've heard a lot of rumours, but never taken them seriously and I've never seen anything... but of course they'd play it all close to their chests. Jesus... I wouldn't put it past the sick bastards.'

'Get hold of her and then call me on this number.' Jairus scribbled down the number and passed it to Black. 'I'm not letting them get away with this, not this time. Their luck just ran out.'

Black didn't waste any time and fixed up a meeting with the nurse within an hour. Jairus headed over to the travel motel near London Bridge, parked and walked with his hands deep in his pockets, taking in the misty shining lights that reflected on the Thames and almost danced a little.

He kept seeing Burdock, smiling at him, sat behind his desk, convinced that he'd won already.

He pushed the glass door and headed across the

red-carpeted reception area and towards the lifts. He was about to step into the lift when his phone begun to vibrate in his pocket.

'Yeah?' he said, stepping away from the opening doors, watching a couple of young suits stepping out.

'It's Rich. Your mate, the prison guard has been trying to get hold of you.'

'Yeah, why?'

'Frank Saunders has been abducted from the hospital. Apparently, some armed masked men went in there and took him.'

Jairus scratched his head. 'Jesus... looks like they're scared. They're trying to clean up after themselves. Saunders is one of the few people who know what's going on here. That's probably why he got knifed in prison, so they could get him from the hospital.'

'Why not kill him in prison?'

'I don't know. Maybe they want him as part of their fucked-up ceremony. Thanks, Rich, but I got to go.'

Jairus hung up, stepped into the next available lift, went up to the fourth floor and found the right room and knocked.

Black himself opened the door carefully and, seeming satisfied, let Jairus into the small, neat room which he knew would resemble all the others in the hotel.

The young woman with dark brown hair, wearing dark jeans and dark red jumper sat on the bed, her arms wrapped around herself, her eyes refusing to stay long on Jairus as he entered.

'Anne Wright,' Black said, an ill-fitting light tone entering his voice. 'This is... Mr Jairus. You can trust him.'

Jairus stuck his hands into his pockets. 'Anne... can I call you Anne?'

She nodded, almost smiled.

'Good. Like Black said, you can trust me. You work for Douglas Burdock?'

'No, not really...'

'Not really?'

'Well, I work for his...father. Robert Burdock.'

'Douglas Burdock.' Jairus took the chair from the desk opposite the bed and sat down facing her. As he had said the name, he'd kept his eyes on her, watching the way the name struck her, registering the effect it had on her as if she were a tuning fork. He saw the uncomfortable movement of her eyes, her hands tighten, her shoulders tense.

Jairus smiled. 'What's Robert Burdock like?'

She shrugged. 'He's not like anything... he's not a well man... well, actually, he's supposed to be sick, suffering from severe Alzheimer's... but...'

Black huffed out a laugh. 'The old bastard's trying to get out of facing a trial for all the illegal shit his media company has been up to.'

Jairus saw her eyes take him in. He smiled. 'You spend a lot of time dealing with his son?'

'Sometimes... I try not...'

'You don't like him, do you? Douglas?'

She shrugged, but Jairus saw the cringe, the eyes that so wanted to let the tears flow. 'It's more than that, isn't it? You despise him, don't you? He did something terrible, didn't he?'

She nodded, and he heard the sob building in her throat, saw her tremble.

'Listen to me, Anne... I'm here to stop Douglas Burdock from hurting anyone else. I need to know if there's anywhere he might be going tonight... maybe he's talked about a place he...'

'He doesn't talk to me about that sort of thing... he

only ever talks to me like I'm dirt... tries...'

'Believe me, I know what sort of person Douglas Burdock is... he's a psychopath. He thinks he's better than the rest of us, superior in every way. He doesn't have our weaknesses. Thing is, he's got his own weakness... he's blind to the little things... like you... he thinks that you'll stay quiet, beaten down and won't fight back... but he doesn't understand the bond between you and your child and your desperate need for survival. He doesn't understand that that makes you stronger than him. That you're better than him.'

Her eyes lifted to Jairus and held him. 'He thinks... he thinks he... destroyed me... that night.'

Jairus had a thought dig through his brain. 'That night... where did he take you?'

'A big house in... Chelsea, I think.'

Black stepped forward. 'In Chelsea? Burdock doesn't own a place in Chelsea.'

Jairus smiled. 'Anne, can you remember anything about the place that stands out?'

She nodded, still trembling, the memories obviously stabbing into her. 'There was a hidden doorway into a much bigger room. I couldn't move... he must have...'

Jairus was patient while she fought back the pain and tears that threatened to pour out of her. 'Do you think you'd recognise the building again?'

'I could try.'

Jairus stood up and faced Black. 'We need to take her on a drive around Chelsea. That's where they'll be having their fucked-up ceremony.'

Black grabbed his jacket and put it. 'I'll go get my car. Bring her down in five minutes.'

After Black had left the room, Jairus sat down and faced her, watched her as she began to cry, letting it all out. 'It's not over yet, Anne. I'm afraid I'm going to need you to do something else after we find this house.'

Her eyes were full of anxiety as they sprang up to him. 'What do you want... I don't know what else...'

'I know it'll be tough... but I need you to go back to work. You need to be there tonight, or Burdock will know something's up. Can you do that?'

She looked him in the eyes, the tears pouring down her cheeks, swallowed and nodded.

'Good. I promise, by tomorrow morning this will all be over.'

CHAPTER 38

Black drove expertly and at speed through the wet London streets, swerving round the bends, seeming to narrowly miss the awkwardly parked cars and the vehicles that had pulled over to let them pass. Jairus never saw him press down on the brake once. He never liked being a passenger when he was being rushed under a blue light, but he somehow felt at ease with the aging Scot at the wheel, a fag hanging from his lips.

Eventually they pulled up in the wide road of luxury houses in poshest Chelsea and sat in silence for a moment.

'Some of these rent for twelve grand a week,' Black said, lighting a new fag with the old one. 'That's fucking criminal.'

'That's our fucked-up society for you. Which house is it?'

'Middle one with the red awning. When's it supposed to go down?'

Jairus sat back, trying to get comfortable. 'I don't know.'

'Well, I'm informed that several cars have arrived covertly around the back over the last couple of hours. So, how do we proceed?'

'Can you get an armed response unit down here?'

Black took a long drag on his cigarette and shook

his head. 'How can I? I try and get an armed response team here, they'll know we're on to them. Like I said before there's a civil war going on behind the scenes and these psycho bastards have got enough clout to stop me doing my job. What are we going to do, walk in there ourselves? God knows how many are in there. And they're all sick bastards, let's not forget that.'

Jairus put his face in his hands, rubbed his eyes and sighed, trying to come up with a plan. He looked up and saw a car parked up the road, a familiar figure coming down the street, the rain soaking them head to foot.

'Wait here,' Jairus said and climbed out, feeling the wind trying to shut the door on him, and the rain digging into his scalp.

He walked towards Tom, who had now stopped, drenched, his crazy eyes now filled with sadness more than anything.

'How did you find me?' Jairus asked.

'I didn't. I've been following one of them. I knew they'd lead me here eventually. It's tonight, isn't it?'

'Yeah, I think so. What are you going to do?'

Tom opened his coat and produced a hand gun and knife. 'Kill them. Kill them all. You going to stop me?'

Jairus looked towards the house, then over at Black, who was watching them, smoking hungrily. 'No, I don't think I am.'

Tom nodded, then crossed the road, walked towards the house, more rain hitting his body, soaking him. Jairus watched him enter the grounds of the house and vanish.

It was a couple of minutes later that he heard the sound of a distant gunshot, and went back to the car and leaned into Black.

'You better call someone and tell them a madman

with a gun has just started shooting people in that house.'

Black looked at him, then over to the house. 'You're joking?'

'No, call it in. Now you've got cause to go in.'

Douglas Burdock was staring at his father, watching the faint rise and fall of his withered chest. How pathetic he seemed lying under the thin sheets; how far removed from the Satan he painted himself as. He knew he could take a photograph of the pathetic, weak vision before him and sell it to his myriad enemies and make another fortune.

He took out his mobile and took a snap, but he would never show it to anybody, just keep it as a reminder of how the mighty can fall.

'You're dying, Father,' he said aloud as he tucked away his phone. 'Your empire is mine. The King is dead, long live the King.'

Douglas turned when he heard the door open behind him, and smiled when he saw Nurse Wright frozen in the doorway, hesitating, looking even more terrified than usual.

'Come in,' he said. 'Don't be afraid. The old pervert will be gone soon.'

She carried on towards the bed, carrying the clipboard and chart in her hand, her eyes avoiding him. Then she stopped, and her eyes, still hardly being able to take him in, looked towards him as she said, 'I don't understand how you... how you can be so...'

'Blasé about my father dying?'

She nodded then walked to the bed and went about her nursing duties.

'You see, Anne... my father created a monster when he took me and introduced me to his world... I don't know whether I was the way I am, or whether it was his influence, but here I am. He taught me there is no God, that there are no consequences to my actions. I could do anything I wanted and get away with it. I chose to carry that on, except I came to the realisation that there had to be some intelligence behind the world, the universe, I just didn't believe there was any good in that intelligent mind.'

She didn't say anything for a while, but he felt her hatred and fear subsiding, giving way to curiosity.

'So, you've had him murdered?' she said, her voice strained. 'So you can have it all?'

Douglas smiled, just because she was so far below him that she would never understand his rationale. 'I'm not murdering so I can have it all... it won't be long before it's mine anyway... I'm killing him because... well, to me it seems the natural order of things... of this world. I can do it and get away with it. I don't have to answer to the ridiculous notions of guilt and justice that you lesser mortals feel so impelled to. Wouldn't you rather be part of a society where there is a truer justice, where a death sentence is delivered swiftly?'

She looked at him as if she pitied him, which made him want to break her nose with his fist. Instead, he smiled.

'I don't want to live in a world governed by monsters,' she said and started taking his father's blood pressure.

'That's rather unfortunate. Because you one day will, and you sort of do already. I know, Anne, that you think I did you a terrible wrong... but I was only doing what our ancestors would have done. I just took you, because I wanted to, and because I could.'

He kept the smile on his face, even when she stared at him, the fire in her eyes, all the terrible wishes of a tortured death he could see blazing there. Then she turned and walked out, leaving him alone with the dying old man.

Jairus stood back, out of the way, watching as the rain hammered everything, soaking everything, flooding the gutters as the Armed Response unit turned up and headed into the house in teams of two.

Black had put on a bullet proof vest and a raincoat under the shelter of his boot. Jairus shook his head when he was offered the same protection, and shoved his hands into his pockets as they all went inside.

The armed officers smashed in the door, then swept inside, pointing their Heckler and Koch submachine guns, their boots slapping against the ceramic floor, then the polished wood staircase. Each room was checked, then a shout went out.

Somewhere above them a shot boomed out and they all froze for a split second, then in one roar of noise, every one of them scuttled like insects towards the sound.

The armed officers entered the large living area and searched every part of the immaculately decorated room.

It was Jairus who headed to the wall on the far side and ran his gloved hands over it, found the pressure point and pressed it.

The door clicked and Jairus opened it, revealing the small opening into the large, dimly-lit room.

'The room must cut into the house next door,' Black said as the armed response officers ducked and headed inside.

Jairus followed Black and stopped behind him when they found themselves in a long narrow room with some kind of stone altar at the far end. Between him and the stone altar, there were several bodies, each one dressed in black robes and a red mask, all lying either sprawled out or curled up in the foetal position. Blood was splashed on the walls and streaked across the tiled floor.

Jairus turned towards the wave of noise that filled the room.

On his right were several antique carved wooden cribs and he could see the naked, pale babies that lay there crying. Kneeling on the floor beside them, were three naked young women and a skinny young lad. Two of the women were crying, sobbing with relief, while one stared at Jairus in disbelief. The young lad was breathing hard, his face scarlet, his eyes full of angry tears.

Shouting took Jairus' eyes from the boy and he looked towards the end of the room.

The armed response team were by the altar, shouting at a figure half hidden by a wall that jutted from the corner of the room.

'Put your weapon down!' one of the armed response team shouted at the man.

As Black went over to the naked young women and began to say something to them, perhaps comforting, Jairus buried his hands into his pockets and began stepping over robed bodies.

'Stay back!' one of the armed team shouted at him, so he stood still and watched as Tom emerged from behind the wall.

He had his gun in his hand, the muzzle pressed hard into the temple of a robed man who was on his knees. His mask had been removed and lay cracked on the floor beside him.

The robed man had his eyes firmly closed, whispering something under his breath that Jairus took to be a desperate prayer to some divine being.

'Put the fucking gun down and put your hands on your head!'

Tom didn't seem to be listening to the commands of the armed response team; his eyes and attention had turned to Jairus as a tear rolled down his cheek.

'They're safe,' Tom said, and he flashed his eyes over to the babies.

'Yeah, they are,' Jairus said. 'You did a good thing today.'

More tears came as he said, 'Do you think I'll be forgiven for the bad things? For all the deaths? For all the bad things I had to do to get there?'

'Lower your fucking weapon!' The armed response team repositioned themselves.

'You'll be forgiven, Tom,' Jairus said and smiled.

Tom pulled the gun away from the man's cheek and allowed him to collapse onto his hands.

'Now drop your weapon!'

Jairus watched Tom, saw the tears in his eyes, saw him take one last look at the babies he'd freed and the mothers that were manacled by them, before he turned the gun on the armed response officers.

The shots punched the air, smoke filling the room, clouding Jairus' vision as Tom dropped to the floor, his chest spotted with patches of fresh blood.

After a few seconds, the armed team had cleared his body, secured Tom's weapon, so Jairus, with his ears ringing, turned to face Black.

Uniformed officers were freeing the women and taking the babies to safety.

'It's all right,' Black said, slapping him on the back. 'I can vouch for the uniforms. They come from my special unit I'm setting up.'

'Good. Let me know what's happening. Take good

care of that boy.' Jairus headed towards the door, taking out his phone as he walked.

'Where are you off to?'

'There's someone I need to deal with.'

Outside the house the rain had loosened its grip on the streets, so Jairus stepped out and dialled Rich Vincent and waited as he watched paramedics helping someone into the back of an ambulance. A uniformed officer also climbed in the back with whoever was being treated.

'Hello?' Rich said.

'It's me. I'm calling to let Terry know that his boy is safe. Tell him it's the truth this time.'

'He'll be glad to hear it. You OK, mate?'

'Yeah, just got something to sort out, then I'll swing by. Talk to you later.'

Jairus hung up then walked across the pavement, getting ready to cross the road.

'Jairus!'

He stopped, with one foot in the road and turned towards the ambulance and picked out the pale unshaven face of Frank Saunders. He was sat up, handcuffed to the stocky uniform, being examined by a paramedic.

Jairus headed over and stood looking into the glowing interior, and the mad evil eyes staring back at him.

'You found the sick bastards then?' Saunders said, grinning.

'Yeah, didn't I say I would? What rock did they find you hiding under?'

Saunders flinched when the paramedic touched the wound that had opened up over his eye. 'Fuck, that hurt. They kept me in the basement like I was animal. Do you believe it?'

'Funny that.' Jairus had had enough of looking at another face of evil, so he turned, ready to walk away.

'Where you going? Thought you'd want to know what was going on in there.'

The rain started again. 'I think I know enough.'

'Oh, come on. Don't be like that, Jairus. Ride in the ambulance with me and I'll tell you all about it. It'll knock your fucking socks off.'

'Yeah, I'm sure it would, but there's somewhere I need to be.' Jairus headed into the rain, the icy beat of it filling his skull.

'What about Karine?!'

Jairus froze, the rain trickling down his skin, as his heart rampaged, his hands turning into fists. He turned around and faced the murderer, stared into the empty eyes. 'Don't say her fucking name! You got me?'

'She would've been ten at the time, I reckon.' Saunders smiled. 'Come on, get in and I'll tell you what I know.'

Jairus stood frozen in time, the torrent of rain soaking him from head to foot, now unaware that the world was still carrying on. 'You're trying to get in my head. I put you away...'

'I know all about her, Pinder, Janine... don't you want to hear the whole story? Yes... there it is in your eyes... the hunger for the truth.'

Jairus felt himself climbing into the ambulance, even though a part of his brain was screaming for him to stop, to run and cover his ears like a frightened child.

The truth will not set you free.

CHAPTER 39

The ambulance started on its way after waiting for a gap in the traffic. For a moment Jairus looked out the back windows, seeing the sheet of rain exploding against the glass. The outside traffic was just a blur of light. He concentrated on anything outside his body, not listening to the terrible whispering voice in the back of his mind, growing louder all the time.

The paramedic sat rocking with the movement, his eyes fixed on Jairus, waiting. Jairus looked at the uniform and saw he was staring too.

'So, here we are,' Saunders said and laughed and slapped his leg. 'At the very end. Just the two of us.'

Jairus looked at the two men with them. 'Not just us. We're not alone.'

'No, you're right. We're not alone. But we're never truly alone, are we? You've got your ghosts and I've got my voices.'

'Tell me about Karine.' Jairus clenched his fists.

Saunders smiled. 'Like I said, she was barely ten or eleven, I think. Tell me, Jairus, do you believe in synchronicity?'

'Just get on with your fucking story!'

'I do. It's funny how things work out, isn't it? As if a supreme being is pushing us around like chess pieces? To think you caught me five years ago and put me inside... then, I join the cult...'

Jairus looked up at him, saw his grin, his nod, while his skull began to ache with realisation.

'That's right, Jairus. Let it sink in. I'm in the cult. We haven't got a name. We just are. Likeminded men who know they are more than the rest of you... superior... and we know there is only one master. Lucifer.'

Jairus nodded. 'Yeah, that's right. You're the leader. Right?'

'You're correct. It's taken me a long time to climb my way up.'

'Of course... It's not how much power you've got, or money...'

'It's what you're willing to do for our cause. Our struggle to make good evil and evil good.'

Jairus sprang forward, grasped hold of Saunders, snarled into his face as he pulled him close.

'I'd be careful what you do.' Saunders' eyes swept over to his left, and Jairus followed his vision and saw that the uniformed officer had a gun in hand, resting on his leg.

Jairus let go of him and sat back, gave a sickening laugh. 'These two work for you. Of course. What's this really been about? All this time I've felt like I've been herded along.'

'That's because you have. Even before I had Burdock employ your services. I knew you'd never stop and I needed you to keep digging. All it took was the revelation that the love of your life was involved and you'd go to the ends of the earth, to hell in fact to find out the truth... to lead you here.'

'What's this about? Revenge? For putting you away?'

Saunders threw his head back, his hard laugh filling the small space between them. 'Revenge? Fuck me. You really think you putting me in prison affected me? You really are up your own arse, Jairus. The governor of that shithole is in our pocket... I come and go when I like, do what I like. I think if you looked hard enough, you'd find a few unsolved cases over the last five years.'

Jairus breathed in, doing his best to keep his fury in check. 'So, what is this all about?'

'Death and rebirth... rebirth into the next life, a life where there is no guilt, no comeback for the pure pleasure we take. This life is just a corridor... A practice run.'

'You really believe all this... this satanic bollocks?'

Saunders' face tightened, his smile completely eradicated. 'It's not a matter of belief or faith... at least not the way those crazy Christian arseholes talk about it. I don't believe, I don't have faith, it just is... I just know. The things I've done... I've seen suffering, I've inflicted pain and taken my pleasure from seeing that exquisite pain and the life flow out of my victims... in those moments I look into their eyes, and do you know what I see there?'

'The reflection of a fucking psycho?'

Saunders looked at the uniform and nodded.

Jairus lifted his hands, covering his head as the butt of the gun smashed down on it. It caught him above the eye, and he felt the burn of it, the trickle of blood that flowed over his brow.

'See,' Saunders said, shaking his head. 'I can do that and there's no comeback. There's nothing you can do.'

'Oh, I'll do something.'

'You're angry?'

Jairus stared into his eyes. 'There's not a word to describe what I am.'

'Good. I'm glad. Aren't you going to ask me about your beautiful Karine?'

'Whatever you say... whatever comes out of your shitty mouth... will be a lie.'

Jairus felt himself rock forward as the ambulance came to a sudden stop. Then there was movement again, going backwards, then forwards, manoeuvring.

'We've come to our destination. Our journey is almost at an end.' Saunders nodded to the paramedic and Jairus watched him get up and make his way to the back doors. He opened them, revealing that they were parked outside an old stone building and a pair of arched battered wooden doors.

'Get out,' Saunders said.

Jairus looked towards the gun that the uniform had pointed at him, then at the paramedic, who had now also produced a gun. He had no choice but to comply.

He climbed out of the vehicle and headed for the arched doors that the paramedic had opened for them.

It was a small stone chapel with worn wooden beams criss-crossing as they reached for the roof. At the far end was a stone altar, but as Jairus was marched inside he saw strange drains that had been more recently fitted into floor. He raised his eyes and saw that there was a large stone cross above the altar, but it was inverted.

Saunders walked past him, lifted his head to look up at the cross, said something in a low voice and then turned and smiled at Jairus. 'Now we're alone.'

Jairus heard the door slam behind him and swung around to see the room was empty. He spun around to Saunders and stormed towards him. 'What's to stop me from beating you to death?'

'There's only one way out of here. Through that door. And my friends will be waiting on the other side. If you beat me to death, they would shoot you. Simple as that.'

'Then why I am here?'

Saunders turned and reached behind the altar and brought out an ancient looking long thin blade. 'You're here because of this?'

Jairus nodded and looked at the floor. 'Yeah, I get it. All that baby, King Herod stuff was all bollocks. That was to bring me in, get me hunting you down.'

'That's right. Here you are, Jairus. Like a great big lamb to the slaughter.'

A thought occurred to Jairus. 'I'm curious. If all that ceremony stuff was all fake, then what about all those robed men who Tom killed?'

'You weren't there. Tom didn't kill them. I did. He killed some... but I killed the rest. Those men gave their lives to be reborn. When the bodies are examined, they'll see that they were all shot in the back of the head.'

'You lot really are fucked in the head. You're willing to die for...' Jairus stopped, the black cloud of fury that had wrapped itself round his mind dissipating. He looked down at the ceremonial knife in Saunders' hand, then up into the black, unforgiving eyes that stared back at him, telling him that he was right in whatever dark realisation he'd just had.

'Jesus... there's me thinking that knife was meant for me, like you were going to try and slit my throat and let my blood flow into those drains in the floor... but that's not it at all. Is it?'

Saunders didn't utter a word. His hand flew out, throwing the knife close to Jairus' feet.

Jairus looked down to the blade and the foreign words that had been stamped into the curved blade and the carved handle. 'You want me to kill you?'

Saunders nodded. 'That's right. Now he finally gets it. Now you get to finish me off. How much pleasure will that give you? To kill the man who tortured and killed all those pretty little things? But you know there's more, don't you, Jairus? You have that feeling in your gut, like acid eating away at your soul.'

Jairus laughed, hearing the sickness in the strange sound of it. 'This is your big plan, get me so angry, so full of hate that I kill you? That's the payoff? Not very original, is it, Saunders? Think I saw it in a film once. Get on with it... spill your guts, give me all the bullshit you've got stored up.'

'You'll be able to tell if I'm telling tales, won't you? Yes, you will. Look into my eyes... when I tell you I was one of them, one of the men who did those unspeakable things to your beautiful Karine...'

'Shut up!' Jairus' fists tightened so much it felt like the tendons might snap, and he trembled all over as his heart pounded, filling his ears with the sound of it. His world tipped sideways, and suddenly he was looking down at himself.

'You want the truth, don't you?' Saunders' face filled with fake pity.

'You need to stop talking.'

'But what else is there to do in here? Let me tell you what she was like... tall even then, caramel skin, skinny awkward limbs...'

Jairus swept his right arm above him, his fist drawn, shaking, while his other hand grasped Saunders by his shirt. 'Shut the fuck up!'

'I think they'd call this irony... that you've been searching all this time for the truth, only to find you'd already confronted the man who raped, beat and eventually murdered the woman you loved.'

Jairus let go of him and forced himself to step back, breathing hard, the images cascading into his brain, unable to stop them.

'Sorry, I couldn't resist... when I found out one of the little girls back then was your lover... well, we had to kill them anyway... so I thought, why not do it myself?'

Jairus spun round and stormed towards the doors, pulling at them, then hammering his fists against them.

Saunders came up behind him and Jairus could sense the deep grin cut into his long face as he said, 'Of course, I couldn't do the things I wanted to... but I forced that little pill down her throat... and she begged for her life. I think she would've done anything I asked, just to have one more...'

Jairus found himself spinning round, sidestepping Saunders and falling to the floor where the knife was lying. He grasped the blade by the handle, held it tight, breathing hard, fighting back the tears that were ready to flow. He was panting as he struggled to his feet and turned to face Saunders.

'Is this it...?' Jairus held out the knife. 'Is this what you want?'

'That's it. Think of Karine... not just that day you argued with her and left... I saw you leave. Slam the door, jump into your car... leaving her all alone.'

Jairus rushed forward, enclosing his hand around Saunders' throat, tightening as he pinned him against the wooden doors. He lifted the knife in his shaking hand, digging the tip of the blade into Saunders' throat.

'Push it!' Saunders closed his eyes then, muttering some foreign words under his breath.

Jairus lifted his head, let out a howl and grasped Saunders tight to him, enclosing his knife hand round him, turning the knife round in his fist. The blade was now pointed at Saunders' back and he pushed it away, then pulled it back, driving it into his flesh.

Saunders flinched and screamed through gritted teeth as Jairus dug it in, then pulled it sideways.

He stepped back, let Saunders fall to his knees, his panting breath escaping his mouth as he collapsed onto his face.

Jairus fell to his knees and then leaned his face in close to Saunders' ear. For a moment he listened to his shallow breathing, and then whispered, 'You're still alive, Frank... how does it feel? I cut into your spine, but I left the knife in, so that should help stem the wound. I'm going to keep you alive... but you're fucked, you'll never move again, trapped in a prison of my making. How's that for fucking justice? Enjoy yourself.'

Jairus clambered to his feet and staggered over to the door and hammered on it. 'He's dead! I've done it. That's what you wanted!'

He stood back as he heard the lock being turned and the heavy doors slowly opening. Light crept in with the rain as the outline of a man came in the room. Jairus saw the gun in his hand, pointed towards him as the uniform stepped in. His eyes fell upon the fallen body of his leader, then he stepped closer and jabbed his foot at him.

The cult member who was dressed as a paramedic stood in the doorway watching.

'What happens now?' Jairus said, looking between them. 'One of you kills me?'

The uniform looked at the paramedic and said, 'It's time. Let's go.'

Jairus stood still, watching them both head towards the doors as if nothing had happened until the roar of an engine and glaring headlights lit up the narrow street. The car ground to a halt and two silhouetted figures came racing towards him.

One was an armed officer who pointed his sub machinegun at the paramedic and the uniform. The other figure was DSU Black, who came and stood, arms folded opposite Jairus' two captors.

'Where do you think you're going?' Black asked them. 'We've got a lot of questions for you two. You all right, Jairus?'

Jairus nodded, shoved his hands into his pockets. 'Yeah, just about. But you better call an ambulance. A real one.'

'Don't move!' the armed officer stepped closer. Jairus turned to see the fake paramedic and police officer raising their guns slowly, bringing them up until they were pressed under their chins. Both men whispered something under their breaths, clenching their eyes shut.

'Put down...'

Both men collapsed to the floor as the shots exploded through the back of their skulls.

Black and Jairus stared down at the dead men while the armed officer secured their weapons and then went into the church.

'What the bloody hell is this place?' Black said, stepping round the bodies, staring up at the building.

'Some kind of church... Saunders is in there. He's wounded in the back. I'm hoping he'll survive.'

'You stabbed him?'

'Yeah, I'm afraid so.'

'I'm sure that can be ironed out. I can make it go away. Self-defence and all that rigmarole.'

Jairus looked at him, starting to question the man's motives. 'Why would you do that for me?'

'I'm putting together a small unit. Operation Hades. Looking into cold and delicate cases that no other bastard wants to deal with. I want you on side.'

Jairus was dumbfounded for a moment, his mouth refusing to find the words. 'You're having me on?'

'No, I'm not. I'm deadly serious. Like I said before, there's a civil war going on in the force. I need people I can trust. Who can't be bought. So, you interested?'

His initial instinct was to grab Black, scream some kind of affirmative into his face, but then came a wave of doubt, bringing with it all the terrible things he'd seen in the job, all the bad things he'd done to get by, or right the wrongs to bring his version of justice.

'I don't know... I thought I'd say yes, but I'm honestly not sure if I'm up to it. I'll think about it.'

'You sleep on it. Call me on this number. We've still yet to find somewhere to base the operation.'

Jairus took the card Black handed him and pocketed it. 'You might want to take a look at Southgate. There's an old station house there. Oh, and there's a DS Kate Wood you might want to recruit. You can trust her.'

'Aye, I will. Right, I better get in there and make sure that bastard doesn't die. Where you off to?'

Jairus pushed his hands deep into his pockets. 'I still have to go and see to Douglas Burdock.'

CHAPTER 40

Jairus climbed out the black cab, paid the fare, then headed, hands in pockets, towards the big glass box they called a reception office that sat at the bottom of the exclusive private hospital. Somewhere up at the top, Burdock's father was dying.

There was one beefy looking security guard who was eyeing him from his little room by the end of the long gleaming reception desk. It looked more like a plush modern hotel than a hospital.

The guard stepped out and blocked Jairus' way, giving him his best threatening stare.

'This where you give me verbal and pat me down?' Jairus asked.

'Na, you can go in. He's expecting you.'

'Bet he is.' Jairus headed on, running everything through his aching, broken mind, keeping the image of a child version of Karine hidden in the deepest part of himself.

He stepped into a lift and travelled up to the top floor and out onto the wood floors and along the brightly-lit glass corridor.

He kept on walking, burying the anger, preparing himself for the smug face of the media mogul.

A young Asian security guard looked up then rose and stared at him with a question in his eyes.

'If you're wondering if I'm Jairus,' he said, walking

round the desk. 'The answer's yes. I take it he's in there?'

'He's there. What's the problem, man?'

'No problem.' Jairus went through the doors that opened for him and walked into the kitchen at the end of the small corridor. Nothing about the apartment said hospital to him.

'Ah, Jairus,' Burdock said as he held a bottle of champagne and began to open it. 'Just in time to join us in our celebrations.'

Jairus' eyes jumped to the quiet figure in the corner, her arms wrapped round herself, hiding in the shadows. She seemed smaller than when he interviewed her.

'Yeah, and what exactly are you celebrating?'

Burdock unwrapped the top of the bottle and pressed his thumbs against the cork. The bottle popped and the foam sprayed and poured over the bottle until Douglas poured two glasses. 'Here, Anne. Jairus, have you met Anne?'

Jairus nodded to her then turned his attention back to Douglas. 'Frank Saunders and the others are dead.'

Douglas sipped his champagne and nodded. 'I'm quite aware of the situation. My father is also dead, Jairus. The empire is now mine. You're looking at the new emperor.'

Jairus stepped closer. 'It's over, Douglas.'

The mogul laughed. 'It's far from over. There are more like him, more men like us willing to do what it takes to make this country great again.'

'Then I'll hunt them down too. I get the feeling you don't really buy into all this satanic shit.'

Burdock sipped his drink. 'It's a means to an end more than anything. I certainly don't believe in God. Evil? Definitely. It makes the world go round. Anyway, with Saunders gone, there'll be room for me.'

'Yeah, so you're planning to lead them from a prison cell?'

Douglas put down his glass and smiled. 'You sound like you're going to arrest me. If I'm not mistaken, you're not a policeman anymore. I gave you the chance, but you turned it down.'

Jairus huffed out a laugh, then found himself laughing even more as he took out his phone and dialled the number he'd been given. 'It's me... yeah, I wanted to say the offer you gave... I'd like to take you up on that offer. Yeah, that's right... OK, I'll see you then. Thanks. I've got to go.'

Jairus hung up and put his phone away and saw Burdock staring at him with raised eyebrows. 'Who was that?'

'My new boss. DSU Black. Douglas Burdock, I'm arresting you on suspicion of murder and conspiracy to commit murder. You do not have to say anything. But, it may harm your defence if you do not mention when questioned something which you later rely on in court. Anything you do say may be given in evidence.'

Burdock laughed again and then handed the other glass of champagne to Anne. She retreated further back into herself, shaking her head. Burdock dropped the glass to the floor where it shattered.

'You see, Anne, DCI Jairus believes he's on the side of good, but he also knows the terrible truth... That my very expensive lawyers will destroy whatever case that is built against me. Yes, look, my darling Anne... look into his eyes, and there you will see defeat. You've lost, DCI Jairus. You've got your job back, but you've got to carry around the truth about what happened to your precious Karine. Did Saunders give you all the juicy details?'

'Turn round, kneel down, put your hands behind your back.'

'Whatever you say, officer.' Douglas did as he was ordered and put his hands behind his back. 'Shame this will all come to nothing.'

Jairus laughed. 'Thing is, Douglas, you've been underestimating Anne here. I convinced her to place a couple of video cameras in here and in your father's room. There'll be enough on there to put you away.'

'Well done, Anne.' Douglas turned his head to face her. 'You've toughened up. Good for you. But it won't make a bit of difference. It won't even reach a courtroom. Jairus knows I'm right, don't you, Jairus?'

'Shut up.' Jairus pulled his arms back and cuffed him and saw Anne crouch down out of the corner of his eye.

Her arm was a blur, shooting out towards Douglas, disappearing past his face.

No, not past, but in, spurting hot blood outwards, coating the wall, his suit, soaking his shirt in seconds.

'No!' Jairus pulled him round, saw the blood oozing down his neck, the confusion on Burdock's whitening face.

Jairus grasped his neck, pressing down on it, feeling the blood coating his fingers in its warmth.

He looked round at Anne, saw that she had fallen back against the wall, her hands over her mouth, her eyes wide with horror.

'Call an ambulance!' Jairus shouted at her, but she didn't move, just kept staring.

Burdock began to shake, his eyes scared and wide, looking downwards, trying to speak as Jairus kept pushing against his neck. He could feel the pulse beneath his palm, beating, pushing out the blood out with force.

There was a change, a slow shadow of realisation passing over them all, or that's what it felt like to Jairus. He looked at Burdock, saw into his eyes and the way they looked slightly upwards. They were empty, glistening, seeing nothing. Even then he stayed with his hand sliding along his neck, carried by the thick river of deep red blood.

He closed his eyes, but the smell of it filled his skull and eyes and his stomach.

He let go and almost slipped backwards in the blood. He clambered up, rested his back on the work surface and kept breathing, thinking, his head now turned towards the horrified face of the nurse.

She looked up at him as if for something, perhaps for confirmation or comfort. After a moment, he helped her up, and walked her out to the security guard who almost fainted at the sight of their blood-splashed clothes.

Jairus left them for a moment, found a quiet place, close to the wall of glass that looked down at the glowing green Thames and the lights of the endless city that surrounded it. He dialled Black, ready to ask for help.

CHAPTER 41

Jairus parked at the edge of the woods on a dirt track that led past the old tumbledown castle and the house built within.

He buried his hands into his pockets and walked along the track, avoiding the deep puddles and the patches of thick mud, allowing the hidden security cameras to get a good look at him as he approached Besnier's hybrid house.

By the time he walked the three hundred yards through the trees that surrounded the house, the dull winter light sprinkling a little sun down on him, he could see two figures stood out the front.

He had no problem recognising the lithe and shapely form of Cathy, dressed in jeans and a tight sweatshirt, her arms folded across her chest. Behind her was the harsh, hard and worn figure of Janine, a cigarette in her hand, smoking nervously.

Cathy stepped back, allowing Janine time to stub out her cigarette, smile and walk towards him.

'You're still alive then?' she said, her voice breaking up.

'Yeah, still alive. Just about.'

Janine rubbed her arm, her eyes looking round at the woods. 'So... what happens now?'

'You'll have to talk to the police, tell them everything you know... don't worry, you can trust them. You'll talk to DSU Black. He's a good man. You'll do fine.'

Janine nodded, her eyes filling with tears. He flinched when she jumped towards him and flung her arms round him, squeezing.

'Thank you,' she mumbled into his coat. 'Thank you. Thanks for... everything.'

'You're welcome.' Jairus' hand hovered for a moment then landed lightly on her back.

She looked up, her eyes wet. 'She loved you... so much. She always said.'

Jairus felt the burn of his emotions trying to find their way out, but quickly swallowed it all down. 'Thanks... that means a lot.'

Janine let go of him, looked awkward for a moment, then turned and walked back towards the house.

'So, they took you back?'

Jairus looked at Cathy. 'Yeah, they did.' He nodded. 'That's if the whole Burdock thing sorts itself out.'

'I'm sure it will... and you'll be back getting yourself in more trouble, taking matters into your own hands... serving your own kind of justice... how long do you think you can keep going before it kills you?'

Jairus looked deep into her eyes, then stepped closer to her. 'A long time. A very long time.'

She huffed, looked around, and he thought he saw anger or fear pass her eyes. 'Well, I'll be around... always ready with the bandages or... well, I'll be there if you need me.'

He smiled, reached out his hand, but she pulled away, her face changing, hardening as she said, 'But I won't be there at the end... when it all eventually comes to a head... and your luck runs out. Because it will, Jay. You know it. I know it.'

Jairus forced a smile to his lips. 'But do the gods know it?'

'We don't believe in God, or the devil, do we?'

'No. We don't.' He turned and took a step towards the dirt track.

'Jay?'

He turned and saw that her face had lightened. A subtle smile grew as she said, 'You can stop haunting her now.'

'Yeah, I know.'

'Maybe one day there'll be room in your ghostly heart for someone else.'

'Yeah, maybe.' He put his hands into his pockets and walked away.

Two days passed slowly, filled with questions, interrogations and blank looks. DSU Black was there, keeping an eye on things as Jairus recounted it all, sat in a small interview room somewhere in the city.

Black spent half the time on the phone, marching up and down, talking heatedly with someone, trying to get Jairus a stay of execution.

Civil war. It was the phrase that kept coming back to Jairus every time he'd see Black on his phone. Strings were being pulled, but Jairus was too tired to dance.

Each day Jairus found himself going home in the dark of night, passing the glowing shops, surrounded by ghostly bodies, a voice in his head that sounded very much like all the psychos combined muttering to him, whispering for him to get a bottle of vodka and pour it down his gullet until he could feel no pain and the images stopped playing in his head on a loop.

On the fourth day, Black called early, sounding tired and told him to dress smart and head for Southgate police station.

'Oh, and bring your ID,' he said and hung up.

Jairus pushed open the battered doors and walked into the narrow and long room that made up the main floor of the station. Desks had been set up along the room with a few computers and monitors and phones installed. A big whiteboard was hung at the far end.

DSU Black came out of the middle office to Jairus' right and stood staring at him, giving him the onceover, seeming not impressed by what he saw.

'You look fucking awful,' he said. 'You dinnae get any sleep, Jairus?'

'None. What's happened?'

Black smiled and came closer. 'The footage taken in the hospital speaks for itself. Burdock raped her, she stabbed and killed him. Good riddance. Unfortunately, a lot of their secrets die with Burdock and Saunders. What a bunch of... excuse my language... cunts. So, you're free and clear...'

Jairus breathed out, shut his eyes. 'Thank fu...'

'Jairus. Look at me, son.'

He opened his eyes to see Black's sharp and clear grey eyes piercing into him.

'This is a closely guarded secret, this unit. I've fought for this... for you. Don't fuck it up. You hear me? No trouble, no big fucking publicity blow ups. Got me?'

'Yeah, I get you. I'll do my best.'

Black stared at him, then shook his head, turned his back on him and headed to his office. 'Do his fucking best, he says. Fuck me. You better or we're all fucked.'

Jairus watched him disappear into the office, then looked round at his surroundings and took out his warrant card. He stared at it for a moment, put it away and shoved his hands into his pockets.

'By the way...'

Jairus swung round to see Black looking at him

from the doorway. 'Yeah, boss?'

'We've got a job on. Two dead pensioners. Here's the address. Wood's already there. A strange one this.'

'Yeah, that's how I like them.' Jairus snatched the piece of paper from his hand and headed towards the door, still fighting off the evil pictures crowding into his mind, pushing out the good memories.

Do the job, he told himself, solve a few cases, make the bad things fade away.

But he knew as he headed down the concrete stairs, the buzz burning through him, that they would never go away, would never leave him alone in the darkness.

JAIRUS WILL RETURN IN JAIRUS' SLAUGHTER

Printed in Great Britain
by Amazon